WITCH TOWER

Lawrence King

Editing by The Artful Editor.
Author photograph provided by the author.

ISBN-13: 978-1533508621
ISBN-10: 1533508623

IMAGE CREDITS

original.

Chapter 9 Image:
"Gfp-lecture-hall.jpg" by Yinan Chen, used within public domain guidelines / Desaturated and cropped from original.

Chapter 10 Image:
"Thanksgiving table.jpg" by Chef Sean Christopher, used under CC-BY-SA-3.0 / Desaturated and cropped from original. Text added by Lawrence King.

Chapter 11 Image:
"Full Moon (9120148155).jpg" by Tony Alter, used under CC-BY-SA-2.0 / Desaturated and cropped from original.

Chapter 12 Image:
"Kraków - ogród botaniczny,.jpg" by Magdalia25, used under CC-BY-SA-3.0 PL / Desaturated and cropped from original.

Chapter 13 Image:
"Christmas presents under the tree (11483513325).jpg" by James Petts, used under CC-BY-2.0 / Desaturated and cropped from original.

Afterword Image:
"Italian Greyhound standing gray.jpg" by christina, used under CC BY 2.0 / Desaturated and cropped from original.

For Daniel Hutchison

PART I

The Interview

PROLOGUE

The four of them are arranged around one end of an enormous conference table in the chancellor's study at Miskatonic University. The study is quite large, designed for meetings of the full board of directors. This formal room, like so many at Miskatonic, creates an impression of long-standing wealth and influence. Its imposing fireplace is lighted today, but the room is hardly cheerful, scarcely warmed by its soft glow.

Dr. Marianne Christianson, head of the Science Department, slides a manila folder across the table to her boss, the chancellor of Miskatonic University.

Dr. Thomas Mason, the chancellor, receives the folder and asks, "Do you think he's a good choice, then? Will Dr. Mackenzie fit in here, Marianne?" Dr. Mason is the head of this small review committee and the head of the college as well.

"I think so," she replies. "He's smart, young, and eager to make his way in the world. He would make a good addition to our teaching staff. He's also a writer; his dissertation at UCLA was compelling. Not many people moving into academia add anything to physics research. His dissertation extends Steven Hawking's early work on black holes in two significant ways. First of all, he calculates the energies involved for creating small black holes in the laboratory. Second, he shows how much Hawking radiation might be produced from them and how we might harness this energy."

"I read the dissertation," says Dr. Shyam Gupta, sitting to the right of Dr. Christianson. He's clearly excited by what he's saying. "If the hole is stable and sized appropriately, the energy production is immense due to black-body radiation being constantly released near the event horizon. It could be a surprisingly safe and efficient energy source."

"Safe, unlimited energy—a nice theory," says Dr. Christianson.

Dr. Gupta continues, "I also saw him present a research paper on creating miniature black holes. The team he was working with at UCLA has made a lot of progress in proving how that might be done."

"So the boy can teach, research, and write," says Dr. Mason. "That certainly could get him a graduate teaching fellowship here. But what about our other projects? How does Dr. Mackenzie fit into our long-range plans?"

"The details are in the folder, Thomas," says Dr. Christianson. "I'll give you the bird's-eye view, though, and you can read the rest for yourself later. First off, he's a lucid, imaginative, and coherent dreamer."

"And we know this how?" asks Claire Barry. Ms. Barry, the fourth member of this review team, has been quietly taking notes.

"I have a friend who was involved with UCLA's dream research program," says Dr. Christianson. "As an undergraduate student, Dr. Mackenzie was one of their paid dreamers. My friend was helping to wind down the research after their grant money ran out. Dr. Mackenzie's participation was distinctive—that was why my friend first called me."

"Did he know the purpose of the research?" asks Ms. Barry.

"No. The students were told they were part of a study to compile a dream dictionary of common themes and symbols that dreamers encounter. They were given basic training on recalling, recording, and summarizing their dreams. They were given information on lucid dreaming and some simple exercises to try to enhance the lucidity of their dreams. They were paid for their efforts as part of a work-study program."

"Is he stable?" asks Ms. Barry. She's looking intently at Dr. Christianson.

She responds, "A good question given the lucidity and directive nature of his dreams. Yes, I think so. As part of the study, the students were required to have quarterly MMPI and other evaluations to test their mental states. Throughout the two-year project he was fine. His scores show that he's a bit of a loner, a bit repressed emotionally and sexually, but quite sane. I would say from his profile that he could be taught to transverse. The copies of his dream diaries that I was given show powerful lucid-dreaming states."

"Transverse potential," says Dr. Mason, thoughtfully. "Anything else?"

"Perhaps just a curiosity," says Dr. Christianson, shrugging her shoulders slightly. "I think he might be one of the Kingsport 'Kings.'"

This gets the attention of the group. Ms. Barry breaks the silence. "And how would you know *that*?"

"That was an easy one. Our routine background check provides a birth certificate," Dr. Christianson says. "Although his last name is Mackenzie, after his mother, his father is listed as James King of Kingsport, Massachusetts. Although it's a common enough name—not in Kingsport. It appears that he's had no contact with his father since he and his mother moved to California when 'Mac' was about three years old."

"Should we consider this an asset or a liability?" asks Dr. Mason.

"Good question. Ultimately an asset, I think. It helps to explain some of the images in his dream journals and speaks to his potential in that area. He may have some of his father's capabilities, although heredity doesn't seem to play a major factor in that."

Dr. Mason closes the folder that Dr. Christianson gave him. He pushes it back to her across the table. He says, "Let's send the young man a letter of interest and set up an interview. Do you think we could have him here during Ostara? It would be lovely to have him here with a full moon! We can interview him for his teaching skills and to get an idea of how well he might fit into life at Miskatonic. If things work out, let's have him teach for a year before we involve him in our greater plans. It would be good to have him think of Miskatonic as 'home' before we complicate things."

Dr. Mason says, almost to himself, "I might have Brown Jenkin interview him as well, to check into the other matter."

The mention of Brown Jenkin simultaneously elicits a smile from Dr. Christianson and a look of disgust from Ms. Barry.

Dr. Mason concludes the discussion, "If nothing else, wouldn't it be better to have him here, working for *us*?"

CHAPTER ONE

Dressed for Success

The beach in Santa Monica is lovely on this spring morning. Although it's only 7:30 a.m., the temperature is already in the sixties, and the sky is blue and clear. It's supposed to be in the high seventies later in the day. I'm wearing cutoffs and a polo shirt. I'm barefoot, and Howie and I are enjoying a walk along the shoreline only a few blocks from our apartment. In one hand, I'm holding my flip-flops. In the other, I have Howie's leash.

Howie is an Italian greyhound. If you're not familiar with the breed, think regular greyhound, only smaller—much smaller. Weighing in at twelve pounds, he's oversized for the breed standard. Some are much smaller. With a short velvety coat and cockeyed ears, we get a lot of comments. I used to think it was all about Howie, but lately I've begun to realize it's the contrast. Where Howie is miniature, I'm tall. It's the combination that sticks out in people's minds: "Look at the tall, skinny man walking the skinny dog!"

I don't mind. Howie's family. Against my mom's wishes, I got him as a high school graduation present to myself. Rescued from an elderly breeder that passed away, Howie came full-grown but with a lot of puppy energy. As an undergraduate, he rode around in my backpack and was very popular in study groups. Now he's ten years old, and I'm trying to start out in college again—this time as a professor.

I finished my doctoral dissertation this last winter and am scrambling to find a teaching job. My PhD in Physics turns out to only be useful in a few areas: the military, energy production, and academia. Not wanting to further the evolution of weapons of mass destruction or promote nuclear energy, I've been looking for teaching posts. My motivation is threefold:

1. I have to make my first student-loan payment in less than six months, and I'm almost broke.
2. I can't really afford to live in my little apartment now that my work-study job has ended.
3. Although she would love it, I do *not* want to move back in with my mother.

Luckily, I'm flying out for my first interview today. Honestly, I don't even remember sending a letter of inquiry to Miskatonic University in Massachusetts. I applied for a lot of graduate teaching fellowships online, though, so it's possible. I remember uploading my qualifications to an academic headhunting website, too. Maybe the referral came from there. In any case, I received a promising letter of introduction from Miskatonic University. They're paying for a two-day "greet, tour, and evaluate" trip to see if they want to hire me.

Howie's enjoying our walk along the beach. He's running off the leash now, along the edge of the water. "Would you like to live on the East Coast, Howie?" I ask. He looks up at me quizzically and pauses for a moment. Then, like a rocket, he launches himself after a seagull.

For a minute I worry about how he'll adjust to New England. Massachusetts has a beach, but it's not like this one. The winters in the Northeast can be brutal. I'll have to do a little research on dog clothing —sweaters and such.

For another minute I worry about my car. Can my 1999 Toyota RAV4 even make it to Massachusetts? I'll have to do a little more research on getting a newer car or see if I can get by at Miskatonic without a car. I've been thinking it would be environmentally responsible to have an electric car. Do they have charging stations in Massachusetts?

"Slow down, Mac," I say to myself. First there's the interview.

I'm checking my suitcase. Not being much of a traveler, I wonder what I've forgotten. I have the usual underwear, toiletries, and socks, of course, but do I have the right clothes? I assume that I need a button-down dress shirt and sport jacket for the interview, but is a tie necessary? Could I wear jeans? I nervously pack slacks and an emergency necktie in addition to more casual clothes. Better to be prepared.

The coordinator of this visit, a Ms. Claire Barry, indicated there would be some kind of "meet and greet" reception party when I get there tonight. "Do you think I need fancier clothes for the party, Howie?"

Howie is sitting on the end of my bed, his paws folded in front of him. He's been watching me intently. He knows I'm going somewhere and knows he's going to be spending some time at Mom's. She's going to come by and pick him up from my apartment on her way home from work.

I get out my tickets, maps, and information about Massachusetts and Miskatonic University. I don't really need the map; a driver is picking me up from Boston airport. Still, it's nice to visualize where I'm going.

Naturally, I've been doing some Internet research on Miskatonic. The campus is a few miles outside of Arkham, Massachusetts, on a 150-acre plot. Founded in 1775, it is one of the few US universities established before the American Revolution. Although it is not one of the Ivy League schools like Brown or Columbia, it's certainly old enough and well pedigreed. It's a small university with about 4,000 students and 380 academic staff members.

The Internet claims that its specialties are literature and oceanography (it is only a half hour from the coast.) The online catalog of classes indicates plenty of physics classes that I could teach. Hopefully they will allow me to concentrate on some of my specialties.

The photos of the campus are impressive, if a bit austere. Many of the buildings are so old that they have that gothic look. If there's Internet access on the plane, I'll see if I can research the architecture a bit. The administrative building looks like a medieval cathedral or castle, and some of the other buildings are quite striking. I wonder if there's on-campus housing or if I have to find a place in Arkham.

The doorbell to my apartment interrupts my thinking. I see that my taxi to the airport has arrived. The driver picks up my small suitcase and backpack and puts them into the back of the cab. I say goodbye to Howie and lock the apartment behind me. The journey has begun.

Later, on the plane, I have a realization: *I'm going to get this job.* Since the letter of inquiry arrived, I've been feeling it getting closer. The job, I mean. I know that sounds a little crazy, or maybe desperate, but it's not that. Sometimes I know things before they happen. Sometimes I can feel when something is a sure thing—and generally it is. I have that feeling about Miskatonic. My life there is "getting closer."

I've also had one of my dreams.

I remember almost all of my dreams. I was trained to do that as part of a work-study research project at UCLA. As an undergraduate I was paid to do dream research. I still keep a dream journal, and I can generally record several of my dreams every night.

My numinous dreams are different, though. They seem portentous. They stand out from the other dreams. They also generally come true. Not in a literal sense, not always, but almost always in a recognizable way. My backpack is under the seat in front of me, and I pull out my dream journal and find my notes on the dream I had about Miskatonic.

It was like this: I'm standing in a lecture hall in front of a green blackboard. A piece of chalk is in my hand. Rows of seats are arranged in tiers going back and up so that everyone has a good view. The hall has high ceilings and is well lit with arched palladium windows. The room is old, stately even. Although it has some modern touches and AV equipment, it looks like it's been in use for at least a century.

The hall is full of students, and they're all looking at me intently. In the dream it's not scary, though. I'm their professor, and they're just caught up in my lecture. It's a comfortable feeling and one that I've had as a graduate teaching fellow at UCLA. The difference is that it feels like home. It feels like it's *my* lecture hall. It feels like these are *my* students.

The classic *Star Trek* episodes had a weird lighting technique. It made a character or scene "stand out." In the midst of the otherwise well-lit Starship Enterprise, one actor (usually Captain Kirk) would have moody, shadowy lighting. His face would be strangely highlighted amid the shadows.

My dream journal says, "Star Trek lighting," because it was like that in the dream. I was the featured actor. I was the one getting the special lighting treatment in my own lecture hall, just like Captain Kirk got special lighting on the bridge of his starship.

That's how I know I'm going to get this job. The lecture hall is already mine. I'm the featured lecturer.

❖

Flights going east across the country take all day. Even with a morning flight from LAX I spent most of the day on planes and then a ninety-minute trip in a hired car. We make it to Arkham near sunset, and as we approach the university gates there's just enough light to admire the campus.

Miskatonic University *is* impressive. It was built over two centuries and features some of America's most monumental architectural styles. Granite, sandstone, and brick are the featured materials, and some of the buildings are like medieval castles complete with turrets, colonnades, cloisters, and bell towers. The grounds are well maintained, and I feel like we've entered the estate of European nobility. Using a circuitous utility driveway, we pull up to the main administration building, University Hall.

Getting out of the hired car, I can't help but stare. The building is imposing. It stands tall at the head of an oblong grassy area and looks like it is carved out of solid granite. A sense of ponderous age assaults my senses. This building will be here long after my passing. It is both solid and graceful. It seems impossible that flying buttresses and filigreed window casings could be made of stone!

A cool wind blows across my face, making me shiver. I realize that I'm not alone, and I step forward to meet a woman standing in the entrance portico.

Extending her hand, she says, "I'm Claire Barry. You must be Dr. Mackenzie."

Ms. Barry looks extraordinary. Although in her fifties, she has a youthful bearing and an energetic handshake. What I notice first, though, is her shock of orange-red hair. This color, clearly out of a bottle, complements her almost-black skin perfectly. With striking looks and an easy-going manner, she seems larger than life. She's wearing a yellow blouse and a russet-colored skirt and jacket that accentuate her slight figure.

"Nice to meet you," I lamely say, noticing that her long fingernails are painted the exact color of her hair.

"You look a little tired," says Ms. Barry, motioning me to follow her into University Hall. "That's not surprising, considering your all-day trip." I take my suitcase and backpack and follow her into the foyer of this grand building, back toward a hallway to the left of the entrance. As I follow, she continues speaking. "Let me show you our visitor's suite and you can freshen up before our meet-and-greet party tonight. This building was built in 1750, and although it's drafty and cold in the winter, it has some beautiful rooms."

At the end of the hall, she opens a tall door, and I see what she means. If this is the visitor's suite, they must have been expecting royalty. We've entered a sitting room with a travertine floor, white paneled walls, a travertine and alabaster fireplace, and lovely modern (and comfortable-looking) furniture. An oriental rug is centered in front of a fireplace and subdued lighting warms up the entire space. To the left, I see an opening into a bedroom with more of the modern furniture to contrast with the three-hundred-year-old dark wood paneling and vaulted stone ceiling. The effect of both rooms is one of amazing luxury.

"I'm sure you'll be comfortable here, Dr. Mackenzie. The bedroom is through there and a bathroom beyond. You have an hour or so to get ready for our cocktail party. I'm not sure if that's enough time for a nap, but you can at least take a shower if you like." She's smiling and getting ready to make her exit. "The meet-and-greet is at seven, and I'll come by to take you there."

I'm putting my suitcase down, still taking in the room. It has arched gothic windows looking into a walled garden. The dwindling twilight barely illuminates a cherry tree in early spring bloom.

As Ms. Barry heads to the door, I stop her with a question. "How should I be dressed tonight?"

She turns to look at me, and her smile widens a bit. "Nervous?" she asks. "You needn't be. Although the university faculty may tend to dress up for holiday parties, it's more a matter of form than it is of judgment. You brought a suit, didn't you?"

I pull my sport jacket and slacks out of my suitcase and hold them up. Ms. Barry looks less than impressed.

"A tie?" she asks.

Reluctantly, I pull my tie out of the suitcase.

Ms. Barry looks from the clothes to me and back again. "Yes, that will do," she says, turning to leave.

"You mentioned a holiday," I say with a question in my voice.

Without turning back, Ms. Barry says, "Tonight's the beginning of Ostara."

An hour later, a chime sounds in the sitting room. I'm almost dressed —just struggling into my necktie. I feel much better after a shower and am looking forward to meeting my colleagues at the party. I fuss some more with my tie, then realize the chime was probably some kind of doorbell.

Ms. Barry is at the door, and she's holding a necktie of her own.

"I hope you don't mind," she says. "This belongs to my son, and it will go much better with your shirt and sport jacket." She's smiling again, and I realize this is probably the way she smiles at her son. Maybe I remind her of him. Maybe he also has trouble dressing properly.

"I don't mind, if you help me put it on," I say. "I'm having a heck of a time getting the two ends to be even."

"Of course," says Ms. Barry. She deftly puts her son's tie around my neck, and ties it in a few seconds. She was right, too, it looks like it was made for my sport jacket.

"I thought you said they wouldn't mind how I looked," I say, inviting comment.

"That's not exactly what I said," clarifies Ms. Barry. "I said that dressing well for tonight was more a matter of form than a means of judgment. I also think that first impressions are important, and I want you to make a good impression."

I'm not sure how to respond to her kindness, so I say, "Thank you."

"You're welcome," she says.

"You mentioned Ostara. I don't think I've heard of that holiday. Is tonight a special occasion?"

Ms. Barry looks puzzled for a minute, then asks, "Did I say Ostara? I meant Easter, of course. It's this Sunday, and we like to celebrate it at Miskatonic. Ostara is just an old word for the beginning of spring. Easter's an old holiday, you know, based on the lunar cycle. It's celebrated on the Sunday following the first full moon after the vernal equinox. The early Anglo-Saxons used it as a time for planting spring gardens and to herald new life and new ideas."

I'm wondering how the resurrection of Christ fits into all this, but not being a churchgoer I make no comment.

"Shall we go 'meet-and-greet?'" asks Ms. Barry, pointing to the door of the visitor's suite.

I follow her down the corridor nearly all the way to the grand entrance hall, but we make a turn down a short hall and through a doorway at its end. It opens into a small, lovely ballroom. The room is square, with twin fireplaces on opposite sides. Both are lit, and they add to the warm glow of the room. An inlayed wood floor is in shades of honey-oak with ebony accents. A rich tapestry covers much of the stone wall opposite the doorway. A bar has been set up near the fireplace on the left, and a few small tables and club chairs furnish the rest of the room. The ceiling is quite high, with amber-shaded lights hanging from imposing wooden beams. Flanking the tapestries, arched windows look out into the same garden I see from the visitor suite. It's dark now, but the garden is bathed in moonlight.

The room has about a dozen people in it, and Ms. Barry guides me toward a group seated at one of the tables.

"Dr. Mason, I'd like to introduce you to Dr. Mackenzie," she says, brightly. "Dr. Mason is chancellor of Miskatonic University."

Dr. Mason is pale and lean and rises to shake my hand. In his late sixties or early seventies, his hair, eyebrows, and small mustache are surprisingly dark. He is wearing a black evening suit and tie. His clothes look like they were tailor-made just for him. I'm clearly under-dressed for this evening.

"Glad you could come out east for a visit," says Dr. Mason, smiling warmly. "It's almost impossible to find good teaching staff these days, and you are highly regarded at UCLA. It's hard to get to know people in just one day, but I hope we can at least start the process."

I'm thinking, *Not well regarded enough for UCLA to hire me*, but I say, "That's nice to hear! I'm looking forward to meeting some of the people I might be working with."

"Then, let me introduce two of your colleagues," says Dr. Mason. "This is Dr. Marianne Christianson, the head of the Science Depart-ment. She would be your boss and advisor. Marianne has had the pleasure to mentor quite a few new faculty members here at Miskaton-ic."

"Nice to meet you, Dr. Mackenzie," says Dr. Christianson. Marianne Christianson is dressed even more extravagantly than Dr. Mason. Although I'm not much on ladies' fashion, it's easy to spot some of the more expensive accessories. Her Hermés scarf must have cost more than my monthly salary at UCLA.

"My pleasure," I say, shaking her hand. She is about five-and-a-half feet tall and a little plump. With an expensive short haircut and mani-cured nails, she is every inch a powerful businesswoman. Her smile is genuine, though, and I can tell that she's more interested in me than in how I'm dressed.

"Your dissertation on black-body energy was most promising. Do you think it might be put to practical use?" Dr. Christianson's eyes gleam in the soft light of the room.

"Science always has real-world potential," I say. "The trouble is how much time and resources must be spent to make it useful. In the case of harnessing black-body energy, containment of a mini black hole will be the first issue to be addressed. It won't be contained using any current techniques, that I know of."

Dr. Christianson smiles broadly as though I've passed some test. "Oh yes, time and resources! Time and resources! I guess everything boils down to those!"

"Luckily, we're teaching the theories that will eventually allow such things," I say, with an encouraging smile of my own.

"Quite right," Dr. Christianson says.

Dr. Mason continues his introductions. "And this is Dr. Horace Alvarez. Dr. Alvarez, this is Dr. Mackenzie."

"We'd be partners," says Dr. Alvarez. "We'd share lab spaces, conference rooms, and lecture halls." With coffee-colored skin and dark hair that has turned mostly gray, Dr. Alvarez must be in his early sixties. He's tall, like I am, and has a strong, confident handshake. He's dressed a little more casually, in a dark brown suit, a cream-colored shirt, and a patterned necktie. I immediately get a good feeling from Dr. Alvarez. His clear brown eyes are friendly and welcoming.

"What is the lab space like?" I ask.

Dr. Alvarez shakes his head. "We have two. They're a bit stuck in classical physics, I'm afraid. One of the reasons I'm looking forward to having you here is to modernize things. The labs are a good size, but the equipment needs updating."

"And I've promised to help with that," says Dr. Christianson. "We have a significant budget for lab equipment upgrades over the next twenty-four months. We're just waiting for a proposal on how to use it."

Dr. Alvarez is looking at me directly, and I say, "I think Dr. Alvarez and I could have fun spending your money, Dr. Christianson."

"Call me Horace," says Dr. Horace Alvarez, with a happy smile.

"I'm Mac," I say, smiling right back.

As we get drinks from the bar, I can't help but notice the tapestry on the stone wall. It's huge, and it's so old that the once-bright colors have faded considerably. It appears to be a coastal scene. The blue, green, and gray colors depict a shoreline with cliffs, a prominent reef, and a small town. It also appears to be a battlefield. The people from town are attacking people from the offshore reef. It's a confusing design, and it's difficult to see whether the townspeople are fighting other townspeople or creatures from the sea. Some of the "people" on the reef look human. Others look more like fish or mythological creatures.

"That's one of our famous tapestries," says Ms. Barry. "It's over two hundred years old and depicts Devil's Reef and the uprising of the

townspeople of Innsmouth against the Dagon merpeople." Ms. Barry is
trying her best to keep from smiling.

"Um, OK." I say. "I didn't realize that tapestry makers would spend
all that effort on myths."

"Oh yes," says Ms. Barry. "They do, actually. There are wonderful
tapestries depicting St. George and the dragon and others featuring
unicorns and mythical creatures. What makes our tapestry unique is
that it is a new-world myth. Stories of the merpeople, or Dagon as they
were called, go back before the founding of America by white settlers.
Innsmouth was one of the first settlements in Massachusetts, and this
depicts how that initial settlement was destroyed."

"By merpeople?"

"That's the myth," says Ms. Barry, peering closely at the tapestry.

We're interrupted by the approach of a shy man of middle age. Ms.
Barry introduces him. "This is Dr. Shyam Gupta. He's one of our
dissertation advisors and one of the true scientists on staff."

I extend my hand and say, "Pleased to meet you, Dr. Gupta. I'm Dr.
Mac Mackenzie."

Dr. Gupta is olive-skinned and has dark hair and shining black eyes.
Ms. Barry leaves the two of us to talk as she heads over to a table of
finger food.

"Yes, I know," says Dr. Gupta, shaking my hand as he speaks. He's
clearly interested in my research, and excitement shows in his voice.
"We've actually met once before. We were at a conference together. You
were part of the team that presented a wonderful paper on miniature
black holes."

Remembering the conference in New York, but not Dr. Gupta, I say,
"Thank you. It was a great conference. Were you presenting that day,
also?"

"No, just an observer," says Dr. Gupta. Brightening, he continues,
"Do you think we'll be able to create mini black holes in the
laboratory?"

"Maybe we already have," I say, slyly.

"Not for real!" exclaims Dr. Gupta, clapping his hands together.

"Well, it's possible," I say. "A mini one would be microscopic. They
would be devilishly hard to detect. With such a small event horizon,
they could remain unnoticed for a long period of time. We may have
already created one as a result of one of the particle collision experiments at CERN or at Beijing's IHEP."

"Wouldn't it siphon off matter, though?" asks Dr. Gupta.

"Oh yes. Little by little. Because it would work its way through matter, it would fall into the nearest gravity well. Then its event horizon would slowly eat away at the matter drawn into that well."

"My stars! But you're talking about the Earth!" says Dr. Gupta. "If the black hole was created here, it would sink down into the Earth's core. It would be digesting the planet from the inside out!"

"Little by little," I say again.

A pause, then we both laugh at my little physics joke. We both know that in theoretical physics most anything is possible. Not likely but possible. As we laugh, I think Dr. Gupta is warming up to having me on campus.

"And what about transversing the realms?" asks Dr. Gupta. "Do you think we can manage it through physics, or will we have to continue using trance states and lucid dreaming?"

I'm completely baffled by his question. Unsure what to say or ask, the conversation halts. Ms. Barry rejoins us with a plate of crackers and Brie and sees my inquiring face.

Dr. Gupta explains, "I was asking Dr. Mackenzie about his thoughts on transversing and..."

Ms. Barry gives Dr. Gupta a Medusa stare that cuts him off in mid-thought.

"Dr. Gupta," she says with a surprisingly cold voice, "Perhaps you would consider refilling our glasses?"

Ms. Barry continues to look at Dr. Gupta as he heads to the bar. Without a word of explanation, she holds out her plate of finger food. "You really should try one of the rice paper rolls," she says. "They're quite good."

After more chatting and with fresh drinks in hand, Ms. Barry introduces me to a table of gentlemen from the Oceanography Department. I must be starting to get tired (or a little drunk), because I almost immediately forget their names. They're all complaining about funding and the expense of submersible equipment. After a bit, I realize that they're talking about Innsmouth. Miskatonic University's Marine Science Center is located in modern-day Innsmouth.

I point to the tapestry and ask the group, "Do you gentlemen know more about merpeople and the Dagon myth? Ms. Barry told me that the tapestry depicts Innsmouth from two hundred years ago."

The gentlemen look at each other in silence. Finally, one of them, a blond professor of oceanic currents, says, "Do you mean the creature or the worship?"

The others at the table look down, but the speaker continues. "The word 'Dagon' pertains to both the mythical creature thought to live off the coast of Massachusetts and also to a cult that worships those creatures."

He says this with such seriousness that I'm not sure how to respond.

"The Dagons still exist," he says, shrugging. "They have a church in Innsmouth."

CHAPTER TWO

Ostara

After the party, after falling asleep in the visitor's suite, and long after midnight, I have this dream. It's an unusual one, and at first I don't think I'm dreaming. I gradually "wake up" in the dream and find myself in bed in the visitor's suite of University Hall. I've never had a dream about waking up in bed before. But it's definitely a dream.

The room has a funny feel to it, a sort of dreamlike, slo-mo quality. I imagine this must be what it's like being anesthetized for an operation. Moonlight streams in from the window, washing the room in pale, silvery tones. I'm awake but not.

Of course, it has to be a dream for the little brown man to fit in. He's quite amusing. At no more than six inches tall, he's sitting at the foot of my bed on top of the covers. Just looking at him makes me smile. He's like an animated character out of a children's movie. Half human, half animated mouse, he's holding his tiny hands in front of him and is wearing a green vest. Although covered in sleek brown fur, his head is human and cocked to one side, peering at me from underneath expansive eyebrows. He's smiling, too, like we're good friends.

"Hello," I say. "I'm Mac."

The little man/mouse smiles more broadly, and he stretches forward a bit sniffing the air. It is a mouse-like movement, and his pointy nose is lifted high.

"I'm Brown Jenkin," he says.

It's hard to place his accent, but I swear he must have flown in from Bristol, England. Brown Jenkin continues to stare at me with both familiarity and intensity.

"Why are you here?" I ask.

"Oh, that's a good one," says Brown Jenkin. "Why am I here? Well, I will not lie to you. It's not my style. I'm here to interview you."

That gets me laughing a bit. I'm being interviewed by an animated mouse! I don't remember having such an odd, funny dream before.

Brown Jenkin joins me in the laughter, then asks, "Will you remember this dream, do you think, Mac?"

"I'm sure I will. I remember all my dreams."

"Do you?" asks Brown Jenkin. "Remarkable. Do you mind if I come a bit closer?"

"Of course not," I say. "Come up, and I'll get a better look at you."

Brown Jenkin edges forward a bit on the bedspread, and it's an odd movement. His edges appear indistinct, and the motion is a hybrid of how a mouse might scramble and how a small man might walk. My mind has trouble understanding Brown Jenkin's mode of movement, but suddenly he's much closer, and I notice that his small round face is really quite handsome. For some reason, I'm feeling almost inebriated, and I say the first thing that comes into my head.

"You're a handsome little fellow, aren't you?"

"Yes, I am quite 'glamorous' tonight, you might say," he replies. "I thought I would look my best for the interview, you see. I owes you that." As he speaks, he's primping a bit, showing off his vest and puffing up his furry chest.

"That's right. The interview," I say.

"Second question," says Brown Jenkin. "Do you make changes in your dreams?"

"Oh yes. All the time. If things get scary, I just change it. Sometimes I change things in a dream just to make it more fun."

"Are your dreams often scary, Mac?"

"Is that one of your questions, Mr. Jenkin?"

"We're friends now, Mac. You can call me Brownie, if you want. Scary dreams, yes?"

"Some are scary, Brownie," I say, almost laughing again. Something about calling him Brownie seems hilarious. "What kind of name is 'Brown Jenkin?'" I ask.

"Oh, it's an old, old name, but then, I'm an old fella. I came to America on a brigantine full of Puritans. Those were the days, eh? A little fellow could take his pick of friends then. People were simple, more trusting, like. But I'm the one asking questions, remember?"

"I remember."

"Do you have dreams about places you've never been to? Places in other worlds or places where people aren't even people?" asks Brown Jenkin.

"Of course," I reply. "Doesn't everybody? Don't you?"

Brown Jenkin smiles broadly, and his teeth come into better focus. They seem sharper than I would have thought for this happy little guy. He doesn't answer my question.

"Do your dreams ever show you what's going to happen?"

The frivolity of this dream seems to be having its impact on me. I think of the Disney version of this question. "Are you asking me if my dreams 'really do come true'?"

"Yes," says Brown Jenkin, pointedly. "Do they?"

"Not always," I say truthfully, hoping not to disappoint my new little friend.

"Can you tell the difference?" asks Brown Jenkin. "Do you know which dreams will come true?"

"Sometimes."

"Is this dream going to come true, do you think?" asks Brown Jenkin, with a twinkle in his small brown eyes.

At first the question seems silly. We're still having this dream, after all! But then I realize he's also asking if this is a lucid dream. He's asking if I have any control over how it comes out. By way of answering, I make his vest disappear.

"Oi!" says Brown Jenkin. "That's my vest! You ought not interfere with a fella's vest, you rascal!" The vest reappears but not under my direction.

"Do you believe in Magic?" asks Brown Jenkin. "Do you believe in summoning spirits, talking to the dead, and scrying the future?"

"That's more than one question," I say, a bit peevishly.

"Answer," says Brown Jenkin, a note of sternness in his voice.

"I do believe that 'There are more things in heaven and earth, Horatio, than are dreamt of in your philosophy,'" I say, remembering the quote from *Hamlet*. I try to match Brown Jenkin's stern tone but end up with a giggle.

"Shakespeare, is it?" remarks Brown Jenkin. "He was a true arse, in my opinion. Thought he was so la-ti-da!" He pauses for a moment, reflecting. "So you *do* believe in the hidden world, eh?"

"Yes. Most of what's hidden isn't magic, though. It's just hidden."

"Always the scientist," says Brown Jenkin, tilting his head and smiling wickedly. "I suppose you'll think more on it after Miskatonic gets under your skin. Have you ever wished someone harm and had it happen?"

"No. Other people create their own bad fortune."

Brown Jenkin thinks and then asks for clarification. "And you, eh? Do you create your own bad fortune?"

The conversation has turned philosophical for a moment. "I believe that we each create our life, bad or good, as a consequence of what we think and believe and expect. If you expect life to be hard, it will be. If you expect and think the best, you'll have a more positive life."

"Oi," says Brown Jenkin, after a moment's pause. Suddenly he's all smiles again. "Sounds like New Age American pap! Good luck with that around here!" He waves broadly, indicating the university or perhaps the world in general.

"Last question," says Brown Jenkin. "Do you have sex with animals?"

We both laugh. This seems like a great joke, but at the same time I see that he requires an answer. Throughout the dream I feel like I've been given a truth serum. It's a fun dream, and answering the questions feels fun, too.

"No," I say, smiling. "That's disgusting."

Brown Jenkin shrugs, then he says, "I think that's enough questions for now, eh?"

"Did I pass?" I ask.

He looks at me, uncomprehending.

"The interview," I prompt. "Did I answer all the questions correctly? Did I pass?"

"Oh yes. The interview." Brown Jenkin reflects a moment. "Yes, you answered all the questions. You did good, and I'm going to tell you a story."

Clearly the story is a reward of some kind. "Is it a bedtime story?" I ask, indicating the bed around us with a sweep of my hand.

We both laugh.

"Yes," says Brown Jenkin. "It will help you go back to your sleep."

Sleeping already, as we are, we both have another quiet laugh.

Brown Jenkin moves a little closer and begins to tell the story. "There once was an old lady what wanted to own the world."

"You can't own the world." I say, but Brown Jenkin silences me with one finger of his right paw.

"She wanted to control the world, then, if you like. To this purpose, she learned the forgotten magic ways. She studied old books. She apprenticed with a cut-wife and learned herbs. Later, she conjured demons and learned the means to control them."

"Did she have sex with animals?" I ask, repressing a giggle.

"Shush," says Brown Jenkin. "Listen to my story." He moves a little closer. He's sitting on my solar plexus now, his perfect little hands clasped together in front of him.

"She learned about the secret side of life. She learned how to bewitch people and have them see what she wanted them to see. She healed people of all sorts of diseases and also could make them sick, when it suited her right. She learned ancient ways of stopping death or at least how to go beyond it.

"As part of learning poisons, many of the neighbors' dogs did disappear. One of her spells made all the milk in the village turn sour. Although she had nothing to do with it, a village babe was born with twelve fingers. These things and more were said to be her fault, and the people of the town grew fearful, like. They called her names and stopped doing business with her. They were afraid of her, but she learned that fear was not enough to keep her safe. One cold spring morn' she heard the old wives talking to each other while hanging the wash. She heard the wicked people of town planning to kill her. A dozen men would come to her home on Sunday, three days hence. After church they'd hang her."

"Hang her," I say, almost to myself.

"Oh yes," says Brown Jenkin. "They planned to haul her right up Church Street to Hangman's Hill. That's the way they did things then."

"In the story," I say, quietly.

"In the story," repeats Brown Jenkin. "So she planned her escape. By Sunday morning she'd be long gone. She put together the things she needed for travel. She'd go on horseback Saturday night and needed to get provisions from the village. The villagers all knew about the hanging, of course, and they were happy to sell her what she needed. They must've figured it was easy money and soon she'd be done."

Brown Jenkin pauses in thought as though remembering the rest of the story.

"She bought herself traveling clothes, jerky, pemmican, hardtack, and other things so she wouldn't have to stop for a league or more. She was a smart one and a good planner, like. She also decided to buy a new saddle, one better for long-distance and damp travel. At the smithy, she came across a fine saddle brought all the way from England. She bought it with the last of her money. Hidden away, in the pommel of the saddle, after four thousand miles aboard a ship, she found her first true friend."

"It was you," I say, somewhat sleepily. The bedtime story is having its effect, and I'm having trouble focusing on the story and on Brown Jenkin. When I blink my eyes, it's hard to see him clearly. One blink, he's all animated mouse character. The next blink, he seems more like an old sewer rat.

"I was her only true friend," says Brown Jenkin, "and someone who could help her." He moves forward again. Now he's on my chest, and I see that his vest is gone and what I thought was sleek brown fur is actually patchy and worn. His front paws still look like hands, though, and they're outstretched to my neck and face as he continues his story.

"Her new friend also knew a thing or two about magic. Even a mouse has its place in the hidden world," says Brown Jenkin, puffing out his chest. "Old World mice have lived through plague and war. While much of London was on fire, mice were underground learning what can only be learnt in the dark places of tomb and grave."

Brown Jenkin's voice is getting quieter now, and I'm half asleep. I've got one eye open, and Brown Jenkin has paused his story for a moment. His mouth is bright red now, as though he's wearing lipstick. Lipstick on a rat! I think, amused at the idea.

As I slip into a half-sleep, back into the dream within a dream, Brown Jenkin finishes his story. "But either the old woman overheard wrong or the villagers changed the plan. When she went out Saturday afternoon to saddle up the horse, her property was surrounded by villains, her horse nowhere to be seen. That lady was desperate, I can tell you, with no means for escape. She ran back into the house. That's when those men decided that instead of hanging, they would burn her up.

"They set her thatched roof on fire and proceeded to barricade the doors. The house went up quick, I can tell you! Whoosh! With the flames coming out the windows, they expected to hear screams. But there was only silence and the sound of burning wood. They guarded the house all the afternoon until it was burnt clean to the ground. In evening they looked for signs of her body in the ashes and smoky remains. They were disappointed! No trace was ever found of Mother Mason!"

I can still hear Brown Jenkin, but my thinking is muddled with sleep, and I find myself overcome by it as I hear the last words of his story.

"I taught the witch to fly!"

Breakfast is uneventful. Ms. Barry has sent over someone from the dorm cafeteria with a tray. She must have forgotten to tell them I'm a vegetarian, because in addition to eggs, toast, and oatmeal, there's a pile of bacon. I pick over the food and wonder how I was at the party last night.

I remember the conversation was a little weird. Something about mythic undersea creatures. I got a bit drunk and indistinctly remember Ms. Barry walking me back to the visitor's suite. Oh, and the weird dream. I wonder if I should explain my behavior or if it was really OK? Distractedly, I look out the window in the sitting room into the walled garden. Today it's cloudy and looks colder than yesterday.

This time I recognize the chime from the door to the visitor's suite. I open the door, and there's Ms. Barry and a young man with blond hair and watery blue eyes.

"Good morning, Dr. Mackenzie," says Ms. Barry. "I hope you slept well."

I do not detect disapproval in her voice or face, so maybe I behaved well enough at the meet-and-greet. Ms. Barry looks fresh and happy. I return the borrowed tie to her, and she introduces the young fellow.

"This is George Marsh," she says. "He's a graduate teaching fellow in the Oceanography Department. I thought you might enjoy having someone your own age give you a short campus tour."

"Call me George," he says.

I smile and return the favor. "I'm Mac."

"George, would you do me a favor?" asks Ms. Barry. "I don't want Dr. Mackenzie to get lost or be late for his interview. Can I ask you to give him a tour, but end the tour at Massachusetts Hall no later than ten forty-five? His interview is at eleven, and I'll walk him there from Massachusetts Hall."

"Sounds fine, Ms. Barry," says George.

Ms. Barry takes her leave, and George helps me finish my breakfast. He eats the bacon, I take the rest.

George is about my height with a narrow face and a slender but muscled torso and lean arms. He's probably just a few years younger than I am. His blond hair is receding a bit, but he's handsome and easygoing.

"I like Claire," says George. "She practically runs the Science Department. I know she's Dr. Christianson's personal assistant, but somehow she's more than just that. She doesn't like me calling her

'Claire,' though. She's all business where Miskatonic is concerned."

While I'm getting ready to go out on the tour, I ask George some questions about the college.

"Are the younger faculty happy here?" I ask, pulling on a sweater for insulation against the outdoors.

"I suppose," says George, thoughtfully. "To be honest, though, there aren't many young professors on staff. I would guess that's one of the reasons they've invited you to interview. Miskatonic could use younger people with new ideas. There are a few other graduate teaching fellows that are in their twenties and thirties, but not many full professors under fifty."

"Is it easy to make friends here, do you think?" I ask, putting my shoes on.

"Oh yeah," says George, smiling. "Every fall there's a new batch of friends—if you know what I mean."

I do know what George means, but I respond, "Yes, but friends that will be more permanent. Not just dating."

"I see what you mean," says George, more thoughtfully. "I guess Miskatonic isn't any different than any other place with groups of transient people. You have to look toward the people who really live there if you want to make lasting friends. I don't think you'll have any trouble with that, Mac. I'd be glad to introduce you to some of the permanent faculty and GTFs. We're all a pretty friendly bunch."

I sense that George is being truthful, and I like the idea that he might be a friend on campus. We make our way to the front of University Hall. For all his fitness, George has a strange kind of shambling walk. From the windowed entry I can see that last night's clear sky has been replaced by heavy overcast. A light rain is beginning to fall. Although it's itching a bit, I'm glad I brought the wool sweater! We borrow umbrellas from the entryway of University Hall and step out onto the portico.

George starts by explaining the overall layout of the university.

"Think of three concentric rings," he says. "The first ring was built surrounding the Green. That's the common green area that existed when the campus was founded." We're standing just outside University Hall, at the head of the Green, with the first of George's rings spread out around us.

"In the early days, there was just this circle of buildings. In the 1800s, a second circle was built around the first circle. The third circle is mostly private residences built in the 1700s and 1800s. They were converted into university buildings and acquired by the school after the original owners died."

"Across the Green is Massachusetts Hall. That's the Science Department where Claire and Dr. Christianson work. That's also where you'd be teaching. I have a few of my science classes there too. Also in the first ring are the buildings for music, natural sciences, mathematics, and an alumni building. The big one to the right is the Solomon Center, which houses the main library as well as a large event auditorium."

George points between two of the buildings in the first ring to a more modern building in the background. "The second ring has a few newer buildings in it, including that modern dormitory complex and the Student Union. The Union is a great place to hang out, get a snack, and meet friends. It also has a graduate-student lounge, which is a nice place to meet some of the GTFs and younger instructors.

"I live in the third ring. If you get the job, ask them to find housing for you. They only take a small portion of my teaching salary and give me a small apartment. It's really quite affordable. Make sure you ask for on-campus housing—driving into Arkham in the winter is not fun!"

We step out into the rain, and George shows me more of the architectural sights. The Solomon Center, in particular, is spectacular. It's shaped like an eight-sided multistory beehive built of brick and sandstone. The sides are stacked gothic arches with leaded-glass windows. Each arch has fretwork and a lightning rod at the apex. The front "door" is three stories high, and George shows me the first floor of the library complex. It's a showpiece of old paneling and antique fixtures but also has modern library facilities and computers.

We end the tour, as we promised Ms. Barry, at Massachusetts Hall. It's a bit of a marvel, too. All granite and brick, it has an unusual five-sided tower integrated into one side of the building and projecting from the top of it. "I think they built the building around that old tower," says George. "You can see that it doesn't really match the rest of the building."

As we walk up the steps to Massachusetts Hall, I get a strange feeling. There's something not quite right about the place, or maybe it reminds me of something from a forgotten dream. I feel a little disoriented standing in the entryway. For a moment I wonder if this whole "moving to Massachusetts thing" is a good idea. Maybe I should change my mind, change my course of action, just get the hell out of here! Then, whatever weird feeling I'm getting passes. I'm just standing at the top of the steps at Massachusetts Hall with George holding the door open for me.

The inside of Massachusetts Hall is quite lovely. It's designed around a central rotunda, ringed with a multistory colonnade. We find Ms. Barry in the rotunda on the first floor. She's behind a reception desk, clicking away at a computer terminal.

"You're just in time," says Ms. Barry, speaking to George. "Let's quickly take him up to the third floor so he can see the physics labs and the lecture halls. Then I've got to get him back to University Hall in time to have him change for his interview." She's eyeing my clothing again. Clearly my jeans will not be adequate for the interview.

The three of us pile into the most interesting elevator I've ever seen. It's a brass cage hanging on the edge of the multistory colonnade and held in place with cables and struts. The controls look like some kind of steam-punk fantasy, but George is familiar with them. He pulls the gate to the cage closed, turns a huge lever, and we begin to rise majestically upward to the top of the rotunda.

We start with the physics labs. There are two of them on the third floor, and I'm a bit disappointed. When Dr. Alvarez said they were designed for "classical physics," I think he was being generous. Sir Isaac Newton would have been pleased with the labs and their equipment. Not me. Major upgrades will be necessary to perform quantum physics experiments in these labs.

Then we walk down the hall a bit farther, and Ms. Barry opens the door to one of the lecture halls.

It's my classroom from the dream. The tiered seating. The palladium windows. The green blackboard. All of it. I feel a chill going down my spine, and it's as though the lights have dimmed, while a brighter light is shining on me. It's that *Star Trek* lighting thing again. Of course, it's only in my head, but isn't that where reality starts?

"This is my lecture hall," I say, quietly, in perfect confidence.

Neither George nor Ms. Barry contradict me.

I'm back at University Hall in the visitor's suite and, once again, Ms. Barry is helping me with my wardrobe. She's borrowed another necktie and a pocket square from her son to go with my sport jacket and sweater. I have to say, Ms. Barry knows what she's doing. Although my look is still casual, it now looks expensive-casual and everything "goes together."

I'm still not sure of her motives. Why does she care how I look? Why does she care if I get this job? Somehow, I just don't have the gumption to ask these questions, and, smiling, she leads me down yet another hallway into a formal conference room.

The room is quite impressive. Ms. Barry calls it the chancellor's study, but it looks more like a medieval boardroom with a long oak table lined with armchairs with high backs. There's a fireplace along one paneled wall, but it doesn't dissipate the chill from this austere room. A wall of leaded-glass windows provides filtered light. High overhead, arched beams hold up a whitewashed ceiling. The main wall is bare granite stonework. The fireplace mantel contains the only decoration, and its bas-relief is a row of winged creatures with spears. Angels? Demons?

The room's chilly atmosphere is broken with a welcoming invitation.

"Come in, come in, Dr. Mackenzie. We've been looking forward to talking more with you." Chancellor Mason is all smiles today. He's dressed in another tailored suit, this time in shiny midnight blue. He motions to the others sitting at one end of the enormous table, and they stand. "I think you've already met everyone here." He motions to each one in turn, reminding me of their names. "Dr. Christianson, Dr. Alvarez, Dr. Gupta, and Ms. Barry, of course."

They all smile and nod as they're reintroduced. Dr. Alvarez (Horace) gives me a small wink.

"Please sit," says Dr. Mason, "and we'll get started. Claire, do you mind taking notes for us?"

Ms. Barry already has a small pad of paper in front of her, and she picks up a pen for note-taking.

Remembering my dream and Brown Jenkin, I wonder if Dr. Mason is going to ask me if I have sex with animals. He does not. Instead, I get a series of questions about my academic record, my research into quantum physics, black holes, dark matter, inter-dimensional mathematics, quantum computers, some of Einstein's paradoxes, and particle accelerators. Most of it pertains to the subjects I'll be teaching, but some of the questions sound more like fringe-science. At one point Dr. Christiansen asks if I think inter-dimensional travel is possible. Is she trying to see if I'm crazy or if I like science fiction? I give her my "anything is possible" speech, but I see that she's not entirely satisfied by it. Does she want me to speculate without any sort of scientific evidence?

Ms. Barry must feel that I'm starting to get flustered, so she asks me a question that's more down-to-earth. It's a hard question, but I appreciate her sincerity. She asks, "Why do you want to leave your home, your family, and your life on the West Coast, Dr. Mackenzie?" She's looking at me with compassion, and I know that this is the only question that matters to her.

"It's time for me to move forward in life," I say, simply. "So far I've just moved along. In school I did well in science, so Mom suggested UCLA. It was close to home, so I could save on expenses. One of my professors said that I had a real talent for quantum physics and started involving me in a team working on black holes and dark matter. Another professor loved my master's thesis and wanted me to help her work on a paper to be presented at a symposium. Someone at the symposium thought we could collaborate on a more fundamental study of so-called 'Hawking radiation.'"

I notice that I'm scratching my neck. That darn wool sweater! Self-consciously, I relax my hand and put it in my lap. "It seems my whole life has been successful—but always doing what other people thought I should be doing." I pause for a moment. I'm not really sure what I'm going to say next, but I plunge ahead, looking at Ms. Barry. "Working here represents doing something just for me. I love teaching, and this would be an opportunity to concentrate on what I love. There's something wonderful about showing new people the wonders of quantum physics. There's a power in helping someone set up proper conditions for a controlled laboratory experiment and utilizing the rigors of scientific methodology."

I look over to Dr. Alvarez and say, "I would so enjoy working with you in upgrading the science labs, Dr. Alvarez. Collaboration is something that I'm good at, and I have friends at UCLA who would help me, help *us*, with lab design. Updated equipment would bring Miskatonic into the modern age. Maybe physics could one day be listed as a Miskatonic 'specialty.'"

Now, looking at Dr. Mason, I finish answering Ms. Barry's question. "Although I don't know much about Miskatonic University, I do feel called to be here. When I went into the lecture hall on the third floor of Massachusetts Hall, I knew it was *my* lecture hall. I don't mean this in an arrogant way. I know you may not hire me for a teaching position. What I mean is that I had a complete sense of owning a classroom. I'm a good teacher. I would be a good professor *here*. I know that I can thrive at Miskatonic University, and I know the university will be better for my participation."

After a bit of silence, Dr. Christianson smiles and says, "So we've grilled you for about an hour, and you'll need to leave for your red-eye back to California in about another hour. Before you go, what questions do you have for us? If you were to accept a teaching position here what would you ask of us?"

So I tell them.

The plane ride home isn't any shorter, but at least the lights are low, and there's no pressure for talking. Most everyone is asleep. I'm pleased with my job interview. I can't imagine answering the questions any differently, and I think people responded well to me. Dr. Alvarez seems relieved that he would have someone to help him upgrade the labs and teach some of the more modern physics classes. Ms. Barry clearly wants me to have the job, and Dr. Mason, the chancellor, seemed friendly toward me.

Dr. Christianson didn't say much during the interview, but she didn't seem negative in any way, either.

My mind is racing a bit, and I realize that "worrying" about my job interview is silly. I either get the job or not. Worry will have no effect on the outcome and is just preventing me from going to sleep.

I also realize that I've been scratching my neck, off and on, for most of the day. It feels like I'm getting a rash on my neck and upper chest. I stop scratching and get out my gratitude journal to calm my nerves. It would be good to focus on all the positive things happening in my life and put my worries aside. A wise teacher once told me that recording five gratitude items every night would increase my awareness of the good things around me. Actually, she said, "That which we are grateful for will increase."

I write my list for tonight:

1. *Claire Barry: Ms. Barry may be too formal to be called "Claire," but I know she's going to be a friend.*
2. *Horace Alvarez: Horace will make a good colleague and collaborator.*
3. *My new lecture hall: It's mine. I can feel it!*
4. *Howie: I'm always grateful for Howie, and I know we'll make a home together at Miskatonic.*
5. *Neckties: I wore two different neckties in two days. That's got to count for something.*

I stow my journal and turn out the reading light. I'm calmer, but my neck still itches. I wonder if one of the flight attendants might have some cream. If it's an allergic reaction to the wool sweater, maybe a Benadryl would help. The seatbelt sign is off, so I unbuckle and move to the forward galley and bathroom area.

"Any chance you might have a Benadryl?" I ask one of the flight attendants. "I think I'm having an allergic reaction to something I was wearing earlier in the day. My neck and chest are really itchy."

She looks back at me, not unkindly. "I'm afraid we're not allowed to give passengers any kind of medication. Not even over-the-counter stuff."

"Might you have some hand cream or lotion? That might take some of the itchiness away."

The flight attendant reaches into an overhead and brings down her purse. "I guess I won't get in trouble for giving you hand lotion." She offers me a tube.

I get into one of the plane's tiny bathrooms. It's so small that I have trouble taking my polo off to check the rash—and it's quite a rash. It's at least ten inches in diameter, centered just above my collarbone. Of course, my scratching hasn't helped things. It's bleeding in the center.

I run some water on a paper towel and blot the small bloody patch where I've been scratching. The cool water feels good, and the bit of blood easily washes away.

Revealing the most curious thing.

There, at the center of this spreading rash, is a mark that's not made from my scratching or from a reaction to wool. It's two small punctures, like injection marks. They stand out white and unnatural against the surrounding rash. I'm dumbfounded. At first I think of spider bites. I've had them before, and they cause this kind of rash if you scratch them. Then I think of bed bugs, but they make bumps as well as itching. Maybe they're not bug bites at all.

In the dim lighting of this tiny bathroom, I peer closely at my neck. Suddenly, I realize exactly what the marks are.

I picture him sitting on my chest chatting amiably, creeping closer, so charming. Now he's leering with red-stained lips, his two incisors suddenly sharper than I remembered.

But Brown Jenkin was just a dream!

PART II

Witch Tower

When age fell upon the world, and wonder went out of the minds of men; when grey cities reared to smoky skies tall towers grim and ugly, in whose shadow none might dream of the sun or of Spring's flowering meads; when learning stripped the Earth of her mantle of beauty, and poets sang no more save of twisted phantoms seen with bleared and inward looking eyes; when these things had come to pass, and childish hopes had gone forever, there was a man who travelled out of life on a quest into the spaces whither the world's dreams had fled.

—H.P. Lovecraft, *Azathoth*

PROLOGUE

In the center of the White Castle, on his black onyx throne, Azathoth dreams. His salt-and-pepper hair and trimmed beard are immaculate. A tailored gray suit and stark white shirt frame a face of aristocratic breeding. His manicured hands sit in his lap. With closed eyes, he resembles a powerful CEO lost in thought.

He is such a CEO, and he's in the business of dreaming. While dreaming, he's at his creative best. He created the White Castle while dreaming and filled it with art, culture, and beauty. While dreaming, he took the very center of chaos and brought it into exquisite order. While dreaming, he became the king of the Outer Gods and laid waste to whole realms of time and space.

Azathoth was once a man like so many others, held hostage by an impoverished working life. Trapped in a meaningless job, ignored, friendless, he withdrew from life. Night after night, in a small, lonely room, he stared at the stars and dreamed of freedom.

One night, the stars took pity on his soul and liberated him. They gave his dreams creative power. But a powerful man, lost for so long in loneliness, anger, and despair, does not always know how best to use power. Azathoth has whims. He likes to exercise control. He has contempt for others.

Now that the Outer Gods have been brought into order, it is time to try something more challenging. In a time when its gods are dwindling in strength and number, humanity's Earth might be an interesting challenge. Should the sleeper be awakened? Should the tomb at R'lyeh be opened?

What means of entry into the fears and beliefs of humanity might suit his whim?

And so, smiling slightly, the demon Azathoth dreams.

CHAPTER ONE

A New Beginning

"License and registration, please."

It's not what you like to hear when you're making a fresh start in life. I had barely passed through the gates of Miskatonic University when campus security pulled me over.

The tag on his jacket says "Security—Justin Taggert," and he's standing, legs wide, in an exaggerated posture of authority.

"Was I doing something wrong, officer?" I ask in innocence, hopefully without showing annoyance.

"Identification, young man," says Taggert. "License and registration."

I get my license out of my wallet and take the registration out of the glove compartment.

"School hasn't started yet, you know," Taggert says, as I hand him my identification.

"I'm on the faculty. I'm just in from the Boston airport."

"The license says 'California.'" Taggert is looking at me with a mixture of skepticism and mild distain. He stands about five-ten and is packed into his too-tight uniform.

"Yes," I say. "I'm moving from California. I flew out from Santa Monica today to start my new teaching job at Miskatonic. I picked up my new car today, too. In Boston." I figure he's wondering about the temporary license plates on my Nissan LEAF.

"The GTFs don't have their orientation until later in the week," he says. "There's really no reason for you to be here, Mr. Mackenzie."

He's talking about the graduate teaching fellows, the assistants to the professors who teach some of the lower-division classes. "It's *Dr.* Mackenzie, and I'm on the permanent teaching staff. If anything, I should have gotten to campus sooner to get ready for classes." I hope I'm saying this with some authority. He's starting to piss me off. I don't like being treated like a kid—just because I'm young for a professor doesn't mean I should be disrespected.

"Just a minute," says Taggert. "Just wait a bit."

He takes my identification cards and returns to his campus security Prius.

"It's OK, buddy," I say, turning to Howie sitting in the passenger seat. "We're not in any trouble."

Howie cocks his ears and looks at me with an intensity that makes me smile. The ride from Boston has been a longish one for him, and he's probably anxious to get out and stretch his legs.

Eventually, Taggert returns and hands me back my identification. As he leans closer to the car, he notices Howie. "You know dogs aren't allowed on campus."

"I've got special approval," I say, hoping it's true. I did not get a formal answer to my request to have a dog in the residence hall. Howie and I may be looking for a place to live in town.

"What kind of dog is that?" asks Taggert, with a touch of a smile.

This is the first sign of pleasantry from him, so I decide to be chattier. "He's an Italian greyhound. They're like the racing greyhounds, only in miniature. His name's Howie."

"He's going to need an overcoat in about a month," says Taggert, getting a better look at Howie, with his bony legs and thin fur.

"I bought him sweaters and a coat in Boston. Maybe I can find some more things in Arkham." Arkham is the closest town to campus, about fifteen miles away.

"Good luck finding pet supplies in Arkham," Taggert says, putting his hands on his hips. His smile and interest seem to be fading. "But then, you might not be around long enough to need those sweaters. New people just don't fit in here at Miskatonic, and *you*," his arm sweeps to indicate me, my dog, and my new electric car, "*really* don't fit in."

This is such an extraordinary thing to hear on my first day in Massachusetts. My shock must be visible. I start to protest, but he cuts me short.

"You'll want to drive up the main access road here and take the fourth driveway on the left. Anna Brown is waiting for you at Grant Hall."

Clearly dismissed, I roll up the window and resume my slow drive.

The Miskatonic campus is from another era. If you've visited Harvard, Princeton, or any of the Ivy League schools in the Northeast, you know what I mean. Although smaller, Miskatonic's buildings were built in the 1700s and 1800s (some earlier) out of stone, brick, and heavy timber. Like medieval castles, they are solid, imposing, and, well, *old*.

The school is laid out in concentric circles with the oldest buildings on the inside, surrounding a common space known as "the Green." The original University Hall was built in 1750 and still stands as an imposing gothic behemoth at the head of the Green and its ring of initial buildings. I can see it far ahead, looming above the landscape.

A second ring of buildings was created at the beginning of the twentieth century containing all the departments needed to round out a full liberal arts and sciences college.

A third ring of buildings was acquired by converting local residences that had been adjunct to the early university. They, too, are of antiquity and of a variety of styles. As I pull into the indicated driveway, Grant Hall comes into view. It is on the National Register of Historic Places, so I was able to find out quite a bit about it. It was designed by the prominent Providence architects Angell and Swift and built in 1884. The university purchased it in 1940, and it was divided into quirky apartments for unattached faculty members—such as myself. It is built of rough ashlar granite with brownstone trim. It has enclosed balconies, a portico, two cupolas, a small conservatory, and a separate carriage house, all made into living spaces.

I pull up to Grant Hall and see that the Internet did not do it justice. The building is phenomenal. I park the car and step onto the porch.

As soon as I ring the bell, the solid oak door opens inward, and a woman with silver hair greets me. I figure her for about sixty-five years old but with a youthful vigor and stance. "You must be Dr. Mackenzie," she says. "I'm Emma Brown."

Mrs. Brown has one of those Massachusetts accents with the long "ays," as though she belongs to the Kennedy family. Although forthcoming, I wouldn't exactly call her manner friendly. *Am I a bother? Am I another stranger to take care of?* She's wearing tan trousers, a blue scoop-neck blouse, and a kind of stiff-looking apron that implies,

"We're all business, here!"

I volunteer, "Call me Mac, if you like."

She seems to miss my invitation. "My husband, Matthew, and I live just a few doors down. He's the handyman for many of the older residences. When things go wrong, you can give us a call." Quickly, she amends, "Within reasonable hours, of course."

Trying to be friendly, I ask, "Have you been on campus long?"

"Forever. We both used to be faculty, and the university lets us stay on as part of our retirement package. We love this old school."

As we step into the entryway, I see that Grant Hall is as lovely inside as out. Dark oak paneling lines the hall. Period lighting fixtures illuminate marble flooring overlaid with a lovely Oriental carpet. Mrs. Brown continues, "I thought I'd wait at Grant Hall to meet you. I have keys, can give you a tour, and answer any questions you might have about your new home. Have you been to the campus before?"

"Only once. I was here for a visit during spring term. The school flew me out as part of the hiring process. I got to see the campus, meet faculty from the Physics, Engineering, and Natural Sciences Departments, and they got to figure out if I'd fit in here."

"They must have decided so," says Mrs. Brown, giving me the once-over. "So, you're part of the permanent faculty now?" Her tone seems to imply that I'm being given something I may not deserve.

"Not tenured. I'm finishing a textbook and will be upgrading the physics labs. This year will be a trial period to see if the students like my teaching."

"Well, I'm sure they'll like you just fine." Mrs. Brown points to a grand staircase that rises from the entryway. "Would you like to see your quarters? I've picked out a nice set of rooms for you."

Ornate railings wind around a staircase leading up to the second floor. Mrs. Brown walks me up and points out the first door on the right side of the hall. "You'll get nice morning light and you overlook the front yard. Normally, that might not be an advantage, but this street is very quiet, and the view is definitely better here than from the back of the house." Mrs. Brown seems to be warming, slightly, to the idea of me living here, and she opens the door to my new apartment.

When I describe it as *quirky*, I mean it in a good way. It occupies an original second-floor bedroom suite. Mrs. Brown shows off the sitting room, small bedroom, bath, and kitchen alcove. It really has everything I need. Better yet, as an incentive to take my new job and partly as payment for my teaching fellowship, it comes at no cost to me.

But quirky also means *old*. I wonder whether the plumbing will provide adequate hot water and the 130-year-old windows will provide any insulation from the cold. I look for the central heating vents and, when I ask about heat am told that its source is a single radiator under the front windows.

Mrs. Brown's husband, Matthew, joins us. "Please, call me Matt," he says. "Matthew was my father's name, too, and it suited him better than me." Matt seems a little friendlier than Mrs. Brown. He has the same broad accent, but his choice of words and inflection indicate a greater interest in me and a desire to put me at ease. He, too, appears to be in his sixties and in good health. With nearly white hair and a ruddy complexion, he has that look of a kindly grandfather or a favorite uncle. He's wearing jeans and a button-down work shirt as though he's just come from a project of some kind.

Matt changes the subject. "I noticed you have a dog and a car that we have to make allowances for."

"Is that a problem? I thought people knew about Howie and that a small pet might be allowed."

"Oh, it's not that. I just want to make sure we take care of everything in the beginning. I took the liberty of making a few arrangements for the dog, actually. Why don't we get him out of the car."

Howie is a little freaked out by the steep stone steps leading up to the porch. He goes up just fine but stands at the top of the stairs looking doubtful about going down again. Maybe we can practice with some treats? Or maybe I'll just throw all pretense of manhood aside and carry him down the stairs?

Matt professes to be a dog lover. Although unimpressed with Howie's winter-worthiness, Matt enjoys some of his tricks. Both of the Browns get a big laugh out of Howie's operatic death scene when I shoot him with my finger (Bang!). Matt shows off the fenced yard Howie can use, and I promise to clean up after him. Satisfied with this arrangement, Matt surprises me by offering to build Howie a dog door into a window in my room.

"That way," Matt needlessly explains, "he can help himself whether you're here or not." Apparently, Howie and I may have the makings of a new friend.

Matt also has plans for the car. He'll provide a heavy-duty extension cord through a basement window for recharging and has dropcloths that I can use if I want to cover the car. My LEAF particularly intrigues Matt. Apparently, electric vehicles have not made their way into northern Essex County.

"What kind of maintenance does it need? How fast does it go? How many miles on one charge? How long does it *take* to charge?"

I explain it all and offer to let him drive it sometime soon.

The Browns are particularly fond of my new home. Mrs. Brown calls Grant Hall the "grand old lady" of the campus. I know what she means. It's solidly built but also has the fretwork, arches, and period detailing that give the building a feminine flair.

"And don't you mind the stories," Matt says, as we continue talking about the building I'm moving into. "Every old house has its secrets. Houses built so long ago have had their share of death as well as life. They've all had a scandal or two. They've also witnessed a lot of love. Your new apartment, for instance, used to belong to Professor William Dyer. He was a professor of geology, here at Miskatonic. He was a single guy, like you, and I hear he was quite the campus entertainer in his day. The story goes that he was never quite the same after the failed expedition to Antarctica in 1930. He and a graduate student made it back alive, but most of the party never survived that tragic trip to the frozen south.

"Anyway," Matt continues, "my point is that you'll hear some stories about Miskatonic. Some wonderful. Some beyond belief. The ones beyond belief, I'd treat just like that. If it sounds crazy, that's probably because it's a fabrication. The students and professors all like a good story, and the stories seem to get bigger with each telling and with each passing generation."

The Browns get ready to leave and give me a quick tour of the rest of the house. "Dr. Simmons lives in the garret apartment on the top floor. He's in the Literature Department and is some kind of Shakespeare expert. He's away for the summer but should be back in the next few days. He's a nice enough gentleman, although he left his place a mess when he took off at the end of spring term. I just left things the way they were. I'm not a housekeeper, you know." Mrs. Brown gives me a look that says, "I won't clean up after *you*, either."

"You share your floor with a new graduate teaching fellow, George Marsh, from Innsmouth. He's in the Oceanography Department, and I think he's working on opening the Marine Science Center back in his hometown. That's quite the project. We all hope it will revitalize that run-down old town. Anyhow, the ground floor has two apartments, but only Samantha Rouse, another teaching fellow, is staying downstairs from you. She's in the one facing the back. Sam's in computer science, but I don't remember much else. Applied systems, maybe? She's a sweet one but a little scattered. I hope she manages her teaching assignments." Mrs. Brown is clearly doubtful that Sam is going to work out and doesn't seem to care who knows. She dismisses her with a sweep of the hand. "She seems a bit flighty to me."

The Browns finish the tour in the basement, where Mrs. Brown shows me how to use the laundry facilities and loans me some fresh towels and a bath mat (which I forgot to buy on the trip from Boston). Matt shows me a storage locker where I can store the things that will be arriving from California via a slow and inexpensive moving service.

I thank the Browns for their hospitality. "You've really made me feel at home today. This is the first major move I've made in my life. I have to tell you, coming across the country and taking on a teaching position has me a bit rattled. It's a lot of change at once. I feel a bit overwhelmed."

"Let me know if there's anything I can do to help you settle in," says Mrs. Brown. Although the words are right, I can see that there's not a lot of enthusiasm in them. Luckily, I receive a friendlier dismissal from Mr. Brown.

"I'll be back tomorrow to work on that dog door. When I find time, I'll show you around some of the other fine old buildings here at Miskatonic."

"I'd like that very much," I say, thankful for his kindness.

As the sun sets, I utilize Matt's extension cord through the basement window and charge my LEAF in the driveway. I bring in the groceries and other items I picked up in Arkham on the way to the campus. It's time to move in.

I set up my new filtered water pitcher and unload the groceries into the refrigerator. I'll have to pick up more supplies for any real cooking, but I'm set for eating take-out and making breakfast. As a vegetarian, I hope Arkham has a few more options than what I saw earlier today. I finish unpacking my bags. I put new sheets (purchased in Boston) on the bed and unload my new set of dishes, flatware, and glasses into the kitchen alcove cabinets. I unbox my new toaster and coffee maker. Now that I've seen my kitchenette, I make out a small grocery list so I'll be ready for more shopping. I can use meal coupons in the cafeterias on campus, but it's nicer and cheaper to be self-sufficient.

It feels good to have everything unpacked. I may not be settled in, but at least I've put a few things in order. I suppose I'm compensating for all that does not feel settled or in order.

I have a microwave, so I test it out by making popcorn.

While munching and drinking root beer, I configure my laptop for the campus Wi-Fi and test Internet connectivity and e-mail. I drop my mom a quick note to let her know I've arrived.

Hi Mom,

Got to Miskatonic just fine. Air travel, even for Howie, was uneventful. The new (used) car is great. It has all the modern gizmos just like we thought it would from all the Internet info. The price ended up being a little less than we figured. Registration is cheaper than in California. Thank you for this amazing gift.

I spent all the rest of your money on supplies in Boston and Arkham: dishes, warmer clothes (including a sweater for Howie), bedding, etc. I'm all set, I promise. I should get my first paycheck at the end of the month and, honestly, I can start paying you back.

I know you're still pissed at me for leaving. You think this is a foolish adventure—especially after the weird interview trip last spring. I just can't afford to pass up this opportunity. They're going to match the payments on my undergraduate loans. With their help, I can pay off my student debt in about five years. They're also going to pay for all the editing and publishing of my textbook, since it will be work-related. I really don't think I'll get an offer like that anywhere else.

My new apartment is amazing. It's small but elegant. I think it used to be someone's bedroom suite in the 1800s. I'll post some pictures online so you can see. Yes, I have a kitchenette, not that I really will use it much. You know me and cooking.

To reach me, there's my cell phone and e-mail (of course). Nothing changes about them. When I check in at the departmental office tomorrow, I'll find out how the postal mail needs to be addressed and send you another note.

Don't worry, OK? Things are going to be great!

Your loving and self-directed son,

M

Mom was not happy about me leaving California and even less happy with my contract at Miskatonic. She thinks I deserve to be at a more prestigious school and in a nicer location, but Miskatonic's offer was better than any of my other prospects. I'm getting a decent salary, free lodging, and have a budget for upgrading the labs in Massachusetts Hall.

I send off e-mails to a few other people, giving them updated contact information. I post a few pictures of my new apartment to social media.

Howie is set up with food, water, and toys. I brought most of his old things along so he would have something familiar in his new environment. He has a new "on-the-floor" bed, but most likely he'll sleep with me. Howie's been exploring the apartment, and it's clear he likes it well enough. He's used to living in small spaces that can be readily understood and navigated, and this one seems to suit him. I push his new bed next to the radiator. If the bed is going to get any use, it will need to be warm.

With everything ready for a fresh day tomorrow, I decide to take Howie for a walk and explore the campus a bit. It's fairly well lit at night. Vintage lampposts create a pattern of light through the trees, and the cement and brick walkways between the buildings are easy to navigate. The grounds are kept up nicely, especially around the older buildings. Some of the rhododendrons and lilac bushes are so old they could be considered trees. Low plantings ring the buildings, and there's grass in the center of the Green. I'm tempted to say that the campus is picturesque at night, but that sounds a bit more optimistic than the truth. Most of the buildings have that gothic look to them, so the overall ambiance is more gloomy than romantic. The exterior lighting casts odd shadows on the walls of the buildings, highlighting the rough nature of much of the stonework.

Howie is lively on our walk—he's always excited to be out, and the still-warm end-of-summer air suits him. He's not as excited by the shadowed shrubbery, though. The campus is deserted before the start of the term, so I have him off the leash. He sticks to the path and seems to focus on getting to the next lamppost and its brighter pool of light. It's probably just the newness of the place—usually he's a bit more adventurous and will take off for a run just for the pleasure of the exercise.

We walk onto the Green at the center of the campus and make a loop of it, passing by the oldest of the buildings. The Green is perhaps the size of a football field, crisscrossed by walking paths, benches, and occasional tables. Above the Green, the moonless night sky is dark and filled with stars. We're far enough away from Arkham that there's little light pollution. You can easily make out the Milky Way. Although the night is warm, the starlight feels cold. I imagine what it must be like to travel between the stars in the impossible midnight depths of space.

When we walk by Massachusetts Hall, I try to imagine it as my new workplace. This is where I will be teaching ten hours of coursework a week, completing a physics textbook, and renovating the physics labs. I'll get keys to the building tomorrow when I meet my contact in administration. For now, I have to settle for seeing it on the outside.

The gothic-style hall was dedicated in 1778 as the university library (long-since moved into the more modern Salomon Center). It looks a bit like a church of red brick and sandstone, with a two-story entrance and arched windows. Adding to the church feeling, the many roof peaks all have crosses on them. The main tower of the building seems a bit odd, maybe five- or six-sided. It's definitely not right-angled, at any rate, and the unusual angles make for unusual shadows in the lamplight. The tower sticks up above the main roofline and has a row of windows under its separate peaked roof.

I try to coax Howie up the steps into the nearly dark recess of the entrance, but he's not having it. It does look a bit forbidding. The twelve-foot doors look like they must weigh three hundred pounds each, and peering through the glass panels in them, I see a dimly lit grand entrance leading into a central rotunda. From my brief tour earlier that summer, I know the ground floor houses departmental offices and a faculty lounge. An open staircase leads up to the second floor and a variety of classrooms and offices, including my own. The shared lab is also on the second floor of this four-story building. They've said I can have part of the basement to build out a small additional lab.

The other thing about the building is that it feels substantial. The tower is made of huge blocks of granite. It feels like the structure has been here long before my birth and will exist long after my death. *Am I really here? Really on the staff of this university?*

We complete our circuit of the Green. At its head stands University Hall, built in 1750. Its tall spires, peaked windows, and stone construction make it look like a medieval cathedral. Last spring I had a chance to stay in its visitor's apartment, meet the chancellor, and be interviewed in its imposing study. Somehow the place is both luxurious and creepy.

As we pass in front, Howie suddenly takes interest. He plunges into a poorly lit thicket of rhododendrons. I hear him start to growl. Fearing an encounter with a raccoon or other night dweller, I push between the shrubbery and find him braced against the sill of a basement window. My sight gradually adjusts to the gloom of this hidden spot, and I see what he's looking at. A well-worn hole in the casement of the window. It's round and about two inches in diameter.

Howie's sniffing and at the hole. I peer closer, noticing its strange, perfect roundness. I reach down and touch the edge of the hole and feel plastic. The hole is lined with black PVC piping to make it more permanent and to weatherproof the wood casing. Is it an exhaust pipe of some kind? Then I notice that at the edge of the window casing, a board has been nailed at an angle from the sill to the ground. *Egress and a runway to the ground!*

The image of Brown Jenkin leaps to mind, and my heart skips a beat. His brown, patchy fur. His lips stained with my blood. His too-sharp front teeth. My encounter with Brown Jenkin on campus last spring seemed like a dream, but in my heart I know he's real enough. I'm not sure *what* he is. A rat, certainly, but a rat with a voice? A rat with a will and a life beyond any natural rat. He conducted his own interview of me!

I pull Howie away from the wall and carry him back out to the Green, back to our apartment at Grant Hall. That's enough Miskatonic for one night.

We've been up for many hours today, and although I'm not particularly sleepy, I *am* tired. I peek out the window to see if the car is still charging (it is) and decide it's time for bed. On the bedside table I put my current stack of reading (mostly trashy science fiction) and my three journals. The scientist in me likes to have a journal handy.

One of them contains ideas, notes, and thoughts for work. Since I'm writing a dissertation (to be published as a textbook), I like to jot down thoughts and ideas for it. It's terrible to forget a good idea!

One is a personal journal that contains significant observations, self-revelations, and grand "ah-ha" moments. I smile when I look at this journal because very few such notations are in it. I guess my self-awareness level could improve. It's also my gratitude journal and has an entry for almost every day.

Tonight, sitting up in bed, I write my gratitude list:

1. *Howie: Our long plane trip was uneventful, and he's snuggled in bed.*
2. *Matthew Brown: New friend?*
3. *Grant Hall: My "grand old lady."*
4. *My New Car: Nonpolluting, me!*
5. *Online Shopping: I'll order Howie more clothes.*

The third journal is my dream journal. I put a pen down next to it, ready for awakening, and turn out the light.

In new sheets in our new place, Howie and I fall asleep.

Sometime during the night, I have this dream: I'm back in the Boston airport, and I've lost Howie. He's gone off exploring, and I can't find him. I retrace our steps and go back to the gate where we got off the plane. Worried, I call airport security to have him paged to return to the gate (this is somehow possible in the dream). I ask if anyone has seen him. Most everyone says no, but one woman says he got back on the plane (which has departed for a red-eye flight back to the West Coast). Another woman, dressed head to toe in pink, says, "No. He got on a flight just across the way. I saw him go down the boarding ramp a minute ago. If you hurry, you can catch him."

In the way of dreams, I try to get to the gate she points out, but I'm in slow motion. It seems the faster I walk, the farther away the gate gets. As I struggle, a sense of powerlessness comes over me. I worry Howie may be lost forever, and panic takes hold.

I make it to the gate, but the ramp door is closed. The gate agent turns off the illuminated signs. There's something familiar about the agent, but I can't put my finger on what. I think I know him somehow or at least recognize his shaggy brown hair, pointy nose, and expansive eyebrows. He's shaking his head at me.

Just then, out the window, I see the plane pull away from the docking ramp and head out to the runway. By now the plane is too far away to be sure, but I think I see Howie in one of the windows. He must be standing on a seat. He's looking out at me with a sad face.

I turn to the gate agent and ask where the plane is headed. He smiles, showing a prominent overbite, and says, "Italy." In the dream, I think this means that Howie's headed home. I know it's a cliché for an Italian greyhound to be going to Italy, but in the dream it seems natural that he's going back to his homeland. He's not happy to have left California and even less happy with the idea of Massachusetts in winter. He wants a stable home that suits his nature. Howie's headed back to his roots, where his thin skin will be warmed by the Mediterranean sun.

I feel guilty, as though I've let him down somehow. It's nighttime in the dream, and out the terminal window I see his plane take flight into a cold, dark sky. He's headed to a warmer climate, but it looks like he's facing a long, lonely journey. He has the promise of a warmer destination but is surrounded by strangers.

CHAPTER TWO

Getting Settled

There's no reason to go to work early today; the weekend before fall term there's no one around. The departmental office isn't usually open on weekends during the school term, but the week before fall term is an exception. Claire Barry, the departmental assistant, said she would meet me there at ten o'clock.

I test out my new kitchen by making coffee (not bad), and toast and jam (satisfying). I put Howie in his new blue sweater and take him for a short walk. The morning is cool and clear. We walk in a rough circle around my new home. I greet Mr. Brown, who is pruning roses at Condon Hall. He seems affable but preoccupied and promises to start on Howie's dog door later that day or "tomorrow at the latest."

"Nice sweater, there, Howie," he remarks.

Howie is more confident this morning. Although the air is crisp, the bright sunshine gives everything a warm, golden glow. Howie's decided that there's nothing to be spooked about, and I'm letting him sample some off-leash time. A squirrel in an elm tree particularly fascinates him, and he's bouncing up and down at the base of the tree trying to get a better view. Unlike many small dogs, he's not a barker. You have no idea how happy I am about that.

"You must be the new guy living at Grant Hall." The comment comes from a young man with sandy hair. "I'm George Marsh. I'm living on your floor, at the back of the place."

George and I look at each other for a moment, and recollection hits us at the same time.

"You gave me the campus tour last spring!" I say, offering my hand.

George is smiling broadly and says, "That's why you look so familiar!"

He is a year or two younger than me. He's about my height, with a pleasant, thin face. His ocean-blue eyes seem a little far apart for his narrow face, but they convey a sense of openness and cheer. He seems unusually pale, as though he spent the summer indoors. His voice is deep, and he has the same broad vowels as most of the people born in this part of New England.

"I ran across Mrs. Brown. She said you arrived and the LEAF in the driveway is yours. Did you drive it all the way from Los Angeles?"

Mrs. Brown has apparently used me as the front-page story of the day. I spend a few minutes answering questions and filling in the gaps for George Marsh. An electric car is a great icebreaker! For the second time in twenty-four hours, I explain all the ins and outs of driving electric in a gasoline-fueled world.

"Our submersibles are electric, of course," says George. "You can't really have internal combustion underwater. This summer I've been interning at the Marine Science Center over in Innsmouth. It's one of the Oceanography Department's big new initiatives to draw more people back to Miskatonic. It's also, of course, a big deal in Innsmouth. We hope it will bring in some much-needed tourism to the area. In addition to a research vessel and laboratories, we'll have a small visitor center where people can see some of our work close up."

"Like an aquarium?"

"More like a working laboratory with viewing areas for the public. We'll have a few things just for the visitors, of course. We'll run movies about oceanic research, and we'll have a permanent tide-pool area where kids can see and touch starfish and sea anemones. The main point of the center is research, though. I'm researching practical uses of kelp and kelp farming."

As we walk back to our common home at Grant Hall our conversation continues. George was born in Innsmouth and so he spends a great deal of his time there.

"I'll only be hanging out at Grant Hall a few nights a week," he explains, "when I have classes here on campus. On weekends, or if I'm working on a project at the center, I just stay at my parents' house in Innsmouth. The bus takes about an hour from Arkham, but I can generally get a ride from someone in the department. There's a lot of back-and-forth activity."

George is an easy talker, but not an easy walker. As we stroll back to Grant Hall I notice that he has a funny kind of rolling gait. He also has unusually large feet for someone of his stature. He's a few inches shorter than me, and I'm six-one. Not sure if his walk is based on injury or deformity, I decide I'll ask him when we get to know each other a little better.

"Let me show you the Marine Science Center later this fall," he says, as we reach the porch of Grant Hall. "Innsmouth is a great little town, and I'd be happy to show it off to you."

I drop off Howie at home. He'll be fine for the rest of the morning while I get keys and inspect my new working environment.

Massachusetts Hall is less imposing during the day. Under blue skies and enjoying an almost windless late summer day, I walk up the steps and enter. The foyer, or entrance hall, is deeper than I could make out last night. In earlier ages, students must have used the area as a gathering place and for storage. Cubbyholes in the paneled woodwork serve as places for books, shoes, rain gear, and other outerwear. Built-in benches and nooks provide informal study and conversation areas. I can easily picture myself at one of the small tables grading papers or reading between classes.

Beyond the foyer lies the rotunda, soaring upward and ringed with columns. At some point this four-story space was retrofitted with an elevator—a great glass-and-cage affair that goes all the way up. The elevator and soaring staircase dominate the rotunda. The dome at the top of the space either has skylights or is cleverly illuminated. It showcases a lovely stained-glass ceiling in amber, green, bronze, and white. The whole place is lit with golden, sunset tones.

Radiating from the central rotunda are the various departmental offices for the sciences. At one time, each of the disciplines probably had its own department with separate areas and staff. Budget cuts and less need for secretarial work reduced the necessity for distinct formal departments. There's one basic reception area for all the sciences and one set of administration offices with simple signage: "Department of Science and Related Disciplines." Across the way, I notice that the Department of Oceanography rates its own offices. Apparently, George Marsh has the right major.

Claire Barry sits at a desk in the reception area. She was so kind to me when I came to interview. Her bright red hair stands out against her dark skin and frames her small round face. She waves me over, smiling in recognition. She wore bright Caribbean prints when I met her last spring, but today she's wearing a solid lime-green dress just about the color of her manicured nails.

"Dr. Mackenzie, great to see you! Glad you're here a bit before the term starts. So, you decided to make Miskatonic your new home, eh?"

"You made me an offer I couldn't refuse!" I reply.

"And what was that?"

"Good pay, a nice apartment, funding for my textbook, and upgrading the labs, for starters."

Being friendly to the departmental staff at a university is always a good idea—but in Ms. Barry's case, it's easy. She has a fun personality. Her New York by-way-of-the-Caribbean accent is charming, and the help she gave me at the interview was heartwarming. I'm guessing she might actually run the Department of Science—only needing a few people like me to do the teaching.

"I'm too busy for a tour," she says, with disappointment in her voice. "It may not look like it today, but a week from Monday we'll be stacked to the top of that pretty dome with foolish, young kids who are away from home for the first time. There's not much to be done about that, of course, but I have to make sure they're scheduled into the right science classes."

She opens a drawer, hands me a set of keys, and has me sign a security form. "This one," she explains, "opens the side door when the main front door is locked. The main doors are opened by security according to schedule, so you don't get a key to them. The three smaller keys are for your classroom, your office, and the main lab, which you share with Dr. Alvarez. Generally, these areas should be locked when you leave the classroom. Although we don't have much theft or vandalism at Miskatonic, we try to limit our exposure by keeping unused rooms locked. The smallest of the keys are for locking cabinets in the lab. You and Dr. Alvarez, of course, need to decide which pieces of equipment or supplies need to be kept under lock and key. The lab has a posted list of safety precautions you should become familiar with."

"Do you have a key for the storage room that I'll be turning into a secondary lab?"

"Oh, that's right." She opens another drawer and pulls out a wooden box. It holds the most amazing key I've ever seen. Looking like a stage prop from a Frankenstein movie set, the key is as long as my hand and made of forged iron. "Don't laugh," she says. "And don't lose it! You have to promise not to lose it! I tried to have a copy made, but so far nobody is up to the challenge. The storage room is in the basement, and the elevator doesn't go down that far. You go through that door." She indicates a paneled door across the rotunda next to the elevator area. "At the bottom of the stairs, turn left, and the storage area is at the end of the hall. It's basically the basement of the tower.

"That reminds me. You'll need to sign for your credit card since you'll be refurbishing the basement there. Although the major charges will require purchase orders, Dr. Christianson requisitioned a credit card for your use. You're allowed to use it for buying hardware-store-type items to get started down there. You know, moving boxes, special cleaning supplies, paint, that sort of thing. I arranged to have the room emptied out by someone from maintenance. It should be ready for a good cleaning, painting, and whatever else needs to be done. You'll have to file a detailed request for any furniture or lab equipment you need." Ms. Barry hands me a credit card and has me sign another form.

"Have you checked your classes yet?" she asks. "Would you like a printout of your preregistrations, or are you one of those nice young men who can do all that on his own?"

Ms. Barry clearly hopes this is the case, and I do not disappoint her. She opens another drawer and gets me a copy of my login and operating instructions for the departmental enrollment, grading, and information system. She turns to her desk for a moment, logs herself in, and asks, "What would you like for your initial password?"

"Howie," I say. "H-O-W-I-E."

"OK. But you better change it when you get home. Within about three days everyone knows everything about everyone around here. If that's your pet's name, you'll be hacked within two weeks."

"Will do. Thank you. Do you have a map of Massachusetts Hall? I'd like to find my dissertation adviser's office and give myself a tour, if I can."

From another drawer, Ms. Barry pulls out a sheet of paper. "Here's a campus map, but I don't have one for this building. It's big but doesn't have all that many rooms. Just take the elevator up and explore. Who's your dissertation adviser?"

"Dr. Shyam Gupta."

"Dr. Gupta is on the third floor. His name is on the door. It's near the end of the corridor. I'm a little pressed for time today, Dr. Mackenzie, and I'm going to have to set you loose to explore on your own." She gives me another big smile as though she might rather spend time giving me a tour than doing her work.

"Could you call me Mac?" I ask.

"Only if it's just us, Mac," she says. "I learned a long time ago that it's better for everyone if we use our titles. It's better for relating to the students and makes things clear around the office, too. When it's just us, please call me Claire, but it won't be 'just us' for long, Mac. Then I'm Ms. Barry."

"Thank you, Claire, soon-to-be Ms. Barry."

"You're welcome." As she turns back to her computer, she gives me one more suggestion. "After you look at your preregistrations and schedule, you may wish to go to the textbook area at the back of the bookstore. We leave it up to the instructors to make sure they're stocking enough textbooks for you."

The elevator is a trip! It was state-of-the-art in 1930 but is clearly a relic today. Like a bird in a brass cage, I rise to the top of Massachusetts Hall and begin my exploration. The fourth floor comprises mostly classrooms. Four large, generic, lecture-style classrooms are left un-locked. All of similar design, you enter at the front where the instruc-tor stands and work your way up into the tiers of seating. This forces latecomers to walk directly by the instructor. I'm not sure that this scheme discourages tardiness or just provides interruptions at the beginning of each lecture. Each classroom has a bank of windows to let in light and (during the summer) air. From the fourth floor, the views are lovely. Among the treetops, you have a view of most of the Green and the picturesque buildings surrounding the inner circle. The big classrooms can hold more than a hundred students each.

The fourth floor also has four smaller classrooms for graduate-level work and six private offices, all closed for the summer.

Rather than call the elevator back up, I take the stairs down to the third floor and continue my tour. As predicted, I find Dr. Gupta's office at the end of the main corridor. A board next to the door shows he's away for the summer and returning next week. I met Shyam when I was here in the late spring (and yes, he says I can call him Shyam). He and I have also been corresponding by e-mail, so I feel pretty good about my dissertation project.

I use the "Dr." title because I already completed one dissertation, back in Los Angeles. My credentials are from UCLA. Part of my employment contract at Miskatonic, however, requires me to work on a second project—a combination textbook and primer to quantum physics. I haven't decided on the title yet. In my head, it's "Quantum Physics for Dummies," but I'm sure the publisher will steer me away from that!

I was hoping to meet Shyam before classes start to chat and negotiate my timetable in person. Clearly, the book will take at least a year to complete, and I hope he will allow me a year and a half to include time for editing and illustration. One of the reasons they've hired me is to bring some national attention and academic scholarship to Miskatonic. I'm not sure exactly how that's supposed to happen—although, when I see what's going on in the Department of Oceanography, I'm getting some ideas of what might be expected. At any rate, a book is a good place to start, and I generally enjoy writing about science in ways that nonscientists find approachable and interesting.

Down another floor and I find my office. I figure out and try to memorize which of the smaller keys opens the door, and I enter my second home. Well, it has a window. It's got to be the smallest private professor's office I've ever been in—but the view is lovely. Whoever had the office before me positioned the desk so it faces the door and has the window to the right. I'm going to keep it exactly like it is. With an amazing view to the north, I can see the top of Grant Hall and a sliver of what might be my bedroom window. To the south, we're in the treetops, and pleasant filtered light fills my small space.

It's a good thing I don't have many books. The small bookcase and two visitor chairs are all that fits with the desk in its current position. I like it, though. It will be the perfect place to hang out between classes and to meet with students. Its small size means I probably won't use it for working on my book. There would be too many interruptions, anyway, with full classes and students trying to drop in with questions. I make a mental note to bring along an additional power strip for my laptop and a desk lamp. When I get time, a nice framed print would help make the office feel more like "mine." A plant in the window wouldn't hurt either.

Continuing the tour of my floor reveals my primary classroom and the lab I share with Dr. Horace Alvarez. Dr. Alvarez has been at Miskatonic for many years, and between the two of us and two graduate students, we'll teach all the physics classes. The classroom we share is fine, and I see that it even has a place where I can store a few personal items or classroom supplies.

The lab is more problematic. As I expected, it's a lab for teaching Newtonian physics. It's clearly stuck in the 1950s, with instruments and facilities to prove some of the basic laws of physics that work in the everyday world. Trouble is, quantum physics deals with the extraordinary world of small and fast particles, of photons and superstrings. The lab is simply inadequate to demonstrate quantum effects. With some additional power circuits (which I see were added according to my late-spring request), I'll be able to run some of the new lab equipment I ordered. For a few of the experiments, we simply need a different kind of space, which I hope to create in a new smaller lab in the basement.

Back down on the main floor, I nose around a bit, waving to Ms. Barry as I pass the reception area. She's hard at work on her computer and gives a small wave in return. I find my way into the combination break room/faculty lounge. I can't say I'll spend much time here—it's mostly junk-food vending machines and microwaves. It does have a nice terrace that opens to the back of Massachusetts Hall. I could see myself sitting at one of the bistro sets on a nice day.

Crossing the lobby and opening the paneled door that Ms. Barry pointed out, I take the stairs down to the basement. It certainly *is* a basement and has all the storage rooms, utility closets, and windowless halls to prove it. About half of the basement seems devoted to the boiler and heating system, which is locked behind doors marked "Plant and Utility Only."

At the opposite end of the long corridor is a door whose lock must match my funky key. Although the rest of the basement is plaster and cement, there's no mistaking the tower. Its mortarless granite blocks are clearly visible, and the carved wooden door fits into the middle of one of its sides. The door, obviously original to the structure, is about ten feet high and nearly four feet wide. The tower must predate the rest of Massachusetts Hall because the door is weather-worn, as though it used to be outside. The carvings are questionable in nature, both for being faded and for depicting a variety of odd and sexually suggestive scenes in bas-relief.

I put my special key into the lock. The mechanism is stiff but oiled and turns with a *thunk*. The large door, rotating on iron pins, swings opens. At first glance, the room is not large. Each of its five sides is about sixteen feet long, forming a pentagon. The room is about twenty feet across, thirteen feet high, and has a false ceiling made of acoustic tiles in a grid pattern. The size of the space is masked, however, by its current contents. Ms. Barry was mistaken about the room being clear. It is full—crammed—with boxes of files and records stacked six feet high and higher. Narrow pathways squeeze between the rows of boxes. I can barely see that the room and floor are painted gray.

"What are you doing here?" comes a voice familiar and yet out of context. It's Matthew Brown, and he has his hands on his hips and a doubtful look on his face. "How did you get the key to the storeroom?" Not content with my startled pause, he asks a third question: "What's going on here?"

Feeling unjustly accused of something, I explain, "This is going to be the new physics lab. Dr. Christiansen said I could use it as a secure environment for the more sensitive quantum experiments we'll be doing with the students. I hope to have it up and running in time for winter term."

Matt is unconvinced.

"Ms. Barry knows all about it. She gave me the key." The mention of Ms. Barry seems to calm him somewhat.

"So, you're the one planning to use the tower room?"

"That's me."

"Well, it's a stupid idea," says Matt. "We've had storage down here for years, and I can't see making this space into anything else. There's no electricity, and heaven knows where all the files will have to go. They told me about this plan, and I decided to ignore it. I figured that whichever fool had the idea, they'd give it up."

"I guess I'm that fool."

That gets a smile from him. My deadpan delivery manages to take the edge off his anger.

"Now why do you want to go and do that when you have some of the best-kept labs I've seen right upstairs in this same building?"

I explain the shortcomings of the upstairs labs and the need for something more secure from miscellaneous radiation and electronic chatter. "Part of what I want to do with my students is re-create some of the essential experiments that have helped shape our ideas of how the quantum world works. Although some of the experiments are not bothered by electromagnetic fields and charges, many are. In particular, this winter we'll be performing the famous double-slit experiment. All sorts of electromagnetic leakage can influence the experiment, so I want to conduct it within a Faraday cage or shield. They're enclosures designed to keep out, or sometimes in, electromagnetic radiation. We need one, and it's not financially feasible to create a large one upstairs. We'd be covering windows and hanging wires everywhere. It would really mess up the labs for other uses."

"So you think you can build one of those cages down here?" asks Matt.

"We'll make the whole room into one," I explain, "lining the walls, floor, and ceiling with conductive material; mesh or even foil will make the room into a Faraday cage. Generally, it's powered by an external electrical current that creates a charge within the cage's conducting material. This blocks radio-frequency emissions and other EM interference from entering or leaving the cage. It doesn't need a large power source, so we can probably wire it without disturbing the walls down here. The electricity can be surface mounted if necessary."

Clearly in professor mode, I continue, "You may not know it, but we use Faraday cages all the time in real life. The reason microwaves are safe is because the interior of the oven is covered in a mesh that contains the energy used to 'excite' the molecules of food into becoming hot. Without the mesh, you'd be cooked, too. It's also the same principle that tends to make your cell phone go dead in an elevator—essentially a metal box with electricity to power its lights and mechanism. Even though it may not be a perfectly formed Faraday cage, it's close enough to keep your cell phone from receiving texts or you from phoning out during an emergency. We really have to move our hands-on laboratory work into the twenty-first century for Miskatonic to be competitive."

Either impressed with my description or baffled by my bullshit, Matt falls silent. Thoughts cross behind his eyes as he comes to a decision. "Well," he says, drawing out one vowel into a full sentence. "I guess we'll start moving those boxes, then. I'm part of the maintenance and utility crew for this building, so I'll get with Ms. Barry and find out where these boxes are going. How soon do you need to have it cleaned out?"

"Ms. Barry said it had already been cleaned out."

"Oh, yeah," says Matt, followed by a sigh. "We did get that notice about a month ago. Like I said, I was hoping we'd talk somebody out of it."

Matt looks hopeful for a moment, then resigned. "I'll have a team in here tomorrow, and we'll have it clean as a whistle for you. Do you have someone from engineering to help you with the new construction? This hall is designated as a National Historic Building, you know. You can't just knock down walls."

"We won't knock down any walls. We won't have to change the structure at all. It's really a task of lining the existing surfaces. We may need to upgrade some wiring, though. Could you be my contact with the Engineering and Maintenance Departments? I could sure use your help."

Asking for Matt's help seems to do the trick. He may still think this is a bad idea, but at least he's willing to help with the bad idea.

"I'll talk it over back at the shop, and we'll see what we can do," he says. "I guess I better get over to the plant and see how many work-study students we have who can put in some hours here tomorrow."

"Thank you, Matt. I sure appreciate it." As Matt walks down the hall to the stairs, I try to see more about this windowless, odd-shaped room. I stand on a two-box-high stack of papers and manage to lift a ceiling tile. A cool draft comes down. It's hard to see how high the real ceiling is. All I see is blackness above the tile. Since the ceiling grid is made of metal, I'll have to get some advice on whether the Faraday cage can be constructed underneath the grid or if it should be above. A few phone calls should take care of that. I wonder if Matt knows how high the real ceiling is.

I close the door to the storage room and leave it unlocked so that Matt's work-study students can get in to move the boxes. Hopefully, it really can be cleaned out in the next day or so. I want to have plenty of time to construct the cage and test it before we use it during winter term.

A few hours later, I've had lunch, and Howie's been for another walk. I put in a call and an e-mail to friends back at UCLA to ask about Faraday shielding with regard to the ceiling tiles. I leave a message with one friend and talk to another—she believes that if the existing metal grid will support it, I could put foil or wire mesh on the underside of the false ceiling.

Howie and I are now headed into Arkham to check out the hardware and lumber supply store. I'm assuming I can get all the ordinary materials there. It would be great if I could also have them order some of the more particular supplies for the cage, too. I've used construction foiling to build a Faraday shield before, but it has to be thick enough and made of the right materials.

A long stretch of the road into town runs along the Miskatonic River. The rushing water adds liveliness to the otherwise still and claustrophobic forest. It's almost a tunnel of trees in places where the tall maples intertwine overhead. Howie is standing on the passenger seat looking out the window. The bumpy pavement has him doing a little dance to remain upright

I enter Arkham about three o'clock. I go back to the supermarket and pick up the few things I missed yesterday. I stop at a department store and pick out some towels. I'll be able to return the ones I borrowed from Mrs. Brown.

I loop back around the main drag and head east until I get to Three Rivers Hardware and Lumber. Usually dogs are welcome at such places, so I leash up Howie, and we go in to see what they have. At the customer-service desk, I say, "I'm Dr. Mackenzie from over at Miskatonic. I'm going to be fitting out a new lab in the Physics Department, and I wanted to see what kind of materials you have and what can be special ordered."

The older man behind the counter frowns. "We're used to working with Miskatonic, of course. Generally, the Plant and Utilities Department contacts us and orders materials. I don't think we work directly with any of the professors."

I sense a dismissal coming, so I pull out my new credit card for emphasis. "It's more of a resurfacing project, not really construction. I'll be buying paint, rolls of specific foil, possibly some mesh. We'll need adhesive to put up the foil and fasteners if we use the mesh. The materials are pretty specific for laboratory use—they won't be the sort of materials that the Plant and Utilities Department are used to ordering."

"Um. OK."

I'm getting that odd look that people give me when they can't decide if I'm old enough or powerful enough to be the one making decisions. Outside of academia, I get that sometimes. It can be a problem.

"Do you mind if I look around a bit?"

With a sweep of his hand, the customer-service fellow indicates that the store is mine to enjoy. "Let me know if I can help you with anything specific," he says.

Howie and I look around. I find plenty of the fasteners that I've used before if we decide to install wire mesh. I stop by the paint aisle and pick out some color swatches. It might be nice to paint my office, if that's allowed.

I do not see much in the way of foil coverings, except that which is already affixed to rolls of insulation. It will most likely have to be a special order. I'd like to stay away from the wire mesh if I can, unless we need it for the floor. The floor may be a little tricky, since uncovered foil will get torn by foot traffic. We'll probably have to cover the foil or mesh on the floor with some kind of concrete "skin" or other material. As long as the cage is continuous, it's fine to cover parts of it on the inside with nonconductive finishing materials.

I pick up some picture-hanging fasteners (which I'll buy with my own money, of course) and head to the checkout. The original customer-service guy waves me over.

"Do you have a minute?" he asks. "If you go out to the lumber yard, you can talk to Brian. He works with the folks at Miskatonic and handles special orders for them. He may even have information on some of the other special laboratory orders they've placed."

I thank him, and Howie and I head out to find Brian. I identify him by his name badge. He is behind an inventory computer in lumber sales. Brian Hoskins is tall and of medium build with russet hair and a short, neat beard. He has a wide face with a few freckles and an open smile. He "fits in" at the hardware store in the way he looks and walks. He has that slow, confident stride that speaks of time on an athletic field.

I introduce myself and explain what I'm trying to do. I can see he's interested. Not just as a building project but also in the idea of the Faraday cage and why I need it.

"We *are* used to working with Plant and Building Maintenance," he explains. Brian does not have a New England accent, and I would guess he's from farther south. He continues, "We can work with you directly, of course, but Building Maintenance has all the invoice numbers and thirty-day billing cycles that tend to make everyone happy. We have a pretty good working relationship with our suppliers and can get all the standard materials within two to three days. Some of the special items will take longer, and laboratory-specific materials may not be on our regular supply lists."

I talk about the specific aluminum foil that I've used before, and Brian shakes his head. "We don't carry that anymore. Too many builders were using it as a vapor barrier on the wrong side of the insulation. It was causing too much mold and mildew in residential applications. I can still order it for you, though, from a different supplier. It would be here within a week."

"That's not bad," I say. "Would it be best if I e-mailed you a list of specific materials and quantities once we've got all the measurements down?"

"Perfect," says Brian. "I can come by and help you check measurements, if you like. I'm familiar with the school. I know that foil's expensive. You'll want to be pretty exact with the square footage you'll need."

I'm having trouble imagining the lumber sales guy making "house calls," but I thank him for his kind offer. He gives me a business card with his phone and e-mail.

"If we can get most of the items on one order, it always helps," says Brian. "When I send out several small orders, it seems like they always lose one."

We finish talking, and Brian holds out a hand to shake. "It was nice meeting you, Dr. Mackenzie," says Brian.

Howie and I leave the lumber yard and walk out to the parking lot. As I lift Howie into the car, I have the distinct feeling of being watched. As I pull out of the parking lot, Brian Hoskins is observing us from the loading dock. Although it's hard to see from across the parking lot, it looks like he's got a smirk on his face.

In the evening, I decide to work on my book. It's been a long couple of days, and the ideas aren't flowing as well as I'd like. I'm trying to explain one of Einstein's theories and why he was so mad when he followed through with its implications. It should be a funny story and a good example. I'm trying to straddle that line between writing an engaging story and teaching good physics. My hope is that the book will open quantum physics to a wider audience. The university hopes it will bring more people to Miskatonic and provide good publicity.

Usually, I can always write. As long as the subject is interesting to me, I can make it interesting for others. Not tonight, however. I find myself sleepy and a little stupid from staring at my laptop. New ideas are not flowing.

I brush my teeth and catch up on e-mail. I send some ideas and questions for the Faraday cage to my friend Tab at UCLA. He's an expert on electromagnetic shielding. I'm hoping for an easy and inexpensive solution for creating the Faraday cage.

I look over at Howie. He's napping in his basket by the radiator. I ask him if he'd like to go for a walk. He doesn't even open his eyes all the way. I take that as a no.

Following his lead, I get into bed myself. I think I had a pretty successful first day at work. Sitting up in bed, I write my gratitude list:

1.   _Claire Barry_: People who help me.
2.   _My Lecture Hall_: It's perfect!
3.   _My Office_: A private professor's office. Just for me.
4.   _Lab Space_: Well, I'll be even more grateful when it's finished.
5.   _My Job_.

I put my journal back on the bedside table and turn out the lights. I snuggle down on the pillow and put one hand underneath it.

I feel the edges of a piece of paper—an envelope. _What the hell?!_

I jump out of bed, envelope in hand.

The envelope is addressed to me. My name is typed out in Courier font from what I imagine is an antique typewriter. The ink does not perfectly fill out the letters, but it is easy enough to read: "Dr. Mac." It sounds like what some of my students used to call me at UCLA. On the next line, it has the address, something an old student could not possibly know. It matches the brass plate on my apartment door. It simply says, "Apt. C."

I open the envelope and discover a single typed page:

Dear Dr. Mac,

I hope you know what you're doing. Many before you have come to bad ends. If you value your little dog and your life, you should go back to L.A. You're not wanted here. You're not safe here. Accidents happen.

Your Friend

CHAPTER THREE

Back to School

Today is the first day of fall term. Matt Brown was able to get Howie's dog door installed, so I feel fine about leaving him alone while I go off to teach my first class. He also followed through with clearing out the basement tower room.

Not only am I ready for classes but also to begin setting up the new lab. With any luck, we'll be able to use it, as planned, during winter term.

I'm teaching four classes over fall term: "General Physics," "Physics Concepts for Nonscientists," "General Physics Laboratory," and "Introduction to Quantum Mechanics." Monday, Wednesday, and Friday mornings I teach the introductory classes, and Tuesday and Thursday afternoons I teach labs and the quantum physics material. It doesn't sound like full-time work, but when you figure in class preparation, office hours, grading papers and exams, writing and committees, most professors work more than fifty hours a week. The good news is that other than the scheduled classes and office hours you can plan your life as you like.

Last week I spent most of my time getting ready for classes. Reviewing notes, recompiling a syllabus for term length, outlining a book I haven't used before—it was an investment in time and attention. For classes that I'll continue to teach, the prep time always pays off.

The campus really feels alive. The Green is full of students, and spirits are running high as the kids find classes, make new friends, and discover some of Miskatonic's peculiarities. Some students hurry to their next appointment or class. Others start later in the day and are just enjoying the fresh air and warm sunshine. Over four thousand people are enrolled this term. Only three times that many people live in Arkham!

It is a lovely fall day, and I enjoy the walk to Massachusetts Hall.

I get to my first class early and warm up the projection system. We're not running any demonstrations today, so all I need to do is set up the projector and microphone. I plug my laptop in and make the necessary connections. Everything is working properly.

As I watch the new students filing into my second-floor classroom, I'm reminded why I enjoy teaching this cross-major class for nonscientists. It's a class with kids of so many backgrounds and interests. They're taking my class to fulfill a science requirement, but they're in for a treat. It's my specialty to make physics interesting to regular people. This is the group that I'm writing my new book for. I hope to use it as the textbook for this class next year. The class is full by the time the buzzer in the hall sounds.

We start the quarter talking about the Big Bang. You might think it would be more appropriate to discuss the beginning of our universe in an astronomy class, but the Big Bang is where the laws of physics start. Thirteen-point-eight billion years ago, within the first few seconds of the existence of our universe, all the physical laws were determined. From the initial explosion, giant clouds of primordial elements later coalesced through gravity to form stars and galaxies. If the initial bang had contained more or less mass or generated more or less heat, everything would be different.

I show short animated graphics that illustrate the Big Bang theory and the formation of the universe. The beginning of the universe and its physical properties and laws also predict the ultimate fate of everything. If we exceed a critical density threshold, we can assume that the universe will eventually stop expanding, ultimately contract, and heat up into another cyclical Big Bang event. If the density of the universe falls short of this critical threshold, the universe will continue expanding (and cooling) forever.

Fire or ice? The correct estimate of universal density determines the fate of everything!

The class goes great. Most of my students are smart and interested in the material. They ask intelligent questions and seem prepared for their first day. Many of them are new to Miskatonic, and some of their questions are more general in scope ("Where's the lab? How do I set up an appointment with you?").

My second class is likewise full. It's the first in a series of physics classes for students who *do* hope to become scientists. They tend to be a less cheerful group. There is generally some competition for good grades, lab projects, and, ultimately, jobs in the scientific community. This class took the most preparation because it uses a textbook that I don't really care for. More of my time was required to beef up the relevance factor for the lectures and class discussions. Even someday-scientists deserve to have classes that are interesting and provide useful applications in the scientific world.

After class, I head to my office to finish out the morning with my first set of office hours. I already have students waiting outside my door. One wants to know if the labs are really required (only if you want to meet the department requirements and get your degree). One wants to know if she can take an oceanography class to meet her science requirement (probably, but she should talk to her official adviser to make sure). One wants to see if I would *be* her adviser (I tell her that advisers are assigned randomly during enrollment and that she should give her assigned one a good chance before she asks to switch).

One young man was intrigued by one of my Einstein stories and just wants to chat. Since he's the last in line, I'm fine with that. He and another student linger, and we talk about Einstein's time on the Manhattan Project and the ethical dilemmas that scientists face when asked to use their knowledge for military purposes.

At the beginning of the term, there are usually fewer students with questions, so I pop next door to Dr. Horace Alvarez's office to visit.

"Do you have many students come to your office hours?" I ask.

"Always," says Horace. "It's one of the ways I know I'm doing a good job." I must be giving him a questioning look, because he elaborates. "I pride myself on being approachable—not one of those professors who are too good to be bothered. I think it's important that students ask questions and that we're available."

"We think alike," I say, nodding. I like Horace and respect what he's accomplished here at Miskatonic. "How long have you been at Miskatonic?" I ask. "Have you taught at other universities?"

"I've been here for all but the first three years of my career. I originally taught at Northwestern but was recruited to Miskatonic almost twenty-five years ago."

Something in the way he talks leads me to believe he sees me as too young to have a professorship in physics. Either that, or maybe he wishes he had more energy to take the department into the next century all by himself.

"How long were you here before you were tenured?" I ask. In academia, tenure is always a big thing. Until then, you're usually on one-year teaching contracts. After tenure, you're permanent.

"Tenure, eh?" He pauses to reflect. "At Miskatonic, tenure might be a little different. In most places, once you've put in a few years, published a book or some articles, you're eligible for tenure. Here, tenure is reserved for those who fit into certain extracurricular activities."

I'm giving him the questioning look again, but this time he doesn't offer any explanation.

"You mean I need to coach a sport or be on a committee or something?" I ask, not really getting his "extracurricular" reference.

Horace pauses again, looking at me intently. "If you haven't gotten a good idea of what's going on here yet, I think maybe you should ask someone else. Maybe Dr. Christianson. One of the other elements of tenure here is strict confidentiality. Let's just leave things at that."

Office hours are complete, so I decide to visit campus security and then treat myself to a movie. This is one of the great perks of being a professor—almost complete flextime. After checking in with Howie, I get in the LEAF and head down the main access road to campus security.

The security office looks like a medieval gatehouse. Attached to the brick wall and adjacent to the ornate front gates, it is a squat affair with double-wide doors and arched windows. The doors are also half-doors, and the top of the door on the right is open. I stick my head into the opening to see who is on duty. Immediately, I see Justin Taggert. *Great.*

"Hello, there," I say. "Is the chief of security around anywhere? I'd like to speak to him about something."

Taggert scowls. "I *am* chief of security."

Double great.

"Oh, I see. I didn't realize." I guess I made assumptions about him, just the way he made assumptions about me. "Do you have a few minutes?"

"Sure. What's up, *Dr.* Mackenzie?" Taggert gets up from his chair and crosses to the window to get a better look at me.

"I have something troublesome to report, and I have a question or two."

"Have at it," says Taggert, without much enthusiasm.

I pull the threatening note from inside my jacket and show it to him. "This was under my pillow last night."

"Under your pillow," he repeats, as he reads the note. "How did it get under your pillow?"

"That's the security question," I say. "My apartment was locked, I live there by myself, and only the Browns and I have keys."

Taggert turns the note over and looks at the paper for a minute. "Typed on an old typewriter. Weird."

"But why would someone do this?"

"It seems clear that someone doesn't want you here. Didn't I say you don't fit in? Seems like someone else has the same idea."

"So, you're not going to do anything, then?"

"I didn't say that. I take my job quite seriously, and nobody should be breaking into anyone else's apartment. I'll look into it. To start with, I'll check with Matt Brown about the key situation. Maybe he's missing some spares."

Taggert's just standing there. "Is that it?" he asks. "You said you had a question or two."

"Oh, right. I almost forgot! You mentioned that pets are not allowed on campus, and I know that I had to get special permission to bring Howie along."

"The Italian greyhound."

"That's right. Well, what I wanted to know is whether anyone else has a pet here. Am I the only one?"

"No," says Taggert. "Dr. Mason, the chancellor, also has one. A weird kind of animal for a grown man to have for a pet, I think."

"A rat," I say. Taggert nods.

"Did you know the rat has visiting privileges?" I explain about the hole in the window casing and the little ramp.

"Yeah, that's even weirder, isn't it? You wouldn't think a rat would go outside and come back in. They're not that smart."

"Maybe this one is," I say, recalling the little vest-wearing hypnotist.

I'm headed into Arkham to visit the Lansdowne Theatre. Built in the 1920s, the Lansdowne is a lovely example of Hollywood as applied to architecture. With its glassed-in ticket booth under a canopy of a thousand lights, it's a reminder of a time when more glamour was appreciated. Parking's a breeze midweek, and I quickly find myself at the ticket booth.

I decide to try out some advice from Ms. Barry. I show my faculty card to the woman selling tickets and ask if they still have the special matinee discounts.

"Monday through Thursday, as long as the show starts before five, you get in for two dollars," she says. "Two dollars more if it's a 3D movie because of the glasses."

Liking the Lansdowne better every minute, I get popcorn and check out the movie posters. There should be some good movies coming up. The theater has been newly recarpeted in midnight blue, and I am pleased to see that the seats look relatively new, as well.

I find a center seat near the front and settle in for the movie. I'm still a little early, and I take in the theater. The main part has column cutouts and red velvet draperies. It holds about three hundred people, but only a few of us are here for the matinee.

I can see they've updated all the speakers, and there is a sign in the lobby that says they're using a new digital projection system. Around the ceiling, a Greek-key motif repeats in gilt.

A few rows back, a pair of middle-aged women are heatedly discussing something, and I begin to tune in to what they're saying.

Woman number one says, "It's disgraceful that they still have those books! They should be destroyed. Some poor student will check out one of them and ruin their life! Don't they know how dangerous they are?"

Woman number two says, "But the books are locked away, surely. Not just anyone is going to 'check one out.'"

At first, I assume they're talking about some book they think should be banned from the local grade school (you know, like *Heather Has Two Mommies*). Then I realize they're talking about Miskatonic and the college library.

Woman number one says, "I know the college prides itself on preserving all sorts of old books. They get people from all over the world who come to study in the library. They spent a lot of money on climate control in the rare book section, and I'm all for it. It brings money to the school, of course, but it also brings money to Arkham. We'd have to close a couple of our motels and restaurants if it wasn't for the parents and out-of-town scholars spending their money here." She's on a roll, and her voice gains passion as she takes a breath and continues. "I just don't see why they have to specialize in *those* books. Why couldn't it be Shakespearean literature, for god's sake? Why couldn't we have the world's largest collection of Victorian poetry or rare copies of the *Gutenberg Bible*?"

Woman number two says, "I don't see how they make money on it, though. You don't pay to see the books—it's a library. How does that make the university any money? I agree that they should just get rid of the books. Especially if they're as awful as you say."

I'm a bit intrigued, but the movie is starting, and the women fall silent. For 110 minutes, I'm pulled into a world of compelling fantasy. Schools, students, labs, and libraries all fade into the background. I open up to a new reality with wizards and magical creatures, and anything appears to be possible. There's something about a good film that opens your heart and mind to new experiences and new ways of thinking.

After the show, I have an idea. I'll follow the women from the theater and see if I can satisfy my curiosity. Before I can catch up, they enter Roxy's, a fifties-style diner on the same block as the Lansdowne.

Roxy's vinyl booths are striped in red and white, and it has black-and-white linoleum in a bold checkered pattern. I walk up to the women, now seated, and strike up a conversation. "Did you two enjoy the movie?" Before they can answer, I add, "I don't mean to interrupt, but I'm new to Arkham and Miskatonic University and just trying to get to know people a bit. I'm pretty sure we just watched the same movie together."

"I'm Shirley, and this is Anne," says woman number one. "Why don't you join us, and we'll talk it all out!" Shirley has a bright smile, permed gray hair, and glasses. She clearly would like additional company. She pats the seat of the booth and scoots sideways to make room for me.

"That's very kind of you," I say, joining them.

"I thought the movie was way too long," says Shirley. "All the plot got used up at the beginning, and the ending was too predictable. It wasn't as good or exciting as the other ones."

Shirley's friend Anne counters with, "I enjoyed it fine. But there were too many special effects. It takes away from the character development. A good movie is about relationships. I liked the characters from the beginning, but there didn't seem to be any further development." Anne also has gray hair, but it is cut in a more attractive style. She's the more proper of the two and probably wouldn't have invited me over if she'd been by herself.

The waiter takes our orders, and we continue to chat about the movie.

When the conversation gets to a quiet spot, I steer it to Miskatonic.

"I couldn't help but overhear you at the theater, earlier. Could you fill me in about the controversy over the university library and its collection?"

Shirley is on it in an instant. "Yes," she says, "I think it's disgraceful." Shirley manages to make *disgraceful* into three long syllables. She continues, "Being known for the world's largest collection of satanic bibles, blasphemous writings, witchcraft how-to books, and obscene hieroglyphics is not really my kind of notoriety. I realize it brings the school some acclaim. I know it's a large collection and that scholars come from all over the world to see it. I just don't think the books, themselves, should exist! I also don't think using obscene materials to generate money is appropriate."

"They have a copy of the *Necronomicon*, you know. And *The Book of Azathoth*." Anne's eyes light up as she names the "forbidden" books at the college, and I wonder if these books even exist. "They have *all* the witch books, carefully preserved. You know, like the grimoire that was used in Salem to conjure up demons and such in the 1600s. And original transcripts from the witch trials. I think they have first editions of all of Cotton Mather's books, too, on witchcraft and how to spot witches and cleanse people of demons."

I've heard of Rev. Cotton Mather from Boston and the Salem witch trials, of course, but the rest of the story sounds like something from a gothic horror novel. I think these ladies are mixing facts and fantasy.

"But what does it hurt?" I try to sound reasonable. "It's not like these things are real. You can't call up demons or cast spells. The Salem witch trials were a dark part of local history, sure, but magic and witchcraft don't really exist except in people's minds. They're like things from the movies—just like the movie we saw today. It's fun on the big screen. I love fantasy, but it's nothing to get upset over. The movie's over. No one's going to get hurt. No demons are going to be raised if a student checks out a book from the library."

Shirley takes the final word on the subject as our burgers arrive. "Well, the Salem witch trials *did* exist. Whether you believe in witches or not, we can agree that many people's lives were ruined over the ideas presented in those books. My fear is that young minds are impressionable. Such books are an encouragement. When someone hears about raising and controlling demons, they might be interested. They might want to try their own hand at such blasphemy. They might check out one of these books and try a blood sacrifice or worse. They might be just crazy enough to believe and take action!"

When I get home, I'm met with a big surprise. Howie is sitting on the front porch of Grant Hall. He's wagging his tail, happy to see me. His collar is gone. I check for gaps under and around the fence in the yard. Everything looks secure. The gate is still latched from the inside. Howie is no help; he wants to play. He's apparently enjoyed his freedom.

Did somebody let Howie out of the yard? I don't see how. Was someone in my apartment? The door is still locked. I suppose somebody could have vaulted the fence and either brought Howie back over or gone through the dog door into the apartment. But why? I repress an urge to call campus security. "Somebody let my dog out of the yard!" doesn't quite seem like an emergency. It's concerning to me but probably not to Security Chief Justin Taggert.

I'll have to watch Howie the next few times he lets himself out into the yard. If there is a way out, I know he won't be able to resist using it. I should be able to catch him if he's discovered an escape route. He enjoys his freedom, especially when he doesn't get enough exercise. If I have to, I guess I can just close up the new dog door.

I check in with my housemates. George Marsh is not in. He's probably in Innsmouth for the evening with his family. Sam, downstairs, is home. She wrings her hands and says, "I just knew something was wrong." Her limp blond hair seems particularly greasy this evening. "It's not like you to have him loose. I should have called you, but I don't have your number. I should have at least brought him inside my apartment and put a note on your door."

"That's OK," I say. "No worries. What time did you first see him out there?"

"He was on the porch when I got home at three-thirty," she replies. "I knocked on your door, but you weren't home."

About the time I was watching the movie in town.

"Sam, would you be willing to help me keep track of Howie if he should get out again? I promise to find and fix any problems with the yard, fence, and gate, but I want a backup plan if he escapes again. You seem to be here more than our other housemates, and it would be wonderful to know there's someone here who might watch out for him."

Sam agrees, and I show her where I've cleverly hidden a key in the downstairs hall. I check, but it does not appear to have been disturbed. Together we go into my apartment with Howie, and I show her how to lock down the dog door. "If he escapes again, just use the key, put him in my apartment, and close the dog door."

I make sure Sam has my cell phone number in case I'm in town and she needs to reach me. She also gets the card with my office and departmental numbers. She seems genuinely happy to help with Howie and offers to take care of him if I go away on a trip.

I check upstairs to see if Dr. Simmons from the Literature Department knows anything. I still haven't met him, and I hear music coming from inside. After knocking twice, I'm about to go back downstairs when he opens his door. Dr. Simmons is about forty and is wearing too little clothing for my taste. I guess this is his house, too, but greeting people in your underwear seems a little informal. He has almost-black hair and a small matching goatee. His stomach and chest are a bit droopy for his current exposure, and I try not to stare while introducing myself.

"Hi. My name's Mac. Dr. Mackenzie. I live just downstairs from you."

"Howdy, there," says Dr. Simmons. Although "howdy" is cowboy talk, Dr. Simmons's accent is upper-class East Coast.

"I haven't had a chance to introduce myself yet. I'm new this term and am a professor in the Science Department. I'm teaching physics."

"You don't say," says Dr. Simmons.

"Anyway, I was wondering if you've been out of your apartment this afternoon. My dog got out of the yard, and I was wondering if you had seen him?"

"Is he the little Italian greyhound?" asks Dr. Simmons.

"Yes. His name's Howie."

"Well, I've seen him before. In the yard, I mean. I haven't been out of the apartment today, though. My teaching days this term are primarily on Tuesdays, Wednesdays, and Thursdays, so I was here all day. I'm getting ready for my first fall class, tomorrow morning." He pauses, then asks, "Did you find him? Is your dog OK?"

"Yes, he's back. I just want to find out what happened and how he managed to get out."

"You got me there, sport," says Dr. Simmons, standing in his tighty-whities.

Sensing that the conversation isn't going anywhere productive, I offer him one of my business cards and add my cell phone number to it. "If you should see him outside the fence, would you mind calling me? I'd really appreciate it. My name's Mac."

I guess I am not allowed to know his first name, but he nods as he closes his apartment door. I say goodbye to Dr. Simmons and go back downstairs.

I feed Howie and sit down at the computer. I'm halfway playing with Howie and halfway doing research on the Internet. Anne used the word *grimoire*, so I look it up. It's a fancy word for a book of spells. So, a "Salem Witch Grimoire" would refer to a book used in the 1600s, supposedly to invoke spirits, communicate with the dead, curse enemies, and perform other "spells."

I ask Howie if he knows any spells. He cocks his head and rolls a tennis ball to me. I guess he *has* cast a spell over me in his own way. Between tosses, I continue researching. The public index of the college library has no listing for the *Necronomicon* (assuming I'm spelling it properly). *The Book of Azathoth* is similarly not present.

In a moment of insight, I log on with my faculty credentials. I have not spent much time using the departmental system because I have not yet had to record any paper or exam grades. After logging in to the Science Department, I see all my students and classes. From here, I navigate the campus hierarchy to the library. Now the search screen has more options. In addition to title and author, I can browse collections and search by a variety of other criteria.

I try "Necronomicon" but get no results. *The Book of Azathoth* is in the catalog and is part of the Ancient Texts collection. It cannot be checked out but may be viewed by permission from the Rare and Arcane Book Specialist. The catalog is not clear whether the book is in English, and there's no publisher or publishing date listed. If it's very old, I suppose it might have been copied rather than published. There's an interesting note at the bottom of the entry: "For Research and Viewing Only. No Photocopies May Be Made."

I pull up Google Translate and set the "From" language to Greek. I set the "To" language to English and type in "necronomicon." It translates to "book of dead names."

I go back to the library catalog and try the translation—no results. I try "book of names of the dead." No results. I try "book for naming the dead." Up comes a cross-reference to *The Book of Naming the Dead*. I click on the link. *There it is!* In fact, we have four versions of the book and multiple photocopies of each version. A sixteenth-century Greek version is the oldest, printed in Italy and donated to Miskatonic University by the Pickman family of Salem, Massachusetts. A seventeenth-century version is in Latin as translated by Olaus Wormius. Another version was translated into English (from the Latin) by a Dr. Dee in 1919. A second English translation was made in 1936 by someone right here at the college. All the versions are attributed to Abdul Alhazred, the author of the original Arabic manuscript. Although copies are listed for all four, you cannot check them out, or at least the system would not let me put a hold on any of them. In addition, the same strange catalog warning is given at the bottom of the screen: "For Research and Viewing Only. No Photocopies May Be Made."

As part of the academic staff at Miskatonic, I feel empowered to call the library. I introduce myself to a librarian in Rare Books and Manuscripts.

"This is Dr. Mackenzie. I'm interested in your polices around viewing and checking out rare books."

"Most of them have been photocopied," she explains. "You can't check out the originals, but you can check out a copy using your faculty ID or view the original in our collectors' room. Many have even been scanned, so you can view them online."

"Well, that's just it. The online catalog says the books I wanted to look at aren't available for public viewing, and photocopies can't be made."

There's a pause. "What department are you associated with?"

"I'm in the Physics Department."

"I think I know the books you want. They're reserved for research and qualified arcane text scholars, only."

I sense that this is all the information my phone call is going to muster, so I thank her and hang up.

My book is going much better tonight. I finish a section on the *time* part of the space-time continuum. I illustrate it with an astronaut story. The faster the spaceship goes, the younger the astronaut stays in relation to the folks left back home on Earth. When the astronaut gets home he's the same age as his son. Of course, the spaceship has to be going really fast. I have some fun explaining just *how* fast.

After writing for a few hours, I take Howie for a bedtime walk. With him dressed in his blue sweater, we make a circuit around the central Green. It's late, and only a few lights are on in various windows. It's nice to have the campus alive with students. It makes the place feel warm, even if the air is a bit chilly. The buildings look less forbidding with people in them. Voices and laughter drift over from the main dormitories. The evening has cooled off, but I'm quite comfortable in my shirt, jeans, and sandals. Howie's getting used to wearing his sweater to keep warm. We pass a few people, but I allow Howie off the leash for some fun.

We play ball on the Green. He can go for hours, and frankly I want to wear him out. I'm not happy about his escape attempt. Keeping him well exercised is always a good idea. He's a little dog, but he's also a racing hound—a greyhound. They have competitions where even the little ones can race. The more Howie runs and plays, the better he sleeps and the better he is about being in the apartment all day. For some reason, seeing him run reminds me of how lonely I've been since coming to Miskatonic. Howie's really my only friend here on the East Coast. How can a twelve-pound dog be my only real connection to life? Am I that much of a loser?

We avoid playing by University Hall. I'm still not quite sure what I want to do about Brown Jenkin. Probably nothing.

After about forty minutes, we head back home to get ready for bed.

I check my e-mail and see that I have a note from my friend Tab at UCLA. Tab has sent me a diagram and parts list for creating a Faraday cage entirely out of heavy-duty aluminum foil. He recommends foiling everything, including the floor. He suggests rubber-mat flooring that comes in interlocking tiles to go above the foil. That way, if the aluminum foil needs to be replaced, you can simply pull up a tile or two for easy access. Tab is really an expert at these kinds of installations and reinforces my understanding of how to construct my "cage." You just need to have a nonconductive layer (like the walls and floor) covered completely by a conductive layer (like the foil). Except for the ceiling (of which the metal grid, unfortunately, *is* conductive), the job is going to be easy. Put up the foil, lay down the floor tiles, and that's it.

I just have to figure out the ceiling grid. Maybe a layer of cardboard or fiberboard glued to the false ceiling, then foil on top of that?

I wash a few dishes in the sink and check on Howie. He's fast asleep in his bed by the radiator. He's curled up in a tight ball, and my heart opens when I think of the day he's had. He looks so delicate lying there, but he's also a plucky little guy. I can't imagine what it must have been like to have a stranger in our apartment and to be locked out.

I bend down to pick him up and put him in the big bed with me. That's when I notice something. The window above the radiator is closed, but not locked. I know it was locked when we moved in on Friday. I rack my mind in vain to remember ever opening it. I lock the window and check the others.

Is this how someone left me the note yesterday? Is this how Howie was let out today? *Who's coming into my apartment?*

CHAPTER FOUR

The Faraday Cage

Two weeks have passed. Matt Brown changed the lock on my apartment, and Howie has not escaped since. No further threatening notes have been left. I'm assuming that the note writer is also the person who let Howie out.

Campus security is pretty sure that the intruder got in through the unlatched window or even through Howie's dog door. I still feel better with the locks changed.Justin Taggert chalks it up to student hijinks. I honestly can't think of any of my students doing these things.

I'm in the rhythm of school again. I conducted my first quiz yesterday, and most of my beginning physics students are doing just fine. I like to have at least one test early in the term. It gives the slower students a chance to see that they might need a little help before it's too late. This week is also the deadline for students to drop a class without any grades or marks against them. That's another reason for having early tests: it gives kids a chance to switch majors or find other options if physics just isn't right for them.

Tab approves of the final design for the Faraday cage. Here's what's going to happen. First, we're going to paint everything with a special flat primer to create an even, clean surface to affix the foil to the ceiling and walls. Then we need to put a nonconductive layer on the underside of the metal grid that holds up the ceiling tiles. The metallic foil can't touch any underlying metal or the cage will "leak."

Tab agrees that we can just use cardboard! When I first thought of it, it made me laugh, but what a simple, inexpensive option. Today I'll try a few different adhesives to find out what will stick the cardboard to the ceiling tiles the easiest. Once the cardboard is up, all the surfaces in the room will be covered in foil. There will need to be some special foiling over the door. When the door is closed, the room needs to be a seamless enclosure.

After the foil goes up, we can put down the interlocking rubberized floor tiles.

Rather than pierce the foil to have electrical outlets (a potential source of EM leakage), Dr. Alvarez suggested we use a drop cord that would simply lie over the floor tiles. If we only run one experiment at a time, a single shielded electrical supply cord should work just fine.

This can all happen pretty quickly once the adhesives prove to be effective. The Plant Department has three guys set to start the painting today, and the same people can help with the foiling. By the end of the week, we may be able to start testing the lab!

I forwarded my materials list to Brian at Three Rivers Hardware yesterday. Brian has been great to work with—he's interfacing with the Plant and Maintenance Departments so that everyone's happy with the invoicing process. I haven't really had to use the credit card, which has our department bookkeeper duly impressed.

As I get ready for the day, I check my e-mail and notice the materials list order has already been confirmed at Three Rivers. Brian must be in early and has already placed the order. With any luck, he might even turn into a friend. He's invited me to go hiking on one of my days off.

After morning classes, George Marsh meets me at the soon-to-be lab space in Massachusetts Hall. He has the afternoon off and offered to help me test some of the adhesives that we'll use to put up the foiling.

The basement tower room looks plenty big enough now that all the boxes are cleared out. I explain the proposed layout to George. "A laboratory table will be located in the center of the room to hold experimental equipment. There will be enough room for about fifteen to twenty chairs or stools so the lab students can see what's going on."

"That doesn't leave much room for equipment," says George, looking around.

"It is small for a lab, that's true. Equipment that's not in use will be stored in a closet down the hall to save space. The less that's stored inside the Faraday cage, the easier the room will be to maintain. It's probably best to have just one experiment running at a time."

Yesterday I painted part of one wall and some of the ceiling. George helps me put some foil over the painted wall using three different adhesives: spray glue (like you would find in a craft store), watered-down carpenter's glue (like you would find in a woodworking shop), and wallpaper paste.

"The carpenter's glue is hard to apply," says George. "I give up trying to apply it to the foil. Can I use a roller and just roll it on the wall, instead? Then, once I have an even coat, I can apply the foil."

"I don't see why not."

While George is working with the carpenter's glue, I'm using the spray glue. It's easy to apply but really makes a mess. My fingers and clothes are already sticky just from putting up my sample piece.

"You know," says George, "if you're going to use the spray glue for an extended period, you'll want to have a respirator. I can't imagine the fumes are good for your lungs."

"It sure smells good, though."

George laughs. "Oh, I see. I bet you became a professor for the easy access to flip-chart markers."

"Oh no! My secret's out!"

George is fun to be around, and I'm enjoying our banter. He tells me about the kelp studies he's working on at the Marine Science Center in Innsmouth, about growing up in that small coastal town, and his close-knit family that still lives there.

We decide to tackle using the wallpaper paste together. Like the carpenter's glue, it spreads more easily on the hard surface first. Other-wise, it's like hanging real wallpaper. With the foil you don't even care how straight things are—there's no pattern! We just make sure to have a decent overlap as we unroll each vertical section.

George defers being on the ladder, pointing down at his feet. "You'll have to start at the top. These feet of mine don't do ladders."

I look down at his feet and once again notice his overly large shoes. They would make it hard to be on a ladder for very long. I go up the ladder with a roll of foil and unroll it downward over the wallpaper paste.

"Were you in an accident?" I ask, hoping not to be callous.

"Birth defect. I was born with syndactyly. It caused my hands and feet to be webbed."

I look at George's hands, and sure enough, fine surgical scar lines are apparent.

He notices my glance and says, "I had six surgeries on my hands and had way too much downtime. I'm happy with the results, of course." He flexes his hands. They seem to work perfectly.

"I'm sorry to bring it up, George. Please tell me if I've been insensitive."

"Actually, it's fine to talk about it. It's much worse when people talk behind your back." He pauses, then continues. "As for my feet, the webbing is more extensive. I couldn't see spending the money and not being able to walk for months. I just get really big shoes, instead. I can walk OK, but my feet don't bend right for ladders."

"Those *are* really big shoes."

George smiles wistfully. "It gives the ladies something to hope for. You know what they say about big feet…"

I laugh at George's joke but am also sensitive to the difficulty he must experience. He's a nice-looking young man, but some women might avoid dating a man with a physical deformity. High school must have been rough.

As far as our adhesive application, the wallpaper paste wins. It is much easier to use than the other adhesives. That's only half the equation, though. We'll have to see how well they adhere once things dry.

Now for the ceiling. George braces the ladder and has my sample cardboard ready. Applying adhesives to the ceiling proves to be less than an ideal process. My hair starts to get sticky from the drips, and the smell of the glue starts to make me a bit dizzy. I reach up to brace myself, and one of the ceiling tiles falls to the ground.

"Holy cow," says George, looking upward.

There's no real ceiling! I get a flashlight from the storage room to make sure, but it's true: the tower room is a simple cylinder. Above the ceiling tiles is only airspace that goes up five floors to the roof. I can barely see the windows set around the top of the structure. They must be painted out because the interior of the tower is in darkness.

"Look how the false ceiling is attached." George is pointing to guy-wires that have been anchored to the walls about five feet above the false ceiling. The wires are holding the metal ceiling grid and tiles in place.

I'm stunned. Why didn't I notice that the tower had no rooms on other floors? Why didn't anyone tell me that the basement room was five stories high? I guess the tower was just built as an architectural feature. It wasn't intended to add usable square footage to the building.

"Does this make any difference to your plan for the lab?"

I pause to think. If we seal the enclosure in foil, EM radiation will be locked out no matter how high the real ceiling is.

"That's a really good question. I'll have my friend Tab, the EM radiation expert, weigh in on this development. But I think we should proceed with our materials test. In the worst-case scenario, we'll just be out an hour or so of our time."

"Then let's try something different. Wouldn't it go easier if we put the adhesives on the tiles when they're removed from the grid? You can hand them down to me, and I'll use a roller to apply the adhesive. Then you can put them back in the grid and apply the cardboard and foil."

"You're a genius! I thank you, and my hair thanks you even more."

George smiles, glad to have figured out a better way of handling this messy job.

"I feel a little like Thomas Edison today," I say, waving my arm to encompass the room. "He tried thousands of combinations of filaments and voltages until he found the perfect mix to create a stable light bulb. Although this Faraday cage won't be a startling discovery, I'm happy to think we might find a new combination of materials and techniques that create an EM isolation cage at low cost and high effectiveness."

George laughs. "You really are quite the nerd, aren't you?"

George and I finish our work in the lab, and he leaves to catch the bus to Innsmouth. It's been really nice to spend the afternoon with him.

I must admit that I'm still feeling lonely. I've been at Miskatonic for over a month, and I don't really have any new friends. Of course, Matt Brown is friendly, but in a fatherly way. Horace Alvarez is friendly, too, but, really, as a colleague. It would be nice to have some friends my own age, like George. I'd like to be with people who share similar experiences and values.

Well, you have to start somewhere. To this end, I decide to spend time in the graduate student lounge in the Student Union. The lounge is on the third floor and takes up quite a bit of space. It has a few small rooms for meetings or quiet study. It has a fireside room with many sofas, small tables, and nooks for reading, visiting, and playing games and cards. Another large room is fitted for study with some long tables and good work lighting. It even has a small kitchen where you can refrigerate (or reheat) a meal or make popcorn and other snacks. The decor is midcentury modern (yes, twentieth century) with chrome light fixtures and blond wood. The fireplace has that pinkish brick that was so popular during that period in America. There's a mirrored starburst over the mantle.

All graduate students and graduate teaching fellows are welcome to hang out in the lounge. It was created as a place to relax, study, read, and make social connections.

And, as my luck would have it, I'm almost the only person here! There's a young woman engrossed in her laptop (I nod and smile) and three people in one of the small rooms working on a project together.

I go out onto the terrace that runs the length of the fireside room. It has a flagstone floor and planters decorated with bloomed-out summer flowers. The terrace has some nice tables and chairs for good-weather socializing, but nobody's outside today.

Back inside, I decide to check out the kitchen area. It has three refrigerators and signs that explain they're cleaned out once a week. We're encouraged to load and run the dishwasher and keep the two microwaves clean. There is free coffee, tea, and hot chocolate available. This helps the teaching fellows stay up all night while grading papers for professors and classes they support.

There are four bistro-sized tables, and I notice a young woman sitting at the one farthest from the door. She appears to be taking apart her backpack and its contents. I make a cup of hot chocolate and decide to engage her in some conversation.

"It's nice that they give us free hot chocolate," I say, somewhat lamely. "My name's Mac. I'm a professor of physics over in Massachusetts Hall."

She looks up, and I see that she's quite pretty in a coltish way. She is long and lean and holds her body with equal parts elegance and tomboy assuredness. Her mid-length hair is chestnut brown, as are her eyes.

"Pleased to meet you, Mister Mac. I'm Ally Wilmarth, your resident folklorist. If there's anything you want to know about fairies, demons, crop circles, leprechauns, witches, or trolls, I'm your girl."

We both laugh. She has a lovely, bright laugh. She's wearing skinny jeans and a hooded pullover in a lightweight blue fabric. She doesn't have an accent at all, so I assume she's not from New England.

"I'm trying to find the power adapter to my phone," she says, surveying the distributed contents of her backpack. "Mine seems to lose its charge about every fifteen minutes unless I keep it plugged in."

We spend a few minutes talking about our electronic devices and not being able to use them at Miskatonic because of the lack of cell service. Ally eventually finds her adapter and plugs in the phone. I show her how I have my phone set up to place calls using the campus Wi-Fi network.

"That's handy," says Ally. "I think you may have really simplified my life. My friends like to stay in touch, and this will be a big help. I've been missing them, and the term's only just started. I'm from the Midwest, and this is my first year at Miskatonic. Seems like it's proving hard to be a full-time graduate student and keep up with long-distance friends."

"What are you studying?" I ask.

"I'm taking my graduate studies in literature with folklore as a specialty," she says, while returning the many, many things to her backpack. "I'm just starting this term working with my dissertation adviser. Do you have any experience with that? It seems like coming up with the idea—the title, even—is the hardest part."

"Yes, I finished one dissertation, and I'm working on another similar project right now. I completely agree with you about the initial idea. It's critical. If you don't work on something that interests you, you're not going to finish it. Even if you do finish it, if you're not interested, the review committee won't be interested."

Ally smiles and puts the last of her things away. "That's part of my problem. I'm interested in so many things! You have no idea how rich the East Coast is for folklorists. In the Midwest, especially Chicago, there's enough history to generate some legends and stories. Here in Massachusetts, though, they've had hundreds of years for scandals, killings, mysterious happenings, and otherworldly influences. I've moved into a hotbed of folklore right under my feet. I really don't know where to begin." Her smile is genuine and infectious.

"Initially," she continues, "I thought I'd write about the Salem witch trials. When you hear about Massachusetts and, more particularly Essex County, you think *witches*. Trouble is, it's already been done. Take a look in the library, and you'll see at least a hundred theses presented right here at Miskatonic with the word *witch* or *witchcraft* in their titles. This university has been here for a long time, and generation after generation of graduate students has researched and documented that unpleasant but intriguing period. It's interesting to me because it shows a sort of reverse-folklore effect. Generally, something real happens and, over time, stories about it become more elaborate and fantastical. In the case of Essex County and witches, folklore was applied to real people and created a huge mess!"

"Do you chalk it up to mass hysteria, then?" I ask. "Did they just pick on some unpopular young women and describe their behavior as witchcraft?"

"That's the popular notion, but I'm a little more open in my thinking. Just because the women they persecuted and eventually hanged were not witches doesn't necessarily mean there *were* no witches."

"I take your point. No, it doesn't. That's a common misapplication of scientific methodology. Let's say you set up a hypothesis that witches exist. Then you look at a list of people accused of witchcraft. One by one, you eliminate potential witches. This one was just a disgruntled wife who was named as a witch by her angry husband. That one was labeled a witch because she was seen talking to chickens, or whatever. You eventually conclude that witches don't exist because nobody is left on your list. That would be a biased conclusion because you don't know if the original list is a representative sample of the control group, which would be *all* potential witches."

"You're quite the scientist, Mac," says Ally, smiling.

She's now started to absentmindedly peer at the ends of her hair. I may have overdone the scientific methodology. It's always hard to know (especially with women) when my passion for science becomes too professor-like. Today, I'm looking for friends, not more students. I decide to change the subject.

"So, what are some of the other folklore topics you might consider for a dissertation?"

"I might write about the Sea Witch of Billingsgate," suggests Ally. "That legend started right here in Massachusetts in the Cape Cod area. The legend of the Sea Witch began in 1715 when an older man seduced and impregnated fifteen-year-old Goody Hallet of Eastham. Nine months later, Ms. Hallet was found in a barn with a dead baby in her arms. The local constable assumed she had murdered the baby, who was conceived out of wedlock. She was taken to jail, lashed, tortured, and awaited her execution."

"Nice," I offer with some sarcasm.

"Then, a handsome stranger shows up at the jail. He turns the bars of the cell window into straw with a wave of his gold-tipped cane. He promises to allow Goody to escape if she'll sign a covenant with the Devil. She does so, escapes, and heads to freedom. She's now the Sea Witch and takes up residence in Billingsgate, where she lures ships aground, taking the lives and souls of drowned sailors. She also creates wind and rainstorms to punish the mariners and townspeople of the cape."

"But how does that turn into a dissertation? I'm not really sure of the purpose of a dissertation in folklore or how you develop a theme from a particular tale."

"Good question. Generally, we would provide analysis to a series of folk stories and show how they attempt to solve a particular problem in society or how they reflect hidden beliefs of the time. In this case, you might say that the Sea Witch of Billingsgate fits into the larger 'mermaid' mythos originating with the sirens of ancient Greek mythology. I could probably suggest that mermaids represent the repressed sexuality of the time, especially for sailors at sea for months." Ally's stretching here, and she knows it. Finally, she offers, "Christopher Columbus reported seeing mermaids in his exploration of the Caribbean."

"You don't sound overly enthused about the Sea Witch."

"Yeah, writing about mermaids seems a little lame, even if I do tie it into a local context."

"Any other East Coast legends that you *do* fancy?"

"Well, there's always the Jersey Devil," says Ally, brightening up a bit. "The story goes like this. One stormy night in 1735, a New Jersey woman named Mother Leeds took to her bed in childbirth. This was to be her thirteenth child. The woman was suspected of being a witch, and neighborhood women gathered to see if the baby would be born normal. The idea was that witches had sex with devils and demons and would produce deformed offspring. Supposedly, the child was born normal, but shortly afterward began changing. The child grew at an enormous rate, becoming taller than a man. It changed into a beast that resembled a dragon but with a head like a horse, a snake-like body, and bat's wings. The now-grown child beat the women, including its mother, and fled up the chimney. After that, the legend grew with local sightings of the beast in the woods and in towns. In the 1800s, the story was used to caution children not to play in the woods alone. Over the years, there continue to be sightings of the Jersey Devil haunting southern New Jersey and parts of eastern Pennsylvania."

"That's quite a story! How would you turn that into a dissertation?" I ask.

"The obvious one's already been done," says Ally. "In the 1950s, someone wrote their master's thesis, 'Birth Defects as Fuel for Myth.' It ties together everything from the Jersey Devil to the Elephant Man. In early times, birth defects were seen as a punishment to parents who were not following a godly path. Having sex with animals, demons, or spirits supposedly caused such defects. Many of the more dramatic birth defects turned into local legends. Without knowledge of DNA and prenatal screening, it was a way of explaining why some babies were born with defects."

"But if that analysis has already been made, what's *your* interest in the Jersey Devil?"

"I think I could take another approach to researching and writing about this subject," Ally speculates. "There's the whole idea of changelings. A changeling is the offspring of a fairy, elf, or other legendary creature that is secretly left in the place of a human child. The human child ends up as a servant to the nonhuman entity. The human parents raise the changeling, generally with great difficulty. I think the Jersey Devil child could fit into this pattern of a changeling/ child swap. A changeling is often ravenously hungry, easily angered, and quite a handful. The changeling is generally killed when its true nature is discovered. The Jersey Devil escaping up the chimney is probably just another way of saying that they burned the deformed baby in the fireplace. I think these stories (including the Jersey Devil's) could be compiled quite nicely into a dissertation called, 'Infanticide and Its Contribution to Myth Creation.'" Ally looks at me, waiting for my reaction.

"Well, that's cheerful!" I say, and we have a good laugh.

"Sorry, Mac. That's one thing that's almost universally true in folklore. It's the disquieting stories, the horrible stories, the stories of death and supernatural influences that almost always turn into myth. There just aren't too many myths about kittens or stable family relationships."

"Maybe that could be your niche," I propose. "Maybe your dissertation could be 'Preternaturally Cute Kittens as Mythic Archetypes in Twenty-First Century America.'"

We have another good laugh.

It's after dinner, and I'm correcting yesterday's quiz from my Basic Physics class. All the students seem to understand what physics teaches, the value of hypotheses, and why the scientific method is so important. The main essay question is to create a hypothesis of any sort and describe how they would use the scientific method to prove or disprove it. Here, some of my students do a great job, even using trivial hypotheses. Others, however, rapidly start losing points when they create hypotheses that cannot be tested or ones that prove a negative.

All in all, the test is a success, most students passed easily, and we'll review the common mistakes next class. I fire up my laptop and log on to the internal department system. Using Ms. Barry's cheat sheet, I teach myself how to add an exam to my class. Then I go to a grading screen and pull up each of my students to record the grade associated with their exam. It's a little harder than it needs to be. Many screens of data are required to record one set of test scores.

It's time for a change of pace, and I decide to pay a visit to the main library at Salomon Center. A light rain is falling tonight, and I basically make a dash for it. I've managed to buy some sweaters and coats for the cold weather ahead, but this is just wet—heavy clothes would not really be helpful. Next trip into town, I really must buy an umbrella.

Salomon Center was built in 1862 and is both the library and an auditorium. The lower story is built of fieldstone, and the upper part, including the tower, is made of wood. The tower holds the official campus clock, with chimes to mark each quarter hour and a gong to count the hours. The main entrance is on the south side of the building and leads to the auditorium, which seats about five hundred people. It is used for public presentations and lectures. The other (east and west) entrances are to the Library Department offices and the library itself.

I duck into the west entrance and shake myself off a little before stepping into the hallway. They've modernized quite a bit of the interior of the Salomon Center, including security systems. We're under surveillance, and I have to use my faculty card to enter the main section of the library. From the posted signs, it appears I use the same card to check out my own books, gain access to the library computers, and pay for photocopies. It's nice to have a well-set-up system for handling this stuff. I just hope there are real people to answer questions.

The main library is lovely. It continues the oak paneling from the entrance lobby and has a terrazzo floor in shades of gray and beige. Oak reading tables with antique lighting fixtures form two rows down the middle. You can tell that the card catalog area has been repurposed; the extensive library holdings are now referenced electronically.

My mission tonight is one of pure curiosity. Based on my conversation with Shirley and Anne (my "movie ladies" from town) and my own exploring of the online library catalog, I'm wanting to see what kind of restricted books Miskatonic has on tap.

I approach the main reference desk at the library and smile (I hope) innocently at the young woman behind the two-hundred-year-old oak-paneled desk.

"I'm Dr. Mackenzie from the Physics Department. I was hoping to do a little research in some of your arcane folklore texts."

"Sure, Dr. Mackenzie. Do you know what you want to check out?" she asks. Her nametag says "Shelley."

"I'm not sure I can check it out, Shelley. It's called *The Book of Naming the Dead*, and from perusing the online catalog, I think I can only read a copy of it here. I was hoping to see one of the English translations."

"Let me just check," says Shelley, as she clicks away at the terminal on her desk. She frowns. "That's interesting. I'm not sure you can even do that. It must be one of our rarest books. Sometimes you have to make a specific request to borrow or view them." She clicks on a few more links. "Yes, that's it. You have to make a request in writing to the library staff to view that book. They review the request, and if it's approved, you make an appointment to come in and see it. The form you have to fill out is online, here. Do you want me to print it for you?"

Although my curiosity is mounting by the minute, my avenues of pursuit seem to be narrowing. What earthly purpose could I claim for wanting to view a book that the townspeople are afraid of? Pure curiosity?

"That's OK, Shelley," I say. "I'd probably want to fill it out at home, anyway. I'll just print it out there."

After thinking a minute, I ask, "Do you have much folklore in the stacks that I could peruse? I don't have a particular book in mind, I just want a sampling of what you have."

"Of course, Dr. Mackenzie." Shelley seems relieved to actually be able to help me with something. She gives me a map and indicates where to find the folklore material.

I guess Miskatonic really *is* a regional center for folklore and associated studies. The folklore section is quite large. I see what Ally means about the Salem witch trials. There must be a hundred books relating the Puritan witch phenomena. I pick out a book at random: *Witches and Witchcraft: A Dark Puritan Legacy* by Laurie Elton.

I continue browsing and run across *The Grimoire: A Recipe for Magic*, and I remember the word being used by one of the ladies in town. Wasn't that the generic description that she gave for the *Necronomicon*? I pick up the book and read from the introduction:

From the earliest times, humanity has desired to better understand and document its environment. Among some of the first books are those detailing what things are and how things work: lists of animals, details of poisonous plants, charts of the stars, and discourse on the nature of humanity.

But early writers also had a desire to document mystical beliefs and practices. After mapping the stars, they wrote about their belief in astrology. After enumerating the physical elements, they devised a system of alchemy. Their desire to write down about the invisible world and its influences eventually led to the grimoire.

Due to the popularity of urban fantasy novels such as the Harry Potter *series and such television shows as* Buffy the Vampire Slayer *and* Charmed, *the grimoire is of renewed interest. There is a fascination with the promise of controlling our environment by magical means. Grimoires offer this possibility using the age-old format of a recipe book. Grimoires are books of curses and charms, of spells and amulets. They provide instructions on how to create magical objects, heal illnesses, confound enemies, and fulfill desires. Grimoires are recipe books of magic...*

I smile: a recipe book for magic. Can a book of magic really have the ladies in town upset? Could a collection of historically preserved, arcane books here at the library really cause a book-burning panic? I decide to borrow this reference book and see if there's more than meets the eye to a grimoire.

Using my faculty ID as my library card, I soon figure out the checkout process and am on my way home. I put my borrowed book under my jacket to protect it from the rain still pattering down.

When I get home, I realize it's late—almost too late to take Howie for a walk. He, however, doesn't seem worried about the lateness or the weather. Why should he? He, at least, has a raincoat. I put it on him, and we briefly make a small circle around a few of the campus buildings close to Grant Hall. I'm still in my light jacket, shivering a bit with the damp night air.

Before long, we're back at home, and I play with Howie for a bit. I'm trying to teach him a new trick. I say "Attention!" and (before long) Howie will salute. Right now, his salute looks more like his "Shake Hands." What can I say, he's a smart dog, but even smart dogs require practice. Armed with some treats, we practice. He salutes.

Howie and I call it a night and find ourselves in bed.

I pick up my personal journal and write a bit about some of the "strangeness" I keep finding at Miskatonic. Is it a mirror of my own strangeness, or is it just this time and place that collects strangeness? I don't have an answer to this question. Perhaps it's both.

I create my gratitude entries for the night:

1. _George Marsh and Ally Wilmarth: Possible new friends?_
2. _My Students: All but one are passing._
3. _The Internet: It's a modern miracle._
4. _Tab Cousins and Distant Friends._
5. _Thomas Edison: The scientific method personified._

I turn out the light and fall instantly asleep.

Sometime in the night I have this dream. Howie and I are down at the seashore. It's not the familiar Southern California coast with powdery sand and warm water. It must be a seashore here in Massachusetts. It's a gray day, and the waves are pounding. Gulls pinwheel overhead. A steady breeze blows from offshore. With the sun obscured by clouds, it's hard to tell, but I would guess it's midday.

There's a long line of rocks, a jetty, I presume, that sticks straight out into the stormy water. The top of the jetty is pretty level, and Howie and I are standing close to shore on the surface of it. To the right is the beach and crashing surf. To the left is a channel leading into a bay or harbor of some sort. I can't really say how we got here or where we are.

Straight ahead is the jetty built of granite and basalt rock.

The dream is unhurried and, side by side, Howie and I watch the rough surf and notice the patterns of the waves as they crash on, and sometimes over, the jetty. The rocks are worn from countless such attacks from the sea. Here and there, patches of barnacles and sea stars cling to the edges of the stonework closest to the water. The channel side of the jetty is choked with sea grass moving with the surges of the water.

Gradually, over the sound of pounding surf and the cry of gulls, I begin to hear the faint sound of music, of singing. I start walking slowly forward to better hear the music. Howie wants nothing to do with it. He stays put, shaking his head.

I continue walking, the music becomes clearer, and I can hear a woman's voice singing over the haunting melody. I can hear her sing— but can't make out the words. When I think of the words, the phrase "sea shanty" comes to mind, but I think that's the flavor of the music and not what she's singing. I take another step or two forward.

It's a lovely song, drawing me closer. Despite the wind and waves raging on both sides, I feel strangely relaxed. The singer has a beautiful voice.

Behind me, I can hear Howie starting to whine. He wants me to come back.

I keep moving forward, trying to better understand the song. I feel sure that if I can understand the words some mystery will be explained, some secret will be revealed.

Soon, the singer is revealed. A young woman, quite naked, is perched on a rock on the surf side of the jetty. She's half in and half out of the water, and her mid-length chestnut brown hair is still wet from swimming. She's not looking directly at me. Her head is inclined slightly to gaze at the surf. She's tall, slender, and coltish with small breasts and thin arms.

I still cannot quite make out her song. The closer I get, the louder the surf roars in my ear, muffling her lyrics.

Behind me, Howie is barking. He's telling me to *come back right now*. He's warning me not to be silly. *The jetty could be dangerous; the woman's a stranger!*

The singer seems to notice me, at last. She turns her head to face me. She continues to sing, and I try reading her lips. She has small, sharp teeth but lovely full lips the color of roses. I strain to read her lips. Somehow, the words have an important message for me.

It's confusing. The song is lyrical, lilting even, but her lips seem to be singing or saying something different. I must have it wrong. He lips are saying that her name is Azathoth. It's a funny name, but I'm sure she says "Azathoth" and that she'd like me to come away with her. That makes no sense. That's not who she is. That's not what she wants.

"You're Goody Hallet, the Sea Witch!"

She smiles as she sings. She's looking straight at me now. I'm close enough to reach out and touch her. Behind me, Howie is bent with his front legs close to the ground and his hips high in the air. He's barking and growling.

A sudden noise distracts Goody. Though she keeps singing, her attention has now returned to the sea. Offshore, perhaps a mile or so out, a small ship is blowing a horn as it makes its way to the channel. Although I don't know much about nautical signals, I would guess it's a distress signal. The deck of the ship is awfully close to the water. The stronger waves toss over its keel. I can dimly make out figures on its windswept deck.

Goody makes a sweeping motion with her arms, and a slight fog blows in from the open sea. The ship all but disappears, although I can still hear its horn and what might be muted voices from its crew. Goody continues to sing, louder, if anything.

I look down, and Howie is tugging at my pant leg: *Come back!*

Goody strains seaward, her song stronger than ever. The ship's horn sounds closer. Goody waves her arms again, and the fog thickens.

The fog is now roiling up and over the sides of the jetty. This startles me, and I step back. I take another step backward, trying to avoid the mist that threatens to obscure the whole jetty. I'm turning now, putting my back to the surf, to the channel, to the singing siren and the floundering ship.

Howie and I are almost back where we started, back to the shoreline and safety, when we hear the crash of the ship on the rocks.

CHAPTER FIVE

Fat Dog Pizza

The rusted iron sign says "Pioneer Cemetery." Howie and I are walking through a part of Miskatonic we haven't seen before. We're almost completely across campus from our home in Grant Hall. The walk has been long and leisurely, and I don't have classes until midafternoon.

Howie's wearing his (now favorite) blue sweater. The colder October temperatures are making his clothing a necessity. For a small dog, he's quite the walker. We must have covered three miles by now and have a similar amount to make it home. The morning has been clear with little wind. When Howie's really enjoying his walk, as he is this morning, he tends to tug a bit at his leash. Since we're well away from the main part of the campus, I decide to give him his freedom and let him run.

If there was a gate or fence to the cemetery, it's long gone. A laurel hedge is about all that marks its boundary from the campus grounds. We slip past two of the laurels and find ourselves among the rows of stones, monuments, stone angels, and crypts. More laurels divide the stones and statuary into maze-like rows and walkways. The cemetery dates from the time when whole families would be buried together over many generations.

Vandals have overturned a few of the gravestones, but largely everything is as it should be. Freshly mowed grass and well-trimmed shrubs indicate that the campus groundskeepers likely have a hand in upkeep

—few old cemeteries would be this well maintained.

As Howie and I walk along we look at the inscriptions on the stones. Here's one for a pastor:

Here lie the Remains of
Rev Mr JOHN AVERY
Who Departed this Life ye
23d of April 1654 in the
69th Year of His Age and
44th of His Ministry and
the First Pastor Ordained in
this Place
In this dark cavern, in this lonesome Grave
Here lies the honest, pious, virtuous Friend
Him, Kind Heav'n to us priest and doctor gave
As such he lived, as such we mourn his end

The first pastor of Arkham? More likely the first pastor of the small village that was to become the Miskatonic campus. And here's another one from the church that used to be where the campus is now:

In Memory of
Dea'n JOSHUA FREEMAN
who died Sept'r 22d 1795
In the 79th Year of his Age
having faithfully served the
Church in the office of Deacon
45 years
Mark the perfect man and behold the upright
for the end of that man is peace

As we continue through the graveyard, it's clear that the older the gravestone, the more likely the epitaph to be on the dark side. Many of them say "Remember Death" underneath the names and dates. Some provide rhymes that we might think humorous today. Here's one for a Mrs. Hannah Rich, who died at thirty-five:

Here lieth Buried in the Dust
In hopes to Rise among the Just

Opposite a large family crypt I see a stone for a young woman who died in childbirth:

Here lies the Body of
Mrs ABIGAIL ADAMS
The amiable Consort of
Dr. SAMUEL ADAMS
Who died in Childbed

July 8th 1774
In the 24th Year
Of her Age
O Death all eloquent you only prove
What Dust we dote on when we Creatures love

Although Howie is enjoying running through the grass and between the graves and monuments, the atmosphere of the cemetery is starting to get to me. The air seems too still. The grass is too perfect. The monuments are heavy and final looking. What few flowers that have been placed graveside are dead and awaiting removal. I know it's silly of me to feel spooked, but I decide to make a short loop and head back. Maybe a warm summer day with friends would be a better one for exploring the Pioneer Cemetery.

Howie and I take a left turn at a mausoleum, the final resting place for generations of a Palmer family. A pink climbing rose, still blooming, covers its doorway. Then we take another left at a stone angel. She sits in a quadrangle with about a dozen gravestones for the Wells family. Based on the dates, many of them are for children.

We continue a bit, and the graves appear to be a bit newer. Many of them are from the 1800s and even a few from the early twentieth century. As we head back toward the opening in the laurels that leads back to campus, the quiet stillness is broken. It sounds like a child crying.

We take a small detour in the maze of stones and monuments, and the sound becomes louder. A right turn—and it's louder yet. A final turn past a large granite tomb, and *there she is*. But, it's not a child. It's a young woman. It's my new acquaintance from the graduate lounge at the Student Union, Ally Wilmarth. She's sitting on a stone plinth at the head of a small plot of graves.

Howie runs ahead and startles Ally. She looks over her shoulder, and I can see that she's been crying for some time. Her face is red, her eyes puffy. She looks disconsolate. Howie's a good caretaker, and he rubs up against her to let her know that petting him might be good for both of them. She reaches down and strokes his head, pats his back.

"Hi, Ally," I say. "Are you OK? Am I intruding?"

"Yes—I mean, no," says Ally. "I guess I really don't know what I mean. I'm OK. Sorry for the tears. Sometimes I get this way when I come to visit the family."

I look down and take in the square plot, ringed in stone, the plinth marked "Wilmarth." The plot has several of her relatives in it and room for more. She's sitting near one that's modern in style and text. It says:

Albert Wilmarth
1875 – 1964
Faithful Servant
to the College
and to the Family
At Rest For Eternity

She points to the stone and says, "My great-grandfather. I never met him, but my grandfather has told me quite a bit. Like so many of our family, he was devoted to this part of Essex County, Arkham, and the university. He was a folklore scholar, like me."

Feeling a little lost, I ask, "Is there anything I can do? Would you like to talk about it?"

"Maybe I would," says Ally. "I'm not really crying for them, you know," she says, gesturing to the graves. "Nobody's buried here that I know personally—it's just an old family plot." She has a sudden idea. "I suppose I could use it someday. That would be fitting!"

Ally is wearing warm-up pants, sneakers, and some kind of sweater with an oversized neck. The bulky clothes are hiding her slender frame and delicate features. She is wearing a stocking hat, but bits of her unruly chestnut hair have come down in back. Somehow, with frumpy clothes and a tear-stained face, Ally still manages to look pretty.

Smiling and wiping her cheeks, she apologizes. "Sorry for the messy look. Sometimes I come here in the morning to meditate. Today I started thinking about complicated things that have been bothering me lately. They're tears of frustration, not sadness, not really. My family has a history of overcommitting themselves, and I'm afraid I'm next in line. Have you ever felt helpless, responsible, frustrated, and obligated all at the same time?"

I smile. "I don't think men are allowed to feel that many things at once." I sit down beside her at the head of the plot. She seems so vulnerable. I put an arm around her shoulder.

She peers into my face for an awkward minute through teary eyes. Is she sizing me up? I feel an odd tension between us, like she might kiss me.

Instead, she abruptly asks, "Are you gay?"

I get this question. I'm not sure if it's the way I look or the way I talk, but it comes up. My answer never seems entirely adequate, but I give it anyway. "I'm not sure," I say. "I've slept with men and women, but it's not been the best of experiences, either way."

"Oh, sex," she says, with a wave of her hand. "That's not so important. According to Kinsey, we nearly all have sexual experiences that cross the boundaries. Who have you been in love with? Girls or boys?"

Ally's manner is so direct, so frank, that I can't help but smile through what would typically be an awkward conversation. With her, it doesn't seem awkward, and I find myself telling her about a girl I was with in sixth grade and a boy in junior high. Talking to Ally is surprisingly easy.

"Those were just crushes," she says. "You wanted to follow them around like you were a puppy, right? You wanted to smell their hair and do their homework. That's not love, though, at least not entirely." She pauses for a minute and makes a pronouncement: "I think you're gay. You just haven't fallen in love yet to know for sure."

There's no arguing with an unproven hypothesis, so I decide to give her a similar treatment. "And you? Have you been in love?"

She tears up again. "High school. His name was Michael. I dated him all four years. We said we'd never be apart. We planted a tree together. We went to Planned Parenthood to get condoms. It was real love, I know it was." She says this as though defying me to contradict her. She pauses for a moment, then continues, "Summer after senior year, he goes on a trip with his parents to Europe. When he comes back, he's applying for school at different universities without even talking to me. He's suddenly busy all the time. He doesn't want to have a real conversation anymore. He doesn't seem to even notice me."

"Sounds like a jerk."

"You're sweet to say that. He's not a jerk, though. I think he just decided that what he felt for me was juvenile—not an adult thing but a teenage thing. When he graduated from school he graduated from me." Ally's crying again, and I hold her a little tighter.

"You're still in love with someone from high school, and I've never been in love," I observe. "We're quite a pair. Not sure which is worse."

"I know which. Although it hurts, I think I'd rather be me. At least I *know* love."

Through tears and conversation, Howie's been staring at us. Now he jumps up into Ally's lap. He always knows how to cheer me up and is trying his luck with her. "So, what's his name?" she asks, drying her eyes with her sleeve.

"Howie. Ally, this is Howie. Howie, this is Ally. " I mug my way through formal introductions. "Bow to the lady, Howie." Howie bows, respectfully, and Ally gives a surprised laugh.

"I haven't heard 'Howie' as a dog's name before. Did you name him, or did he come with it?"

"Neither. Howie told me his name when I first got him."

Ally looks puzzled, so I demonstrate. "Howie? What's your name? What's your name, boy?"

I look intently at Howie and tilt my head slightly upward to remind him of the trick. Howie looks back at me, lifts his head to heaven, pushes out his small but deep chest, and opens his mouth.

"Hooooooowwieeeeeeee!" he proudly cries.

My afternoon class goes great. We're discussing quantum entanglement and nonlocality. Albert Einstein called these remarkable features of the invisible world "spooky actions at a distance." He didn't believe that these odd effects postulated as part of quantum theory would ever be proven. The scientific world marches forward, however, and the practical experiments by John Clauser and Stuart Freedman in 1972 seemed to show they are, indeed, real.

First, I go over what entanglement is. We cover the basics of how electrons are naturally entangled within a stable atomic structure. I show an atomic structure where mathematically we've proven the total spin must be zero. If one particle is found to have clockwise spin on a certain axis, then the spin of the other particle, measured on the same axis, must be counterclockwise. Through bombardment, we can change the spin of one electron, and the other electron will automatically change its spin so that the total is still zero.

Then we have to cover nonlocality. Initially entangled electrons are "local" to one stable atomic structure. They orbit one atom's nucleus. When such electrons are removed from their initial structure they are no longer local but still may be entangled.

I continue with my lecture. "The final proof of quantum entanglement and nonlocal interactions came at the end of 2015 when multiple research teams conclusively demonstrated the phenomenon."

On the overhead system, I display a pair of industrial diamonds.

"Ronald Hanson from the University of Delft used a pair of diamonds with a gap in each diamond's atomic matrix. It allowed each diamond to trap a single electron stolen from another atomic structure."

An illustration of the diamonds' structure is then displayed, and an electron is added to each. "The diamonds were then taken one-point-three kilometers apart. Electrons from a stable atomic structure always have corresponding characteristics, and when a characteristic of one electron is changed—the spin, for instance—the other electron will change its characteristic to maintain the quantum equilibrium."

I continue with a slide showing Hanson and his team. "The team was able to observe that changing the spin of the electron of one diamond simultaneously changed the spin on its entangled electron on the diamond located across town. This proved that 'spooky actions at a distance' are real."

The next slide shows another group of scientists. "A similar experiment this last fall was completed by the University of Vienna. They separated the entangled particles even farther—by one hundred forty-three kilometers. This allows any possible uncertainty in the experiment or its setup to be minimized even further."

I acknowledge a raised hand in the second row. The student asks, "Does quantum entanglement help to explain any everyday things, or is it just something scientists do in the lab?"

"Good question," I say. "There's a current theory that says quantum entanglement of electrons and atomic structure is what causes entropy in the universe. What we observe is that energy dissipates. A coffee cup loses its heat to become the same temperature as the room around it. We see buildings crumble over time. We see stars eventually shed all their fissionable material and burn out into a lifeless cinder. What's interesting is that it never works the other way around. There's nothing in classical Newtonian physics that would say it shouldn't happen or couldn't happen the other way. There's nothing in prequantum physics that says a coffee cup couldn't absorb some of the ambient heat from the room and make the coffee hotter over time. We're used to the idea of entropy but don't really have a good way of explaining how and why it happens.

"But Sandu Popescu, Tony Short, and other colleagues working together at the University of Bristol reported a discovery in the journal *Physical Review E* in 2009, arguing that objects reach equilibrium, or a state of uniform energy distribution, by becoming quantum-mechanically entangled with their surroundings. Quantum entanglement, then, is the cause of what we see as the dissipation of energy over time. Without quantum entanglement, we might not age, or we might view time in a very different way. On a more speculative note," I say, and smile brightly, "quantum entanglement might allow for the possibility of faster-than-light communication. With large sets of entangled and separated electrons, we could create a quantum telecommunication device. We'd be able to instantly communicate across vast distances of space in an instant. Of course, initially the entangled electrons would have to be separated the old-fashioned, slower-than-light method.

Once in place, though, instant communication to the opposite ends of the universe would be possible."

The final part of the presentation is a short clip from the classic *Star Trek* television series starring William Shatner and Nichelle Nichols. "Uhura," says Captain Kirk, "put through a call to Star Fleet. Tell them it's urgent!"

The kids laugh, but another hand is raised. "Can macro objects be entangled? I know that consciousness plays a big part in quantum effects, so could consciousness, itself, be entangled? Could entanglement be the reason for the life-experience similarities between twins raised separately?"

"Another good question," I say. "Drs. Huping Hu and Maoxin Wu proposed such entanglements between people and other macro structures in 2006. They proposed that such entanglements could explain the 'twins-raised-separately' effect. They also said it could explain documented cases of telepathy, such as a mother getting a mental message from her daughter, thousands of miles away."

"So far," I continue, "these are just speculative theories. They're also pretty hard to test. Why would some people be entangled and some not? How can we know if someone is entangled with someone else? If you were entangled, why wouldn't you have telepathic communication all the time? We may never be able to prove or disprove such theories, but it makes for great science fiction."

After I finish up my day of teaching, it's time to make a trip into Arkham. I give Howie a short walk around the campus but decide to leave him home. I'm going to be stopping at Three Rivers Hardware and Lumber and am not sure if I'll be filling the car with materials or if I can have things delivered.

The trip to Arkham has become routine. Initially, the campus seemed remote from town, but with repetition, the few miles go by quickly. We're in October now, and fall colors are starting to show. The red, yellow, and orange leaves help brighten the trip through the hardwood forest to town.

It's about four thirty, and Arkham's rush hour has started. I smile at the thought—nothing in Arkham is ever a rush, and there are only a few dozen cars on the streets downtown as I head over to the store. There are plenty of spaces in the parking lot at Three Rivers, and I pull in near the lumber loading dock, hopeful that some of my materials will be ready.

I poke my head into the lumberyard and see Brian working with another customer.

Today he's wearing a rust-colored flannel shirt with the arms rolled up and jeans. The shirt suits him perfectly, and I can't help but think he picks out his clothes to go with his light skin and reddish hair. To top off the studied-but-casual look, he has a New York Yankees baseball hat on backward.

After finishing up with his customer, he calls over to me, "Hey, Dr. Mackenzie. I have most of your materials in."

"Just call me, Mac," I say.

"Floor tiles, sample adhesives, wire, paint—everything's here but the rolls of foil," says Brian. "You can take any of it with you, or if you're not in a rush, I can have it delivered to the college. You'll definitely want the foil delivered. The rolls are pretty heavy in the thickness you're getting."

"How soon before the foil comes in?" I asked.

Brian is at one of the store's computer terminals now, and he clicks away on the keys. I can tell he knows his way around computers. "Just a second," he says, "and we'll see."

He flips through a few more screens and says, "It looks like it shipped two days ago, so we should get it tomorrow. I can put it and the other materials on our delivery list for tomorrow if it comes in before noon, or if later, we can have it delivered to the campus on Saturday."

"That sounds perfect." I'm happy to avoid loading things into my car. If it's delivered, the Plant Department will probably take it over to the lab for me.

"I wanted to thank you for all your help, Brian. You've made this pretty easy on my side. By invoicing the department, it's saving me from using the credit card and creating a lot of reimbursement forms."

With our business finished, we chat a bit. I learn that Brian was born in the DC area. He moved to Massachusetts and Arkham after high school, about nine years ago. He has worked at Three Rivers for almost as long. Although he has criticisms of Arkham and Essex County, I can tell he also has a pride associated with living here. This is where he has made his home. He's captain of a bowling team. He helps organize kids softball. This is his town.

We finish making arrangements for delivery just as the lumberyard is closing. As a friendly gesture, Brian suggests we get a bite to eat at local pizza place. He pulls down sliding security blinds, turns out some lights, checks in with someone inside the hardware store who is in charge of closing up, and we head to the parking lot. I follow his black Jeep Cherokee to the pizza place.

Much to my surprise, Fat Dog Pizza is a bright spot amid Arkham's general air of twilight and decay. The place is spotless, with a lively Italian decor. Red-and-white-checkered tablecloths top each table, and there are white cloth napkins. The menu is not just pizza. They have a variety of traditional Italian specialties as well as their signature pizzas fired in a wood-burning oven. The food is good! I have a vegetable calzone and explain my vegetarian habits. Brian has two slices of "Death Valley" pizza and explains his love for spicy food.

We both have salad and red house wine.

As time passes, I realize we're talking like old friends. With nothing particular in common, we discover how much we *do* have in common. We both love eighties synth-pop music. We both love sci-fi and horror. We both love dogs. We both feel *just fine* about living a long way from our families.

"So how did you get roped into being the captain of a bowling team?" I ask. "Or have you always been a bowler?"

"I'm pretty good at most sports," says Brian, "but I prefer team sports without a lot of knocking around. I don't really think football and hockey are very good for kids. Too many injuries. Teams are great, but physical dust-ups, not so much. In America, that leaves softball and bowling."

"I bowled in high school," I offer. "It was really an experiment on the part of my aunt. I think she saw me as a lonely kid and thought team sports would help me get out of my shell. Since I didn't like football and baseball, she took matters into her own hands one summer. She enrolled me in a summer bowling league and told them I was the team captain. I was so shocked that I went along with it. I invited some friends and some people I hardly knew from school and we played all summer."

"Did you know how to bowl?"

"Well, I did after that summer!" I laugh. "Actually, my aunt showed me the basics, including how to keep score, before the league started."

"Did you have fun?"

"Oh, yes. I never really got good at bowling, but when you score with handicaps, skill levels even out. I think the real bonus of that summer was that it taught me self-reliance. With only a little preparation I was able to put together a team, learn how to bowl, do all the team paperwork, and interact with lots of new people. It was an experience I fall back on when I'm feeling overwhelmed."

"She sounds like a smart lady—your aunt, I mean. Are you feeling overwhelmed now?"

"A little," I confess. "Moving across the country to a new place for a new job is a bit crazy-making. I feel confident in my work, of course. I love physics. I think where I'm overwhelmed is with my new position and my current lack of a support system. Sometimes I feel like I'm just pretending to be a professor and someone at Miskatonic will catch me."

That leads us to ordering another glass of red wine and talking about Miskatonic.

At one point, Brian says, "Three Rivers sends all kinds of materials to their Plant Department, including some surprisingly intense security equipment for the library."

"Yes, the library. I'm beginning to think something weird is going on there. Between books that nobody is allowed to look at and the quantity of books on witchcraft and folklore, it's downright strange." I tell him a little about my own experiences at Miskatonic in the library and elsewhere—the weird vibe of the whole place. I tell him about the threatening note I received and some of the odd characters I've met on campus.

I look at Brian more directly. "And I swear, I must be working in one of the restricted buildings, too. I'm trying to remodel the basement of the tower section of Massachusetts Hall, and you'd think it's some kind of historic landmark. I mean the building *is* an historic landmark, but I don't see why there's so much fuss about remodeling the basement." I explain Matt Brown's shock at my plans and some of the difficulties I've had getting boxes moved and other work accomplished.

I ask Brian about his job, but he starts his story a little earlier. "I came north on a bus three days after my high school graduation. When the bus stopped at Arkham I could see a hand-lettered 'Help Wanted' sign at Three Rivers. I got the job that same day. I just never got back on the bus! At first they were a little hesitant to let me do much. They thought I was too young or stupid, so they put me out in the lumberyard. That was fine with me. I enjoy working outside. Pretty soon, though, they discovered I have a knack for computers and inventory. You'd be surprise how hard it is to predict how much lumber you should have on hand. Too much and your inventory costs soar. Some of the materials degrade with time if they're not sold quickly. Too little inventory and you piss off builders who can't wait for materials to come in from the wholesale lumber suppliers."

Brian's eyes light up as he talks about his work. He animates his speech with his hands and explains how his job at Three Rivers has evolved. He's proud of his work, and I bet he's good at it.

"In the end, they put me in charge of outdoor sales and the whole lumberyard. Last year they asked me to put in extra hours to help install the new ordering and point-of-sale systems. That way our inventory is directly tied to our sales. We know ahead of time when we should order common things without having to do a physical count. I guess you can tell I enjoy my job," he says a little self-consciously. "What's it like being a professor?"

I tell him about my graduate fellowship and teaching. "It's really just the start of a teaching career," I explain. "Although I teach classes, I'm not a full professor. I've finished one dissertation back at UCLA, but the department head here at Miskatonic wants me to create something that could be published as a textbook. If I stick things out, I could become a full professor in two or three years. That's not a promise of tenure, of course. These days you have to work at a university for years before they grant you tenure. Basically, if they think you're not pub-lishing enough or bringing enough prestige to the school or they just don't like you, they can cut you loose."

"That might be a good thing in the case of Miskatonic! You might want to be cut loose!"

We continue to talk, and I begin to have the oddest feeling. Brian is smiling at me with an intensity and warmth that is both familiar and confusing. It feels like I'm on a date! Am I imagining things, or is Brian flirting with me?

My question is soon answered. As we finish our food and pay our separate checks, Brian asks me back to his place.

Not entirely sure if the wine is speaking for me, I say yes. We both seem surprised but happy with this one-word statement of intention.

I follow Brian into the parking lot where our cars are parked side by side.

"Just follow me," says Brian, "My house is only a few miles from here."

I get in my LEAF and follow Brian's Jeep through the mostly desert-ed streets of Arkham.

As we cross the downtown area and head northwest, the residential area begins to thin out. The sidewalks end, and the city takes on a more rural feel. We turn onto River Road, one lane but paved, running along the Miskatonic River. After a mile or so Brian pulls up at a small place cleared from the maples and oaks that line the riverbank. The front yard is simple and filled with native shrubs. We get out of our cars and survey his home.

"I just bought it last year," he explains. "It is a ruin, but it's my ruin! I think it used to be a fishing shack. I'm using my employee discount and renovating it, little by little. So far I haven't done too much more than the outside of the house. I had to put on a new roof and new siding. While I was doing that, I put in new windows and insulation so my heating bill won't be too bad."

Brian's place is very small but nice for a "fishing shack." Back in California, I would call it a bungalow, but I haven't really seen many places like it here in Essex County. It has a porch across the front and a simple pitched green metal roof. The siding is of stained cedar shakes and glows a soft amber color in the porch lighting. Most everything on the outside is new and looks to be handcrafted with great care.

As we enter the main living area, I see proof that the space is largely unfinished. The layout is complete, but sheetrock has not been put up in the main room. You can see the studs and thick insulation. Wiring and plumbing are still exposed. A few skylights in the main room show overhanging trees and a spot of clear sky and stars.

"On the inside, I'm doing one room at a time as I can afford it," explains Brian. "The whole thing is only twelve hundred square feet." His hand sweeps across the room. "So I plan to make every inch count. I haven't done much in the main living room, but I'm nearly done with the kitchen alcove." Brian continues his description of small-space living. "The kitchen fits on one wall. That allows me to use a big table island for either food prep or a big dining table." He shows me some of the cabinets with built-in drawers for spices and sliding shelves for pots and pans. Even with his employee discount he's spent a lot of money on high-end appliances and surfaces. The counter is reddish granite with silver flecks. Based on all the cooking gear, it's clear he not only knows how to remodel a kitchen but also enjoys cooking.

"Oh, yes, cooking's a passion! It's relaxing to work my way through a recipe and create something wonderful. It's great to have people over for a meal. I guess it's what I like about remodeling, too. You make a plan, you get the materials, little by little, and you end up with something really wonderful."

"I'm glad you like cooking. I like eating! I must confess: my best meals generally come from a take-out carton. I've never had an apartment with a full kitchen. I don't even have a stove where I am now."

The back of the house is mostly sliding windows with a view of the Miskatonic River below. There's a nice deck with outdoor furniture and a barbecue. Brian shows me how the entire wall of windows can slide open. We step out on the deck and take in the rushing river. Partial moonlight shines down on the water illuminating the rocks and vegetation. The river is beautiful and silvery. The night is cool and peaceful with only the sound of the water below. We're holding hands, and Brian leads me back inside.

The tour ends at the bedroom. It's the only other finished room of the house and is in quiet colors of tan, brown, and deep blue. There are small stained-glass lampshades on the bedside tables that cast a golden light and jewel-tone highlights across the room. He opens the window slightly so we can hear the river and smell some of forest. His bed is made up with high-quality sheets and has a view down to the river. There's a skylight over the bed, and when we look up we see a sprinkling of stars framed in maple leaves.

The sex is good—a bit wild and at the same time tender. Maybe it only makes sense that way when it's two guys. I haven't been with a man since my sophomore year in college, but somehow it feels good tonight—right and exciting. There is no forgetting how things work or how to give pleasure to my new friend.

"Can you stay the night?" he asks.

I had not really thought about this. The whole evening seems a little unreal, and I pause in thought.

"You don't have to," he says. This phrase rings out in my mind. With his good looks and easygoing manner, I had thought of him as the worldly bachelor. I had him pegged for casual sex and friendship. Now I'm seeing something different. This man worries that his charms might be all on the outside.

I think of Howie back at the college, but I remember that he has plenty of food and water and the use of his new dog door. It seems I'm not going home tonight.

"I'd like to stay," I say. Changing the subject, I ask, "Why did you come here? To Arkham, I mean, on that bus after high school?"

His smile fades, but I can tell he's still enjoying lying next to me. "Oh, yeah, that story. Truth is, my parents kicked me out for being gay. They caught me with a friend in high school. I had to live with my grandmother my senior year. I was glad to get out of that tiny town and away from those people. My father still won't talk to me, although my mom and I trade phone calls every so often."

My heart opens. I can't imagine Mom kicking me out of the house. My whole world would crumble. No wonder he's proud of the life he's created in this small city.

"Is it difficult to be gay in Arkham, too?" I ask.

"No, not really. Massachusetts is pro-gay marriage and all that. Arkham's treated me well. And I'm not that insecure kid anymore. I'm not afraid of what other people think. I haven't had any problems here. Everyone at work knows I'm gay. It's no big thing."

"And dating?"

"Yeah, that *is* a problem. How do I meet people? Arkham's small. I've grown to love it, but there are no social outlets for meeting men."

"Well, you met one," I remark, sleepily, "at the hardware store."

I look over, and it seems Brian is also about half asleep. He has a satisfied smile on his face and one arm draped over my stomach.

As I settle in to sleep, I mentally prepare my gratitude entries for the night:

1.   *Brian Hoskins: A new friend or more?*
2.   *Fat Dog Pizza.*
3.   *Good Coffee.*
4.   *Dog Doors.*
5.   *Albert Einstein: Always grateful for him.*

As we lie side by side, I notice nothing's happening. Just breathing. Just being in each other's space. Such peace.

Then the most curious thing happens.

I thought Brian was already asleep, but I distinctly hear him whisper a word, a name. He speaks it not as a question or for my benefit. In fact, he may not even know that he has spoken aloud. But there it is, in that most intimate of spaces, my name: "Mac."

CHAPTER SIX

The Double-Slit Experiment

"Guess what I've got in my hand!" I've been teasing my mom on the phone and it's working.

"Stop! You know I can't guess! Is it something important?" She's curious as hell.

"It's just a piece of paper, but's it's worth sixty-two hundred dollars."

"Oh, I can't guess!" she says, but she does anyway. "Is it a rare stamp?"

I miss hearing my mom laugh. I guess I miss quite a few of things about California.

"No, silly. It's my first real paycheck."

"Honey, that's wonderful. Really: sixty-two hundred dollars? For a month?"

"Well, before taxes, anyway," I explain. "Now do you see why I can start paying you back for the car?"

"You don't have to pay me back."

"But I want to."

"Let's discuss that after you get the quarterly statement on your student loans," she says with typical concern in her voice.

It's been great to catch up with Mom. She has a lot going on and is angling for me to visit her during the winter holidays. We chat for most of an hour.

It's Saturday, and I'm expecting Brian to come by the lab and help me finish installing the shielding on the door. Everything else is complete. It turns out that the wallpaper paste works fine as the adhesive on all our surfaces and materials.

The Maintenance Department was able to do all the work with student labor. The lab is now one big five-sided cavity. The door is the only thing remaining to make my Faraday cage complete.

Brian has only one Saturday a month off from the lumberyard, so I feel very happy to have his help and his company on this sunny but cold fall day.

I'm meeting him at ten o'clock, but I want to get an early start on the lab. After loading my backpack with some tools, I decide Howie might want to spend the day with us. I pack a bowl for water, a ball, a blanket, and a baggie with some kibble. Howie's getting used to Brian, and I'm sure he'd rather be with us than in the apartment, alone, for most of the day.

With his brown nylon leash and matching coat, Howie's quite the sporting dog. He's lifting his front paws high in case anyone is watching. He's really become quite silly about wearing his clothes. I'm getting used to being seen around campus with him and don't mind the sidelong looks.

We take a circular walk to Massachusetts Hall so I can get an espresso at the Student Union's coffee window. Now I have a stuffed backpack, coffee in one hand, and Howie straining on the leash in the other. I struggle up the steps. The main doors of Massachusetts Hall are unlocked on Saturdays until five, so we enter and cross the rotunda to the stairs leading down to the maintenance level.

As I approach the lab's ancient door, I try fumbling in my pocket for the oversized key. It's wedged in my jeans pocket. About ready to spill coffee, I decide I better put my coffee and backpack down while I unlock the door. I bend over to let Howie off the leash and notice something curious.

Has someone been trying to break into the lab?

The unusual antique key cannot easily be duplicated, but there are scratch marks around the keyhole. Were they there before and I just didn't notice them?

Leaning farther down to pick up my coffee, I see more evidence. Someone has been trying to pull the pins out of the door hinges. The doors have a unique handmade system of hinging. The pins are notched into the doors themselves rather than part of an external hinging mechanism. I can clearly see that someone has tried using a chisel or other woodworking tool to attempt to remove the pins. The ancient oak must be like stone, however, for the pins stubbornly refused to give in. The gouges in the wood look fresh. A few loose specks of wood on the floor reveal that a recent, incomplete, cleanup of wood shavings was made.

I unlock the lab, open the doors, and reassure myself that the break-in was unsuccessful. The lab is the pristine foiled masterpiece that I expect it to be. None of my equipment or tools have been taken or even moved. Howie can tell I'm a bit nervous, and he sniffs around the lab as if to satisfy himself in some way.

I make a quick call to Matt Brown in the Plant Department.

"Matt, this is Mac. There's been an attempt to break into the basement lab. I don't think they've taken anything, but I want to know if we have any security reports or logs for this building. Are there any cameras?"

Matt is silent for a moment, then replies, "No cameras in Massachusetts Hall. We do have night security, but they make infrequent rounds of the buildings. Unless they see lights where they're not supposed to be or suspicions activity, nothing would be logged. You could call campus security and ask if anything was reported last night."

Now it's my turn for a short silence.

"Matt, do you think we could install a camera? We've just put some pretty expensive equipment in this new lab. I hope to finish all the shielding today. For all intents and purposes the lab is done, and I'd like to start using it, knowing it's secure. We probably also need to somehow get more than one key so campus security can have one, as well as Dr. Alvarez."

"If you don't mind locks on the outside, we can certainly fit the door with a new secure lock. I suppose it could be pried off, but that would take a lot of time and make a lot of noise. I think I have one around here, somewhere. If you want I can bring it around for you to look at. Also, I think there's an electrical outlet on the wall opposite the door. That would be a good spot for a security cam. We don't have one, mind you, but if you get one, I can help you hook it up."

Matt promises to come by later in the day with the lock, and I thank him for his trouble.

I put in a call to campus security to let them know about the attempt. After talking to one of the junior security people, they put Chief Justin Taggert on the phone. He asks me a lot of questions:

"What's the value of the equipment in the lab?"

"Have any students been in the lab or asked about it?"

"Are you sure the scratches and wood shavings are new?"

Taggert checks security logs for the night shift, but neither of the night security officers had anything to report.

I ask for advice, and Taggert says that a campus security lock should definitely be installed. Campus security does not install video equipment or other special security devices—if a department requires them, it must provide its own.

Before I start my work in the lab, I put in one more call.

"Hi, Brian. It's Mac."

"Hey there!" he says, with a smile in his voice. "I'm looking forward to seeing you soon."

"That's why I'm calling," I explain. I tell him about the scratches on the door lock and the wood shavings and gouges around the hinge pins.

"Are you OK?" Brian asks.

"Yes, nothing's stolen, I'm almost certain they didn't even get in."

"But do you *feel* OK? Safe, I mean?"

It feels nice to have Brian worried for my safety. I think it's been a long time since anyone has cared about me in that way. "Yeah, I guess so," I reply. "I'm a little spooked, that's all. I do have a question for you, though. There's something that might make me feel a little better about being in the lab and knowing the equipment is safe."

"What is it? What can I do to help?"

"Does Three Rivers have security cameras? I seem to remember a section of security hardware and other products. Do you carry cameras?"

"Sure," says Brian. "Actually, we have several models. Some are stand-alone units, others are part of a wireless security system and include door and window break-in sensors. Tell you what. How about I pick up some supplies from Three Rivers on my way to the college? I'll bring you a variety of cameras, and we'll see if any of them will work. What you don't use I'll take back, and what you do use I can invoice to the school. You're still under budget for your lab remodel, aren't you?"

"Yes, I am, thanks to my handsome friend," I say, smiling.

"Even after the additional foil?"

"Not sure what you mean," I say.

"The Plant Department called last week to order more foil to finish the room. I was afraid it might put you over budget."

"That's weird, they didn't tell me about needing more foil."

"We got the foil overnight and just added it to your invoice. Maybe they messed up cutting the foil and needed more. Just let me know if you need information about the extra order or invoice."

"Will do. What time will you be by today?" I ask.

"I might be a little later than my original estimate. Do you want me to bring you some lunch?"

"You're really sweet, you know that?"

"Aw, shucks," says Brian, in his best imitation of a shy country bumpkin. "I guess I'm just sweet on you."

"You must be a little freaked out!"

Matt Brown has come by sooner than I would have imagined, and I show him the damage to the door. "Nothing was stolen," I explain, "and I don't think they even got in. I am a little worried, though. It seems someone has an unusual interest in me and what I'm working on. I guess I *am* freaked out, a little."

"Well, let me show you the lock I've brought. It's a sturdy one. To begin with, it's rock solid. It's a surface-mount locking mechanism that's large and modern. It's to be countersunk slightly into the wood of the doorframe so it can't be pried off without major tools and time. It's made of hardened steel with rounded edges so it can't be gripped by a vise or bolt cutter. The other nice thing is that it's part of the university key system. Reputable locksmiths will not duplicate such keys, and a computer keeps track of how many there are and who has them."

I think the new lock will be perfect. It really is a security set: even the bolts are recessed and are tamper resistant. I work on setting up the new lab table in the center of the room while Matt installs the lock.

When everything is complete we take a look. It certainly seems solid. It's difficult to imagine anyone removing the lock without a lengthy sledgehammer session or plastic explosives. I think it would be easier to saw through the door than remove the lock.

Matt also came with a surprise for me. Though used elsewhere on campus as "kick plates," he brought some metal hardware that we can screw over the countersunk hinge pins of the door. The plates have one-way screws. That should prevent further attempts to remove the door by removing the hinges.

"Matt, you're the best," I say, with some awe. "You must have better things to do on your day off than help me!"

"I'm never too busy to help a friend," says Matt, wiping sweat from his forehead. I can tell this little job has tired him out. He's not a young man, and even with power tools this has been intensive.

"Can I take you and your wife out to dinner to thank you?" I ask.

"I think I just need to take a nap," he replies, smiling. "Maybe some other time."

Matt gives me two lab keys, one for myself and one for Horace Alvarez. He even has the campus security-key forms with him. I sign one and promise to give one to Horace to sign and turn in sometime next week.

I help him pack up his tools, most of which he puts in a storage closet at the boiler-room end of the hallway here in the basement of Massachusetts Hall.

After Matt leaves, I sweep up the remains of his woodworking and work on setting up some of the equipment for the double-slit experiment I want to demonstrate next term.

Brian's just in time. I'm starting to feel really hungry. He enters the lab with a backpack and a large box. From the second he enters, you can see he's admiring the Faraday cage. He hasn't seen it since the materials were delivered.

"It looks like an inside-out Airstream trailer!" he says.

I laugh, because it's true. "You're right. Have you ever seen so much aluminum foil in your life?"

Brian puts the box down on the lab bench and takes off his backpack. Before anything else, he moves across the room and kisses me. I'm still feeling a little shy about dating a man, but he warms me up pretty quick. Brian's a good kisser, and I can tell how he feels about me.

He lets me go and reaches into the box. "For my starving friend," he says, producing a cheese sandwich, hummus, pita chips, soft drinks, and some kind of homemade dessert in a little plastic container. I'm impressed that he remembers I'm a vegetarian. I'm sure I mentioned it, but we didn't really discuss it much, and we've only had one meal together.

"And for my other friend," says Brian, reaching into the box and producing a package for Howie. He peels back a plastic strip and produces a rawhide chip. "Can I give it to him?" he asks.

"Of course," I say. "But remember that you're setting up expectations."

"I'm good for my half of the relationship," says Brian. "I haven't had a dog since my yellow lab passed away. I miss her dearly and hope Howie and I will be good friends."

Howie's already chewing on his treat, tail wagging furiously. "I think you're off to a good start."

Brian and I chat while we're eating. I show him how the Faraday cage works by isolating a conducting layer of aluminum foil inside the nonconducting shell of the cardboard-lined room. It's really just two thin layers covering all the surfaces. You just can't have a break in the layering or any conductive material that pierces the cardboard. Brian can see that even the floor, underneath the rubber-mat tiles, is the same sheath of aluminum.

"I think I understand the shielding, Mac," says Brian. "I even think I understand the idea of the electromagnetic waves that you want to keep out of the laboratory. Can you explain more about your experiments, though? Why do you need the shielding? What will you accomplish in this 'cage'?"

I pause to come up with a good example.

"Why don't I walk you through one of the so-called slit experiments? They'll give you an idea of why shielding is important. I hope you don't mind me turning into the college professor for a few minutes."

"Not at all. I've always wanted to kiss a college professor," says Brian, grinning.

"OK, here goes. Back in 1900, the age of quantum physics was born when Max Planck postulated that everything is made up of little bits he called *quanta*. Matter had its quanta but also the forces that kept material together and the energy and light of the universe was built of quanta, as well. Einstein took things further when he successfully described how light interacts with electrons. At the smallest level of the universe, everything is made up of bits we call quanta."

I take a breath to check, but I can tell Brian's still interested. "In the early part of the twentieth century, scientists spent a lot of time classifying the quanta, their various properties, and how they work together to create the world around us. One of the things they hoped to explain was the unusual characteristics of light. In particular, they wanted to determine if a quantum of light, called a photon, behaved as a particle or as a wave. Earlier experiments appeared to show that they behaved as neither or both.

"The modern double-slit experiment shows that light has even more unusual behaviors. Here's how it works: a coherent light source, such as a laser beam, illuminates a plate pierced by two parallel slits, and the light passing through the slits is observed on a screen behind the plate. The wave nature of light causes the light passing through the two slits to interfere, producing bright and dark bands on the screen. They look like waves on a pond when two rocks are thrown in. This is a result that would not be expected if light consisted of particles. However, the light is always found to be absorbed by the detectors at discrete points, as individual particles and not waves. Even more puzzling, versions of the experiment that include detectors at the slits find that each detected photon passes through one slit, as you would expect from a particle, and not through both slits, as would a wave.

"And, if that's not enough, in one experiment, detectors were placed throughout the room, some even behind the laser. Although very infrequently, some photons were detected everywhere throughout the space. A few made U-turns in order to be detected behind the light source."

"You're talking about light, right?" asks Brian. "I know it disperses, like with a flashlight."

"Yes, but it also curves and can make a U-turn. Not a lot of it, but some of it. That's why we need to have a Faraday cage. In early versions of the experiments, some of the odd results were blamed on the lab conditions where leaky shielding was likely allowing outside radiation to trigger the sensors. With a Faraday cage, you know the results are from quanta inside the enclosure. In the mid-part of the 1900s, more elaborate equipment allowed scientists to send a single photon at the slits at a time. Guess what happens?"

"I give up," says Brian, holding his hands out.

"You get the same interference pattern. It's as though each photon interferes with itself or as though they produce the pattern based on probabilities rather than actual trajectories of the photon. In the 1970s, more elaborate equipment allowed for photon detectors within the slits themselves. It was an attempt to see if the photons acted as particles when they went through the slits. Can you guess what happened when the photons went through the slits with the detectors?"

Brian shakes his head.

"Those photons didn't appear as part of the wave patterns. Because they were forced to behave as particles, the buildup of the wave pattern was degraded by the amount of light detected going through the specific slits."

This last bit of information may be a bit over Brian's head. He's already understood as much as many of my first-year students. That's enough science for one day!

I show and describe some of the test equipment to Brian. I turn on the laser and show him how tight the beam is. It's not like a flashlight; the coherent beam does not measurably disperse over the length of the path through the double slits and the collector.

"This laser will self-align to the slit aperture," I explain. "That used to be the tricky part of setting up the experiment. If the laser is out of alignment, the experiment will give strange results. The light isn't dangerous, but you wouldn't want it to shine directly in your eyes. It could be harmful to your retinas. The laser moves freely on its base, and the alignment is motor-controlled by this device."

I show him the servomotors and how to align the laser using the controls. Then I show him how the beam is directed through mirrors to the slit array and how the photons are recorded with a photon detection system. I have some pictures from previous experiments to show him the wave patterns from the experiment done with two slits and the built-up set of photons when you have a single slit.

"I don't know that I've dated anyone as smart as you," remarks Brian. He's thoughtful, as though this might require some special consideration on his part.

"Well, it *is* how I make my living," I say, shrugging. "Is that a problem?"

"No, not at all," says Brian. "I just never thought about having scientific discussions with anyone. I'm sure it's a good thing. I assume you're interested in me talking about home improvements and bowling, right?"

"Absolutely," I say, with complete truth in my voice. "So far, I like you exactly as you are. One scientist around here is plenty."

We put away the lab equipment and finish our work for the day. We have to finish foiling the door so it overlaps well onto the walls. This doesn't take much time. We use duct tape to make overlapping flaps on all sides of the door. We then paste the aluminum foil over the door and flaps. When the door closes, the room is now a solid aluminum box.

We then inspect the various security cameras that Brian brought.

"You have many choices," he explains. "The least expensive one must be wired into a monitoring system. From looking around here, I don't really see where you'd have the wires go or where you'd set up the recording equipment."

"You're right. That won't work. What else have you got in that box of yours?"

"This one is more like a nanny cam. It wirelessly connects to a Wi-Fi network, and with the proper IP address the viewing or recording can take place anywhere on the network."

"That's more like it," I say. "Is it battery operated or does it plug in?"

"Plug in," says Brian. "The battery-operated ones don't have infrared capabilities for night viewing."

"Night viewing. Wow. You think of everything."

"Well, you said the break-in attempt was at night, so I figured we should have the option of a camera with night vision. You might also want to check out the most expensive option. It's a part of a whole security system. It also connects to Wi-Fi, but it has capabilities for adding additional sensors, such as motion detectors and door and window alert mechanisms."

"How expensive?" I ask.

"Before I answer, let me give you one more selling feature. It has a phone app. You can get an alert on your phone and actually see what's happening through the camera on your smartphone. It uses the same protocol as FaceTime."

"Sold!" I say. And after we talk a little more, I *am* sold.

It's surprisingly easy to hook up the equipment. I decide on the system I can have running in my office upstairs in Massachusetts Hall. This will record the video and any information from the sensors and provide a log of all activity. We unpack the camera, which we mount near the ceiling on the wall opposite the door to the lab. It plugs discretely into the outlet on the same wall, and we run the cord down a seam in the cement. We also unpack a motion detector that I install farther down the hall in a location even less noticeable. It will detect anyone walking down the hall toward the lab door.

Brian may think I'm the smart one, but he's got the Wi-Fi part of things configured in less than an hour. We're using the regular university Wi-Fi network and a user ID and password for Massachusetts Hall.

Finally, we load the free iPhone app onto my smartphone.

We clean up our mess and test out the new security system. We go down the hall and initialize the system from my phone. We start walking toward the end of the hall with the lab door. About twenty feet from the door, my phone produces a ping, letting me know that motion near the door has been detected. As we get closer to the door, I can see us on my phone. The image from the camera is at a strange angle, but it's clearly us. Brian gets a step stool and adjusts the camera angle so our faces are easier to see when we're in the hall. When we're actually at the lab door, you only see the backs of our heads, so the hall view will be more important.

We move the motion sensor just a bit so it will pick up movement when people first start walking down our end of the hall. We try our entire test again with better results. I'm notified of the motion sooner, and it's easier to see and identify us on the camera.

Howie's sound asleep on the blanket I brought for him, so we temporarily leave him while Brian and I go upstairs to install the recording equipment in my office.

This also goes pretty fast. It's about the size of a small notebook. It just needs an electrical outlet and access to the Wi-Fi network. Brian sets it up to record just the video when motion is active. He configures it so that when the storage media fills up it will give me a warning. After that it will replace the oldest video with the newest video.

The afternoon has led into early evening. The golden light of sunset is shining through my large office window. I show Brian my beautiful office view among the tops of the trees looking across the campus. He holds me as we watch the sunset, and we spend some time canoodling.

Brian invites me to dinner, but I decline. I have papers to grade and haven't looked at e-mail all day. I know if I go with Brian it will be hard to get anything else done.

"Can we make another date, then?" asks Brian.

"Of course. What do you have in mind?"

"I'm thinking of a bowling night."

That surprises me, but I'm not opposed to it. "Tell me more," I say.

"Halloween's coming up. It's on a Monday night, which is league night. We're supposed to be in costume, and that has one of the guys freaked out. He's not coming, and I need a substitute. It would be great to have you along," says Brian.

"You have interesting dating ideas," I say. "I think that might be fun. Costumed bowling, is that what you're proposing?"

"That's the offer," says Brian, with a smile. "We can have beer and bowling food to make the evening complete, if you like."

"I was thinking of other ways we could make the evening complete," I offer. "Maybe we could spend another night together?"

"After bowling?"

"After bowling. My Tuesday classes don't start until midafternoon, so we can even sleep in."

"You're good at the whole date-planning thing, aren't you?" Brian says.

"One more idea," I suggest.

"What's that?"

"Would you mind if I invited a guest? To watch?" I ask.

"To our date?"

"Just to watch the bowling part, I promise," I explain. "I think I've made a new friend named Ally. She's a GTF here on campus. She's been under some stress lately. Beer and costumed bowling might be just the ticket to cheer her up. Besides, if I get to meet your friends, you should have a chance to meet mine."

"That's a deal," says Brian, smiling from ear to ear.

Howie and I walk Brian to his Jeep, and I give him a kiss and thank him for spending the day with me. I watch the Jeep head down the street into the night. I'm thinking how much I like Brian Hoskins.

On the way back to Massachusetts Hall I let Howie off the leash. It's after seven, and most students are either back in their dormitories or off campus. It's a quiet, cool evening, and Howie is enjoying the walk. We take our time.

I get my engineering aptitude from my great-grandfather. During the Great Depression, he was the millwright of a combination sawmill and paper plant. With repair budgets and supplies nonexistent, he was known for his ability to fix things with bailing wire, prayers, and liberal amounts of wood glue. He was a local hero and kept the plant running and the workers employed through most of the hard economic times.

One of my favorite memories of him was sitting in a large recliner after a noonday supper. He would sit back to meditate (as he would call it), and after about half an hour the meditation would turn into a light snoring. The meditations worked, though, or so he claimed. He could take a problem into one of those meditations, and when he woke up, the solution, or at least the start of it, would be present in his mind.

I use this contemplative technique myself with excellent results. Of course, it's just a form of relaxation. It allows my imagination and creative self to work on an issue in a nonlinear form.

After a long day working on the lab, I'm tired. It was great spending much of the day with Brian but also frustrating when I think of the attempted break-in. I'd like some answers to many questions.

So, in a cheap plastic chair, in the middle of my just-finished Faraday cage, in the basement of Massachusetts Hall, I sit down to "contemplate." Thinking of my great-grandfather, I begin by asking some questions:

Who is trying to get in my lab?

Why am I getting threatening notes?

Which of my students or colleagues has some reason to interfere with my work?

Who's been gaining access to my apartment?

And, after a few minutes, like my grandpa, I must have fallen asleep. I have the most striking dream.

First of all, it isn't quite *me* in the dream. I have the impression of being myself but not entirely as I usually am. For one thing, my senses are not working properly. My depth perception is off as though my eyes are farther apart or have different lenses. Things from far away suddenly appear right before me. Things that seem within my grasp recede into the distance as I reach for them.

And reaching for things is most disconcerting, because I seem to have no arms or hands. I have the sense of reaching normally, and things do generally come to me but with no visible means of conveyance. I feel embodied but with no feedback that could prove the existence of a physical body.

Sight and touch are not the only senses that are strange. My hearing and color perception are somehow intermingled. Colors seem to have sounds associated with them (or maybe the other way around). Yellow, for instance, is associated with an almost piercing high-pitched noise or frequency. The brighter or more pure the color, the more intense the sound that goes with it.

Geometry and physical properties are also different. This is the part that's really hard to explain. The nature of shapes seems to have an emotional component. Shapes convey meaning and nuance of feeling in the dream.

For some reason, none of this frightens or troubles me. I feel like an explorer, and there's an exhilaration of discovery welling up inside me. Although everything is unfamiliar, it also feels natural somehow, as though this "not me" and "not here" are parts of a fun puzzle to be figured out.

As I look around, it seems I'm still in the basement lab. The familiar five-sided room is around me. The shape of the room is foreboding, though, as if there's something off about it. Another difference is the texture and color of the walls. Instead of the foiled cement, the walls are red stone, and the red feels like pain. There's a noise associated with the red stone blocks, too. It feels like a heartbeat or a drum beat. I know I'm describing this poorly, but my senses seem to be jumbling things up. The stone color seems to be beating with that low noise we associate with our own heart.

As I observe the walls, they retreat, and I find myself in a much larger five-sided enclosure. The ceiling has vanished or moved so far above me that I fancy I can see stars between it and me. There's a whole constellation trapped within whatever contains the space. If I reach out across this vast space, I have a sense of touching or sensing even the most distant objects. The little stars seem cold, lonely, and piercing. The wall opposite me, leagues distant, seems alive with a leathery feel to it.

My initial feeling of exhilaration has turned to caution. There's something not quite right about this place. I feel as though there's something I've forgotten or something hidden from me that I really ought to know.

I began to perceive that I am not alone. Contained within this five-sided infinity, I feel the presence of something or someone. At the periphery of my senses I feel something welcoming or comrade-like. I suppose like meeting someone for the first time that you seem to already know. In this case, it appears as a floating, solid object of gemstone-like color and purity. It is violet, and the violet color sings with a friendliness and fondness. I would say that it is shaped like an amethyst crystal that my mother used to wear, but that's not quite right. It also seems like something stolen from an ornate lead-crystal chandelier, but the angles are not quite right for that, either.

What is right is the feeling I get from the violet crystal. Here, in this frankly creepy place of shouting colors, alien geometry, and distorted senses, I get a feeling of companionship.

The violet crystal and I explore our surroundings. A low plateau before us is filled with objects. Part way across the plateau, I realize that we are exploring some dream-expanded version of the table in the middle of the lab. The objects are simply distorted or expanded versions of the objects that are on that table. A green physics book seems to be a softly moaning green door, asking to be opened. A yellow pencil (I assume that's what it is) has a high, piercing yellow whine associated with it and seems somewhat dangerous. In the dream it is almost one dimensional, as though only length exists for it.

My crystal "friend" begins to push some of the objects around with an invisible force. The objects are pushed over to me, and I discover that I can push them back. We continue in this game until I realize the familiarity of it.

"Howie," I say, "is that you?"

There's no real speaking in the dream, so I don't really know how this communication is taking place, but I get a message of, "Yes!" Wanting a more concrete verification, I try one of Howie's tricks.

I visualize a gun and say/think, "Bang!"

The violet crystal turns black and wobbles, then tips over. Howie and I laugh as comrades in this quirky dream world.

After exploring some additional items on the plateau, we sense the entrance of another being. This time I do not sense friendship. The soft violet sound that Howie has been making changes a bit, as does his color. Instead of fondness, Howie is sending me a sound and color of warning.

At the far limit of my senses, I feel it beginning to approach. It comes with a wriggling or undulating. Although it moves constantly toward us, it nonetheless travels like a snake or some creature from light-starved oceanic depths. As it comes nearer, I began to hear its color. It has an angry orange-ness to it that is both a laugh and a gibber. Usually a laugh is a good thing, but here it is the laughter of insanity. It is the laughter of a maniac held in a cell for too many years. It is the laughter of rotting fruit and sibilant protestations.

Although the circumstances are so strange and the creature so abhorrent, there's also a familiarity to this scene. It's like I've met this horror before in some midnight terror.

The creature is calling to me, commanding me. Suddenly, I realize the command is one of ownership. As an angry, muttering vagrant might seize a coin from your outstretched hand, the being wants to take me, to have me. Anxiety and fear kick in, and I try to move backward, to escape this horror in front of me.

I turn around but sense no exit from this five-sided prison. I could retreat, but where? I think of ways to defend myself. I try to push the approaching maniac away as Howie and I pushed objects on the table. The being continues its inexorable approach. It feels like it is leering at me and begins to outstretch appendages, tentacles, toward me.

Howie tries to intercede, to help me avoid the looming menace, but he, too, seems unable to alter its course.

"Howie," I cry/think. "Run! Get away! Move!"

As the screaming orange maniac comes close enough to touch, terror rises from my stomach, to my heart, and to my mouth. I scream a blue scream of terror and anguish and hopelessness.

I awake, sweating, in my chair. Howie, standing on the edge of the lab table, is gently tugging at my sleeve.

CHAPTER SEVEN

Trick or Treat

Before my morning classes, I stop by the Browns' to see if my costume is ready. Emma Brown offered to alter it, and I decided to take advantage of her kindness. I still don't know what to make of Mrs. Brown. Unlike her husband, she's a bit prickly. She tends to see the downside of most situations and has a dim view of most people's pastimes and personalities.

I plan to impress Brian and his friends tonight with both my bowling and my costume. To take advantage of my skinny frame and dark hair, I'm trying for a sexy Ichabod Crane look. You know, the guy from Sleepy Hollow.

I've rented a long brown frock coat and matching trousers, white ruffled shirt, a ponytail-and-bow wig, and a tricorn hat from a local costume shop. My footwear won't be authentic, but at least my bowling shoes are brown. I'll see if I can manage to wear the hat and bowl at the same time. The hat may have to come off.

Although the costume is nice, the jacket was too big in the chest and waist, so Mrs. Brown has taken it in a few inches for a more tailored look.

"What do you think?" she asks.

I look in the mirror and nod. "It's great." I've let my beard grow for a few days, and I'm almost pulling off that five-o'clock-shadow look that's so popular. With my tailored costume and dark brown stubble, I should at least cut a striking figure tonight.

"I have something for you," says Mrs. Brown. She goes to the kitchen and returns with a boutonniere. It's a simple cluster of blue asters from her fall garden. It's tied with a bit of brown ribbon and looks charming.

"It's wonderful," I say, as she pins it to the jacket.

"I know you want to look your best tonight," says Mrs. Brown. "Matthew says you're a bit lonely, so I'm glad you've joined the bowling league."

"I'm subbing for someone," I say. "It's mostly an evening out with friends."

"In any case, things haven't been the easiest since you've arrived here. I'm surprised you've stayed, frankly." Mrs. Brown looks down at Howie and says, "This little dog must really be your best friend."

"Howie has been with me since he was only a couple years old."

"Matt was telling me about that horrible dream you had in the lab. Even in your dreams, Howie is there to guide and protect you."

Mrs. Brown, as usual, is starting to make me feel a bit uncomfortable. I really don't care to discuss my dreams with her, although Matt clearly told her about the unsettling one I had in the lab.

I decide to use Howie to good advantage to change the subject.

"Howie," I say. "Bow to the lady."

Howie obligingly sits on his haunches, tucks one "arm" across his chest, and bows.

"Thank you so much for altering my costume," I say.

Mrs. Brown smiles as I take my costume and head to my first lecture.

After a busy morning lecturing and meeting with students, I'm left with a stack of papers to grade and thoughts of Halloween bowling. I haven't bowled in some time, but I used to be pretty good. Do you forget how to bowl? Will I embarrass myself in front of Brian? Will Brian and Ally like each other? Am I doomed to have a teenager's feelings of inadequacy my entire life?

While already thinking ahead to the evening's entertainment, I'm also trying to grade papers. Howie and I are camped out in my office at Massachusetts Hall. I asked Brian if he would pick me up here for a number of reasons. I hope to finish the papers and post the grades outside of my office door, for one thing. For another, I'm planning to have Howie stay in the locked lab while we're bowling. Since I found the note under my pillow, I still worry about strangers accessing our apartment. I think Howie will be safer in the lab with its new lock.

Another reason I want to meet Brian at Massachusetts Hall is I want Brian to make sure everything about the lab security system is still working. It seems to be. I look at the video logs over the last two weeks, and I see a janitorial guy on video almost every day. Although he doesn't come down to the end of the hall as far as the lab, he does set off the motion detector when he opens the janitor closet. I see a short video of him getting and stowing brooms, mops, and other gear about nine o'clock in the morning nearly every day. Twice I see Ms. Barry entering the storage area where the records that used to be in the lab are now being stored. Once I see Matthew Brown going down to the other end of the hall—I think that's where the heating and cooling system for the building is located. I also see a couple of unidentified people entering the storage area. They have keys, so I assume they're helpers of Ms. Barry.

I plan to ask Brian to tilt the camera slightly so I can see faces better. The camera is tilted a bit too much toward the lab door. This means that I mostly get a side view of people in the hall. If we tilt it slightly, I'll still see the lab door, but I'll get a better view of people as they come down the hall toward it. Brian also said it would be possible to block out the phone alerts during certain times of the day. Every day when the cleaning guy comes, my phone goes off. I'd like to ask Brian if we could weed that notification out based on time.

I finally finish grading papers about five o'clock. Using my laptop, I record them in the university's grading system. I use the small printer in my office to print off the grades. I verify the grades against the papers, then post the grades on a small cork bulletin board outside my office door. Papers will be returned in class next week, but some students want to know their grades as soon as possible.

I get a text message from Brian about six. He's parking in the ten-minute spot at the back of Massachusetts Hall, typically reserved for deliveries. I head upstairs to the back door to greet him.

He's in full pirate regalia! He's wearing a shoulder-length reddish wig that matches his beard and a full pirate costume, including breeches, a vest over his smooth chest, and a cutlass hanging from his belt. We'll see if he can bowl with *that*. He comes up for a hug, which is just long enough to show me he doesn't mind if people are watching and think we might be more than just friends.

"Avast, ye, matey," he says, in his best pirate speak.

I silence him with a kiss, and we enter Massachusetts Hall. We go up to my office and talk about the security system while Brian plays with Howie. You can tell they enjoy each other's company.

"I'm not sure about turning off the alerts by time," says Brian. "It would be hard to pinpoint exactly when the cleaner comes, so you would have to leave the alerts off for an hour or two every day. If anyone was watching, they might wait until he leaves. That would be a good time to break in, and then you wouldn't get an alert.

"Another option," suggests Brian, "is to just set your phone to 'do not disturb' when you're in classes or you don't want to be bothered with alerts."

As we're talking, I'm getting into my Ichabod Crane costume. I get another, longer kiss midway through my wardrobe change. Brian compliments me both in and out of costume.

Then we head down to the lab. Howie leads the way; he's familiar with Massachusetts Hall by now and has a bed in both my office and the lab. We take his water and food bowl down with us.

In the downstairs hall, I explain my idea of adjusting the camera, and Brian agrees. With a step stool, the camera is just within his reach, so he tilts it slightly outward to line up more with the hall.

"Try your phone," he suggests.

I activate my phone and choose the video camera app. I see us standing in front of the camera. Brian walks down to where the motion detector is first triggered when people enter the hall.

"Can you see me better?"

"Yes," I reply. "That is better. Can you head the other way, like you're going to the equipment room?"

Brian complies, and the camera captures his image for a few steps before he goes out of its range. I can see his face well enough to recognize him.

"I think that's the best we'll do with one camera," I say.

"Great! Shall we head out for bowling?" asks Brian.

We make sure Howie is comfortable in the lab, with water and food. The door, with its new security, is locked, and I can see that the camera is watching us as Brian and I head down the hall, up the stairs, and out into the night.

Brian says that on league nights, parking at the bowling alley can be difficult. The lot's not big enough when the lanes are full. He and I have a little trouble finding a spot, but we still manage to get there before the league starts. As we walk across the parking lot, I notice how clear the sky is. A full moon is just rising in the east, and the night's velvet backdrop is scattered with stars. The air is still and cold, and I can hear music and voices coming from the bowling alley.

Arkham Bowl was no doubt built in the 1950s at the height of America's passion for bowling. As with so many bowling alleys, this one is just a big box with a flat roof. An arched entryway and neon lights help make it a little more interesting, but only just a little. Inside, it's all wood, linoleum, ceiling tiles, and indoor-outdoor carpeting. To the left is a place for renting shoes and the bathrooms, to the right a restaurant and bar.

Straight ahead and down a few steps are the lanes and a wide assortment of costumed bowlers and their friends. Although it's a men's league, many of the men have brought their wives and girlfriends. Costumes and people of all sorts are present. I discover that there will be prizes for the best costumes later in the evening and think Brian might have a shot. He really does look handsome as "Redbeard."

Many people have taken pains to make or rent great costumes. We have a very nice "Pope" straight ahead, and "Elvira" is carrying some beers to a table near the shoe rental stand. In the distance I see what must be "Ronald McDonald," and there's a stunning young woman ahead of me who looks like she just stepped out of a gothic romance novel.

Suddenly, I realize it's Ally, and she looks amazing! She's wearing a dark green satin dress as big as a sports car and an almost-black wig that contrasts with her pale skin. With scarlet lipstick and scarlet opera gloves, she is resplendent.

"It's a princess outfit," she says, but it must be a gothic princess. The material looks dusky and ripples over full underskirts so that it is voluminous and breathtaking. The neckline is both low and wide so her shoulders are almost bare. A garnet necklace highlights her long, lovely neck.

Almost speechless, I say, "Ally, you look stunning. Where did you get that amazing dress, and how did you get here wearing it?"

"We all have our secrets, Mr. Mac. But I'm counting on a ride back to campus."

"That's the plan," I confirm. "Brian's taking us both back after bowling and dinner." Although I'm not sure why, I haven't really told Ally about Brian and me—except that we're friends. She doesn't know that the plan also includes Brian staying the night at my place.

Ally and Brian stand out with really good costumes. Other people have put forward less effort. A few look like they bought a vial of fake blood, smeared it on their regular clothes, and called it "good enough."

Although Brian and Ally have heard about each other, this is their first meeting. I make introductions. "Ally, I'd like you to meet my friend, Brian. Brian, this is Ally from the college."

Brian extends his hand to Ally. She accepts it, and he kisses the top of her hand. "Enchanted, my dear. You're stunning! It's too bad there's no dancing tonight. You look made for the dance floor."

Ally blushes and smiles. Brian does have the charm.

He takes us over to the alley where we'll be playing to make further introductions.

"This is my friend Mac, who's subbing for Ryan tonight," he announces. "The escaped convict is Will, you might recognize him from the hardware store. The vampire is my hiking friend Steven, and the man of undetermined bloody nature is Arnold. We've been friends since I first moved to Arkham."

"Call me Arn," says Arnold. "And I'm a butcher, remember, Brian?"

Everyone, of course, wants to be introduced to Ally. She arrived only a few minutes before us and has been turning quite a few heads. "This is my friend from Miskatonic, Ally Wilmarth," I say, showcasing Ally and her magnificence. "She's a graduate teaching fellow in folklore."

"She's a beauty, is what she is," says Brian, in his best pirate speak.

Ally says hello to the boys, and we all trade a few words about our jobs and our lives.

I borrow a rack ball with a reasonable fit and take a few practice throws.

A woman dressed as a sailor comes by and takes a drink order (beers all around) and sells us some raffle tickets to win gift certificates at local restaurants. The tickets benefit a local children's charity.

Soon, we're drinking, laughing, and bowling.

They have good music at Miskatonic Bowl. Over the clatter of pins, a DJ is doing a wonderful job of keeping the mood upbeat and party-like. With ambient lighting, good music, and fun costumes, this is becoming a night to remember.

My bowling skills are a little rusty and, as a substitute bowler, I don't get the advantage of a handicap. It's clear I'm one of the weaker bowlers on the team, but nobody seems to mind. Although many men's leagues are competitive, this one seems friendly and easygoing.

Our team, the Arkham Alleycats, is playing the Bowling Stones tonight. Based on their handicaps, I would say that the Stones are the better bowlers, but tonight we seem evenly matched. We definitely have the better costumes, but that's not much help on the scorecard.

As with most bowling leagues, it's half bowling and half socializing. The beer and costumes have things weighted on the socializing side tonight, which is fine with me. It's a good chance to meet Brian's friends and some of the Arkham locals.

Brian asks the convict, "How's your girlfriend, Will? Does she still work with fire and police?"

"Yeah," says Will. "They're training her to help with police reporting procedures. After that child went missing last year, they've had to revamp how they investigate the disappearance of minors. They want to devote more office personnel and beef up their analysis staff."

"Did they do something wrong in the investigation last year?" I ask.

"I don't think so," says Will. "It's just that the state is beginning to take notice of Essex County. Apparently, we have more missing minors, especially young children, than the rest of the state combined. I think they're just trying to make sure everyone knows how to handle a missing child case and that we have the resources to quickly and thoroughly investigate."

"Missing children: I'm sure that's not how we want Essex County to be remembered," says Ally.

"No kidding," replies Will, as he gets up to retrieve his ball. Then, he asks me, "What do you do up at the college?"

"Mac's a physics professor," says Brian, with an arm around my shoulder. "They're lucky to have him."

I'm starting to blush, but it goes unnoticed, as Will takes his turn to bowl.

"Doesn't your wife work at the college?" Now Brian is speaking to Steven, the vampire.

"Yes," says Steven. "Deb. She works in Oceanography. They got a big grant a couple years back and hired her to do their internal accounting. It has the biggest departmental budget at Miskatonic. Deb's great with numbers, so it's a good fit. Can't say she likes the college all that much, but the pay is good, and her office friends are nice." Steven looks at me and asks, "Do you believe all the weird stories about things that go on up at the college? I've heard that some of the buildings are haunted and the library is full of satanic books."

"I haven't heard about hauntings. Have you, Ally?" I ask.

"No," she says. "But we do have a large collection of restricted literature in the library. People from all along the coast come to view the antique books and texts. They're very old and valuable. They also have original manuscripts for much of the Salem witch trials. I guess that's where the notion of satanic books comes from."

"Now there's a lovely period of Massachusetts history," says Steven, as he gets up to bowl.

It's near the end of our three games, and it looks like our team will win. Will, Brian's coworker, is having a particularly good evening. His current game will end upward of 250, I'm sure.

Brian is reminding me how the final frames are scored when his hiking friend, Steven, sits down next to us. "It's nice that Brian's finally seeing someone," he says, looking at me. "It can't be easy being single and gay in a small town."

I'm still getting used to the "I'm dating a guy" concept, but I smile and nod. I appreciate the fact that Brian's friends know he's gay and support him so openly. I hadn't really thought about what it might be like to be Brian, a gay man in a traditionally straight man's job.

"He's a great guy and a good friend," says Steven of Brian.

As we finish up, they turn down the music to announce the winners of the drawing. The owner of the bowling alley introduces himself, and the dining gift certificates are given away.

Then he announces that the prizes for best costume are to be given.

"Will the following bowlers or friends please come forward?" he asks. "We'll let the crowd pick from among the top five. Will 'Dark Cinderella' please come up?"

He's pointing at Ally, and I nudge her. "They want you," I say, not surprised at all. Ally moves forward, up the few stairs to the raised lobby area.

"Will 'Gandalf the Gray' please come up?" A convincing *Lord of the Rings* wizard joins Ally.

"Will 'Nosferatu' please come up?" At first, I think they mean Steven, but I see a better-costumed vampire go to the front of the lobby.

"Will 'Billie Holliday' please come up?" A striking African American woman goes up in a beaded, tight-fitting dress and a dramatic hairstyle from the 1930s. She even *looks* like Billie Holliday.

"Will 'Carmen Miranda' please come up?" This time it's a fellow in drag. It's not pretty drag, but the costume is well executed, and the fruit-salad headdress is towering. Could the guy really have been bowling in that outfit? Amid a catcall or two, "Carmen" joins the others on the stage.

The five contestants are lined up, and the owner of the alley highlights each costume in turn, having the crowd applaud for the one they like best. The crowd, mostly men, favors the beautiful ladies. Billie

Holliday wins first prize, but our Ally wins second prize and $150. She's surprised and elated. I don't know that I've seen her so happy.

"You look so amazing tonight, Ally," I say, when she joins us back at the bowling lane. "Congratulations."

"You've definitely added some class to the sport of bowling," says Brian, smiling broadly.

As the bowling crowd disperses, we pack up our gear and head over to the restaurant. Though it's getting late, we decide to have a bite before we head back to the campus. We find a booth toward the back and order drinks and finger food.

"You know," Brian says, "I have an idea. Maybe we're looking at everything from the wrong angle. You know, all the weird stuff at the college, in Arkham, and in Essex County. Maybe we're being too black and white about it all."

Ally and I are intrigued, and Brian continues. "Remember when you were telling me about the double-slit experiment, Mac?"

"Yes," I say, and briefly explain the concept to Ally.

"It seems to me," says Brian, "that we're trying to define the weird happenings around here, past and present, based on two primary characteristics. Just like particles and waves. Some of us want waves. We want missing children, dangerous books, and mysterious break-ins to be of a supernatural nature. That would be the folklore position," Brian says, nodding at Ally.

Ally smiles and quotes Shakespeare, "There are more things in Heaven and Earth, Horatio, than are dreamt of in your philosophy." She toasts us with her soft drink.

"Exactly," Brain continues, with a wink. "Others of us want particles. We want to know the fixed details of how everything happens with no mystery and no nonsense. We want books to have a realistic purpose, we want to know the who, what, where, when, and why of a failed laboratory break-in." Of course, now he's looking at me, the scientist. I shrug in assent.

"But what if it's both?" asks Brian. "If I understand the double-slit experiment, Mac, sometimes the answer is not 'either or' but 'both.' What if the weird things around here are both supernatural *and* scientific? Maybe they follow a logic of their own, but it's not bound by the scientific laws that we understand today."

Brian's point is not lost on me. "Maybe it's not the difference between supernatural and scientific causes," I propose. "Maybe it's just a difference between supernatural and scientific interpretations. I'm thinking that the causes may not be in question when we have more information. Then it will just be how we choose to describe the causality."

"You mean like global warming?" asks Ally. "Where people want to make the problem either climatic cycling or human intervention?"

"Yes," I say. "Nobody's questioning the rising temperatures, and mostly scientists agree that it's because carbon dioxide in the atmosphere is building up. We're just having trouble interpreting the data in ways that help us find solutions."

Brian is less than convinced. "You're giving us humans too much credit. Part of the planet hasn't really even agreed that there's global warming to any degree that something must be done. I still think that it's an 'either-and' situation, anyway. The planet may be in a cycle, *and* we may have significantly contributed to it."

That stops the conversation for a moment, but Ally starts it back up.

"Talking about global warming reminds me," she says. "I want to plan a picnic at the beach before our New England cold season hits! Do you have things planned for the first weekend in November? While the weather is still a little nice, I'd love to get away for a day to the beach. Could we plan for that first Saturday or Sunday?"

"Sounds fun," Brian and I say, almost in unison.

We check the calendars on our smartphones and choose Saturday. Brian says he usually works Saturdays but will trade with someone who does Sundays. We start to plan more about our picnic, but our phones start buzzing like crazy.

"It's the lab," says Brian.

"Someone's set off the motion detector," I add. "Can we switch over to the camera?"

"Yes," says Brian. "Just press the camera icon."

I do, and a very curious image pops up. A video time stamp is displaying the date/time in the upper right-hand corner: 11:45 p.m. (the current time). A man wearing a Halloween costume is standing in front of the basement lab in Massachusetts Hall. He's wearing one of those black robes and a droopy-faced commercial costume like the villain in the *Scream* movies. You know, the one that looks like the figure in Edvard Munch's famous *The Scream* painting. He has his back to the outside of the lab door and is looking up, straight at the camera. He comes forward a bit, reaches up, *and switches it off!*

Brian must be watching, too, because we gasp at the same time.

"How fast can we get to the lab?" I ask.

"Good question," says Brian. "I think we could be back to the college in about twenty minutes. Shall we see how fast?"

"I think we should," I say, getting up from the table. "Ally. Will you think us terrible heels if we cut the evening short?"

"That's fine, boys," says Ally, also getting up. "You have me intrigued, though. You have to promise to fill me in on what's happened. Remember, you're taking me back to campus!"

Brian's gathered his bowling bag, and we're heading out to his Jeep.

As we drive back to campus, I phone campus security to let them know what's happened. They, of course, can get there before we can.

I also fill Ally in. I tell her about the scratch marks on the lock and hinge pins. I tell her how we installed a new lock and the electronic monitoring sensors, and I show her the bit of video we got from the camera.

"Perfect," she says. "Campus security should have them red-handed by now!"

Brian drives safely but gives us quite a ride back to campus.

There's no parking on the inner circles of the campus, but Brian gets us as close as he can. We try our best to hurry to Massachusetts Hall, but since Ally didn't have to bowl, she's wearing real princess shoes. When we get to the building, all the lights are on. A campus security officer meets us at the door.

"The building's being secured from a break-in," he explains. "No students are allowed."

"We're not students. I'm Dr. Mackenzie, and my lab's in the basement of Massachusetts Hall. I'm the one who called campus security."

The officer gives us another good visual examination. "Well, I'm not the one who took the call. Taggert's downstairs." He pauses a minute. "Halloween party, eh?"

"Yes," I say. "We were at a party in Arkham when the security system reported movement outside the lab. We recorded part of the break-in on video."

"You'll have to wait here until the area's secure."

But we don't have to wait long. Security Chief Justin Taggert joins us in a few minutes.

"I don't see anything out of the ordinary," he says, when he comes up from the basement lab and we identify ourselves. "The entrance doors to the hall were locked when we got here, and all the lights were out. You identified the break-in area, so we went downstairs to investigate. The lab's still locked, and there appears to be nobody in the building. I had Officer Blake watch the door while I went through the building, room by room. It's empty."

"Maybe they're still in the lab," I offer.

"Checked in there, too. Now that the lab has one of our security locks on it, the master key opens it. I went inside and verified that nobody's there."

"But we can show you part of the break-in. We have it recorded." I explain how our motion detector started up the video camera. "Although it's a live feed to our phones, the server in my office should have recorded what the camera saw."

While Officer Blake remains at the front door, the rest of us troop up to my office. I unlock the door, and Brian shows us how to access the video on the server. We watch the video. The feed shows that the hall light was on. The intruder walks down the hall from where he (or she) activates the motion sensor. Almost immediately, you see the person looking up, noticing the camera. As they approach the door, they turn to face the camera, reach up, and turn it off.

Chief Taggert watches the video twice. He looks again at the three of us in our costumed finery and asks, "And this person wasn't part of your costume party? Could they have just left early?"

I start to protest, but then I think. Was there a "Scream" costume at the bowling alley? It really is a common commercial costume.

"It was a big party at the bowling alley in town. I don't remember anyone costumed like that, but I suppose it's possible."

"Could one of your students be playing a prank, Dr. Mackenzie?" Taggert asks. "Everything's secure. Could they just have wanted to freak you out a little?"

It has certainly done that. I say, "I don't think any of my students are involved. We just finished refurbishing the lab, and none of them have even been in it."

"Do any of your bowling friends know about the lab?" he asks.

"No," I say, but Brian stops me from saying anything further.

"Actually," he says, "I've been telling the team about helping you at the lab the last few weeks, Mac. I can't imagine they're involved, but they do know about the lab."

While Chief Taggert looks at Brian, I'm thinking about the evening. Could one of Brian's teammates have driven to the lab while we were in the bar having a bite? Could they have told other people? Was there time to drive back, change costumes, and get caught on the video? Steven's wife would have keys to the building if she does after-hours work in the Oceanography Department.

"Could we go down to the lab?" I ask. "I'd like to examine the door and make sure nothing's really missing."

We go down three flights to the basement and stand outside the lab door. I reach up and turn on the video camera and realize it immediately starts recording. It makes sense: we're moving in the corridor, so it would start recording.

"I relocked the door," says Chief Taggert, pointing at the entrance to the lab. "It was locked when I got here, so I opened it, did a quick survey of the room, and locked it up again in order to search the rest of the building."

I get out my keys and unlock the door. I turn on the lights. It's now 1:05 a.m., and the room seems harshly lit. The foil reflects all the light, and we can see wavy versions of our costumes in the walls and ceiling.

"Crazy-looking lab," remarks Taggert.

I continue looking around the room, but all the equipment seems to be in place. The laser, the calibration guides, the receptor array. It's all there. I turn my attention to the lower half of the room and notice something: a water bowl.

"Howie!" I exclaim. "*Where's Howie?!* I left my dog in the room before we went bowling. I didn't have time to take him back home, so I left him here until we got back. Did you let him out?"

I'm looking at Chief Taggert, but he just shrugs. "There wasn't a dog here when I unlocked the door." Taggert pauses and asks, "Is this the same dog that was loose when some student left you the threatening note?"

I'm not really listening to Taggert, because I notice Howie's dog bed under the lab table. His food dish is there, too. It looks like he ate most of his food while we were gone.

Now I notice something else.

Under one of the lab chairs is a little piece of blue material. It's a blue sweater. Next to it is a strip of leather, a collar. I pick it up, knowing what I will see. The tag says "Howie."

This creates more questions from Taggert:

"Are you sure you left the dog here? At what time was that? Do your students know you have a dog? Does anyone dislike the dog? Has it caused damage or bothered anyone?"

As I answer the questions, the initial adrenaline rush associated with the break-in and working with the security officer begins to fade. I realize, really feel, that Howie is gone. I hold his sweater and collar in my hand. A weight feels like it has been put on my heart. Howie's gone.

More questions and answers are exchanged. Taggert takes a description of Howie, and I explain about his identification chip.

Brian and I decide to walk Ally over to the dormitories. It's almost 1:45 a.m. I can tell she's tired. Her feet must be killing her. She gives me a kiss and says, "I'm so sorry about Howie. I know you'll find him, somehow. Maybe he got loose and is waiting for you at home."

I know she doesn't really believe this, but it's the best she has to offer, and I hold her for a minute. It helps to keep back the tears I feel behind my itchy eyes.

Brian holds my hand as we walk to my apartment in Grant Hall: Redbeard and Ichabod Crane. We must look like a playful pair, but I'm not feeling playful.

There's no sign of Howie on the way back to Grant Hall and no lights on, either. There are no notes on my apartment door and, of course, no Howie.

"We'll put posters up, tomorrow," says Brian. "The security guy may have let him out. He may be wandering around the campus."

We both know that's not likely. Even if Chief Taggert let Howie out, he would have been wandering around Massachusetts Hall, and we would have seen him. All the doors were locked, except the main door, which the other security officer was guarding. We checked the whole building.

"And let's call Arkham animal control tomorrow," Brian continues. "No matter where he is, if someone turns him in, that's where he'll end up."

"That's a good idea. And thank you for being here, for trying so hard to make things turn out right."

"Things *will* turn out right," says Brian. He means it, too. I can tell he's sincere as he looks into my eyes with concern. "Tell me about Howie. Tell me what it was like when he first came to live with you."

I tell Brian about the Italian greyhound breeder who died, leaving nobody to care for her fourteen dogs. I tell him about the animal shelter calling all the people on their rescue list and the scrappy little dog that came to live with me. Brian's already heard about Howie "naming" himself, but I tell him some more stories about young Howie. I tell him about Howie riding in my backpack to my classes when I first started college. I tell him about how much Howie loved the beach and running along the shoreline.

Eventually, I also tell him about my father leaving my mother.

Somehow the words just tumble out without me thinking about them.

"Mom doesn't talk about it. It must be too painful. She was on her way to the hospital to have me when he left. Ironically, it was here in Essex County. One of the small beach towns, I think. My father's from Massachusetts. He just left her. She was on her way to the hospital, and he just left her."

I remember that Brian's parents kicked him out of their home. Although I never had the presence of a father, Howie and my mother have always been there for me.

Talking and crying have relaxed me a bit. I feel calmer. I know we'll follow through with all Brian's suggestions on looking for Howie. He almost has me convinced we'll find him in the morning.

Noticing the hour and feeling my exhaustion, I suggest we go to bed. We're still in those early stages of being together, and our bodies instinctively want to have sex. It's fast and hot and pleasurable but without the sensuality we've felt before. I look forward to a better sleepover with Brian. This was certainly not the date either of us had imagined.

Afterward, we lie, spooning, with Brian wrapped around me. It's comforting. I feel his tenderness. I feel cared for. It's early morning, with the full moon shining through the window, spilling onto the quilt on the bed.

Soon I fall into a sleep where any dreams I have are not remembered.

CHAPTER EIGHT

A Day at the Beach

Howie's been gone for over a week. Despite my desire to hang around campus in case he turns up, Ally, Brian, and I decide to go ahead with our picnic plans at the beach in Kingsport. I make sure the Browns, Samantha (downstairs), and Ms. Barry know where we're headed and how to reach us.

It's a perfect autumn day—sunny and clear, with bold cumulous clouds dotting the sky. Cold temperatures at night have turned the leaves to wonderful shades of red, yellow, and orange. Tourists travel from all over the globe to see New England in its fall colors. Here, it is unfolding in front of me.

In Southern California we didn't have a real set of seasons. It was lovely but always about the same. Here in Massachusetts, the seasons have distinct flavors and textures. The summer can be hot—too hot at times. The winter, I'm promised, will be cold and include snow, likely a snow storm or two before Christmas. But right now we're in a blaze of autumn leaves, and I welcome this authentic bit of Massachusetts splendor.

Ally and I drive to Brian's house to take advantage of his Jeep's snap-together top. Ally and I help with the many, many snaps, and *voila*—we have a convertible! With the top down, the twenty-five-mile ride southeast from campus to the beach is glorious.

Brian looks handsome with wind ruffling his hair. His easygoing smile seems on the verge of a good laugh. Today he's in his usual jeans but is wearing a maroon plaid button-down shirt over a vintage tee. A baseball cap finishes off his studied casualness, and I can't help but think of how attracted I am to him.

We travel through picturesque woods. We loop around one of Massachusetts's famous "round hills," although they seem quiet today (Ally explains the local legends about the noisy hills in New England). Brian is a polished driver on the slow but easy road to Kingsport. We follow the Miskatonic River, sometimes on the left, sometimes on the right, as it makes its downhill trip to the sea.

Ally is also dressed in jeans today. On top, she has a white blouse and a button-up sweater the color of the sky. She's in high spirits. Her classes are going well, and she's enjoying that wonderful feeling of making major progress in her chosen field. Her eyes light up when she talks, and she's really chatty today. Not with nervousness but with pleasure in the company of friends. Her moods may be mercurial, but today it's all smiles and perfectly authentic.

We come through another forested rise, and suddenly the Atlantic is spread out before us. Although it's not California or the Pacific, the ocean has a strong pull on me. The extended horizon, the endless waves, and the salty tang of the air all have a giddy effect. It feels like coming home, and I realize, like Ally and Brian, I'm smiling. A day at the beach seems like an unusually good idea right now.

The Jeep winds its way through light forest and grassy fields. We go over another rise and shortly find ourselves in front of the "Welcome to Kingsport" sign. It's the original home of saltwater taffy and has a population of twenty-five hundred. We wind down into the natural harbor that forms the heart of Kingsport. It sits sheltered from the stormy Atlantic with high headlands on both sides and access to a beach to the south. The Miskatonic River has a low falls, just east of town, and rushes into the ocean with a vigor and enthusiasm you can hear throughout the small town.

Colonists from southern England and the Channel Islands founded Kingsport in 1639. In early Massachusetts history, it was known both as a seaport and also for its shipbuilding. In more modern times, the economy shifted first to commercial fishing and then tourism. Its small, enclosed harbor has a wharf area full of picturesque shops and small restaurants. The rest of the town radiates back from the wharf in tiers of streets, shops, and houses that work up the hillside. Many of the buildings are over a hundred years old. Several of the streets have bridges to link the town that is neatly divided by the Miskatonic River.

We drive across the town, over the main bridge on Front Street, and head south past the jetty, down Ocean Avenue to the beach. We park at the foot of Ocean Avenue and survey the landscape. The beach here is wide and lovely. White sand, gentle waves, and almost windless air make the perfect backdrop for a picnic. We unload our stuff. After a bit of a debate, we pass on a picnic table and spread our blanket on the sand. It's a cool day, but with sweaters and jackets we're perfectly comfortable on our blanket at the beach.

With sandwiches in hand, cold lemonade, and a bag of chips passed between us, Ally tells us a little more about herself. "Mom and Dad live in Chicago, but I had to come out here for graduate school. And, I mean, I *had* to—it's one of the stipulations of my trust fund. The fund pays a hundred percent of my education at any university I choose, but I have to end up at Miskatonic for graduate studies. I also have to study folklore, anthropology, and literature. Luckily, I've always enjoyed those classes best. I love reading about old myths, beliefs, and how people lived their lives in ancient times."

"Oh, a 'trust fund girl,'" teases Brian.

"It's not exactly like that," says Ally. She's wearing a sort of boater's hat, and her hair is sticking out in disarray. Combined with her white blouse and sweater, she's all angles and elbows. She manages to be both pretty and awkward-looking at the same time. As she talks, she absent-mindedly examines the ends of her hair.

"It's a weird family thing. Not from my parents—something set up for educating Wilmarth family kids from long ago. There's a lawyer in Arkham who administers the trust, and my grandfather, on campus, took advantage of it, too. Next term I may have some study time with Grandpa. He works in the library and is one of the university's folklore experts."

"Wait a minute," I interrupt. "How many Wilmarths are there on campus? We visited your great-grandfather's grave, but your grandfather is here on campus?"

"Yes," says Ally. "I don't know Grandfather terribly well—we've always been in the Midwest, and he's always been here at the college. We have lunch sometimes, but he keeps mostly to himself. Next year, I'll study with him. Eventually, I'll be working with the library's rare books. Miskatonic has more arcane and esoteric early texts than any other university on the East Coast, and Grandfather's an expert on them. Acquisition, preservation, promotion, and security of rare books are his specialties."

"Is he in charge of protecting the *Necronomicon*?"

Ally peers at me for a minute. "Nobody really calls it that," she says. "I don't even think the Greek translation has that on the title page. It's *The Book of Naming the Dead*. I haven't seen it, but it's something Grandfather has access to and has studied. It's a full-on grimoire with directions for casting spells, summoning demons, raising dead spirits, and so forth."

"People from town were talking about it, and I looked it up in the library catalog to see if it was even a real book."

"Oh, it's real. The library is quite amazing in other ways, too. They have a graduate student working almost full time on the 'Voynich Manuscript.' It's an illustrated codex handwritten in an unknown writing system likely from the Italian Renaissance period. The vellum on which it is written has been carbon dated to the early fifteenth century and proves that it isn't a hoax, or at least not a recent hoax. The student here at Miskatonic hopes to either crack the code or at least correlate the diagrams in it to natural phenomena. We also have a complete copy of the transcripts of the Salem witch trials and many other original Puritan diaries and manuscripts. People come from all over to read and study *that* unpleasant part of American history."

"You're just a geeky mess when you talk about this stuff," Brian interjects. Ally blushes, but you can tell how much she loves the topic and how much she knows about it. Abruptly changing the subject and with typical Ally boldness, she asks, "How long have you two been together?"

Not knowing what to say, or even how to answer, Brian answers for us, "We met at Three Rivers Hardware and Lumber at the beginning of fall term when I started helping him with his lab remodel. We've been dating for about two months. We've been boyfriends since the first of October." Brian has a bright smile and is somehow enjoying this exposé.

"Way to go, Mac!" Ally says, with a grin. "I told you that you were gay!"

I'm blushing, but pleasantly so. It feels good to have a new friend like Ally, so open in her opinions and thinking. It also feels nice to hear the word *boyfriend* come from Brian. I guess we *are* boyfriends. It sounds right and good. I notice Brian looking at me, and I give him a wink.

"The reason I was asking about local legends," continues Brian, switching back to our original topic, "is that I wondered if they might have some bearing on our present situation."

"What do you mean?"

"Well, it seems we have quite a mystery with Howie's disappearance, the strange marks on the lab door three weeks ago, and the break-in on Halloween. There's also the really weird dream you told me about, Mac. Oh, and let's not forget the threatening note you found under your pillow! I thought there might be a connection to some of the local stories and our weird happenings."

"There's not likely to be a connection between folklore and Howie's disappearance," I assert. "Folklore doesn't unlock doors and steal dogs —people do. You're not really thinking Ally's stories are real, are you?"

Ally scoffs at the comment. "We may end up in a discussion about what's real and what isn't, if we're not careful," she warns. "Since none of us are philosophers or logicians, we may wish to avoid that subject. Seriously, though, what we believe will always color our perception of the world. The witches were real enough to the Salem population. They believed in them, they looked for them, and they found them. A few of the women who were hung or burned believed *themselves* to be witches. Folklore is a gateway into understanding what people believe, and their beliefs are a reflection of what's real to them."

"That makes sense," I say. "A personal kind of reality is something I understand. It's like two people describing an event that happened to them in completely different ways. They saw the same thing, they witnessed the same event, but the personal reality of it is quite different for them. It's like two separate realities that are both true to the people involved."

"Exactly," says Ally. "The events happening in the Salem witch trials are not in question. They're well documented. The *reality* in Salem at the time was that there were witches. Today's reality of those same events is something else."

"Maybe we should ask Ally's grandfather for information," says Brian. "Howie may not have disappeared through supernatural means, but whoever snatched him may be acting on out-of-the-ordinary impulses. Seems like a lot of odd things happen at Miskatonic and in Essex County. Somebody seems to want to get into the lab for some reason that isn't related to physics! Maybe Dr. Wilmarth can give us some ideas why."

"Or at least an historical perspective," concludes Ally.

I'm unconvinced, but in such pleasant company I agree to contact Ally's grandfather, Dr. Wilmarth, when we get back to campus. If nothing else, it will be fun to learn more about Miskatonic and anything he knows about Massachusetts Hall. Wilmarth may have some of his own stories to tell about the campus or the *Necronomicon*.

After finishing our lunch, we play in the surf and walk along the shoreline as far as we can go—the beach ends where a sheer cliff extends out into the water. On the way back, we collect a generous assortment of shells for Ally, who is new to the idea of beach combing. The wind has picked up a bit by the time we get back to our picnic spot. I'm also missing Howie. It's hard to be at the beach and not think of our many walks along the shore in Santa Monica. Brian notices that I've started crying again and wipes my cheeks with a corner of his wool jacket.

We get more blankets from the Jeep to wrap up in while we watch the surf. Brian and I snuggle a bit, and we all watch the clouds sail by in the still afternoon. It's a perfect afternoon in early November.

It's a day to remember. Although worried about my first and best friend, I realize and really *feel* new friends surrounding me.

About three o'clock we pack things up. It's a short drive back to campus, so we've been savoring the day—stretching it out as long as possible. Ally is supposed to be back before dinner to preside over a "study hall" in the early evening. Brian has plans for laundry.

On the way through Kingsport, Ally is telling more legends of Massachusetts and the early Puritans. She points to the top of a particularly high sea embankment that overhangs the north side of the harbor. Terrace on terrace, the craggy cliff climbs skyward until the northernmost tip hangs high above the town. At its base, the Miskatonic pours into Kingsport harbor. Where the harbor meets the Atlantic, crashing waves create a mist that rises up the full side of the cliff. Despite the sunny afternoon, the cliff top is shrouded in mystery.

"There's even a legend about that cliff. Supposedly, there's an ancient stone house on the summit. It's inaccessible unless you have wings," says Ally, smiling. "People report seeing lights in the windows at night." Ally clearly enjoys telling the story. "You can see it better from out in the water, of course. From there you can see the whole house. But, if you strain your eyes a bit, you can just see one wall and part of the stone roof from here."

We comply, and, yes, there is a suggestion of something that might be the side of a small house made of stone and a peaked roof atop it. There's a hint of a possible window opening toward the side facing the sea.

"It's supposed to be haunted," says Ally, with a shrug.

The trip back to Brian's house is uneventful. The day has grown colder, and I'm glad for my warm jacket. After our wonderful beach trip, it would be nice to spend the night with Brian, but he has other plans, and I want to check in and see if Howie (or news of him) has turned up.

I drive Ally back to her dorm for dinner and to prepare for her study hall. Our conversation has slowed down. We're enjoying the silence of our company and the end of a wonderful afternoon. Ally squeezes my arm and gives me a sisterly kiss when I drop her off near her dorm. I stop for a quick bite at the Student Union café. Over a veggie burger and fries, I think more about our folklore discussion. Maybe a trip to see Ally's grandfather would be useful after all. Brian could be right. Whoever took Howie might be involved in something weird or something related to the campus. I'm really at a loss to think of other reasons for stealing a middle-aged Italian greyhound or trying to break into our new lab.

Before bolting off to the Salomon Center and its library, I take a few minutes to check up on Dr. Albert Wilmarth on my smartphone. The online catalog of internally published papers and articles shows Wilmarth published his first scholarly article in 1925: "Extraterrestrial Folk Legends of Rural New England." Even if he got his doctorate at age twenty, that would put Wilmarth well over 110 years old! Obviously, that can't be true. I see published works appearing intermittently throughout the years, including "The Round Hills of New England" and "Sea Shanties and Drinking Songs: Musical Folklore of Massachusetts." Wilmarth is quite a prolific writer in his field. There's even one article published this year: "End-of-Times Legends and Their Precedents in the Americas."

Among other items in the online catalog is a photo of Wilmarth from 1966 when he held the Chair of Literature at Miskatonic. He's receiving a chancellor's award for something. He looks about seventy years old in the picture.

The college directory shows that he is no longer teaching. He is listed as a library consultant with English literature, folklore, and arcane texts as his specialties.

Getting in to see Dr. Wilmarth is not as easy as I would have imagined. As I enter the administrative part of Salomon Center, the departmental secretary, Ms. Evans, is his first line of defense. "Dr. Wilmarth is quite elderly, you know," she says. "He doesn't see many people—he can't. His health is just not up to it."

"But it's really important! He has information that can help us with a problem we've been having at the physics lab."

"I don't see how a folklorist can help you with physics, young man," Ms. Evans replies.

I try again. "It's not so much the physics as it is the lab itself. The building seems to be causing some of our experiments to have anomalous outcomes."

"It still sounds to me like you've got the wrong department. Maybe if you stick to your science, you'll figure it out."

One more try. "Ms. Evans, I've been told that Dr. Wilmarth knows all about the history of Miskatonic University, all its buildings, and even about the land before the university was founded. I think Dr. Wilmarth might be able to help us clear up a problem we have."

"I don't see how—"

"A research assistant has disappeared during an experiment [I hate lying about Howie, but *this is important!*], and his granddaughter says Dr. Wilmarth might be able to help."

"Oh," she says. "You've met his granddaughter? Well, why didn't you say so?"

Ms. Evans then reviews a "protocol" to use with Dr. Wilmarth, and I begin to wonder if Ally's grandfather is a centuries-old vampire or, more likely, crazy. "You can't turn the lights up, young man," she explains. "His skin and eyes are photosensitive. You just have to deal with however much light he has on when you enter his office. And don't expect him to get up or shake hands. Although he's friendly, he's not friendly in that way. And, his voice takes some getting used to. Since I mostly talk to him over the phone, I used to think his line was bad. After a few visits, I learned that that's just the way he talks. He's a kind man, though. If you can't quite catch something he says, just ask him to repeat it, and he will."

The more Ms. Evans talks, the more I can tell she has a kindly view of Dr. Wilmarth. She gives me brief directions on finding his office and says she will phone him as soon as I leave to let him know I'm on the way.

"Are you sure he's in his office?" I ask.

"He's always in his office."

I recross the main library and enter a hall that leads to an older part of the building. At the end of another short corridor is a door marked "Stairs." As directed, I descend two floors into what must be a basement or even sub-basement. This hall is short, too, and Dr. Wilmarth's office is clearly marked, "Dr. Albert N. Wilmarth." On a line below, "Folklore and Antiquity Texts."

I knock twice, and the most peculiar voice invites me in.

Describing my interview with Dr. Albert Wilmarth is not an easy thing to do for several reasons. Firstly, the windowless room is dark. Not completely dark, but very dark. There's a small, dimmed lamp on his desk, another on a credenza, and some kind of a nightlight plugged in near the door. In fact, the major source of light in the room comes from his computer monitor: a largish, late-model Macintosh sitting squarely on his desk next to a bowl of lemons. As my eyes adjust to the gloom, a cluttered but fairly standard professor's office comes into view. In addition to the desk, I see several bookcases full of antique oddities and an Oriental rug overlaying the cement floor. There's a love seat next to the door (which I am invited to use) and a big, old-fashioned wooden desk chair pulled back from the desk and against the wall opposite me.

Dr. Wilmarth is sitting in the shadowed desk chair. The illumination is just enough to hint at his appearance. He's wearing a lightweight hooded jacket, and a thick patch of white hair is poking out in front. The jacket must be two sizes too big—all of him seems covered in baggy layers except for the ends of his hands and his weather-beaten face. His lean, liver-spotted hands sit in his lap. His eyes stare out with a strained expression of what must be tiredness. I would guess Dr. Wilmarth to be about seventy, maybe eighty, years old.

The idea of someone Wilmarth's age wearing a hoodie would normally invite me to smile, but his voice puts off any frivolity.

"Pardon me for not rising to shake your hand, Dr. McKenzie," he says. "I limit my energy a bit these days. I'm afraid you will have to put up with the low illumination, too. The light hurts my eyes, you understand."

There's a kind of low vibration or bass rhythm in the room and in the air that interferes with listening to Dr. Wilmarth. It's like being on an old telephone line with a poor connection, just as Ms. Evans described it. Sounds seem strangely muffled in the room as though the air has a deadening quality to it. Dr. Wilmarth's voice is a buzzy whisper. I've tried thinking of better ways to describe it. The whisper part is right, but it's a kind of stage whisper. I don't really have any trouble hearing him, yet he sounds like he's whispering or out of breath. The difficulty with understanding him is the slight buzzing. It's more than just sibilant *s* noises or a lisp. I can only describe it as a buzzing around the edges of his words, as though insects were somehow involved in speaking or his vocal chords vibrate in some unusual manner. So, one part whisper, one part buzz, then add in the room's undercurrent of vibration, and that's what it's like having a conversation with Dr. Wilmarth.

Oh, and the smell! It reminds me of a visit to a mushroom farm! I must have noticeably sniffed at the peculiar odor of the room, because Dr. Wilmarth whispers, "This old, musty basement. I really must request a good spring cleaning this year."

To end any further discussion of the dark office, odd smell, weird voice, or listless appearance, Dr. Wilmarth changes the subject. "Anna says you've met my granddaughter."

"Yes. We met on campus about a month ago and have been hanging out. She's told me a little about her situation and the local folklore that the Wilmarths have collected over the years."

"I see. So you know about the three Dr. Wilmarths on campus?"

"Two, surely," I offer. "Even if you count the one buried in the cemetery, you can't count Ally, yet. She doesn't have her doctorate."

Dr. Wilmarth sighs. "Two, yes, of course. Two Dr. Wilmarths, and that's quite enough, I should say." He pauses, then says, "Well, young man, maybe you should tell me why you're here and how I might be able to help you."

Not sure of what Ms. Evans may have told him, I hesitate to tell the story. Or hesitate to tell the whole story. In the end, I figure that what's going on in the Wilmarth family can't be much weirder than my problems in the physics lab. I just blurt it all out. The threatening letter. The weird lab dream. The break-in and Howie's disappearance. Ally's suggestion to talk to him. All of it.

Wilmarth takes it all in. His face seems strained, as if he's listening for something in particular. When I tell him about the dream, he nods as though I'm confirming something he already thought to be true. When I talk about Howie's disappearance, his face relaxes, and I catch a whispered, "Yes."

But when I finish the story, he offers no readymade solutions or suggestions of a practical nature. Sounding a bit like his granddaughter, he offers some folklore.

"I suppose you've heard of the Salem witch trials?" he asks. "Most everyone has. It wasn't just Salem, of course. Across New England there were plenty of young women and men burned and hung as witches. Plenty of documented cases of demonic possession and sorcery right here in Arkham. At least two witches were burned, and a collaborator was hung near the cemetery. There were many corroborated descriptions of demons being summoned, of paranormal activity, of magical powers, and of solstice rituals. Today we try to forget that period of Massachusetts's history. We want to think that a small group of Puritans punished a few women who wouldn't conform to period ethics. We'd like to think that demonic possession was just undiagnosed schizophrenia. Unexplained disappearances of the time we attribute to death by natural causes or people simply leaving the area. We'd prefer to distance ourselves from anything that cannot be explained through science.

"Yes, I know who you are and what science means to you, Dr. McKenzie. I know that talking to a folklorist for advice about unexplained phenomena is unsettling. That's why I'm not going to give you any advice. What I *am* going to do is give you some historical background on the Miskatonic River Valley that you might find useful. My grandfather collected quite a bit of material about the college and the grounds before his death. I think I have a few newspaper cuttings I can ask Anna to give you right now and a few call numbers for books that I'll have pulled from the library stacks. I can have them sent to your home or office. I'll let you come to your own conclusions about what's going on."

Sensing a dismissal, I get up to leave. Now accustomed to the gloom, I notice that in addition to books, there are a variety of strange artifacts, objects, and machines on the bookshelves and the credenza. There's a small stone tablet with curious hieroglyphs. There's a fertility statue, I think, but with tentacles where the goddess's head should be. A bronze or copper medallion hangs from a hook on the wall. A row of nineteenth-century diving helmets (only smaller) lines the top of one bookcase. Several control boxes or some kind of steam-punk computer components sit on the credenza. All antiques, I'm sure, but of what original purpose?

We say our goodbyes somewhat stiffly. Dr. Wilmarth smiles and asks me to tell Ally to come by and see him sometime soon. I find myself outside his office breathing air that is pure and fresh. As I walk back up the hall to the stairs, I reflect on the curious conversation with Dr. Wilmarth. Could whatever causes his light sensitivity also limit mobility? Could the weird smell be coming from him or one of his antique collectables?

By the time I reach Ms. Evans's desk, she's ready for me with two newspaper articles in hand and the call numbers for a couple books in the library. Obviously, Wilmarth phoned her the minute I left his office. The call numbers she hands to another worker in the office. "Colin, could you pull these books from the stacks for Dr. Wilmarth? He'll want them right away."

Ms. Evans leaves the office for a minute to make copies of the articles. When she returns, she asks me about Dr. Wilmarth. "Is he all right, do you think?"

Not having met him before, I am hard pressed to answer. "He seems tired and a bit stoic."

"Oh, he's always been stoic! I think that just runs in the family. His grandfather was exactly the same, I'm told. I just worry because he doesn't seem to get out much or have many friends. I thought maybe you would want to invite him to something or collaborate with him on a project. Maybe you and Ally could take him for an outing. It would do him some good, I think."

I, naturally, have other thoughts on this subject, but I say, "He does seem a bit withdrawn. How long has he been at Miskatonic?"

"Oh, since his grandfather died. Around 1970, I think."

"And his grandfather was Albert Wilmarth, also?"

"Yes. A family name, I imagine. Even his granddaughter is named 'Albert,' you know."

I *didn't* know. I see that Ally has a few more stories to tell me about her family and her trust fund.

Ms. Evans takes down my campus address and assures me that the books will be delivered as soon as possible. "I'll have Colin drop them by later today."

I head home with the two newspaper articles and the urge to visit Ally's study hall. We really need to discuss her grandfather!

The first article is from the *Arkham Advertiser* (the local Arkham newspaper) and is dated November 2, 1935:

Students Reported Missing

Arkham police took up the search Thursday for Aaron Triplett and Anthony Marchetti, students at Miskatonic University, who were last seen on Oct. 31 by classmates on campus.

Det. Glenn Woosey is investigating to determine whether the young men might be involved in a prank disappearance as part of Halloween revelry. Books, a rucksack, writing materials, and other items belonging to the men were found Nov. 1 in a disused basement room of Massachusetts Hall. Playing cards were laid out in patterns on the floor, but no alcohol was found. Their dormitory rooms still contain the bulk of their belongings and roommates anticipated their return.

Any person with information pertaining to the location of the young men is encouraged to contact the Arkham sheriff's office. Parents of the men have been notified of the disappearance.

Triplett, 22, is described as 5-5, 140 pounds, wavy light brown hair and slender but muscular build. Marchetti, 23, is 6-1, 180 pounds, black hair and slender.

The second article is a little more recent and is from the *Miskatonic News* (the university newspaper), dated June 23, 1991:

Massachusetts Hall Break-In

Campus security reports vandalism at Massachusetts Hall during a break-in on Tuesday night. Junior Security Officer Justin Taggert reports that a basement window was forced open on the south side of the building. "They didn't do much damage getting in, but they really trashed the tower basement," says Taggert. "They spray-painted satanic graffiti on the floor and walls. It's hard to say whether we can scrub it off or whether we'll have to repaint the whole thing."

The tower basement is primarily used for storage. The Physics Department is trying to determine if anything has been stolen. As photos show, a large pentagram was painted on the floor with various other arcane symbols and drawings. The purpose of the break-in remains unknown.

After dinner while I'm looking at some student papers, the bell rings at the front door. I call out the window to let them know I'm coming and see a young man with a parcel. It must be the books that Dr. Wilmarth was sending over. I thank Colin, open the package, and find two books. The first one is of modern origin, titled *Miskatonic University: Legacy through Time*. It's an edited collection of essays and articles on Miskatonic University since its inception. There are a few articles about the Miskatonic tribe of Native Americans that had the land prior to the university. Dr. Wilmarth even has a folklore piece in it (or at least one of the Albert Wilmarth's do. I'm a little hazy about which one, since the book was published in 1940). But it's not Wilmarth's article that has been bookmarked. Little slips of paper poke up from the book's spine in two other sections.

The first marks an article from a Native American historian that tells of the selling of land to the white settlers. It is not exactly the usual tale of white settlers taking advantage of indigenous peoples. This historian's view was that the Miskatonic tribe (of the Algonquin Nation) was glad to sell the land. They got what was then a reasonable price in cattle and horses and had only one stipulation with regard to the sale.

The Miskatonic chief made plain his desire to be rid of the land and its obligations. The chief insisted that the treaty would bind the land, its ancestors, and its "influences" to the white settlers. He made the transla-

tor and negotiator set forth these intentions with great care. The Miska-
tonic tribe would no longer care for the land or be responsible for it. The
new owners were directed to use the land for their own purposes but at
their own peril.

The second bookmark was in a chapter about the original plans for
the university. It had been started at the site of a small town, circa
1730. Over the next twenty years, the town was relocated and the plans
for the college were put in motion. University Hall (the first of the
large existing buildings) was completed in 1750.

This chapter also has the first mention of Massachusetts Hall. Before
its current use for physics and related sciences, it was the university
library, built in 1878. This tallied with what Matt Brown had told me
about the place on my first day. But the book also talked about the site
before 1878. A church had been torn down on the site of what would
be Massachusetts Hall. It had been torn down because it was purport-
ed to be involved in the New England witch controversy of 1692 and
1693. This book is no doubt the source of Dr. Wilmarth's report of
local witches. In what would be modern-day Arkham, two witches
were put to death by local magistrates. They were part of a coven that
had taken over—you guessed it—the old church built on the land sold
to white settlers by the Miskatonic natives. The church was somewhat
large for the area and had a prominent five-sided tower that rose above
the village. According to the historian's account:

Four additional witches were cornered in the church tower awaiting
arrest by local guardsmen. When the magistrate and guardsmen entered
the tower, all they found were discarded garments belonging to the
suspected witches.

The church was burned to the ground, but the tower was made of
immense interlocking stone blocks that resisted disassembly and destruc-
tion. The stone tower remains as a symbol of this unique period of
colonial Puritan history.

A reproduction of a detailed drawing of the old church is in the
book. Faded and in sepia tones, it shows a gloomy-looking Anglican
church of medium size but with a stout tower on the right side. It's not
clear if it's a bell tower, although there are window openings at the top,
behind which church bells might be rung.

What is clear to me is *it still exists.* Unmistakably, it is the tower on
Massachusetts Hall! Its five-sided geometry is clear. When the university library was planned sometime before 1878, they just included the
tower in the design! It has a different roofline, and the window openings have been made into real windows, but it's the same church tower,

all right. No wonder the stonework on the tower looks a little different from the masonry on the rest of Massachusetts Hall. No wonder the door to the tower is so old.

The other book that Dr. Wilmarth has loaned me is a reprint of a very old book by Rev. Cotton Mather. Many people believe that Mather's writings inspired local Puritans to begin gathering the evidence that led to the Salem witch trials. Mather was born in 1663 and was a prominent Boston Puritan minister. He published several manuscripts that catalog evidence of possession and witchcraft. Rev. Cotton Mather's book is titled *The Invisible World* and was originally published in 1693. He is often cited as an expert for the witchcraft trials in Essex County and was asked for his advice during the prosecution of suspected witches. *The Invisible World* confirms his influence. He says about himself:

I have indeed set my self to Countermine the whole Plot of the Devil against New-England, in every Branch of it, as far as one of my Darkness can comprehend such a Work of Darkness. I may add, that I have herein also aimed at the Information and Satisfaction of Good men in another Countrey, a Thousand Leagues off, where I have, it may be, More, or however, more Considerable Friends, than in My Own And I do what I can to have that Countrey, now as well as alwayes, in the best Terms with My Own.

Dr. Wilmarth has marked several portions of the book where Rev. Mather mentions the Essex County witch trials by name and in detail. Here is one such reference that he attributes to one Samuel Gray, testifying against one of the witches:

Samuel Gray testify'd, That about fourteen years ago, he wak'd on a Night, and saw the Room where he lay full of Light; and that he then saw plainly a Woman between the Cradle and the Bed-side, which look'd upon him. He Rose, and it vanished; tho' he found the Doors all fast. Looking out at the Entry-Door, he saw the same Woman, in the same Garb again; and said, In Gods Name, what do you come for? He went to Bed, and had the same Woman again assaulting him. The Child in the Cradle gave a great schreech, and the Woman Disappeared.

Wilmarth marked a few other places where testimony indicated that one or more witches or specters vanished. Toward the end of the book, he also marked the following short paragraph, the last of Cotton Mather's material that he wished me to read:

The Devil which then thus imitated what was in the Church of the Old Testament, now among Us would Imitate the Affayrs of the Church in the New. The Witches do say, that they form themselves much after the manner of Congregational Churches; and that they have a Baptism and a Supper, and Officers among them, abominably Resembling those of our Lord.

I have several dreams in the night. This one was the most interesting.

A winter landscape is covered in snow, and the wind is howling through leafless trees. I'm standing on the porch outside my house—some kind of log cabin or rustic structure. Trudging through the snow is a short, stout woman of middle age. She's dressed and wrapped up as I imagine peasants from the old country to be. She waves at me and calls me by name. "Dr. Mackenzie! Dr. Mackenzie! You got to hurry! She's having her baby right now!"

"I'm not that kind of doctor," I say.

"Mother Leeds can't be that picky," she says, motioning me to follow her out into the snowy cold of what looks like early morning. "The real doctor in town won't come, anyways," she adds. "This is baby number thirteen, and everyone knows it belongs to the Devil."

In the way of dreams, this makes some kind of sense. I begin to follow the woman out into the country lane in front of my house. The land here is farmland, and the road is not improved. I'm dressed for it, though. I'm wearing a heavy woolen coat, pants, and thick boots. Gloves cover my hands, and a headscarf is keeping my ears warm. We trudge through the snow, down the lane. We pass one house, then another. I'm starting to wonder how far we'll have to travel when we turn from the lane into a house on the left. This one, like mine, is rustic. I would call it an elongated log cabin, except it also has some lean-to additions on one side, and the other side looks like it is attached to a stable.

I'm ushered into the house, and it is full of women. It seems all the neighbor women are here to attend to the birth.

The house is small inside, basically just one room for living, cooking, and sleeping. A fire is burning in the hearth, and the air in the cabin is overly warm. One woman appears to be boiling linens in a large kettle. Another is preparing a bassinet or crib for the infant. A third is making tea or soup or something. Several of the women are on their knees, praying. Everyone seems to be talking at once, but I can still easily hear the moaning and yelling of what, I presume, is the mother in labor.

On one side of the house is the sleeping alcove, a series of shelves set into the wall. Each "shelf" is a bed. The middle shelf is occupied, and two of the women are attending the painful birth.

I walk across the crowded, noisy space to see the mother, and I'm shocked with recognition. I know this woman! In the manner of dreams, though, I don't have a name for her. I don't know who she is, just that I know her and that she doesn't belong in this setting.

"What are you doing here?" I ask. "You're not Mother Leeds."

"The hell I'm not!" hisses the woman. "And what are you doing here?"

"I'm here to help deliver your baby."

Mother Leeds laughs and laughs. Her laughs are not pleasant, and she displays rotten teeth to go with her overall appearance of poverty and filth. "I think I'll do better on my own, *Doctor*," she says, jeering at me.

The two women attending her begin chanting something in a foreign language—Latin, maybe. Mother Leeds resumes her panting and groaning but at a higher intensity. The whole room turns to the bed alcove as Mother Leeds screams in pain. She twists on the bed, and the women move closer to her. She screams again and arches her back, almost hidden by the watchful women.

Although summoned to help, I'm clearly not wanted or useful here. I turn to leave, but I hear the baby, now delivered, start to cry. I turn back to look. The baby issues a pitiful cry, wholly human sounding. One of the women takes the boiled linens to the bed to clean up Mother Leeds and the baby. Mother Leeds should be exhausted, but she looks fully alert. Although obscured by the women, she's looking straight at me. She has a malevolent look in her eyes as she points a finger at me.

"You!" she says. "Don't you think of leaving! You're to blame for most of this trouble, and you're not about to escape your punishment." She's now been given the baby wrapped in a clean blanket. The baby has quieted down a bit. It's still making soft noises, but they don't sound like crying anymore. More like snuffling.

"Here!" she commands, and I find myself drawn close to her. The women shrink back from her powerful voice, and Mother Leeds and I are alone. She's smiling, almost gloating, and sensing her power over the situation. "Sit and hold the baby," she says, showing her teeth again.

Although not wishing to, I sit on the edge of the rough bed. She holds out the bundled baby for me to comfort. As I lean closer to accept the bundle, I look intently at Mother Leeds. With a jarring sense of familiarity, I suddenly realize why I know her. She's my landlady.

She's Emma Brown!

"Mrs. Brown," I say in a small, bewildered voice.

She laughs and looks at the baby.

I look down, too, at the baby in my arms. It's tightly wrapped in the blanket and fussing over the covers. I unwrap it a bit, and the fussing intensifies. The baby kicks the blanket away, and I'm holding the baby on its back. It settles down some now, and I look into its eyes. It's clearly a boy, but the face is an odd shape—the nose too long and his ears positioned toward the top of his head.

The baby starts to cry again. "Oooooooowieeeeeeeeee," it sobs. "Oooooooowieeeeeeeeee."

With another start, I realize it's not Mother Leeds's baby at all. It's mine. I pull the baby up from the bed and start to flee the cabin. The sudden movement sets the baby off again. "Oooooooowieeeeeeeeee," it cries. "Hooooooowieeeeeeeeeeeeeeeee."

And I look down—*and it is. It's Howie!* My little Italian greyhound. I'm holding Howie as I run out of the wretched cabin into the snowy, cold, gray landscape of my wintery dream.

CHAPTER NINE

The Unexpected Visitor

He slipped in quietly, but it's hard not to notice latecomers to a lecture. He made his way up the gallery and sat on an aisle seat near the top of the lecture hall. Students are often late, of course, but this person was not one of my regular students. This late in the term, I've met all of them and know most of them by name. Trying not to stare and trying harder not to lose my place, I make an occasional glance as I continue my talk and draw illustrations on the whiteboard. It's my Wednesday morning "Physics Concepts for Nonscientists" class. Today we're talking about space-time and some of Einstein's theories of gravitation.

I continue my lecture. "In February of this year, astronomers announced the first proof of Einstein's theory of gravitation and how it warps the fabric of space-time. One would assume that after the Big Bang the universe would simply spread outward in an expanding sphere. Since astronomers observe this is not the case, in 1916 Einstein postulated that gravity acts to warp this expansion process. Rather than an expanding sphere, the universe might be more like a bunched-up four-dimensional fishing net."

As I turn to the overhead projection system, I notice more about the latecomer. Elderly, white haired, he clearly isn't one of my students. I try to come up with other ideas, but I'm stumped. There's something familiar about him, though. I could swear I've met him.

I move to the next slide of my presentation that shows the LIGO installation at Hanford.

"The Laser Interferometer Gravitational-wave Observatories, or LIGO, at Hanford, Washington, and Livingston, Louisiana, were upgraded earlier this year. Their Faraday shielding and remote locations enable them to detect changes in gravity at microscopic levels. They use two-and-a-half-mile-long tunnels with mirrors and lasers to measure minuscule disturbances created by gravitational waves as they pass through the Earth. This February, they were able to detect the gravity waves produced from two black holes as they merged. The gravity distortion is so large that it produces a space-time wave that can be detected at great distances."

The next slide is an animated model of the two black holes circling each other, closer and closer. The gravitational waves are depicted with intersecting lines that writhe and swirl about the two rotating gravity wells.

The older gentleman is perched on his seat, intently listening, as I take out a piece of fabric that I use for demonstration. I pull a thread that begins to scrunch up the fabric until it is all ruffles. The center of the fabric is compacted (simulating denser gravity), and the outer edges are flared and fluted around the center in wavy cascades.

"It's a little easier to visualize in three dimensions," I explain. "When gravity pulls part of the fabric of space-time closer together, such as when the black holes merged, the rest of space-time begins to warp and fold in on itself. What might have been a perfect four-dimensional sphere becomes a loopy, ruffled structure. One of the more speculative ideas in science is that wormholes or quasars might represent places where the folds of space-time intersect and allow a connection or even a movement between layers or overlapping parts. Many great science fiction stories have used folded space-time as a shortcut for navigating the universe."

I push a straw through one of the fabric folds and into another.

"The idea is that we might move vast distances, not by going faster but by simply punching through one fold of space-time into another." I'm smiling a little. Students enjoy remembering some of the movies that have used this as a plot device.

"Don't worry if your head is hurting at this point. We don't have the science to show how we could go from one fold in space-time to another. The exciting thing is that we've proven they exist. The folks at LIGO have even put the gravitational waves into a sound synthesizer to give voice to the undulating gravity of the universe."

At this point, a slide shows a synthesizer playing an audio snippet of one of the gravitational waves. Every student is visibly straining intently to hear the voice of the universe chirping and hissing as the sound file is played.

I continue with some of the math involved in measuring changes in space-time and explain how the LIGO sensors actually work. I can see that my visitor has now become less interested. By the end of class, he's sitting back in his chair and waiting for the bell. He loiters as the students file out.

"It's good to see you again, Dr. Mackenzie," he says.

The face is more familiar than the voice, and I still feel as though I've met this man. Sensing my confusion, he clarifies, "I'm Dr. Wilmarth. You remember. We met in my office at the library. You can call me Albert, if you like."

Could it really be? It *does* look like Dr. Wilmarth. He has the same shock of white hair, the same tanned, thin face. But this Dr. Wilmarth is so active! Although elderly, he marched right up the steps in the lecture hall. He's holding his hand out for a shake. Could this really be the Albert Wilmarth I met in a basement office at the library?

"Oh, of course," I stammer. "Dr. Wilmarth—I mean, Albert. It's great to see you again. And, please, call me Mac. I have to say I didn't recognize you out of context. Your assistant made it sound like you don't get away from the library much."

"Yes. Ms. Evans," says Albert, thoughtfully, "she tends to be a bit protective. At my age, we all tend to slow down a bit, you know, stick close to home." He changes the subject. "Ally was telling me more about your classes this fall and left one of your curriculum sheets. I noticed you were going to be lecturing about the space-time continuum, and I wanted to hear it. I love to keep track of how myth and science tend to converge in the long run."

"I'm not sure what you mean."

"Well, I'm not sure I have the scientific words to explain myself very well," says Albert, "but I'll give it a try. At first, science and scientific methodology tended to disprove myth. It showed that the sun and stars don't move around the earth. It showed that gravity works evenly on everyone. It showed that light and sound are like waves on a pond that flow evenly and predictably. Then Einstein came along and suggested that on larger and smaller scales things are not so easily understood. His theories predict that light works like both waves and particles—depending on how the observer looks for them. Although uncomfortable with it, he predicted that entangled electrons could influence each other instantly and at great distances. Today, you added to my knowledge by showing how Einstein's theories of gravity might allow transference of matter from one part of the universe to another in a way that would appear to also be instantaneous."

"I see you enjoy science fiction, as well as science," I say, but in a gentle way, all smiles and inviting the conversation to go further. "The theories do show that these universal structures exist. We're not quite up to using them, though. Although there is some work on faster-than-light communication devices using entangled atomic structure, I assure you we're not beaming people to other planets quite yet."

That gets a return smile from Albert. "No. Of course not," he says. "But I wonder if that's because we're always trying to figure out how we'd create a contraption to punch through folds in space. We want a *machine* that takes us faster than light. But what if it's a natural phenomenon? What if the very nature of space-time, folding back on itself, creates points of weakness or thinness?"

"I think I follow you. And I want to congratulate you on your understanding of some of the basics of quantum physics. Having said that, I don't think that where folds of space-time come together you'd find a natural gateway. And, if you did, I don't know that you'd be able to just slip through it. Maybe that's what a black hole or a wormhole is: a gateway to another part of space-time. You'd hardly be able to slip through, though. I think the result would be destructive to any form of life."

Albert muses, "I was thinking of something even more natural. Since gravity interference is now shown to be in waves, what if it's more like waves on the beach? Sometimes they're stronger, sometimes weaker. Sometimes the patterns converge to make exceptionally high tides. Maybe gravity waves are predictable, too, once you know more about the variables. And maybe when the 'tides' are just right, the space between the folds of space-time become vanishingly small. Maybe, if you know the right time and are in the right place, space-time simply overlaps. At such a time, maybe you just pick which of the two options for 'here' you wish to claim."

I finally figure it out. It's his voice. Today in the lecture hall, Albert's voice seems significantly different than it did in his office. No buzzing, no odd quality that impedes understanding. At best, you could say this voice sounds familiar, but not really the same.

"It's a nice theory," I say. I'm not really sure how to ask about his voice. Maybe he was ill when I saw him at the library? "But it's one of those theories that I don't see how we'd test."

"What if I told you that I think you have been testing it?"

"What do you mean?"

"What if I suggested that certain times of the year, or in a combination of times and on some years, different folds of space-time do come together right here on Earth? More specifically, right here on campus in the basement of the tower in Massachusetts Hall."

He drops this like a leaden weight, as though I might say, "Of course! Why didn't I think of that?" Instead, I say, "Now we're back to folklore, Albert."

"Bear with me for a minute or so, Mac," he says. "Throughout the history of humanity there have been well-documented reports of people disappearing. From locked-room vanishings to cases of multiple witnesses to a disappearance—this thing seems to happen. The other surprising thing is that it seems to happen more frequently in certain locations and at certain times of the year. Anecdotal evidence that disappearances are more common in the fall, especially during Hallowtide, the winter solstice, or Yuletide holidays. Not every year, but often people disappear during these seasons. There's even some statistical data that suggest missing person reports are more frequent during these holidays."

Although I'm enjoying this conversation, it seems like we're headed out of science and back into folklore. "Yes," I explain, as patiently as I can, "the statistics may show that more people go missing on these days. There might be a million reasons why this is true. Suicides are also more frequent on these days. What if missing persons are just suicides where a body wasn't found? What if people choose these intense family holiday seasons to go missing on purpose?"

At this point, I figure Albert and I are in the same space. Each wanting to be "right" about something that we feel should be obvious to the other person. I do not want Ally's grandfather to go away mad, so I try my best to make peace.

"There's no reason to think what you're suggesting is impossible," I say. "It's just not something we can prove. It's not even something I can see how we would test to see if it's true."

"I think you've already performed the test. I think that's how Howie disappeared."

I start to speak, but he waves me into listening.

"Ally's told me all about how you've built a full Faraday cage in the basement of Massachusetts Hall. A Faraday cage, as you've explained today in your lecture, creates a shielded environment. It's free from interference from cell towers, Wi-Fi, and other man-made electronic devices. This may be helpful in allowing the natural overlapping space-time structures to be navigated. Howie disappeared during Hallowtide."

"Halloween," I interrupt.

"Yes, that's what it's called today. It used to be called Hallowtide. It starts on October thirty-first and runs through November second. It was appropriated by the Roman Catholic Church for a celebration of martyred saints and renamed All Saints Day about the year 600. Before that, though, it was a season for remembering those who had departed, for family members who had passed on, and especially for those who simply 'went missing.' Here, in Kingsport, for instance, November first is a festival for fishermen who are lost at sea. Today, of course, Halloween has taken it away from its roots with all sorts of ghostly nonsense and paranormal inferences. But, what if it's not paranormal? What if it's just 'normal' that people disappear this time of year?"

"OK," I say, with some forbearance, "but why Howie, and why in Massachusetts Hall?"

"Yes, Massachusetts Hall. This very building. I think you've been given a few references to it, right?"

"You sent over two articles and a couple book references."

"Yes, I did!" says Albert, in an odd, little voice. "And they should have documented at least two disappearances in the basement of the tower room. The book references should have also explained the questionable acquisition of this land from the Miskatonic native tribe, the building of a Satan-worshipping congregational church on this site, and the eventual building of Massachusetts Hall, incorporating the church's Witch Tower."

"The Witch Tower?"

"Oh, sorry...maybe I didn't send you all the articles."

"Or maybe I didn't read my way through enough of the book."

"In any case," he continues, "over the years, many people have disappeared in this building's tower basement. Documented disappearances have generally been during Hallowtide or Solstice. It's happened enough that Puritan people called this structure the Miskatonic Witch Tower. It's not clear if the Satanists built it because of the legends surrounding this piece of land or if the legends began once it became known as the Witch Tower. The term 'witch tower' is common in Europe and to a lesser extent in Puritan New England. It refers to a tower, or tower addition to a building, where witches were known to perform satanic rites. It also refers to towers where witches were confined and in some cases executed. In Puritan times, perhaps as many as forty people, considered witches, vanished from this location.

"Ally also told me about your dream experience," Albert says in a quieter voice. "You and Howie were alone in the Faraday-caged tower basement. What if your 'dream' was a view into that other space? What if Howie had a preview of another dimension in reality and, when it was presented again on Halloween night, decided to go exploring?"

"Let me try to put this together," I say, doubtfully. "You're thinking that every so often, and generally on October thirty-first or thereabouts, the fabric of space-time becomes situated so the tower cellar of Massachusetts Hall is a point of convergence. Two separate points in the universe come together due to immense gravitational folds and, if you choose, you can find yourself in the other place in space-time. You think that dozens of witches have vanished from this so-called witch tower." I pause for effect and look directly into Albert Wilmarth's eyes. "And, somehow, you think Howie celebrated Halloween by choosing to go through this rift in space-time to explore a remote spot in the universe."

Albert nods. "Yes," he says very quietly, "and I think we should try to get him back!"

When I get home from class, I sit on the front porch to think for a minute. I'm frustrated by Albert Wilmarth and his theories. They're really nothing more than folklore pretending to be science. There's no reason to think his ideas have much merit, even as speculative science. Yet, a part of me would like to think that they hold open a possibility of seeing Howie returned.

I go inside to check my e-mail, but I can't get Wilmarth's visit out of my mind. Does he really think we can get Howie back into the Faraday cage on the next alignment of folds in space-time? I start to do a load of laundry but get another idea.

I call Ally and manage to reach her between classes. I ask her if she has time to meet me at the Student Union for lunch. I tell her about her grandfather's visit and explain that I'd like to talk about it. She agrees to lunch and is curious about her grandfather dropping in on my class.

The Student Union is fairly crowded today. Students are in line at the grill, ordering burgers and sandwiches. Others are at tables with books and notes.

Ally's already there, and she waves me over to a booth that she's managed to stake out. She's wearing a heavy winter overshirt, in brown, and leggings. Her brown eyes sparkle from underneath a loose fringe of hair. I take off my coat, and we hug. We take turns holding down the booth and getting food from the grill. We reserve most of our conversation until we're both seated with our lunch. As we begin to eat our sandwiches and share a large pile of French fries, I give a complete rundown of Wilmarth's visit and his theory of Howie's transportation across the galaxy. I try not to add sarcasm to the story, sensitive to the fact that I am speaking about her grandfather. I thought Ally might defend the older Wilmarth out of loyalty. Instead, I get a competing theory!

"Oh, he's partly right, especially about the witch tower concept. I was going to tell you about it. I did a little research on my own. There are dozens of witch towers in Europe, especially in Germany. A fairly famous one is in Wildensteiner Burg and was active in the fourteenth century. We think of Salem as *the* witch trials, but they were common in many places in Europe during the Middle Ages and later. At the site in Wildensteiner Burg, nobody dared enter the tower because it was considered protected by dark magic. Multiple disappearances were reported before and after the tower was built. I think witch towers, and the sites where they're located, represent potential portals into other dimensions. They represent places where the division between dimensions or alternate realities is thin, places where it's easier to break through. Given the right place and a favorable date and time, the gateway opens."

With a quick bite of her sandwich, Ally continues. "Grandfather's right about *our* witch tower and its interdimensional potential. Where we differ is this: I think witches have been using this site and others like it to communicate with unseen forces and to summon beings from beyond."

"I'm speechless, Ally," I say, which I disprove immediately. "This is the twenty-first century, and you're an educated woman. You don't really believe in witches, do you?"

"Oh, completely," she says, and emphasizes it with a fist of French fries. "Don't get me wrong, though. I don't mean pointy hats and broomsticks. We're not talking Harry Potter. Here's what I believe: I believe that some places on the planet are natural vortexes where the separation between this world and other dimensions of reality is thinner. I believe that some people are naturally predisposed to notice and be affected by these locations. Based on your dream, you're probably one of them, Mac."

I start to interrupt, but she clears her throat.

"I also believe there are people who would like to use these special places to gain power in this world by harnessing allies in the other. Although I don't believe in magic, per se, I do believe that people have devised certain rituals to facilitate the communication between this world and creatures from beyond. Such rituals have been documented and—"

"You're talking about the *Necronomicon* again, aren't you?"

"I wish you'd stop calling it that! It's *The Book of Naming the Dead*!" She looks around the room to see if anyone has heard her raise her voice. "In fact, the name is an important part of the rituals described inside. To control someone from beyond, you have to 'name' him. By using his secret name, you can control a demon or whatever the creatures from beyond *really* are. Anyway, I believe the tower in your science building is a true witch tower, that it's a special place where creatures from beyond may be more easily summoned and controlled. I also believe there's clear evidence suggesting that people have used our tower for this purpose at least twice in the last century."

She pauses for more sandwich, then continues. "The first time was in 1935, during Hallowtide. Two students disappeared from the tower. They found tarot cards arranged in a specific way on the floor. The floor, need I mention, is a perfect pentagram. You have noticed that your laboratory is five-sided, right?"

"Yes."

"The use of tarot cards, or other archetypes in visual form, is one of the ways of invoking particular 'demons' as prescribed in *The Book of Naming the Dead*. Once you have the images laid out, you may safely invoke a demon to serve you. Of course, it might be easy to lay the cards out wrong, and the process might not be so safe. The second modern use of the tower was in 1991. A break-in occurred during summer solstice. Satanic writings were found on the walls and floors. What wasn't reported in the newspaper is that the vandals had a copy of *The Book of Naming the Dead* with them. They stole it from the library. Grandfather was on the scene and collected the book before police took any notice of it. I think they were using the location and the book to perform a ritual to unleash powerful demons or creatures from the other realms. Again, they were unsuccessful and most likely paid a high price."

"So these unsuccessful attempts are fatal?" I ask.

"I guess fatal is right. Or maybe the people just get pulled into the other dimension. We could call it 'hell,' I suppose," Ally says, shrugging.

I'm starting to be angry with Ally and her absurd theory. My anger turns to compassion, though, when I realize my friend is completely serious. She really believes this is possible.

"And Howie?" I ask. "How does Howie fit into all this? Howie doesn't have a copy of *The Book of Naming the Dead*. Howie isn't a witch, and he certainly doesn't have a pack of tarot cards lying around." I'm trying my best to follow Ally's reasoning but can't quite manage it.

"Let's not be patronizing," she says. "*The Book of Naming the Dead* says that the summoning of spirits works both ways. After all, they're spirits or demons in our world. Who knows what we represent to them in theirs? Anyway, the book says that if they know our true name, our secret name, they can summon *us*. We can be drawn into *their* world."

"How would demons know Howie's secret name, Ally?" I ask. "I don't even know his secret name, and I'm not a big blabbermouth where demons from another galaxy are concerned."

"Oh, but you *do* know Howie's secret name. He told it to you. Remember his trick where you ask him his name and he tells you? That really is how it happened, isn't it? When he first came to live with you, you playfully asked him his name, and he told you, Hoooooowwieeeeeeee!"

She imitates Howie and his naming trick poorly, but I remember the morning in the cemetery when we showed it to her.

"Did you use his name in your dream? When you fell asleep in the pentagram in the basement of the Witch Tower? Did you call Howie by name?"

Brian is coming over for dinner. He surprises me by wanting to spend some time in the lab at Massachusetts Hall. He says he has an idea and wants to "return to the scene of the crime" in the Witch Tower.

We meet on the steps of Massachusetts Hall. Evening classes are still going on, so the main doors are unlocked. We make our way down to the basement. Both our smartphones get a notification from the camera in the basement hall: the security system is busy at work. I unlock the door to the lab, and we enter. As usual, it's empty: no Howie.

Brian begins his explanation. "I guess I'm more used to detective stories than ghost stories. While I was growing up, my parents' favorite TV shows were *Monk* and *The Closer*. I was raised on cheap mystery novels and had read all of Agatha Christie's mysteries by the time I was fourteen. I figure we can make some progress if we treat this as a mystery to solve. We're back where Howie disappeared, and I feel like we should play detective and create a murder board."

I help Brian clear space on the lab table.

"I suppose," says Brian, "in this case it would be a kidnapping board." He looks at the cleared table and pulls some prepared index cards out of his coat pocket. "First, I created an index card for each of the suspects. I'll put them across the top of the table. Underneath each one we need to list their means, motive, and opportunity."

"We don't have any suspects," I start to complain, but Brian silences me with an index finger.

Brian continues, "Campus Security Chief Taggert thinks one of your students is likely to have broken into your apartment and left the weird note that first day of school. That same person may have followed up by kidnapping Howie."

Brian flips over the first card. He has labeled it "Student X."

"For means, we can put 'dog door' for entering your apartment, but I'm stumped on how a student would get into the locked lab at Massachusetts Hall. I didn't put anything down for motive, because you said no students have a grudge against you."

"That's true," I say. I mentally review the students I've given failing grades, but there aren't many, and I've worked with all of them on study plans or placement in other disciplines. I don't think any of them blame me for their academic performance.

"For opportunity, I put 'while we were bowling,' but it doesn't really cover how a student could use this opportunity without knowing, ahead of time, about the new security system."

Brian gets out another index card and says, "Because of the campus lock on the lab door, we should put another index card next to Student X." Brian flips over the second card. "This one I've titled 'Campus Security X.' For means, I have 'dog door' for entering your apartment and 'master key' for entering the lab. A campus master key might also open your apartment door. For opportunity, I also put 'while we were bowling.' This seems like a more likely fit, too, because campus security knew about our plans for the new lock and would be better trained to spot things like a camera."

I see that Brian has the motive blank again. What possible motive could someone in campus security have for stealing my dog or leaving me threatening notes? Security Chief Taggert? Officer Blake? But why? My head swirls with other ideas. Could Dr. Alvarez have some jealously about me displacing him by bringing fresh ideas to the Physics

Department? Could Emma Brown secretly hate me for not cleaning up Howie's poo quickly enough? Could George Marsh want Grant Hall to himself and be willing to try to scare me away?

All these ideas seem silly.

"Then," says Brian, "I began to wonder if we've been too hasty with the information that Ally and her grandfather gave us. Not about Howie's disappearance being supernatural, of course, but maybe about a distinct motive. If people really have broken in to what they perceive as a 'witch tower' before, could access to said tower be a motive? Could someone we don't even know want to access the tower to perform some kind of satanic ritual?"

Brian flips over the third index card. It is labeled "Satanist X."

"If someone wants to use the Witch Tower for Satanic purposes, they *would* have a motive," explains Brian. You can see he's given a lot of thought to his kidnapping board. I'm beginning to think his methodology might have its merits.

Satanist X finally is a card with a motive on it: "to access the Witch Tower." Their opportunity is, "while we were bowling," but this seems a little iffy, since a stranger would hardly know about the camera or other security measures. Their means for entry is blank.

"So, this time we *have* a motive. Not much for means or opportunity, though," I say.

"Agreed," says Brian, nodding. "Next, I decided to examine the forensic evidence." With each piece of evidence, he places another card on the table:

1. A Dog Sweater and Collar. "Howie's sweater and collar were clearly removed by a person. On a cold night in October, Howie would never have taken his sweater off. Dr. Wilmarth thinks that traveling between dimensions may only allow organic material to pass from one realm to another. Howie's sweater and collar were just 'left behind' when he chose to go into the other realm."

Yeah, right, I think.

2. Keys. "You called Dr. Alvarez, and he has his key. You have your key. Other than campus security, nobody else should be able to get into the lab. How many people at security have access to the keys? Could someone else have access to a 'master' key? Do you fully trust Dr. Alvarez?"

3. Eaten Dog Food. "Howie was clearly in the lab long enough to have gotten hungry and eaten some food."

4. Camera Footage. "By the actions of the person wearing the

Scream mask, they knew about the camera. They had either already seen it or assumed there would be one and was looking for it. Was the person on video definitely a man, or could it have been a woman? Either, I think. Because the camera was also streaming live, we know what time the break-in occurred: 11:45 p.m. That fits in with Howie's eaten meal. He had been in the lab for some time."

5. The Note. "The note under your pillow on the first day of school seems to indicate that someone has something against you. Was it really from a student who returned to school that day? If so, what's the motive? If not a student, who else?"

Although pleased with himself and his index cards, I can see that Brian has run out of steam.

"I'm sure we'll find that one of these is the kidnapper," he says, indicating the suspect cards. "We just need to make a list of people who fit into these categories and see if they have alibis. Eventually, we'll be able to put a real name on one of them."

"Brian, you're amazing. I can't believe you did all this work to help find Howie. But, before we round up suspects, let's round up some dinner. I'm starving." I give Brian a big hug. He wants so badly to solve this mystery, to bring Howie back to me.

His methodical approach to the crime is interesting. He's given me some new ideas for both suspects and possible motives that I had not thought of. Brian is quite as smart as I am. I realize how lucky I am to have him in my life.

We tidy up the lab before we leave. I know it's silly, but both Ally and her grandfather say I should leave the lab as close to the configuration that it was in when Howie disappeared. They think that during the next "convergence" or "time of overlap" there will be an opportunity for Howie to be returned (or he can choose to come back).

The lab looks just like it did on Halloween night. I'm feeling a little foolish thinking that somehow this lab might magically return my dog on solstice or Holyrood Day or the night of some auspicious lunar eclipse.

But I'm not without hope or ideas.

We lock up the lab in the basement of Massachusetts Hall and begin the short walk home.

It's mid-November, and the sun is setting as Brian and I cross the campus Green, holding hands. The sky is a dark gray with even darker layers of clouds. The forecast has been for snow, but so far we've only had cold and mostly overcast weather. The wind is even and strong tonight, blowing my icy breath away in an instant. The darkening sky barely lights my way, and I'm glad the streetlights have already come on.

As we approach Grant Hall, I see that nobody is home. George Marsh has been spending most nights in Innsmouth with his family. Sam Rouse has already finished her term and headed out of town for a long Thanksgiving vacation. Dr. Simmons's apartment on the top floor is dark, but that's not surprising: he prefers teaching night classes.

I'm momentarily startled by the porch lights coming on as we walk up the steps, but it's just they're set on a timer. As we stand on the porch and look out for a moment in the dim light, I see the first flakes of snow for the season start to swirl down.

I've made a simple dinner for us. I have store-bought lasagna, which is now being heated in my toaster oven. I discovered that a Caesar salad can come in a kit, and when the lasagna is ready, I toss the salad.

"This is pretty good," says Brian. He's sweet to say that. I could blame the lack of home cooking on my kitchen, but that would be stretching the truth. He knows I'm not much of a cook.

As dinner continues, so does the snow outside. Brian decides to make it an early night and head back to Arkham before he gets snowed in.

I hate advice. It's given so freely by people who can't possibly know what you're going through. Wilmarth's off calculating the next alignment of the realms so he can predict Howie's potential return to the Witch Tower.

Ally thinks I should spend more time building up my occult "powers" so I can find Howie using witchcraft.

Brian has a more conventional plan for catching a real-world villain using the kidnapping board and techniques from classic TV.

Now that Brian's gone home for the evening, it's time I check out an idea of my own. With something from Three Rivers Hardware and Lumber, I'm going to try and get Howie back myself. *Well, almost by myself.*

I've set a trap, you see. A literal trap.

I put on my boots and winter coat and pick up my backpack and I head out into the snow. There's not much of a moon, but it's plenty to light up the white-blanketed landscape. Everything is silver, midnight blue, and cold calculation.

I make my way up the path from Grant Hall to the Green. The snow is light and powdery, and it packs down under my feet, making small scrunch noises with each footfall. The sidewalk around the Green is almost invisible, and I find myself walking more by memory than visual guidance.

At the head of the Green looms University Hall. Its dusting of snow renders it even more stark than usual. It's a black-and-white silhouette in the moonlight. The few trees around it are casting strange shadows. I walk to the side of the main entrance to see if my plan has worked. There, under the branches of a rhododendron and next to a certain window casing, is where I set my trap.

Last week I asked Brian to bring me a live-capture rodent trap. I told him we'd found mouse droppings in the basement of Grant Hall. A little fib. I didn't want to tell him my real plan. I've not told him about Brown Jenkin; not as a dream and certainly not as a real creature possessing occult powers. I'm still not sure myself what I believe about Brown Jenkin.

Creeping under the rhododendron, I see that at least the first part of my plan has succeeded. The trap has been sprung. I've been checking twice a day since I set the trap: once in the morning and once before bed. Finally, tonight, I've caught something.

I pick up the cage and peer inside. In addition to the bait, I also put some rags and straw in the trap. After all, I want to capture the rat, not freeze him.

Artfully wrapped up in the bedding is a small figure. Two angry eyes peer out at me.

I take the cage in hand and pick my way carefully over to Massachusetts Hall. If we're going to transverse the realms, I think it's more likely to be successful in the Witch Tower.

I stamp my feet to release some snow and use my keys to let me into Massachusetts Hall, down to the basement, and into the tower room. I put on the lights and a portable heater. While things are warming up, I set up the room as best as I can remember to match the night that Howie and I had our dream together. If Ally is right, it was no dream. Howie and I were "transversing" that night.

Then I get the supplies out of my backpack:
- My dream journal
- Rodent food
- A small bottle of scotch and a tumbler

I put the cage on the top of the lab table in the middle of the room and open the door.

"You can come out, Brownie," I say, remembering his invitation to call him that. "I have some food for you, and I'd like to talk."

No response.

"I won't hurt you, and I promise to let you go. The door's locked now, but I'll open it and take you home after we've chatted. I give you my word."

Eventually, a slim leg and forepaw is extended out of the bedding. One slim finger points to the bottle of scotch.

"Do I have to be a bit drunk, then?" I ask.

Brown Jenkin's snout extends so I can see that he's nodding.

"Does that make it easier to talk?"

He nods again.

I pour a shot of scotch in the tumbler and down it in one gulp. It warms me up almost immediately, and I pour another shot to drink more slowly. I also put some of the rodent kibble into the cage, since Brown Jenkin seems reluctant to emerge.

He looks at the kibble and shakes his head in annoyance.

I finish the second shot, pour a third for sipping, and settle in my chair. I suspect I need to be tipsy for this to work. I also have to trust that Brown Jenkin will cooperate.

It's been a long day, and the combination of tiredness and alcohol is having its effect. I feel drowsy and a little muddle-headed. I look over at the cage and see that Brown Jenkin still has his paw extended. He's making little circular motions with it, little figure eights. I watch as his hand goes left to right, up and down. He's tracing the symbol for infinity in the air before him. Left to right, up and down.

He points a finger back to my scotch, and I take another sip. He makes more circles in the air. His hand is slowing down now, and I realize that it really *is* a hand. I can easily see his fingers. It reminds me of a baby's hand. Perfect little fingers.

The effects of the alcohol, and perhaps something else, are beginning to settle in. The outside world is the slightest bit fuzzy. I'm feeling oddly happy.

Suddenly, as though I've turned to a different channel on the radio, I can hear Brown Jenkin speaking to me.

"...able to hear me? Try closing your eyes if you can't hear clearly."

But I can hear clearly.

"I hear you."

"Right, then, exactly what do you want from me that requires a kidnapping?"

The rat is now emerging from his wrappings in the cage. As in my first encounter with him last spring, he walks with a strange movement. Half scurrying like a rat, half walking like a small human, he approaches the bars of the cage. With each step, his fur gets sleeker, his head rounder, more human-shaped. As he grasps the bars of the cage, his front legs are now arms, and he stands like a perfectly upright cartoon mouse. To complete the picture, a green vest pops into view. Against my mood of quiet determination, I can't help but smile at this affectation. Brown Jenkin is quite the dandy.

Trying to figure out the reality of what's happening, I ask, "How do you appear so human to me right now? And how are we 'talking'? You're not really using your mouth to speak, are you?"

Brown Jenkin shrugs. "It's called the Glamour. I learnt it from a sea hag in Exmoor. You don't think mermaids are actually beautiful, do you? All that time underwater! Oi! They developed the Glamour to lure the fisherfolk. It's an old skill what can be learnt from person to person. The drink helps, too. It blurs the outside so the Glamour can shine through better."

"And how are we talking?"

"I don't know the how of it. You're the scientist—you figure it. The more we talk, the easier it is, though. Come a time we'll talk when we're not even in the same room. A bit of blood helps, too. With practice, you'll not need the drink."

"You're a witch's 'familiar,' then?" I ask, seeking confirmation.

"Didn't you know that last spring at your interview?"

"Ostara," I say, thinking back to the cocktail party and some of the odd events of the evening.

"Ay, the full moon made it easier to talk. The power of the goddess was strong that night!"

"You belong to the chancellor, Dr. Mason?"

"I'm not a pet. Tom and me belong each to the other," Brown Jenkin says, with his hands on his hips and a certain air of impatience. "So, again, what is it you want from me?"

"When we talked before, you said you'd taught Mother Mason to fly."

"That was a story."

"But you don't fib. I remember you said that, and I think it's true. It was part of a story, but it's a true story, isn't it? You taught the chancellor's ancestor to fly, didn't you?"

Brown Jenkin pauses, then nods.

"I want you to teach me to fly. With your help, I want to fly and find Howie."

"So, this is about that *animal* of yours," says Brown Jenkin, his lips curling. "He means that much?"

"Does Chancellor Mason mean much to you?"

Brown Jenkin considers this and nods again. "But I don't think much of your plan," he says. "Flying is taught once a bond is made. It's not a thing to be taught in a night or with a stranger." He thinks for another moment. "But if you promise to let me go, we could fly *together* tonight. Finding your cur is possible. Especially if you're bound to it."

"We're bound," I say, without hesitation. I *am* bound to Howie and I'm beginning to see that he's always been more than a pet. We've shared our lives together and, perhaps, something deeper.

"Let me out of this cage, and we'll see what can be seen."

"You won't get out of this room if you hurt me, you know."

"There's no reason for hurting more than a little prick."

I reach across the table and unfasten the cage, leaving the release door open. Brown Jenkin crawls/steps out of the cage and approaches me.

"Where do you think the cur has gone?" asks Brown Jenkin.

"His name is Howie," I say. "He left from here, from this room, but I don't know where he's gone. Ally says he used Halloween to go visit other realms."

Brown Jenkin takes this in and says, "The timing is right. Hallowtide is meant for flying. But you say his body left too? That's not a way for beginners. You start with your soul doing the work. Not many witches can fly their whole selves away. Tonight, it's just our souls that fly. You see that, don't you?"

"I don't know anything about this stuff."

"Tonight, if we find Howie, you'll talk to him, locate him, even. But if he's to return to this place," Brown Jenkin waves to indicate the room, "it will happen outside of flying. I can't drag him back with us."

I nod.

"Then be quiet now. Flying is done relaxed."

"Meditation?" I ask.

"Contemplation," says Brown Jenkin. "We start by thinking of the dog and some of the good times you've had. Then I'll see if I can get us to fly."

Brown Jenkin has been moving closer to my chair and points to one of my hands resting on the lab table. "A prick," he says. "A small bite. Just close your eyes, and I'll take care of it."

My eyes are closed. I feel an odd crunch and a sharp sting on the pad of my thumb. I know he's bitten me to draw blood. I don't want to see Brown Jenkin with my blood on his lips. I try not to think of it. Instead, I try to think of Howie. As if Brown Jenkin can read my mind, he says, "That's it. The dog. Picture the dog running."

And suddenly, we are! Howie's running up ahead of me, darting in and out as the waves wash gently ashore. We're in Santa Monica, he's racing after a seagull, and I'm laughing at his antics. But I'm also not really there. I have no sense of my body. At a dog's-eye view, I'm following alongside as he runs. *Of course! I'm flying!*

I feel Brown Jenkin's presence flying next to us.

"Is Howie back in Santa Monica?"

"No, we're flying through a memory," he says, "but it's good practice for what's to come. Now put yourself atop this building. Think you're sitting on the roof and looking out at the Green."

At first nothing happens. I feel a little disorientated when I think of the rooftop of Massachusetts Hall. I can picture its high gables and ornamental ironwork, but that's about it.

"Don't picture the roof from the ground looking *up*," Brown Jenkin says, as though it's obvious. "Picture being on the roof looking *down*."

Giddily, the scene changes. I'm at the edge of the tower roof looking out across the campus. The light snow is still coming down. From my vantage point the Green is all black and white. The partial moon hangs above us, creating the contrast of snow, buildings, trees, and shadow. The stark, cold beauty of the scene makes me think of shivering, but I realize I'm still without a body. I'm not cold. I'm also not sitting on the roof's gable. I'm just a point of view existing above it. It feels like I'm floating above the highest point of the tower.

"Easy now. You can't fall," says Brown Jenkin. He can tell the perspective is unnerving me. "You're safe in the lab. It's your soul what's flying. Let's practice with someplace we can see. What about the library? See the clock? You can…"

A sense of being pulled through the air assaults my senses, and I find myself next to the clock atop the Salomon Center. *Wow. That's flying!* I'm looking out over the Green again, this time looking back at Massachusetts Hall. *Is this really happening? Is my "soul" really flying high above the campus?*

A moment later and I can feel Brown Jenkin next to me, just like when we were flying next to Howie in my memory of Santa Monica.

"Lad, you don't need teaching! You did that by yourself!" Brown Jenkin is clearly surprised by my solo flight. "Were you not fearful you'd fall?"

"Is that a possibility? Our 'soul' can't fall, can it?"

"No. But our senses trick us into thinking we might fall. You didn't feel like you'd jumped off a cliff?"

"Maybe a bit. It didn't seem too bad. But what about Howie? How do we find someone who's hidden from us?"

"That requires building a picture of Howie in your mind until you feel the pull. For it to work, you have to feel pulled to Howie. Then we'll fly."

I Ignore the view from the top of the library and begin to think of Howie, imagining him in my mind's eye.

"Remember what he looks like. Think about how he moves. Feel the feelings you have for him. Once you feel for him, you'll get the pull."

I try this for a while, but I do not have the sense of being pulled that I felt when I flew across the campus Green.

"Feel your connection," Brown Jenkin commands.

I don't feel a pull, but I do gradually begin to have a sense of Howie before me. It's like I'm looking into an old photo. His head is cocked to one side, as though he's listening for something. He does a quick pirouette. The rest of the scene is blurred out. I know that I'm still atop the Salomon Center, but I also have a sense of Howie in front of me.

"Is it you, Howie?" I ask. Howie seems straining to hear. The more I focus on Howie, the clearer things are. When I look around me or Howie, everything is in soft, blurry pastels. It's like a watercolor where the details have been washed away.

"Do you not feel the pull?" asks Brown Jenkin.

"No, but I can see Howie, sort of. It's like a translucent image of him, hanging out before me."

"It's the far-sight. You've got the far-sight." Brown Jenkin sounds thoughtful. "You're seeing pictures of Howie, then. Can you see the room he's in? Maybe sideways, like?"

I have a sense of what Brown Jenkin is getting at. If I stare intently at Howie, my peripheral vision gets a sense of his surroundings. When I look at them directly, though, they disappear. I try to look a bit "sideways," and I get the impression of a cellar or stone room. He might be in a basement. The word *castle* comes to mind. Stone blocks. Cement or stone floor. An odd chair in some black material. I can just make out a ball at Howie's feet. A toy?

"Can we get closer?"

"That's the devil of it," says Brown Jenkin. "We're not flying. This is your own doing. Instead of flying, you're seeing pictures with the far-sight. We're right where we are."

The rat seems confused, and I guess a part of me is, too. I had thought we'd bring Howie home or at least find out where he is.

But another part of me is feeling something completely different: hope.

Howie is alive!

CHAPTER TEN

Thanksgiving

Today is Thanksgiving, but I'm not feeling it. When I was a kid, Thanksgiving was my favorite holiday. Mom would start cooking early, and the house would be filled with wonderful smells by the time I got up. She would be up baking bread or cinnamon rolls, getting ready for a day of food, family, and friends.

We had numerous aunts, uncles, and others join us on Thanksgiving, so that our usually quiet house was full of people. Some would come early and stay all day. Others would come for the meal but stay to play cards or watch TV.

There's no trace of Thanksgiving smells or family in my little apartment in Grant Hall. I make myself some coffee and have a leftover doughnut. Peeking outside, I see that a light snow is falling. We've had snow off and on for the last week, so I'm not surprised.

With Brown Jenkin's help, I've tried twice to locate Howie. We can't fly to him, but I can usually see him and a bit of his surroundings. Some kind of stone room. Brown Jenkin can't tell if Howie has transversed into some other dimension or is just living down the street. More than once it seemed like Howie knew I was sensing him or that I was near. It has been frustrating, but I continue to take hope from these glimpses.

I have not mentioned my "flights" with Brown Jenkin or my "far-sight" glimpses of Howie to anyone. I'm still not sure what to make of

them or what Brian or Ally would say about my use of the chancellor's
rat. I think they would believe me, but I'm not sure I'm ready to admit,
myself, what's happened.

Later today, I'll go over to Brian's house. He's invited me to stay the
weekend. Tonight, he's also invited Ally and her grandfather to join us
for Thanksgiving dinner. Brian loves to cook, so with any luck I'll get
to eat some of my favorite holiday food. He quizzed me earlier in the
week about my favorites: candied yams, pumpkin pie, cranberry sauce,
and garlic mashed potatoes. In addition to the no-meat dishes for me,
he'll make a turkey for everyone else.

For now, though, I'm in a bit of a funk. I look at a photo of Howie
taken one fine spring morning on the beach in California. I'm missing
Howie with a profound heaviness.

I decide to call my Mom and wish her a happy Thanksgiving. I reach
her at my Aunt Susan's house. "Hi, honey," she says. "Since you're not
coming home for Thanksgiving, I hope I can count on you for Christmas." I haven't figured that out yet, so I don't say anything. After a
pause, she asks, "Are you getting a nice dinner today?"

"Yes, Mom. I'm going to a friend's house later in the day. There will
be four of us and plenty of food."

"Is Brian cooking?" she asks.

My mother is amazing. In less than a month after Brian and I
started dating, she had things figured out. Turns out, she thought I
might be gay or bisexual. She's fine with the idea of me dating a man!

"Yes, he's making a turkey with all the trimmings and even some of
my favorite side dishes."

"You mean, you're eating turkey again?" she probes. My mother has
always been skeptical of my vegetarian lifestyle. She always thinks I'm
too skinny and figures my vegetarian diet is the reason.

"No, I'm still vegetarian. He's making turkey for everyone else."

"Should I send him the recipe for the roasted potatoes you like so
much?"

"I'm sure Brian knows how to roast potatoes. He's a great cook." We
continue in this vein for some time. We both like food, and talking
about it is comfortable for us. If we stick to food (or, more recently,
Brian), she's all smiles.

"Have you thought about coming back to California?" she asks.

"No. This is where I live now. I have a job, and I'm paying off my
student loans. I have friends now and a boyfriend. In the spring, I'll be
part of a bowling league. I'm not coming back to California. I like it
here."

"Well, you might like Brian, but I can't see you staying at Miskatonic. It's hardly a real university anymore. I've been reading about it. It used to be quite the East Coast showplace. Now it's just a relic."

"I do like it, though. Even with Howie gone, it feels good to be here. I like teaching and my classes. I enjoy my friends. It really is better for me here. I'm feeling useful and cared for."

"You were cared for here, too, honey," she says. "You had a good life in California."

"That's not what I mean, Mom," I say. "I'm creating my *own* life here. It feels like I belong at Miskatonic."

She sighs, then asks about Howie. I haven't told her about Brown Jenkin or trying to find him. She already thinks there's something wrong with Miskatonic.

"He hasn't turned up, then?" she asks.

"I'm not sure he will. It's been almost a month."

"Have you checked the humane society?"

"Yes, Mom, every week."

"Have you been checking the lab?" she asks. Ever since I told her Ally's theory of the Witch Tower and Howie's disappearance, Mom has been stuck on the idea that Howie will be returned. "He's bound to come back during the next convergence of planets."

"Have you been using your tarot cards again?"

"Don't be smart with me, young man," she quips. "When he comes back, you'll just be grateful to have him. You won't care where he's been or how he got back."

She's right about that. I am missing Howie. I would do just about anything to get him back. I promise to check the lab on my way to Brian's house. I promise to give Brian her regards when I see him. I tell her how much I love her and ask for her to say hello to my California relatives.

Next I decide to go for a walk and check Massachusetts Hall.

Walking is my daily exercise. For my own peace of mind, I generally include a walk by Massachusetts Hall and the Witch Tower. My mom and Ally think Howie may supernaturally be returned there. Brian thinks that since that's where he "got loose somehow," that's where someone might return him. I'm not sure what I think, but Massachusetts Hall is the one place, other than our apartment, where he spent most of his time. He knows it and might return to it.

There are two inches of snow on the ground. Because of the wind and cold, the snow is a light powder and tends to swirl around. I'm bundled up more than usual to keep out the cold. I'm thinking of going on a nice long walk before I go over to Brian's in the early afternoon.

The campus is eerily quiet. With so many of the students off campus for Thanksgiving, there's virtually no movement beyond the falling snow. The day seems like a movie filmed in black and white. The snow makes such a contrast to the dark buildings and evergreen trees on campus.

I decide to make the loop around the Green before checking out Massachusetts Hall. As I walk by Condon Hall, I see Matthew Brown going inside from the porch. The door clicks shut before I can wish him a happy Thanksgiving. He seems distant lately. I can't recall having seen him around as much as usual.

Most of the buildings around the central Green are shut down. The buildings will be locked throughout the long Thanksgiving weekend. The holdout is the Salomon Center Library. It's on shorter hours but remains open for those few graduate students still needing access to materials or study space.

In fact, the library seems oddly busy. The small handicapped-only parking lot is full of the little campus security Priuses. Two police cars from Arkham and an emergency response vehicle are also there. I wonder what's going on. As I walk by, I notice Security Chief Justin Taggert on the steps and wave.

"Chief Taggert," I say, catching his attention. Do I notice a scowl? Or is it just a sign of recognition? "What's going on?" I ask.

"Break-in at the library," says Taggert.

"What's happened?"

"I think I'll leave that to the library folks, if they want to talk about it," says Taggert, in his most unhelpful way. Then his face softens a bit, and he says, "I noticed you put 'missing dog' posters of Howie around town."

"Yes," I say. "I'm hopeful that whoever he's with will realize that he belongs to somebody. Without his sweater and collar, someone might have just thought he was a stray."

"It is odd that we haven't found any evidence of him by now. I'm really surprised he wasn't taken to the humane society. I looked up his breed, and it's not a common one. It's hard to think that if someone found him they wouldn't either want a reward for finding him or at least know that he's not a stray."

I'm surprised Taggert went to the trouble of reading about Italian greyhounds. He's right: they aren't very common in the chilly Northeast.

"Thank you for asking, Chief," I say, and he nods.

I descend the few steps back to the sidewalk that goes around the Green. I continue my walk, but before I've gone far, I hear the double doors on this side of Salomon Center bang open. Two paramedics are wheeling a stretcher out the door. Chief Taggert helps them carry it, with some difficulty, down the side steps and into the handicapped parking lot. A third EMT opens the emergency vehicle and helps them load the stretcher. I hear some dispatch chatter coming from the vehicle as the paramedics get in, but I can't understand what's being said. I've turned around in time to get a glimpse into the back window of the emergency vehicle, and I dimly see them holding an IV bag aloft. I assume the patient is about to begin receiving fluids of some sort.

Now the emergency vehicle is in motion, creeping over the snow in the parking lot and edging its way to the outer ring of the campus buildings and the roadway that connects to the main entrance of the campus.

I continue my walk, completing the ring of buildings around the central Green, and hear a siren start up, leaving the campus on the road to Arkham. It's a little more than just a break-in, I think.

But now I've made my way to Massachusetts Hall. It's locked and dark for the long weekend. I go to the small side door and use my key to gain entry. I cross the darkened lobby to the stairway and head down to the basement. Finding the light is hard, and I almost stumble at the top of the stairs. I descend and turn on the set of lights along the basement hall. I notice the camera in the hall, and almost immediately my phone starts vibrating. The motion detectors are working as they should, alerting me to the presence of someone in the building. In this case, it's me. I smile. Technology often makes me smile. A hundred years ago, it would have been magic. Today, we take so much for granted.

Using my key to unlock the laboratory door, I enter the Witch Tower. It, too, is gloomy and dark. As I reach for the light switch something brushes against my leg. I jump back. Do I hear a rustling? In the shadows, I see the hint of something crouching under the central lab table.

Suddenly, it rushes forward. In the gloom I see it gather momentum and bound off the floor, headed for my chest. Just as I am about to strike out at whatever is attacking, I realize: *it's Howie!*

❖

I couldn't be happier or more surprised. It looks like Howie is just as happy as I am. He's jumping up and down. He also makes it clear that he needs to go to the bathroom. We take a walk upstairs and outside. He pees, but it's too cold for his bony little body, so we almost immediately go back in. He's still jumping up on me, glad to see me, and wanting to be held. I get down on my hands and knees and stroke his glossy short hair. Wherever he's been, he seems well fed and looked after. We spend a few minutes in the entryway of Massachusetts Hall just enjoying each other's company. This is the happiest day I can remember.

I text Brian and Ally with the good news, then head upstairs to my office. I want to check out a mystery. Howie and I navigate the hall and stairs (Howie doesn't care for elevators) finding light switches and using my keys to get up to my second-floor office. The office is locked, as I would expect. I open the door and turn on the lights, and everything looks fine. Desk, chair, bookcase—everything seems the way I left it. Nothing looks moved or disturbed.

Now I use my computer to connect to the security video server that's supposed to be monitoring the basement hallway. It says that it's operating in "standard mode." It does not show that anyone activated the camera this morning other than me. I see a video of myself opening the lab and discovering Howie. I clearly see myself jump back when Howie brushes my leg.

I look back through the logs and see that very few people have been in the lab or its hallway in the last week. I'm there every morning. A maintenance person swept the hall floor on Monday. Someone went into the storage room late Tuesday afternoon. There's nothing in the logs between me checking the lab Wednesday morning and me discovering Howie today on Thursday morning. I check my cell phone for any of the alerts that would indicate the motion sensor in the lab hall had been activated today. There's only the one that I triggered myself. I check the live feed for the camera. I see the lab doorway just as I left it a few minutes ago. The lights are on, and the door is ajar. The camera seems to be working perfectly.

I look down at my little friend. "How did you get back into the lab, Howie?" I ask.

Howie cocks his head and rubs against me. His eyes are bright and inquiring. He jumps into my lap, and I hold him as my mind goes over possibilities.

Something occurs to me. I simply unplug the video server from the wall. I wait a minute and plug it back in. The server reboots and begins scanning the network for video feeds. It restarts the scheduling and alert software just fine. It's now back in standard mode again. It's waiting for the motion sensor in the downstairs hall to start a video recording.

But what if it was unplugged when someone went into the downstairs hall?

My mind is reeling. What are the chances that someone would have the knowledge, keys, access, and technical know-how to sneak Howie back into the lab unnoticed and without a video trail? Am I stuck with the reality of Howie being gone a month in some unearthly realm? Has my sweet dog been dimension-hopping? Brown Jenkin wasn't sure. I'm clueless.

My phone rings, and I pick up the call from Brian.

"Is it true? Is Howie really back?"

"Yes, it's true, but it's a complete mystery. It's like one of those sealed-room murder mysteries you enjoy so much. I honestly have no idea how he was returned to the lab."

"You mean, the camera—"

"Exactly. I'm upstairs in my office now, and there are no video entries on the server for today except my own. There's no indication that anyone else activated the camera. My phone doesn't show any activity either, and no video was saved until my motions activated the camera when I got here."

There's silence on the line for an extended moment as Brian is thinking.

"But he's OK, right?"

"Yes. He appears to be just fine. Well fed, anyway. He's minus a sweater or any identification—just the way he was when he was spirited out of the lab almost a month ago."

"Spirited. Hmmm," says Brian. He pauses for another extended silence, then asks, "Do you *really* think he's spent a month in some otherworldly dimension?"

"I don't know what to think. I do have a question for you, though. Could someone with the proper keys and knowledge turn off the video server in my office? Could they then go downstairs, open the lab, put Howie back in, lock the lab again, go upstairs, and restart the video server in my office? Could all this be done if you have the right keys and access codes?"

Brian thinks, then answers, "Yes, that's possible. Someone with that level of physical access and technical knowledge could possibly even find an easier solution. If they brought down the wireless network for a few minutes, it might have the same effect. Without the network, the camera would not be able to connect to the server. Even if the motion detector activated the camera, there would be no video saved, no log entries on the server, and no alerts sent to your smartphone. The camera would have been running but without a network, so no way to save the video. This might be possible by cutting power to the Wi-Fi router or unplugging it for the necessary timeframe."

"I would not have thought of that. Is it likely that a student or faculty member or even a campus officer would know how to utilize this flaw in our security plan?"

"No. I don't think it's likely at all. Perhaps only you and I would have thought of a way of sneaking Howie into the lab without a video trail."

"Did *you* put Howie back in the lab, my sweet boyfriend?" I ask, playfully and seriously at the same time.

"*Boyfriend.* I think that's the first time you've used that word." Brian pauses, then answers the question. "I did *not* put Howie back in the lab. I've been cooking all morning. Did *you* put Howie back in the lab?"

"No," I say. "I did not."

I'm putting Howie into his sweater and getting ready for the drive into Arkham for Thanksgiving. It's been snowing off and on throughout the morning, so I'm putting him into a thicker blue sweater. He's a very happy boy back in our apartment with his familiar toys and food. I idly wonder if you need to eat where he's been.

I pack overnight things for both of us. Brian's invited Howie and I to spend four days at his place. I'm bringing some DVDs to watch and a book I've wanted to read. Brian says he has games we can play and plenty of food for the long weekend. I pack dog food and an extra coat for Howie and start taking things out to the car. I also pack a folder containing all my notes about "the case of the stolen/missing/returned dog." I'd like to talk over some of Brian's ideas with the Thanksgiving dinner guests.

Howie doesn't like the idea of being left alone. I can scarcely blame him. He's underfoot as I make a few trips out to the car. I can tell he doesn't want me to get out of his sight.

The snow has accumulated to a depth of several inches. The electric car seems to do fine in the snow, but I'm also driving slowly in case I hit a patch of ice. Howie is sitting on the heated seat next to me looking out the window. The black-and-white theme from earlier in the morning persists. Leafless trees with snow-covered branches are white against a dark gray sky. The road has not been well traveled today. I find it hard to pick out the road as it winds around the low hills that create the twists and turns of the Miskatonic River. Although approaching midday, it's a dark day. I turn the headlights on, but it's hard to tell if they make much difference.

Arkham is practically shut down for the day. The QuikMart is open, but the rest of the businesses are closed until Friday or, in some cases, Monday morning. The way to Brian's house skirts the main part of Arkham, so I turn off Church Street and head northeast.

Brian's house looks lovely in the snow. With the leaves now gone, it's easier to see the river winding through this area. With snow on the roof and tree branches, it looks like a winter scene from a picture book. Brian's shoveled his front walk of snow, and a wisp of smoke in the chimney indicates that he must have a fire in his wood-burning stove.

After parking, I let Howie out of the car. He picks his way across the snow. Brian must have heard us pull up; he opens the door and greets me warmly with a kiss. Today he's dressed in a striped polo shirt and jeans. His ginger-colored hair is getting long and untidy. He bends down to look at Howie. "How's it going, Howie?" he says. "Are you OK?"

Howie wags his tail.

"I have a surprise for you," Brian says, smiling at me. "Since you were here last, I've made a home improvement just for you." He takes me over to the side of the house closest to the driveway area and indicates a new electrical outlet. I look quizzically. "It's for the car," he explains. "You can charge your car."

For some reason, this seems like the most romantic of things to me. Imagine someone caring enough to install an electrical outlet just for my car. "You can plug in whenever you want." We plug the car in.

Brian's house is warm and smells delightful. His kitchen counters are so crammed with appliances, utensils, and food that I wonder how long he's been cooking.

"I've been cooking all morning," he says, reading my mind. "You know how much I enjoy entertaining! I think I've managed to cook most of your favorites."

I put one of Howie's plush beds in the corner by Brian's wood stove.

Howie should be comfortable there with the warmth of the fire. He's more interested in exploring now, of course. And making sure I'm not out of his sight.

For the Thanksgiving party today, Brian's moved the furniture around in his small home. His dining table doubles as kitchen preparation space, so today he's set up an additional dining area in the living room. The usual sofa and chairs have been moved to the window wall to make room. The dining table is spectacular. A burlap tablecloth and white linens show off a collection of beautiful blue-patterned Thanksgiving china. "They were from my grandmother," Brian says, proudly. There are silver votive candleholders and raffia pumpkins down the middle of the table. Bronze pinecones have name tags to indicate where we should sit. The table looks like it came out of a magazine on gracious living.

I'll have to make sure I don't break anything.

"Can I help you with something?"

"Of course. Do you like food prep?"

"I don't really know. Maybe. With you, probably."

Brian puts white cotton aprons on us, and I do my best to help. I grate cheddar cheese, trim Brussels sprouts, and, with careful directions, make cranberry sauce. Although not much of a cook, it's fun working with Brian, and his simple, easygoing directions and banter make the time go quickly.

Before I realize it, it's midafternoon, and the cooking that can be done ahead is complete. At the last minute, the turkey comes out of the oven, the rolls go back in for warming, and the mashed potatoes are whipped.

For a break, we decide to take Howie out for a walk. There's now about six inches of snow on the ground. Howie's bundled up pretty good, so he's enjoying himself. He's never been in snow until today, and he's not quite sure what to make of it. He's hopping and bounding more than walking, since the snow comes midway up his long, thin legs.

"Does he look skinnier or unkempt to you?" asks Brian, studying Howie as he plays in the snow.

"I've been wondering the same thing. I think he looks fine."

"Is their proper dog food in the alternative universe, then?" Brian quips.

As we walk, Howie continues racing and bounding but always backtracking to make sure I'm close by.

"It does take the drama out of the whole disappearance thing, doesn't it? If he had come back starved or with scars or with some of his fur missing, somehow it would add to the idea of a transdimensional trip. When you've been dropped into a dystopian hell where you have to fend for yourself, it should show *somehow*. It's hard to think that the alternate world reached through the Witch Tower is filled with dog treats and grooming parlors."

"So, you noticed that his nails look trimmed, huh?" asks Brian.

"Of course," I reply.

"But if the unknown is unknown, why couldn't it be a welcoming unknown? Why do we assume that another dimension is filled with fire and demons? Couldn't it be filled with creatures that are happy and helpful?"

"And enjoy cutting little doggies' toenails?" asks Brian, smiling at me.

"I thought you were in the alternate-world camp, Brian. I thought you were siding with Ally and Wilmarth about other dimensions and portals into the unknown."

"Oh, I still am," says Brian, picking up Howie, who's cold and starting to shiver. "I definitely think such things probably exist. Now that I've seen Howie, though, I'm wondering if that's what really happened to him. Just because I think alternate worlds exist doesn't mean Howie came back from one."

"So, you're on my side, now!" I say, smiling.

"Honey, I'm always on your side!"

"Did you just call me, *honey*?"

"Is that a problem?"

"No. It sounded nice."

"Not dopey?"

"Not dopey. Nice."

Ally and her grandfather arrive at five o'clock, as expected. Ally's dressed in layers. All puffy eiderdown quilting on the outside, she turns out to be wearing navy blue Capri pants and a simple red sweater on the inside. Her hair is growing out a bit, and she's wearing it pulled to one side. With only lipstick for makeup, she looks pale but fresh and luminous.

Albert is wearing a white button-down shirt and tie, and he's making me feel a little underdressed. Do we "dress" for dinner at the Hoskins house? Should I see if I can find a tie in Brian's closet? I think they'll just have to take me the way I am.

Howie is the center of attention, of course! Although I texted Ally to tell her of his reappearance, I have to tell everyone the full story. Howie is a bit nervous at so clearly being talked about. I'm holding him in my arms, and he doesn't even want to get down and greet the Wilmarths.

Brian makes everyone at home, and before long we're all chatting amiably and sipping white wine. Brian puts me back into service in the kitchen as the last-minute food prep is accomplished. Albert offers to carve the turkey, which is a relief to me, and Ally begins taking the food over to the table. I'm making the mashed potatoes while Brian dishes up gravy and gets the cheese rolls in the oven. Who knew that a hand mixer could whip up potatoes so quickly and beautifully?

At six, we're seated at a wonderful Thanksgiving dinner.

Brian surprises me by saying grace.

"I bless this food and the many hands that bring it to our table this Thanksgiving. I express my gratitude for friends and family who are absent from us—but never far from our thoughts. I'm grateful for other friends and family with us here tonight and dedicate this meal to friendship and love."

We raise our glasses in blessing, and I realize how thankful I am for Brian and my new life here in Massachusetts. For all the weirdness going on, now that Howie's home, I am happy and content.

For about five minutes, the silence of the table is only interrupted by the clinking of glasses and the passing of food. The food is amazing, and every face is alive with the simple joy of a good meal. After Brian receives many thanks for his wonderful food and beautiful home, conversation begins to drift to campus-related things.

"Howie seems remarkably well for his trip," says Albert Wilmarth.

"Yes. We discussed that before you arrived. We've started to change some of our theories," says Brian.

"It seems the other dimension into which Howie was flung has good food and pedicures," I say.

The Wilmarths listen as I explain about Howie's reappearance this morning and the possibility of avoiding the cameras and other security measures. Ally examines Howie, and she, too, thinks he's physically sound. Howie is a bit nervous at her handling him. He keeps looking at me to make sure it's OK.

I can see that Ally and her grandfather are disappointed, in a sense. They had, perhaps, hoped for more evidence to support their theories of transrealm travel or other dimensions.

"It doesn't mean the Witch Tower isn't a point of convergence between two universes, of course," mutters Albert. "But I see your point. Demons are unlikely to attend to dog hygiene." After a pause, Albert proposes a new idea. "Of course, do we have to assume that time works the same in both universes?"

I must be looking blankly, because Albert continues. "Six weeks may have passed here, but what if it was only a day or two for Howie? Maybe his toenails didn't have time to grow. Maybe he didn't even have time to get hungry?"

"Or he was kidnapped by someone who had good kibble and didn't like their hardwood floors being scratched by his nails," Brian suggests.

Ally laughs and says, "It does seem more likely, doesn't it?"

Albert asks, "Well, if you suspect a human agency, do you have any ideas?"

Brian puts his fork down for a minute and tells everyone about his attempt at sleuthing with the kidnapping board. They're mildly impressed with his awareness of the police methodology of means, motive, and opportunity but less than impressed with the list of suspects: Student X, Security Officer X, and Satanist X.

Dinner continues, and we're left with choices for dessert. Ally and Albert brought a lovely pumpkin pie, and Brian made a sort of custard tart. I opt for a portion of both, to be polite.

About a minute into our dessert, Albert turns to Ally and asks, "Do you think we should tell the boys about the break-in?"

"At the library?" I ask.

"You know about the break-in this morning?" asks Ally.

"I talked briefly with Security Chief Taggert this morning on my way to Massachusetts Hall," I explain. "There were security vehicles parked outside the library and an ambulance, too. Taggert wouldn't tell me what happened—just that there had been a break-in. When I was walking away from the library, though, I saw two EMTs taking someone away on a stretcher."

"Yes," says Albert, "that was Terrie Woolworth. She's the designer in charge of the rare book exhibit that we're putting together in the archives section. We checked on our way into town: she's still unconscious but will hopefully recover from the blow to her head."

"What happened?" I ask.

"We're not totally sure," says Albert. "We think that Terrie came in early. She's finishing work on some of the book mountings for the exhibit. As near as we can tell, someone, most likely with keys, entered the building at about eight-thirty and ran across Terrie. Whoever it is knocked Terrie out, stole a book that was to be the centerpiece of the exhibit, and left the library. The library didn't open today until ten, so one of the workers spotted Terrie about nine-forty-five and phoned campus security. They called the police in Arkham."

"That explains what I saw about ten o'clock, then," I say, shaking my head.

"Let me guess," says Brian, "they stole the *Necronomicon*."

In unison, Ally and Albert say, "Don't call it that!" Albert continues, "Yes, a copy of one of the corrupt English versions of *The Book of Naming the Dead* was stolen from the archives. The reason this is worth discussing, here, though, is that it might have bearing on your issues in Massachusetts Hall."

"I'm not sure I follow," I say.

"What if Howie's kidnapper is the same person who stole *The Book of Naming the Dead*?" asks Albert. "Maybe your analysis of means, motive, and opportunity would be a good way of solving both issues at hand. I can't imagine, somehow, that they're not related."

Brian retrieves the kidnapping board material and makes a space on the tablecloth to spread out the suspect and evidence cards. "I'm not sure how solving both issues simultaneously will make things easier," I say. "If we had real suspects, we could see if there were common motivations or means that one of the suspects had for both crimes. With an unknown intruder, it's hard to see how this will help."

Suddenly, looking at the suspect cards, I do have an idea. I retrieve the folder of notes I've brought from my backpack and pull out one of the newspaper articles Albert gave me early in November, when we met in his office. "Remember this article, Albert?" I ask. I offer him the article, and he picks it up.

"Um, sort of," says Albert, quickly scanning the article from the school newspaper. "Did I give you this when you came to visit me in my office?"

"Let me read it to everyone," I say. "This is from the *Miskatonic News*, dated June 23, 1991."

Massachusetts Hall Break-In

Campus security reports vandalism at Massachusetts Hall during a break-in on Tuesday night. Junior Security Officer Justin Taggert reports that a basement window was forced open on the south side of the building. "They didn't do much damage getting in, but they really trashed the tower basement," says Taggert. "They spray-painted satanic graffiti on the floor and walls. It's hard to say whether we can scrub it off or whether we'll have to repaint the whole thing."

The tower basement is primarily used for storage. The Physics Depart-

ment is trying to determine if anything has been stolen. As photos show, a large pentagram was painted on the floor with various other arcane symbols and drawings. The purpose of the break-in remains unknown.

"Notice anything from 1991 that applies to our situation today?" I ask. I'm getting blank looks, so I move two of the suspect cards together on the table. Now Security Officer X and Satanist X are overlapping. "What if Chief Security Officer Justin Taggert is a Satanist?" I ask. "Don't you think it's interesting that he was involved in the case in 1991 and in the case today? He has the keys, he knows about the Witch Tower and our security measures. He knows about security at the Salomon Center. Does he know about the *Necronomicon*?" This time, neither Wilmarth objects to my use of the book's more common name.

"Justin's been our security consultant while we've been putting the exhibition together," says Albert. "He knows where we store all the books and has master keys to Salomon Center—even the rare book section."

"He also has a surprising interest in Italian greyhounds," I say. I retell the conversation that Taggert and I had that morning on the steps of the library. "Did either of you tell Taggert about my strange dream and about Howie having a 'preview' of the other realm that night? Might Taggert have thought that Howie had some special ability to pass between this universe and some other? Could Taggert have kidnapped Howie to help him with some occult ritual?"

"It's possible I might have mentioned Howie, when Justin and I were just gabbing," says Albert, sheepishly. "Justin Taggert does tend to get me talking."

"Now that we have a real suspect," Brian says, "let's look at our board." He writes "Chief Security Officer Justin Taggert" on an index card at the top of the table. He writes "Means" on an index card below it.

"He has all the keys," says Ally. "Probably even the ones to your apartment at Grant Hall. Security has keys to everything."

"He knew about the camera at the lab," says Albert Wilmarth. "He told me as much after the Halloween break-in."

"Which he no doubt staged," I postulate, "in order to see if the Witch Tower would be active on Halloween."

"He also would know about the video server and the Wi-Fi setup," says Brian. "That would be standard information for someone in security. Taggert would be familiar with similar surveillance cameras elsewhere on the campus."

"And he knew about the *Necronomicon*, its location, and security arrangements," I continue. "Means and opportunity all point to Taggert. I'm still a little hazy on motive, though. Knocking out Terrie Woolworth seems extreme just to obtain a book that might help you visit other realms. Does anyone have an idea of why a Satanist might have an interest in this whole thing? What's the real motive?"

"What about ultimate power over life and death?" suggests Ally.

"What about eternal life?" suggests Albert.

"You've got to be kidding," I reply.

"No, really," says Ally. "*The Book of Naming the Dead*, among other things, has summoning spells. If you summon certain demons properly, they can wield great power for you. Azathoth, for instance, is named the king of the Outer Gods and is capable of killing with a thought. Other demons are supposed to be able to raise the dead or to make gold out of other materials."

I say, "So, if you really believe in the summoning spells in the book and the natural power of the Witch Tower—"

"It might just be motivation for all kinds of weird behavior," finishes Brian.

After a significant pause, Albert says, "I feel responsible for this whole mess. I've known Justin Taggert for at least fifteen years and never thought twice about his loyalty to the college. I see how all the pieces fit, though. I don't see how it could be anyone else. He's always seemed very interested in the occult and has asked many questions about *The Book of Naming the Dead* over the years."

"I have an idea," I say. "Brian used police methodology to help us come up with a suspect. Let's use the scientific method to help us catch him." I'm getting blank looks, so I explain. "The scientific method is a way to ask and answer questions by making observations and doing experiments. The steps of the scientific method are: Ask a question, do background research, construct a hypothesis, test your hypothesis by doing an experiment, analyze your data, and draw a conclusion and communicate your results."

I realize I'm starting to give a lecture, so I tone down the professor-speak a bit. "Our question would be, 'Who stole *The Book of Naming the Dead* and kidnapped Howie?' We've already done a bunch of research, or I should say, Brian has." I smile at my boyfriend. "Now we're ready to construct our hypothesis. I think our hypothesis is a simple one: 'Chief Taggert stole the book and the dog.'"

"And an experiment?" asks Ally. "What kind of experiment could we devise to test our hypothesis?"

"The faculty Christmas party," says Albert, with a determined smile on his face. "It's on winter solstice this year." Now Albert's getting blank looks, so he continues. "If Justin Taggert really is using the grimoire to summon demons in the Witch Tower, there's only one place he'll be on winter solstice. We just have to catch him."

"Let's run the experiment," I say.

Plans were made, and the Wilmarths have gone home. Brian and I have cleared away all the Thanksgiving dishes, and his dishwasher is churning away on a last load of pots and pans. His kitchen is mostly back to normal. All the furniture is back where it belongs, and we're sitting on the sofa with a view to the snowy Miskatonic River. There's enough of a moon to illuminate the wintry landscape, and the scene is lovely, if stark. Howie's enjoying his bed next to the wood stove, and its warmth can be felt throughout the living space. Brian and I are snuggled under an afghan enjoying each other's company.

"A great day," Brian says.

"More than just great," I say, looking over at Howie. "Really a day of Thanksgiving." On a sudden urge, I ask Brian, "Name five things you're grateful for. That's something I do every night in my journal, but tonight, let's both share. What five things are you most grateful for this Thanksgiving?"

"OK," says Brian, "but you know you're at the top of the list." He pauses, then makes his list:

1.   Dr. "Mac" Mackenzie, boyfriend.
2.   Three Rivers Hardware and Lumber.
3.   My House.
4.   Arkham, Massachusetts, and my friends and life here, and today, especially I thank
5.   Julia Child, for her cooking help.

Brian smiles and turns to me. "And you?" he asks.

"I suppose tonight's list could start and end with Howie," I say. "And you, of course. It really was a wonderful dinner and party. It might sound strange, but there's also someone else I'm grateful for today. I'm grateful for whoever took such good care of Howie while he was gone."

"You mean the demons from beyond the fourth realm of Neptune?"

"Whoever."

"You *do know* that whoever was taking care of him is probably the same person who stole him?"

"Whoever," I say, looking down at my sleeping best friend.

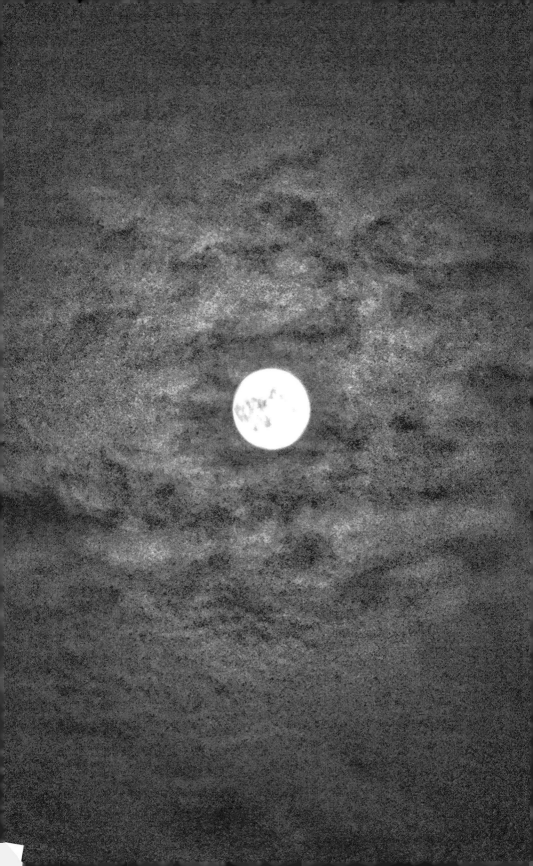

Chapter Eleven

Winter Solstice

When the invitation first came, I nearly threw it away: an invitation from the chancellor's wife to a black-tie Christmas faculty party. I don't even *have* a black tie, and as a very junior faculty member, I'm pretty sure that I wouldn't have been expected or missed. Albert Wilmarth, however, has talked me into it.

Because it's on the solstice, Albert feels sure that Chief Taggert will make another attempt at using the Witch Tower. I guess winter solstice is the most auspicious of all times for pagan rituals, and Taggert won't be able to pass it up. Wilmarth says all department heads are required to attend the party, so Taggert, as head of security, will be there. If we're all there too, we can follow Taggert when he leaves the party and stop him from using the *Necronomicon*. Albert and Ally will have memorized some warding spells to keep us safe should Taggert start a summoning spell before we stop him. If a summoning is in progress or a demon is present, they feel that they will be able to handle it.

In Albert's mind, it's all about spells and counterspells and prevent-ing something awful happening when demons come to conquer the Earth. It sounds crazy to me. Watching Chief Taggert the night of the party *does* sound like a good idea, though. Surely the four of us can retrieve a book from Taggert. Worst-case scenario, I'll just call 911 and pull in Arkham police. Taggert, after all, should be accountable for breaking and entering and assaulting Terrie Woolworth.

Albert and I are staff members and received plus-one tickets to the party. I'm bringing Brian, and Albert will bring Ally. That way all four of us will be there. With all of us watching, it seems unlikely that Taggert can sneak away unnoticed.

That just leaves one more guest: Howie.

After all Howie's been through, I refuse to leave him home alone (and certainly not in the lab). I checked with the Browns, but they're going to be away for the evening. Sam, downstairs, has already left to be with her family over the holidays. My other housemates seem a little on the flakey side, so Howie's going to the party!

Brian's theory is this: if it's a fancy party, people will be too classy to say anything about a well-groomed and well-behaved dog being there. If the party isn't that classy, Brian says I'm to say that Howie is a service dog. We both got a laugh out of that one!

As I hear the door buzzer, I realize it's time to start getting ready. Brian is downstairs, and I let him in. He's gotten off from work a bit early today so that we can have a snack together and get ready for the party. I may need his help with the cufflinks and shirt studs that go with my rented tuxedo.

Howie is almost as excited to see Brian as I am. Brian enters the apartment; his evening clothes are in a zippered bag slung over one shoulder. We kiss, and I hang his garment bag in the closet.

"Hi, boy," says Brian. "Are you ready for the big party?"

He's talking to Howie, and Howie jumps up and down. After a month back home, he's more his old, confident self. Tonight he seems full of energy. He gets an old tennis ball and brings it to Brian, and the two of them chase around the apartment for a bit.

"I brought something for Howie," says Brian. From inside his garment bag, he brings out a smaller bag. He opens it up and holds something in front of Howie. "I may need some help with this."

I look over and I see a dog tuxedo shirt. Or at least, that's how I would describe it. It's made of white dress-shirt material and wraps around to fasten under a dog's chest. It has pointed collars, like a tux shirt, and Brian shows me the little black bow tie that goes with it. "Do you think...?" asks Brian.

"We can certainly give it a try. He's worn Halloween costumes before." We struggle with Howie a bit, but the costume fits and looks cute. Howie seems willing to cooperate. "Where did you get this?" I ask.

"You can find anything on the Internet. Anything."

"I made us something to eat," I say, tentatively. I'm a little nervous.

It's clear Brian's a real cook, and I'm not. The reality of this meal is that I got a lot of stuff from the deli counter at the store in town, and I've arranged it on two plates. If Brian's smart, he won't ask for a recipe.

We chat and eat. We go over my simple version of the plan:

1.   We watch Chief Taggert. When he leaves the party, we leave.
2.   We follow him to Massachusetts Hall and watch him go in. We wait a few minutes to make sure we can catch him in the basement (there's no alternative way out of the basement).
3.   We catch him in the basement.

"I know that Ally and Albert have a more detailed plan involving spells, countercurses, and the 'warding' of demons, but I'm going to focus on the simple plan."

"I'm with you," says Brian.

As we start getting ready, Brian says, "Your jacket seems a little tight through the shoulders. Will you be able to dance in that?"

Suddenly, I realize that confronting demons and summoning spells are not the worst possibilities of the evening.

"Dance?"

"Dance. You know, waltz, foxtrot, that kind of thing. I'm pretty sure they have a band for the party."

I'm stunned. I had not thought for a moment that there might be dancing.

"Do *you* dance?" I ask.

"I'm best at waltz and country two-step. I *can* foxtrot if I have to, but I'm better at following than leading."

"You've had dance lessons," I say, accusingly.

"Of course. A gentleman should dance. A gay gentlemen should learn to lead and follow." Brian says it just like that, like it's a rule. "You dance, don't you?"

"Not a step," I say, lamely. "Do you still care for me?"

"Yes, of course, although I had thought you would dance."

"Are there places where we can dance here? Guys dancing, I mean?"

Brian looks at me. "Honey, this is the twenty-first century and we're not in the Midwest. Massachusetts was the first state to allow gay marriage. If there's dancing, I'll be dancing. Preferably with you."

I'm amazed by this man.

"If you help me with my studs, I'll help you with yours," says Brian.

"I thought you'd never ask."

❖

Now I'm really nervous. We're outside Marston Hall waiting for the Wilmarths. So far we've seen two Mercedes and a Town Car pull up in front of the tall colonnade that fronts the building. Elegant ladies in evening wear have ascended the steps accompanied by impeccably dressed men in tuxedos. No young people. No dogs. No nondancing pretenders! I can imagine Brian going up the steps, of course. He's standing next to me elegant in his tuxedo. He has a woolen overcoat and cashmere scarf around his neck, protecting him (and Howie, underneath) against the cold winter. How did he know how to shop for these clothes? How does he look so good so effortlessly? I stand there in my California overcoat, shivering, bothered by the way I look and my general level of unsophistication.

Across the Green I see two figures, and one of them waves. It must be Ally. They cross the Green from the dormitory block, and I see that Albert is also in a tuxedo and overcoat combination. Although not dressed as nicely as Brian, he does look good. The black formalwear highlights his silver-white hair.

Ally is enveloped in a black wrap that hangs nearly to the ground. I can only make out a bit of ankle to go with her black high heels.

Now assembled, we go up the steps to Marston Hall to begin our plan.

Marston Hall was built as an alumni club and reception hall in 1849. Designed to impress potential donors and to honor the richest givers, it's quite stunning inside. The foyer has a cloakroom, and tonight it is attended. We all leave behind our overcoats and scarves. Howie is revealed beneath Brian's elegant wool coat and is being led on a slim, black leash to match his black bow tie.

Ally's dress is revealed and so is a fair amount of Ally. On a bustier woman, the dress would be indecent. With Ally's slight frame, the plunging neckline is perfect and beautiful. The dress is belted tightly at the waist and accentuates her slim hips. In evening makeup, she almost looks like a model ready for the runway: high cheekbones and graceful legs.

We can already hear the band, and I'm grateful that it's a piece of music I know from the twenty-first century. Maybe this party will be nice, after all. At the entrance to the ballroom, we wait to meet the chancellor, Dr. Mason, and his wife, Elizabeth. They do a great deal to put my mind at ease. They are charmed by Howie ("Bow to the lady, Howie"), and Dr. Mason has nice things to say about my work in the Physics Department. They accept my date, Brian, graciously and enthusiastically. Albert, of course, knows them both well, and they exchange pleasantries. Everyone is charmed by Ally.

No mention is made of Brown Jenkin, and I wonder if the rat has said anything to Chancellor Mason about his kidnapping or my flying lessons.

I'm breathing easier as we enter the ballroom. The room itself is stunning. Rectangular in shape, it has a large raised stage at one end where the band is playing. The stage has pillars on both sides holding up a carved wooden proscenium. Arched palladium windows have white draperies tied back. Their sills hold candles in silver holders. The room is ringed with round tables decorated in white and silver. White lilies grace each table and provide an intoxicating scent. Silver votives dot the tables and cast a shimmering light that matches the overhead crystal chandeliers.

We find a table and sit as we get used to this lovely space and the party unfolding around us. A waiter comes by and offers us drinks. Apparently, wine and champagne are provided. Mixed drinks are available at a nominal price at the bar. Howie settles down underneath the table at my feet.

The small orchestra is doing a lovely job of creating a comfortable, upbeat mood. Within a few minutes, Brian has asked Ally to dance. The song, according to Brian, is "The Lady in Red." It's slow and sensual, and my friends are dancing something called nightclub two-step. As I watch, I have to admit to a bit of jealousy. At first I think it's because I can't dance—because I'm not as accomplished in this area of my life. Then I realize I'm just jealous. Brian is so handsome tonight. I've heard it said that there's "something about a man in a tuxedo," but I never thought it would apply to me, at least not in this way. I know that Brian is not particularly bisexual, so I don't think Ally represents competition in my relationship. When I look at them, I see friendship, not romance. The source of the jealousy eludes me. Is it just not being the center of attention in our group of three? Am I that shallow?

Lost in thought, I don't even notice him sitting down next to me.

"Hi Mac," says Chief Security Officer Justin Taggert. "I see you brought Howie tonight."

I sputter into my glass of champagne. "Officer Taggert," I say. "Great to see you." Am I being too friendly? Should I be more reserved? "What brings you here tonight?" Oh dear! That sounded stupid!

"Oh, I come every year," says Taggert. He leans down to pat Howie on the head. Howie backs up, avoiding the hand.

"Being head of the security department, they invite me every year. Besides, it's a swell party." He pauses. "I see your friends are having fun on the dance floor."

"Yes. I wish I could dance that well."

Albert, who is sitting on the other side of Taggert, adds, "Don't we all. I haven't danced in years!" He pauses, then asks, "Doesn't my granddaughter look lovely tonight?"

Taggert either doesn't hear Albert or chooses to ignore him and asks, "Is that your boyfriend from town?"

I wish I were better at reading people. Is Taggert taking a jab at the whole gay thing? Brian is right about Massachusetts being the first state to legalize marriage between same-sex couples. That doesn't mean everyone is OK with the whole issue, though. I look at Taggert for more clues about his question, but his face is impassive.

"Yes," I say, feeling braver than usual. "He works at Three Rivers Hardware."

"Well, I'm glad you're finding your way here in the area. Sometimes you're not always welcome in a new town. Sometimes people can be downright troublesome."

The words sound neutral, almost pleasant, but do I detect something else behind Taggert's conversation?

Before I can say more, Taggert stands up. "I'll see you later," he says. "I'm going to get a drink. I'm also the security detail for tonight. I want to make sure everyone has a safe, enjoyable evening. Enjoy yourself, Mac. You also, Albert. Take care, Howie, don't get stepped on."

When Ally and Brian return from the dance floor, they pump us with questions. Did he ask why we're all here? Did you find out about his plans for the evening? Does he have a date?

I explain what little I learned from the encounter.

"I'd bet anything he's the one who left you the threatening note on the first day of school," says Brian. "'Sometimes you're not always welcome in a new town,' indeed!"

I wish I were more sure about my feelings about Taggert. It seems like I'm missing something from the conversation.

The waiter brings us another round of champagne, and we decide to take turns watching Taggert so we don't miss his exit from the party. Whoever stays at the table will also sit with Howie.

Brian has the first watch, and Ally asks me to introduce her to some of the people from the Physics Department. Since Horace Alvarez is nearby, we start with him.

"Horace," I say, holding up a hand and getting his attention. "It's wonderful to see you outside of Massachusetts Hall. This is my friend Ally. Ally Wilmarth, this is Dr. Horace Alvarez. He's the other physics professor in the department. He and I share the labs and oversee the graduate teaching fellows."

Horace extends his hand and shakes Ally's.

"Good to meet you, miss," says Horace. "Let me introduce my wife, Elena. Elena, this is the Mac you've heard so much about and his friend, Ally Wilmarth."

Elena does not seem as friendly as I might have thought. I wonder what she's "heard so much about," as she shakes my hand, somewhat limply.

"Are you related to the other Wilmarths?" she asks of Ally.

Ally blushes. "Yes. Albert is my grandfather. He's a consultant in the library. You might know him from there."

"Unlikely, miss," says Elena Alvarez. "I can honestly say I've never set foot in that library."

Ally is taken aback by the surprising comment. Before she can think of anything to say, Elena Alvarez has pulled her husband toward the bar. Horace looks back at me, shrugging, as if to say, "Sorry, but what am I to do?"

"Remind me why we don't think they're suspects," says Ally. "It's clear Elena knows about some of the books in the library—why else avoid it? You said that when you first got here, Horace was a little freaked out about you taking over." Is Ally shifting her suspicions from Taggert to Horace and/or Elena Alvarez?

"I think the Alvarez family was away during the Thanksgiving holiday," I say. That would leave them off the hook for Howie's return."

"*If* Howie was returned," says Ally. "I still think he might have returned himself. From the other realm, I mean."

I see Dr. Christianson and Dr. Gupta in conversation, so I steer Ally over to meet them. They are quite chatty. Ally enjoys meeting my dissertation adviser, Shyam Gupta, in particular. "You look beautiful tonight," he says, appraising her. "Are you on the faculty?" he asks.

"Someday, maybe," Ally responds. "I'm a graduate teaching fellow in folklore."

"Oh, Wilmarth! Of course!" Dr. Gupta says in recognition. "I've no doubt that you'll be welcomed when you're ready, my dear. The Wilmarths have always been so talented, so useful to the library and to the college in general."

Although I'm not sure I entirely follow this conversation, Ally flushes with pleasure. She's clearly charmed by my dissertation adviser.

Dr. Christianson, my department head, is also in a jovial mood. "I keep hearing good things about you, Mac," she says. "Some of the student surveys from fall term are already coming in. Not only do the students like you, they're also getting better grades."

"That's nice to hear, Dr. Christianson."

"Call me Marianne."

"Of course," I say. Now I'm buddies with the department head?

"How's his dissertation coming along, Shyam?"

"Good," says Dr. Gupta. "Mac is producing quality work. Last time we met he'd nearly completed the first draft of the entire textbook. He has some innovative ways of illustrating quantum physics, too. I think it will make it more accessible to our students."

Now I'm the one riding high. I wish my adviser was more complimentary when we meet one on one!

Ally and I are headed back to the table. It's almost time for her to watch Taggert. Cutting across the room with his awkward lope, I see George Marsh approaching.

"Mac," he says, enthusiastically. "I didn't know you'd be here tonight."

Everyone is dressed well this evening, and George is no exception. His tuxedo is clearly a cut above my rental-grade suit. His has been tailored for an exact fit, and with gold cuff links and shirt studs he looks quite handsome.

"Is this Ally?" he asks, looking more at her than at me.

"Yes, this is my friend Ally Wilmarth."

"I've seen you on campus, of course," says George. "You look amazing tonight!"

"Thank you, George!" says Ally. "You live in Grant Hall with Mac, don't you?"

"Yes. I have the back half of Mac's floor. I'm not there often, though. I'm working in oceanography. Most of the time I'm at our research facility in Innsmouth. You know, the new Marine Science Center there."

Ally nods and starts to say something, but George interrupts. "Oh, listen! I love this song! Would you dance with me, Ally?"

Ally nods again and is immediately escorted over to the dance floor. She looks back at me, smiling. She's enjoying the attention she's getting this evening. She deserves it.

I make my way back to the table. Brian is sitting with Howie. Albert must be chatting with colleagues.

"Hi, honey," I say. "Has Taggert done anything to further our suspicions?"

"No, but I think he knows I'm watching him. In fact, I think he's watching me as much as I'm watching him."

I look to where Brian indicates, and sure enough, our table is under the watchful eyes of Chief Taggert.

"Well, that's not good. How can we follow him if he's onto us?"

"I'm also wondering if you ever considered your housemate George Marsh as a potential suspect in this whole thing." Brian is gazing out to the dance floor where Ally and George are dancing. George is not the best dancer. His feet probably don't allow him enough flexibility. Rather than some form of ballroom, he's doing a simple sway to the slow music. He's holding Ally, and they're making a small circle, swaying, in each other's arms.

"What do you mean?" I ask Brian.

"Well, I've thought of a few things to consider," says Brian, thoughtfully. "First off, he's in an ideal position to have knowledge about your comings and goings. He could have easily left the threatening note and known when Howie was alone in the tower on Halloween. His frequent trips to Innsmouth are a good cover. We really don't know if he has an alibi for any of the nights in question." Brian is staring at George on the dance floor. "Plus, how can a graduate student afford a suit like *that*? There must be something fishy going on!"

"You're too funny. George's folks are prominent in Innsmouth. His mom probably took him clothes shopping!"

"Innsmouth, right. That's the other thing. We're looking for someone with occult interests. Someone with a taste for the supernatural, right?"

"Yes, that's the theory, anyway."

"Innsmouth is the very *heart* of occult controversy."

"Oh, I didn't know."

"Oh, yeah," says Brian. "In the way that Salem is famous for witches, Innsmouth is famous for Dagon."

"Dagon?"

"I don't know that much about it," confesses Brian, "but most of the Arkham folks avoid Innsmouth like the plague. Back in the twenties and thirties, apparently there was a cult there that worshiped something called Dagon. Or maybe the cult was called Dagon. Anyway, I'm not sure you need to look any further than our friend George Marsh if you want to find someone connected to the occult."

"You're just jealous because he's dancing closer to Ally than you were."

Brian gives a big laugh and says, "Oh, you noticed!"

We peek over, and George is still dancing, somewhat tightly, with

Ally. The song is just ending, and Ally and George share a few words. Ally laughs. George smiles, shyly. Ally hands George something and returns to our table.

"So, what was that?" asks Brian.

"It was my card," says Ally.

"You have cards?" I ask.

"Yes," says Ally, "and I don't see the big deal. George is sweet, and a girl has to keep her options open!" She pauses to see if we're serious and realizes we're just giving her a hard time. She smiles. "It's not like I'm gonna be dating one of you two!"

The evening continues with another round of champagne and more conversation. I take Howie outside for a quick pee break. He still seems to be enjoying the people and the music.

Later, I notice that the crowd is starting to thin a bit. The party is officially over at midnight, but it's eleven thirty now, and only about twenty people are left. It's been Albert's turn to watch Taggert. Ally and her grandfather are in conversation and standing so Albert can unobtrusively keep Taggert in his line of vision.

The orchestra starts another slow song, a waltz, and Brian tugs at my sleeve. "Please," he says. "Waltz is easy. We can do the country waltz, and all you'll have to do is walk in time to the music. One, two, three."

"OK. But can we have lessons together before the party next year?"

"That's a wonderful idea!" says Brian, leading me out to the dance floor. He takes me into a dance frame, and it's clear he'll be leading. He holds me close and whispers in my ear, "Just remember that when we start, you'll be stepping back on your right foot, and I'll be stepping forward on my left. Basically, it's just walking in time to the music."

They're playing the theme from *Brokeback Mountain*. How fitting, I think, a bit sarcastically. The orchestra is making a beautiful, haunting waltz out of it. Brian's right, it *is* basically walking in time to the music. He must be a good leader, because I can feel the motion of our partnership without thinking about it. I was tempted to look at my feet, but Brian raised my chin so we were looking at each other.

"This is fun," I say, but lose the rhythm, and we start over. I remember to step back on my right foot, and we're gliding across the floor in time to the music. I realize how easy it is to be with Brian. I also realize how big a step this dance is for me. Not only am I dancing in public but I'm also announcing to the world that Brian and I are a couple. I make a misstep again, but Brian gently starts us up again, and I'm feeling the passion of the music and the man in my arms. I'm thinking that the dance lessons will be a wonderful addition to the things that

Brian and I share.

Suddenly, Brian steers us off the floor. He breaks frame and points to Albert. Albert is making a "come here" motion, and I notice that Chief Taggert is no longer visible.

When we get to the table, Albert quietly says, "He just left into the coat room. Let's get ready to follow."

Trying not to call too much attention to ourselves, we cross the room quietly. Albert is in the lead, and I'm at the end with Howie on his leash. We're just ending our night at the party; there's nothing unusual going on here. "Keep dancing" is the signal I hope we're sending to the room.

We wait for a bit at the entrance to the ballroom. Albert is closest to the door and, at last, gives us a signal. "He's just left the building. Quickly, let's get our coats and follow him."

We enter the foyer and the cloakroom and get our overcoats and scarves. We wrap up, then line up at the exit closest to the Green. Brian has Howie again stashed warmly under his coat. We peer out into the full-moon brightness of the Green, but there's no sign of Chief Taggert. He must be headed over to Massachusetts Hall.

"Well," I say, with a touch of drama, "shall we catch our Satanist?"

Ally giggles, and we head out into the cold December night.

The full moon hangs overhead as we cross the Green to Massachusetts Hall. It has a slight halo from ice crystals in the air reflecting the moonlight. Although the rest of us are snug in our overcoats, Ally's elaborate wool wrap doesn't cover the bottom part of her legs. She's shivering in her high heels. The sidewalks have been cleared of snow, at least.

As we arrive at the doorway to Massachusetts Hall, it's easy to see that someone has entered. Although there's always an outdoor light to illuminate the big side door, tonight there's a light burning inside the entry portico, as well. I point to it, and Brian nods.

Ally whispers, "You see! I knew he'd try something tonight!"

We step into the entrance, and Brian extracts Howie from his overcoat and puts him on the floor. Howie looks about, sorry to leave the warmth of Brian's coat but clearly recognizing where he is. We cross the rotunda toward the stairway that goes down to the basement level. Albert points out another light left on in a service area. I can't remember if that one is usually left on at night or not, so I shrug.

Now we're all lined up at the door to the stairwell going down.

"Grandpa, let's get our copies of the warding spell out," says Ally.

"You've already memorized it," he says. "It's better if we go from memory. Who knows if there will be enough light to read. He may just be using candles or a flashlight."

Brian offers something more practical. "I've got my smartphone ready. I'll take video of whatever Taggert is doing and be ready to call 911."

Suddenly, from behind, a hand reaches out to touch my shoulder.

"I wouldn't worry about calling 911 just yet," says Chief Security Officer Justin Taggert.

Ally yelps, and we turn around to face our lead suspect.

"Can you explain what you're doing here?" he asks. He seems more curious than angry or defensive. Can this really be a man ready to summon demons?

Albert saves me from voicing it. "We were following *you*, Justin."

Taggert looks quizzical. "What have these young folks gotten you into, Albert?"

"We thought you were breaking into the Witch Tower to perform some kind of ritual," Albert replies, apologetically.

Taggert laughs. "Well, you might be on the track of something, all right. This won't be the first time someone has snuck into that old tower room." He points at the light burning in the foyer and then at the door to the stairway down. "And it looks like tonight might be another one of those times. I didn't get here much ahead of you. The door had been unlocked, and the light was on. I was just headed downstairs when you folks stumbled in."

We all look at each other.

"Let's see what's going on, then," says Ally.

"Wait a minute," says Taggert. "Security is *my* job. You folks wait up here."

"But we have to retrieve *The Book of Naming the Dead*," says Albert.

"Holy shit," says Taggert. "Really? You think the break-in at the library is connected to this?"

"Absolutely," says Albert. "We have to get that book back. Whoever's here is probably going to use it tonight."

Taggert stiffens. "OK," he says, surprising me. "I guess you and Ally can come along. I may need your help if the *Necronomicon* is involved." He says this like it's the most logical thing in the world and opens the door and starts down the stairs. Albert and Ally follow him.

I turn to Brian, not sure if we should be afraid or intrigued. He shrugs.

"Don't you want to see what happens?" he asks.

I start to answer but notice that Howie has already made the decision for us. I see the end of his leash disappearing down the stairs. Brian and I follow.

Before we reach the bottom, I already know something is wrong. The hallway lighting has been shut off. When I click the switch, nothing happens. "Whoever it is must have flipped the breakers to cut power to the video camera," whispers Brian.

Taggert, Ally, and Albert are ahead of us at the end of the hall, opposite the door to the tower room. I can see that Taggert has a flashlight, but that doesn't explain the light I see coming out of the doorway to the tower. It looks like a red emergency light is flashing inside. Suddenly, I have a thought: the laser! Has someone turned on the laser for the two-slit experiment?

As we catch up to Howie and the others, I start to hear a familiar voice. Someone is loudly reciting some formula or poem. It sounds like a street preacher ranting but in a voice I know. Brian and I crowd a little closer to the door. Everyone is bunched up there, but I'm a bit taller and get a good view over the top of the others.

My brain struggles with what my eyes show me.

It's the Browns! My neighbors, Matthew and Emma Brown, are inside the tower! I notice a variety of disturbing things at first glance, but the most disturbing is that they're *naked*! My friends claim that I am overly self-conscious of my body, but this is a sight best not seen. Matthew Brown has a farmer's tan, and his red neck and arms stand out against his usually hidden torso and legs. His white skin, flabby stomach, and hanging genitals are shocking in the context of my laboratory.

But not as shocking as Emma Brown. Is this the woman who helped me with my Halloween costume? Is this the woman in the faded pinafore with her gray hair tied up in a bun? Her skin is fish-belly white, and my eyes are drawn to her pendulous breasts. Then my eyes shift upward, away from the shock of her nakedness. The gleam in her eyes and the set of her smiling mouth are too much. They tell a story of mania, of madness.

Mr. Brown's "lecture" is from a large book, no doubt the *Necronomicon*. This must be the "summoning" part of the ritual or spell. The words that he is speaking are English but with a curious sentence structure. It's hard to understand what he's really saying.

More prominently, is the laser light show. One of the Browns has activated the laser without controlling the alignment. The laser is slowly revolving on its base. Its red pinpoint of light is turning like a lighthouse, bouncing off the foiled walls in crazy patterns.

We all watch from the doorway. The Browns seem oblivious to us, and we seem to be frozen in time.

I become more aware of Mr. Brown again and notice that he has repeated the same phrase twice. "Azathoth," he repeats, loudly, "Lord of Outer Gods, I summon you!"

As he repeats this the third time, something curious starts to happen. The laser light show seems to shift. It's still creating a dazzling display, but now it seems to be shining through the foil to the underlying structure of the room.

The walls start to glow with a soft, pulsating red light, and I'm reminded of how they looked in the dream I had in this same room. I don't know how the light can be reflected in the foil *and* go through it, but that seems to be the case. As I edge forward and look up into the tower, I can see the laser light shining up into the empty space. In fact, if I crane my neck, I would swear it is going past the roof of the tower and out into the heavens.

Matthew Brown stops his recitation and stares upward. "Azathoth!" he commands.

And there is a response. I recognize it instantly. It is the wriggling, undulating entity from my dream. "Azathoth," I say, almost whispering.

My whisper is enough, though, for Ally and Albert to shake off their frozen state. Albert nudges Ally and starts reciting something in Latin. She picks it up, and their voices sound strong, though not loud.

It may be too late. Azathoth approaches, wriggling down out of the sky and into the tower. It's hard to describe Azathoth. There are some things that our senses are not meant to interpret, and he must be one of them. I have a sense of several hideous elements: of tentacles, scabrous skin, a gaping mouth of needle teeth, and far too many eyes. My mind is used to seeing symmetry in nature, so I must conclude that Azathoth was not created in any natural way.

He approaches with the sound of a squelch as though air is being quickly evacuated to make room for him. With him comes the smell of forest rot and some kind of flowers: lotus, I think.

More important than my outward senses, I feel an inward dread, the same fear that I had in the dream. This is insanity. This is the madness that comes from isolation, from too much power and too little love. This is the fear that a small forest creature must feel in the presence of a predator. I have never felt this frightened.

The naked Browns kneel to receive their descending Lord. Matthew opens another section of the *Necronomicon*. Then, clearly louder than the recitation of Ally and Albert, I hear him say, "I now command thee, Azathoth. Knowing thy true name, I command thee to do my bidding. I command thee and control thee as Baal!"

"Holy shit," says Ally, gasping, then continuing her Latin recitation.

Azathoth gives a big laugh. It's the laugh of a malicious child squeezing a bug to death. It's a laugh right out of an asylum, and it's just inside the door.

And then the Browns are taken. I use the word *taken* because I hesitate to give a real description. They certainly *are* bodily taken, but clearly there's no chance of survival. Eaten might be a more appropriate word, but eaten with a flourish, their insides torn out in one swift movement. Azathoth laughs again, pleased with his conquest.

Then Azathoth turns his attention to the tower door. His scrutiny is fixed on the six of us crowded at the end of the corridor. He begins to smile with teeth made for rending, and a small sound of anticipation clears the back of his throat. His many eyes seem to focus on us separately and clearly.

Albert and Ally have reached an important part of their recitation. They, too, are repeating a phrase in Latin. It sounds like the conclusion of something.

But that's when Howie decides it's time for action. That's when we make a big mistake.

Between Albert's legs, Howie bounds through the door into the tower, dragging his leash behind him. The clock atop Salomon Center strikes midnight. Not willing to lose him again in this awful place, I react without thought. I push my way into the tower room, into the Witch Tower, into the midst of its pentagram as the clock's bell atop the Salomon Center counts to twelve.

CHAPTER TWELVE

The White Castle

Howie and I are in the center of the lab. The light from the laser is still shining crazily around the room. The vibration of the table the laser sits on makes for a shimmering display against the reflective foil. There's just enough light to see that the lab is clear. The Wilmarths' warding spell must have been effective. Azathoth has left, taking the remains of the Browns with him. Just Howie and I occupy the space now. The odd optical sensation persists, though: that feeling of two laboratories existing simultaneously. I can see the foil-lined walls, the lab table, the furniture, and the floor tiles. Even with the weird lighting, I can see things as they are. Now that I'm inside the pentagram, I can also see much more.

It's like one of those paintings or pictures with two versions of reality. When you look at the picture one way, you see two silhouettes. When you look at the picture another way, you see a cup. The lab's there, but something else is also there if I just bend my mind a bit.

On top of the reality of the lab is another world, and now that I've seen it, it starts taking the predominant view. I can still glimpse the old lab through the flashes of the laser, but on top of that I'm in the five-sided Witch Tower. Between flashes of the foiled walls, I clearly see/feel the red, pain-filled pulsations of the centuries-old stone blocks. The geometry here has meaning, and I realize the walls are telling me I'm in the midst of an auspicious moment. Only a few minutes every year have this level of possibility.

Like the dream I had here two months ago, I realize that I am bodiless in the usual sense. I feel embodied, but when I look down, I do not see myself in the usual way. When I reach out, I do not see an arm or a hand, but things do come to me, and I can observe them as though I had picked them up. Also, like my dream, I see that Howie is here with me. At least there's the amethyst crystal-like being before me radiating that sense of fondness.

"Is it you, Howie?" I ask/think.

"Yes," comes the answer. I'm not quite believing it, though. I remember that in the dream I had Howie do one of his tricks to prove his identity.

"Commando, Howie," I improvise. "Commando!"

The friendly, pulsating violet entity tilts down to the horizontal and makes back-and-forth movements as it crawls toward me.

"Good dog!" I say/think. "We're back in the dream, Howie."

"Not dream," says/thinks the violent crystal that is Howie.

I look up and notice that I can see through all the foiling and even the roof of the Witch Tower. It's like we're at the bottom of a well. Cold stars shine far above. Then, through a shift in perception, I realize I'm not looking up so much as down a long corridor. The Witch Tower is more like a witch hallway, with Howie and I at one end and the cosmic emptiness of space at the other. A hallway that can be transversed.

Howie and I move a bit down the hallway (or up, toward the stars, depending on how you look at it). After the horror of the Browns' leave-taking, this is a place and time of calmness. It feels like we could spend eternity examining the walls of this hallway. Howie and I drift, slowly, down its length. It feels like many have made this transition, and I realize that's why the stone walls have the sense of red/pain associated with them. Many people, the Browns included, have made this journey in pain and suffering.

But there's no sense of pain for Howie and me. It's almost a sense of welcoming, of hospitality and curiosity that I feel. If it weren't for the negative residue in the walls, I would think we were in the entrance hall to some great and wonderful palace.

As we get closer to the end of the corridor, I see that what I thought were stars in the sky are really gemstones fixed into the fabric of some kind of curtain. My mind reaches out to the curtain, and I feel expensive velvet. My mind moves the curtain gently aside, and Howie and I are, indeed, in some kind of castle or palace.

The entrance room is quite large with many of the star-and-velvet-draped openings along its walls. A golden pillar separates each one. As we go past some of them, I realize that each might be another doorway into another hallway, another witch tower, and another place with a star-studded sky. In this strange room, the pillars give off a scent of cinnamon and lemon as we pass. The scent seems to be directing us across this entrance area to one set of columns that does not have the velvet curtains.

As we move through the columns into a new area, a sense of awe is produced. It feels like we're standing on the edge of a mighty waterfall or gazing across the Grand Canyon. That's what it feels like, but it's a simple enough space. The room is of alabaster and is pure white. As we enter, atonal piping begins, and I realize that up until now, all had been silent. This is not music, though; it sets my nerves on edge. It is the sound of too much time and loneliness reflected as music.

Midway across the dazzling room is a dais, a raised section of the floor. On it is a black onyx throne. On the throne is a small man dressed in a dark gray suit.

I look down and notice that Howie and I are now in our usual bodies.

The man is about fifty years old, I would guess, and has short gray hair and a neatly trimmed gray beard. His clothing gives the impression of an expensive business suit. He regards us impassively as we approach.

"Hello," I say. "I hope we're not disturbing you. My name's 'Mac' Mackenzie, and this is Howie."

"Oh, we've met," says the man. In a flash, Howie and I are on the jetty again with Goody Hallet as she sings the small ship onto the rocks. Hallet turns her head and laughs.

"Azathoth?" I ask.

"You *do* remember," says Azathoth, nodding. In another flash, he's the small man on the black throne. "Not many people remember their dreams, Mac. I appreciate that. The human existence is short and small enough without losing a third of it to unremembered dreams. In dreams and visions lie the greatest creations of man, you know."

I'm not sure what to say.

He continues. "But I expect you'd like more explanation and less philosophy. Perhaps you'd like to know why you're here. Perhaps you'd like to know about the plans I have for you."

Again, I'm silent. I'm not sure what I can say.

"I was once just like you. I was born on Earth in a nondescript city not that far in time or space from your own. Each day I would go to a dead-end job full of obligations and responsibilities. Times were hard and I had to work many hours. I would come home exhausted, not so much from the work as from the tedium. Earthly life has such a weight to it." He pauses to see if I have a comment, then continues. "Each night I would sit near my one window and look out into a light well in my building. If I craned my neck just right, I could see the stars. Night after night, I would look at the stars, and eventually they became friends. I learned their names and nightly patterns and could imagine that I heard their silvery voices calling to me.

"One night, they did call to me, and a mighty gulf was bridged in consciousness. One of the outer stars reached down to my lonely watcher's window. An infinity of colors, emotions, shapes, and possibilities was presented to me. I was given an unusual gift and a great opportunity. After many cycles, I was left in this place, albeit with a more naturalistic view of it."

As he says these words, our environment changes in another flash. I now see the black throne on a verdant stretch of land bordering a shore fragrant with lotus blossoms. A sea of green everywhere, with the white water lilies punctuating the landscape like stars.

Howie barks, and Azathoth smiles. "It *is* a good trick, Howie! All that we can sense of our human environment is easily manipulated by our consciousness, given the right training. The star-spawn entity that brought me here to rule the Outer Gods pictured it like this," he says, highlighting the field of green and lotus blossoms. "I show it to you like this," he says, and we flash back to the throne room of alabaster, "because I thought you would relate to it better. Now it's your turn, Mac. I thought I'd reach down to you tonight. I could have destroyed you like those foolish devil worshippers. I could have allowed or even encouraged some of the other entities in this realm to take charge of you or to feed on you. Instead, I invited you here. Instead, I invite you to be an apprentice, perhaps a friend."

Finally able to find a word or two, I say, "I don't really think—"

"Let me finish," commands Azathoth. "I want to put some clarity around your visit here. While you're deciding on your participation, you have free access to the White Castle and its grounds. Since Howie has been here before, he's allowed to be your guide, although he may pursue interests of his own, of course."

I look down at Howie, but he is not reacting to Azathoth's speech.

Azathoth continues. "You will find all the time you need to adjust to your life here, Mac. The castle has many wonders and is a useful place to learn about this realm. To be a master of the realm, however, will require my mentorship. To become one of the Outer Gods will require a sacrifice. You must bind yourself to this place and to me. If being a god does not interest you, then simply give me your true name, and I can use your essence as I wish. Afterward, I will give you your freedom as I have done with Howie."

I'm not entirely sure what to make of all this, but I know what to do when someone is talking crazy.

I walk out of the throne room.

The White Castle has few windows, but after some exploring, Howie and I make camp in a midsized room with a series of small windows along one wall. After a time, I notice that it is night outside. As I gaze out, I see an unbroken sandy landscape and a black sky with stars. There is no moon and only a few scrubby trees in close proximity to the castle walls.

The castle interior is well lit. The alabaster walls have an internal glow that provides constant illumination.

Howie and I settle down to rest on a wide sleeping couch at one end of the room. I've got Howie tucked under one arm, with his head nestled across my chest for comfort. I start to make out my gratitude list:

1.   Howie: *Thank God I'm not alone in this stark place!*
2.   Brian: *I know I'll find my way back!*

But I only get to the second item before I start to cry. Howie looks up at me, but there's nothing to be done, little comfort to be had in the moment.

There's also no sleep. We lie there without either of us feeling sleepy or tired. I rest for a bit with my eyes closed. Suddenly, light streams in through the windows. It's as though someone flipped a switch. I jump up from the couch to look out on the same scene of featureless sand extending to the horizon. Now there's simply a well-lit blue sky. No trace of a sun to mark the passage of time.

I soon discover that there is no real day or night in the White Castle. They are arbitrary and somewhat random lighting effects that Aza-thoth uses as a stage setting. There's also no real time. Or rather, I should say, there is infinite time. There is only "now." Howie does better with this concept than I do. He doesn't seem to mind that there's no need to eat or sleep or accomplish anything. Oh, of course, you *can* eat. Some of the rooms are laid out with banquets containing elaborate meals. The food tastes wonderful, but you're never hungry, and you never feel full.

You can also lie down to rest, but without a need for it and without dreams, why bother?

That's my problem. As Howie learns to enjoy a variety of adventures in the White Castle, I say, "Why bother?" He seems to be entertained by the various rooms, gardens, activities, and happenings. I'm just missing my life.

I've tried using my far-seeing, like I did when I was searching for Howie, but nothing happens. There must be something in the castle that blocks my ability to view my friends beyond it.

Azathoth has also removed any idea of friendship with others within the castle. Besides Howie and himself, the castle has no other inhabitants. Sometimes I think I hear other people. Sometimes I get a glimpse of someone else when I walk into a room. But either the castle reconfigures itself (quite possible in this realm), or it's just my imagination. The sound turns out to be a fountain. The room turns out to be uninhabited. This might also be part of Azathoth's plan. He may be using loneliness as a tool to help in his conquest of me.

That's the way I think of it, anyway: his *conquest* of me.

Periodically, he appears. The conversation generally starts out amiable, as though we're two friends. After a bit of chitchat, he moves the conversation around to some invitation for me to find meaning in my life in his realm. Would I like to be in charge of a world? Would I enjoy creating a pocket universe? Would I like to learn how to manipulate space and time? He appeals simultaneously to both my scientific intellect and my need for companionship. Sooner or later, he winds down the conversation with one of two demands. Either I make a binding agreement to stay with him forever, or I give him my secret name.

I always end the conversation by simply saying no or walking away.

I have no intention of spending my life in the White Castle as an Outer God. I want my life back, and there's some part of me that thinks it's possible. Some part of me knows that Azathoth's powers are not unlimited, or he would have already taken what he wants from me. Intuitively, I know there's some way home.

I also have no intention of giving Azathoth my secret name. I suspect it's my Christian name, which no one in Massachusetts has heard or seen. I'm pretty sure if Azathoth can "name me," he can have his way with me. If I've learned anything from Ally Wilmarth, it's the mystical power of naming. To properly name something is to summon it, to control it, and perhaps to rule it. That's not going to happen.

Sometimes Azathoth appears to me as Brian or Ally or even my mother. He's stopped doing this, because I refuse to interact with him in these forms. He thought I would be attracted to these people and therefore more compliant. He was wrong.

❖

One time I wander by the throne room in time to see Howie and Azathoth in the throes of an argument.

"Do as I will, Dog, or I will consign you to a realm of fire and boredom!" The threat is momentarily illustrated as Azathoth transforms the room into a sweltering pit of flame. It could be a picture of hell as described by Dante. The flames are everywhere, obscuring all form and meaning in the room. This would certainly be a hellish existence.

Howie barks, and the room is transformed back to the throne room.

Azathoth, in his visage of middle-aged businessman, turns red in the face and pounds a fist against the arm of his throne. "Enough defiance on your part," he bellows. "Sooner or later, I *will* have him. The longer this takes, the less valuable he will become. You may as well aid me!"

Howie holds his ground and does not respond.

Azathoth returns the room to flames, and a wave of heat belches out of the room, making me retreat a few paces. My eyes sting from the heat.

Howie barks, and the room is back to normal. But this time Howie is not his diminutive twelve-pound self. With the change of scenery, he's super-sized himself! He's larger than Azathoth and rears up to knock him off the black onyx throne.

Azathoth disappears.

Howie can fly here, and he can breathe underwater. I have seen him do almost everything that I have seen Azathoth do. I'm not sure if this is comforting or troubling. Maybe I should be content with having powerful friends in high places.

And Howie *is* still this man's best friend. When I'm depressed or upset, he's always there to comfort me. When I'm lost in the castle, Howie will patiently take me back to familiar territory. He has led me to see some of the most marvelous wonders in the White Castle and its grounds. We have seen rainbow waterfalls full of silver fish that can swim up as well as down the current. We have seen gardens with plants that are mobile. We have seen some of the most architecturally stunning rooms in existence.

I would trade all these experiences for a minute in Brian's arms.

Periodically, I practice my flying. Although I cannot fly beyond the reaches of the White Castle, I can bring myself to other rooms just by visualizing myself there. I feel the "pull," and there I am, body and soul. Howie and I sometimes fly together. We'll fly right out of a window and soar about the castle. All that we ever see are the featureless dunes, stretching to infinity.

One time, Howie comes to me when I'm lost in thought. I'm somewhere in the White Castle. He's worried about me. In our wordless communication, he says that I should be enjoying myself. I should be making the best of our time in Azathoth's castle. He does a little dance in front of me, but I'm not interested in playing.

More forcefully, he pokes me with his nose until I look down directly at him. I realize he's turned into a small green lizard. The lizard blinks, and it's Howie again.

"That's a good trick, Howie." Howie barks enthusiastically.

Then Howie gets down like he's going to do some other trick, maybe "Commando," and barks once, sharply. In an instant, the castle is gone, and we're on the street where my mother lives in Santa Monica.

"That's a *very* good trick, Howie," I say, startled. As I look around, though, I see that it *is* just a trick. The landscape isn't real. He's created it from his doggy memory. The scale is all wrong. He's created California from a foot off the ground. Everything looks impossibly tall. The bushes seem unusually attractive, the ground more finely detailed. Mom's house is too big, almost out of view it's so far above us.

"Thank you, Howie. It's almost home. I can *almost* visit Mom. It was nice to see your picture of California." Howie senses the sadness in my voice. He barks, and we're back in the castle. My cheeks are stained with tears.

Howie climbs into my lap, asking to be stroked. I know it's for me, not him, but I'm grateful for his presence. If it wasn't for Howie, I would have gone mad long ago in this sterile, alabaster prison. Holding him, I do feel better, and after a bit the tears dry up.

Howie gets back down on his haunches again and barks. In an instant, the world becomes the dog park near Venice Beach. When he first came to live with me, it was a favorite place to go when I got home from school.

He barks again, and the scene changes into our apartment in Grant Hall. Again, the view is from one foot off the ground, but it's definitely our apartment. The bed seems impossibly high up, but there's the radiator, and there's one of his now-impossibly-large dog toys.

Howie barks, and we're at the edge of a sea of white lotus blossoms. This is the scene that Azathoth showed us of his first arrival here in the castle. From Howie's perspective, low to the ground, the scent of the lotus flowers is powerful. You can feel the warmth of the water in which they float.

Howie barks again, and we're back in the castle. What he's doing finally dawns on me! "Howie, I'm such a slow learner. How do you put up with me? You're trying to teach *me* a trick!" I can see that he's waiting, almost smiling the way that dogs sometimes do. "I'm not sure I know how to 'bark' that way," I say, apologetically. Howie looks at me as if to say, "You have to at least *try*."

So I get down on all fours on the alabaster floor of Azathoth's White Castle and bark. Nothing happens. I bark again, and nothing happens. Howie comes closer to me. We're side by side. He barks, and we're in our apartment.

I bark, and we're still in the apartment.

Howie barks, and we're at the dog park.

This time, I try a more internal bark. I don't really know how to describe it, but I know that Howie's bark starts in his brain. It's like when he barks for a treat. He knows he's going to get it. It's more like announcing what's going to happen than willfully creating something. These scene changes of his must be triggered by some mental source of bark desire. I try to think a bark, but nothing happens. I say nothing, but Howie gives me an encouraging look, so I try again.

We're back in the castle. At first, I'm disappointed, but then I realize I have accomplished something. *I did this!* I inwardly bark, but nothing happens—no, wait, we're on the other side of the castle. I see Azathoth's black throne. We must be in the throne room! Or, I should say, we're in *my* version of the throne room.

Howie is wagging his tail, obviously delighted with teaching me a new trick.

I practice a bit more, and Howie shows me, silently but patiently, how to create my surroundings through the power of my thought, desire, and will.

❖

One time, I seek out Azathoth in the throne room. I have only approached him once or twice in my stay at the White Castle. He's sitting on the black onyx throne in his business suit. His eyes are closed, but as I approach, he opens them and regards me quietly.

I surprise him by changing the scene. Using the trick that Howie has taught me, I change the throne room into the green embankment and lotus field that Azathoth claimed was his first view of this realm. We're in the midst of a rolling, grassy expanse bordering a marshy lotus bed of infinite length. As he showed it to us before, I make the lotus flowers into perfect white stars dotting the landscape. The sky is a deep blue, the air is warm, and the lotus flowers are giving off a rich scent.

"Don't you like it this way?" I ask. "Don't you remember when you first came here?"

"Yes," answers Azathoth, "I remember." He points to the many lotus stars. "These are the very stars that bent down to bring me here. They came to me in a dream of longing. They came to my rescue. They came as friends."

"Because you had none of those things," I state. "They were giving you what you were lacking. They pitied you."

Azathoth has no reply. His silence affirms their truth.

"But *I* have those things," I say. "I have a place to be useful, to have a purpose. I have friends. There are people who love me and miss me. I don't need or want this life." I wave my hand, indicating the castle. Then I look at the middle-aged man with gray hair and neat beard and say, "You came here because your life was unbearable, and I'm sorry for that."

A cloud passes over the sun. Ripples form on the surface of the lotus field's water.

"But I do not share your need for control or dominion. I did not come here to seek a better life or to escape a bad one. I did not come here hoping to give meaning to my life. My life *has* meaning."

More clouds begin to fill the sky.

"I do not wish to be your mentor, your partner, or your colleague."

The sky darkens, and there's a flash of lightning, followed by thunder.

"If the circumstances were different, I might at least be your friend, but friends are not held captive. Friends are not prevented from living the lives they choose. Friends do not use the 'essence' of one another for selfish reasons. You have no friends beyond these!" I say, pointing to the white lotus blossoms.

Staring at the turbulent lotus field and amid lightning and thunder,

Azathoth roars, "Friends!" and a sheet of rain begins to fall from the sky, obscuring everything. Another crash of lighting highlights his angry face. He sees the truth of what I'm saying, but his heart does not know how to respond. His hands are balled into fists. "Friends," he says again, quieter this time. His suit is stained from the falling rain, and he looks up at the sky.

I decide to leave the lotus field. I change my view back to the usual throne room, back to the white alabaster and black onyx throne.

Azathoth is gone.

One time, I'm at my wit's end. I'm pretty sure I'm either dead or dying. Our outsides don't change in the White Castle, but we do change on the inside. I've changed. From the beginning, I was afraid to give Azathoth my secret name because he would use my essence to increase his own power. Trouble is, I'm not sure there's any of my essence left. I'm not sure who I am any longer and not sure who I can be in this place.

I find my way to the throne room to talk to Azathoth. I will not agree to his terms, but maybe he will at least release me to death or some form of dissolution.

Initially, the room looks empty, the throne vacant.

Then I see that the throne does have someone seated in it. It's Howie.

Weary of Azathoth's tricks, I cautiously approach the throne. "Howie, is that you?" It seems like Howie, but I have been fooled before. Azathoth has the knack for imitating my friends. Azathoth has never been good at imitation friendship, though. Without experience as a friend, Azathoth cannot pretend for long.

"Is there an end to this place? Or maybe a better question: Is there an end to *me* in this place? I really don't think I can continue."

Howie looks up at me with the saddest eyes. I know it's him. Azathoth would be gloating at my weakness.

"Is there no way back?" I ask. "I understand if we're stuck, we're stuck. I know that you're OK here. I think, in some ways, you like it here or at least feel powerful here. But I'm lost, Howie. I feel less than nothing. If it weren't for you, I probably would have died of loneliness. Is there really no way back?"

Howie continues to look up at me.

"I've tried going back to the entrance hall, Howie. I've used your trick to make a view of the velvet curtains full of stars. I know that behind each one of them is another universe, another portal to some-where. I tried one at random, but it was locked in some way. I could not penetrate the velvet."

A thought occurs to me, and I ask, "Could I just go to sleep? I know there's no death here, not really. I know this is a place of pure con-sciousness, so I can't take my life in the usual sense. But could you help me to go to sleep until there's some other way of release?"

Howie has such love in his eyes that I find mine watering. He barks, and the throne room turns into the lotus field. It looks like late after-noon. A golden light shines over the green grass and green lotus leaves. The white blossoms are like the stars that drew Azathoth here from his life of despair on Earth. I realize how this realm brought *him* new hope and a sense of dominion. Silently, I forgive him. Not for my capture, not for my imprisonment, but for his fallibility. Like all of us, he's just doing what he knows how to do. He's trying to find his way in the universe without proper training on how to be openhearted and loving.

The lotus flowers are luminous in the afternoon light. They give off an almost hypnotic scent. There's a moon in the sky that I've never seen before, but it reminds me of the moon on that long-ago solstice night when we confronted the Browns in the Witch Tower. That was the night that Azathoth led Howie and me into the White Castle.

Thinking about that journey to the White Castle reminds me of Azathoth's journey here. It ended right here in the lotus field.

"Howie, is the lotus field another way back to home?"

He looks at me sadly and tilts his head in assent.

"The lotus flowers are like the stars back home, aren't they? Aza-thoth came from Earth."

Howie agrees but does not seem excited.

"What's the matter? Can't I just dive in and get back home?"

Howie barks, and a new scene is before me. Murky water and endless lotus stems clog my vision. Although I don't need to breathe, foul-smelling water fills my mouth and nose, and I feel like choking.

Howie barks again, and we're back above the water on the green grass of the embankment.

"I see. I'm not really ready for this kind of adventure. I'm still too bound to my senses. You're more at home here and can go as you like without being attached to the 'view' of things. Give me a view of deep water, and I'll start drowning. Give me view of murky water, and I'll lose my way. I understand, Howie."

Howie senses the defeat in my voice. He gets down off the throne and trots over to me. I sit down on the steps of the dais, and he gets into my lap to be stroked. We both know it's for me.

After I calm down a bit, Howie gets off my lap and crouches at my feet. He has that "pay attention" look. I observe him carefully, and he goes through several of his tricks. He ends with "shake hands" and offers me his paw.

"Those are your tricks, Howie. Your 'Earth tricks.' You're beyond all those now."

He tilts his head and extends his paw again.

"Oh, I see. You'd like to teach me another trick. Is that it?"

Howie wags his tail in assent and crouches farther down. He's doing his "commando" crouch, but his eyes are closed tight, and his back legs are moving slowly up and down. He's swimming.

"Do you want me to swim? Is that it?" Howie continues wagging his tail and extends his paw, pointing right in front of him. "Right here?" I ask, and Howie gives a little excited sound.

I get down on all fours, lowering myself to the ground. Now I'm the one doing the "commando" trick. Howie gets in front of me and wriggles back until my hands are touching his flanks. I think I understand.

"So I'm to hold onto you and swim? I just keep my eyes closed, and you'll find our way to the bottom of the lotus pond—to our stars and our home?"

Howie looks at me as if to say, "We have to at least *try*."

Before I can make any objections, Howie barks, and I feel the water from the lotus field close in around us. I close my eyes and mouth against the dirty water. At first, it seems like there's more mud than water, and my legs can't really help to propel us. After a time, though, the water becomes deeper and less choked with weeds and lotus stems. My legs start making long, strong swimming strokes. I can feel Howie's fur beneath my hands, and I can feel him reaching out with his front legs. Howie knows how to take us where we're going.

After more time passes, I lose the sense of being in the water altogether, and I open my eyes. Stars have replaced the lotus field. Behind me I see the lotus-stars that first made contact with Azathoth. I think of him there in the heart of the White Castle. Ahead of me I see a bright band of stars stretching like a path to lead our way. It's the Milky Way, I realize, and we're following it home. Farther ahead, some of the stars are twinkling more wildly and vividly than others, and Howie steers toward them.

Something is happening to Howie. Although this travel requires no physical effort for him, I see that it does use his resources. Something about him is lessening. He feels less substantial beneath my hands. Is it my imagination, or can I even see the stars *through* him?

Oh, the stars! We're headed for a wildly shining group of stars at the end of a darker patch of the Milky Way. It almost looks like we're entering a darkish tunnel with flashing red stars at the end. Then my sense of orientation shifts, and I realize we're heading down a dimly lit tunnel and the flashes of light are below us.

Down we go, quickly, gently. I begin to notice that I'm breathing the cold night air around me, as though breathing for the first time. My eyes are smarting from the passing air as we descend farther. Our descent begins to slow and then nearly stop. I realize we're descending through the transparent, permeable roof of Massachusetts Hall and into the Witch Tower. The flashing red stars are the flashing of the laser from the double-slit experiment shining off the crazy foiled walls. For a moment I see a superimposed view of both the Milky Way tunnel and the Witch Tower. I see myself drifting down, and I see another me lying prone on the ground. I see the almost-invisible Howie I'm holding tightly, and I also see a substantial but limp-looking Howie just below.

Then I'm at the bottom of the Witch Tower, and I pass out.

Chapter Thirteen

Christmas Eve

I wake up in a hospital. Brian is here, and as I try to get up, he gently pushes me back down.

"Hey, there," he says. "Wait a minute. I'm glad you're back, but I don't think you're supposed to get up. The doctors were worried. It's not usual to pass out for three days."

I look around, and he says, "You're in Essex Country Regional Hospital. It's about forty minutes south of Arkham. The EMTs weren't sure what was wrong, so they brought you here instead of the smaller hospital in Arkham."

I dimly remember seeing signs for it on my trip in from Boston. That seems so long ago. The room is a bright celery green with peach-colored drapes. They frame windows looking out on a landscape of white and gray. There's snow on the ground wherever I am. It looks bitter cold outside, and I'm glad to be under a vivid blue blanket in this safe place of comforting colors. Brian is wearing bright colors today, too. I almost laugh at his orange-and-green plaid shirt contrasting with indigo blue jeans.

"Did you say three days?" I ask, hoarsely. "Not more?"

"Isn't three days long enough?"

"It seems like I've been gone a lot longer than that."

"To me, too," he says, looking at me carefully. "Do you feel OK?"

"I think so. Maybe a little dry. Can I have some water?"

Brian pours me a cup of water as I get used to being back on Earth.

"Do you remember what happened?"

"Yes, of course," I say, but with some hesitation in my voice. "The Christmas faculty party and our plan to trap Officer Taggert, the Browns using the *Necronomicon* to summon Azathoth, the laser light bouncing off the foil in the lab, Azathoth's rampage with the Browns, and their death. I remember it all."

"You remember them dying?"

"Yes. Horribly. That's not something I will ever forget."

"That's just it. The police say that nothing really happened in the Witch Tower. There were no bodies, no blood, no *Necronomicon*, no damage to the lab. They found a pile of their clothes in the utility closet, but that's it."

"Well, Wilmarth probably has the *Necronomicon*," I say, scratching my head, still clearing my mind as though from an overly long nap. "But you remember how they died, don't you? The blood? You remember the demon Azathoth?"

"Yes, although it seems dreamlike, somehow, or as if I saw it in a movie with really good special effects." Brian pauses for a moment, reflecting. "When the police got there they were tempted to accuse us of giving false evidence to the 911 operator."

"What?"

"We told them to expect blood and bodies, a laboratory in shambles. All they got was you, passed out. They smelled the alcohol we drank at the faculty party and assumed we were drunk. None of us were brave enough to tell them that a demon from beyond ate Mr. and Mrs. Brown!"

"Azathoth," I say, blankly. I'm speechless for a while. Then I ask, "But Chief Taggert—didn't he tell the police what happened?"

"There wasn't any evidence to support it. I think Taggert was afraid to say anything. The police just treated him as a bystander. Since he had been at the party, they made him take the Breathalyzer test, too."

"Is everyone else OK? Are Ally and Albert OK?"

"Yes, completely. But not Howie. You *do* remember what happened to Howie, right?"

I'm less clear about this. I remember spending an eternity with Howie in the White Castle, but I also remember a broken, lifeless Howie on the floor of the Witch Tower. "He's dead," I say, tentatively, almost as a question. I tear up and continue with a constricted throat. "Azathoth wanted to keep him in the White Castle forever, so he left his body behind."

This little speech gets a significant look from Brian. I think better of adding to it. Describing my life in the White Castle will have to wait for another time, if at all.

"You've been having quite the dreams over the last few days."

In dreams and visions lie the greatest creations of man. I remember Azathoth telling me that. I don't share this tidbit with Brian.

"It was one of the reasons the doctors weren't as worried as they might have been. They said it was normal REM sleep. They put you through about a dozen tests, including an EEG and MRI. They tested your blood for just about everything, including stroke. They said your blood-alcohol level was minimal. All the tests came back fine. They honestly don't know why you were out for so long. Just the shock of what happened, I guess."

"Only three days."

I'm looking at Brian. I suddenly realize that I love him. Not just that he's handsome or good in bed or a caring friend. I love him.

"I love you," I say.

"I love you, too, honey," says Brian, as he wipes one of his eyes. "I love you, too."

"Did you just call me honey?" I ask.

Brian looks down, smiling.

"It sounded nice."

"Not dopey?"

"Not dopey. Nice," I say, as Brian holds my hand, and I close my eyes to rest.

Surprisingly, they release me that same day. I think the hospital is short-staffed for the holidays, and they want to take care of only the critical patients. Brian asks me if I want to stay at his place for a few days. I think of the snowy, cold Miskatonic campus and the Witch Tower. I say, "Yes, I'd like to stay with you."

The trip back to Arkham in Brian's Jeep is uneventful. He keeps the heater going. I seem to have trouble staying warm.

When we get to Brian's, he puts a fire in the stove and busies himself around the house. He makes some tea. He notices me looking at Howie's bed next to the stove. He notices me starting to cry.

"Stupid of me," he says, moving it out of sight.

I'm thinking of Howie in the White Castle, wondering if our experience there was any less real than what I'm experiencing right now. My sense of reality has taken a beating over the last six months, and I'm not as sure about things as I used to be.

I notice that Brian bought a Christmas tree. It's a small one, fitting his small house. It hasn't been decorated yet and is standing next to the bookcase near his kitchen alcove. A stack of boxed lights and decorations is on the table. A few presents, already wrapped, are underneath the tree.

"I started decorating last week," Brian explains, his voice trailing off. "I thought maybe we could finish decorating it tonight, if you like. It *is* Christmas Eve."

"You've been with me all three days, haven't you?" I say, realizing for the first time how worried Brian must have been. "Did I mess up your work?"

At first, he doesn't understand, but then he replies, "Oh, no worries. Christmas week is not a big lumber sales time of year at Three Rivers. They were glad to give me a few days off, really, and the store is closed today and tomorrow for Christmas. I don't have to be back until Saturday."

I nod and pull the afghan up to my chin. The room is starting to warm up. It feels so nice to be here in Brian's house.

"Would you do me a favor? Would you call my mom and let her know I'm OK? You don't have to tell her the whole story, just that I was in the hospital, and I'm fine now."

"She already knows you were in the hospital," says Brian. "I called her on the twenty-second. I got the number out of your phone. At first, she was going to fly out right away, but with snow and airport closures, she decided to wait for a few days. She'll fly out on the twenty-eighth."

I picture my California mom trudging through the snow and hating Massachusetts. I picture her complaining about my small apartment in Grant Hall and the bleak landscape of Massachusetts in winter. I imagine her telling me all the reasons she left this lifeless place nearly thirty years ago.

I look out Brian's picture window and see the rushing Miskatonic River running cold and clear beyond his deck. The birch and maple trees create a network of bare branches against the overcast sky. The white pines are dusted with snow. The scene is breathtakingly beautiful but perhaps not the best time to show Mom why I want to stay in Massachusetts. I want to take her to the beach at Kingsport in the summer. I want her to see the lovely fall leaves of New England.

"Could you still talk to her for me? Tell her I'll call her tomorrow, and we'll discuss her trip. Tell her I'm fine, but I'm resting. It's not even much of a fib, I do want to be quiet and rest today. Tomorrow I'll be ready for more."

Brian goes into the bedroom to make the call, and I decide that Christmas decorating would be good therapy. He has a nice selection of lights and ornaments. I see that last week he must have outlined the kitchen alcove in icicle lights. I turn them on and discover they're not white, but multicolored. They look lovely. The tree is a small fir of some kind, and I decide it should also have multicolored lights. I start at the top and work my way down.

Brian joins me in a bit, and we work on the tree together. All the bright colors speak to me as we finish the lights and work on adding ornaments. A small tree doesn't take that long to decorate, and we finish and admire our work. The tree and the alcove icicle lights make Brian's whole house warm and vibrant. I help him put some more icicle lights along the top of the picture window. The permanent hooks there tell me that Brian takes his decorating seriously.

"It all looks very much like Christmas," I say, surveying his living area. "All that's missing is the smell of an apple pie baking or ginger snaps."

"It sounds like someone's hungry," says Brian. "Why don't I start making some dinner for us? Do you like clam chowder?"

"Clam chowder?"

"It was a Christmas Eve traditional dinner when I was growing up. I can make something else, if you'd rather."

"Chowder's great," I say, mustering some enthusiasm. I don't feel all that hungry. It's not the clams; I do eat some shellfish. "Just skip the bacon," I say, remembering that most chowder recipes use bacon for flavoring.

My appetite is awakened in a few minutes as Brian begins sautéing onions and garlic in butter. I had forgotten what a good cook he is. I offer to help Brian peel potatoes. Midway through this job, there's a knock at the door.

It's Ally and her grandfather. She rushes in and holds me in a tight hug. "Thank God you're all right. You don't know how dangerous it was for you to step into the pentagram. I was so worried that your body had been left behind. I've been bugging Brian every day as your tests were coming back. I wasn't sure if they really could tell that you were in normal sleep or something else."

She looks at me critically. "You really are OK, aren't you? You look even more pale than usual."

I shrug and hug Ally again. "I think so. But right now, I'm hungry."

Brian, is there enough chowder for everyone? Can the Wilmarths join us?"

"Of course," says Brian. "If you feel you're up to it."

I give Albert Wilmarth a big hug, too, and help both of them get out of their winter overcoats and gloves. Soon we're all in the kitchen helping Brian with dinner. Before long, the chowder's in a pot, and we're waiting for the potatoes to cook through before adding the clams.

"Are those cheese rolls you made for Thanksgiving difficult?" I ask, hinting.

"A great idea." Brian starts pulling ingredients out of cupboards. While Brian works on the rolls, he suggests that Ally and I work on a salad. Ally wants to know what I remember about solstice.

"Oh, everything, really. Brian and my accounts of solstice match up, so I don't think my fainting spell had too much of an effect on me. I remember the party, interrupting the summoning ritual, the Browns being torn apart by Azathoth."

"And after that?" asks Ally. I can tell she thinks there should be more to the story.

I shrug.

Over dinner, I steer the conversation to the *Necronomicon*. At first, Ally and her grandfather refuse to talk about it. Finally, they give in. The folklore professor in them both takes over, and Brian and I get quite an academic lecture on *The Book of Naming the Dead*.

"It was written, we believe, circa the year 700 in the city of Sana'a, Yemen," says Ally, starting the history lesson. "The author is the poet Abdul Alhazred, well known for his ballads and devotional poetry during the period of the Omniade caliphs in Arabia. He supposedly took a sabbatical from writing poetry and spent ten years visiting the ruins of Babylon, the subterranean secrets of Memphis, and the great southern deserts of Roba el Khaliyeh and the so-called Crimson Desert of ad-Dahna. On these lonely desert treks, Alhazred is said to have begun his communication with spirits."

"It's also where his madness is believed to have started," adds Albert. "By the time he moved his home to Damascus in the early part of the eighth century, he was no longer writing poetry, at least not of the usual or devotional sort."

"Or at least not devotional to any *known* god," interjects Ally.

Albert continues. "His death is fully recorded in Damascus in AD 738, but sometime shortly before his death he wrote the 'Al Azif,' as it was originally called. Supposedly 'Al Azif' is the word that Arabs of the day used to describe the nocturnal sound made by insects that heralds the approach of demons. It's supposed to have been a 'channeled' book, that is, he's supposed to have used some form of automatic handwriting technique to transcribe it in one long night."

"During this same period, his mental instability deteriorates. He was known to talk of monsters and demons and of visiting the lost city Irem, the City of Pillars." Ally is enjoying her turn at professorship and continues for Albert. "One legend is that even his death is mysterious —that he was seized by a monster in broad daylight and devoured horribly before a large number of fright-frozen witnesses."

"Azathoth," I say, and get no disagreement.

Ally says, "So the 'Al Azif' is commonly dated to the year 736 or 737. In AD 950 it was secretly translated into Greek by Theodorus Philetas of Constantinople. He took the current title from the subtitle of the original, *The Book of Naming the Dead*. The original was lost or destroyed around the year 1000, but not before a Latin translation was made. It's unclear whether the Latin was created from the Greek or with access to the original. The Greek version badly translated *The Book of Naming the Dead* into the *Necronomicon*, which is its common name today. Since then, bad translations have been made into German, English, and Spanish using the Latin version."

"So what is it, exactly?" interrupts Brian. "Why is it so important?"

"More like, dangerous," says Ally.

Albert picks up the discussion. "It's more or less a recipe book. It's a precursor to some of the grimoires found in the Middle Ages."

"A book of spells," I say.

"Yes, but more than that, Mac," continues Albert. "The book starts out, luckily, with defensive spells. You learn how to prevent the incursion of demons and it features descriptions of warding off unclean spirits. Then the book turns to offensive spells. You learn how to summon and control spirits. You learn how to prolong your life by taking the essence of life from others. You learn how to transmute both physical and metaphysical substance. Finally, the last quarter of the book is a list of names."

"Secret names?" I ask.

"Very good, Mac. Yes, secret names," says Albert. "In the sections on summoning and controlling demons, it shows you how to manipulate demons by using their hidden or secret name. The demon that we call Azathoth, for instance—"

"Don't name him, Grandfather," says Ally.

"Quite right," says Albert. "This section of the book is what makes it so unique. It's why it's more properly called *The Book of Naming the Dead*. You really *are* naming them. You name them, summon them, and ultimately command them."

"Then things get tricky," says Ally. "The names are sometimes mucked up in translation."

Albert nods. "Exactly. The original 'Al Azif' has everything written phonetically. The spells are all spoken. You need to name a demon verbally. Since the original manuscript was lost, we're relying on versions that have better or worse translations of the names. The Spanish version, for instance, translated all the secret names into names common in Spain in the seventeenth century."

"And," says Ally, "if you name a demon incorrectly, you're pretty much at his or her mercy. You can summon them using their 'public' name, like Azathoth, for instance. But to control a demon requires using their true secret name."

"So when the Browns summoned Azathoth?" I ask, tentatively.

"They were using the cobbled-together English translation by Dr. Dee," says Ally. "We presume he used the Latin version as his source. Dr. Dee made little attempt to phonetically reproduce any of the names. For many of them, he used versions of their names from the King James Bible."

"He called Azathoth 'Baal,'" I say, remembering.

"Exactly," says Albert. "Ally and I were reciting one of the warding spells from early in the book. We hoped it would cut off Azathoth from the Browns and send him back to the White Castle."

"You've mentioned the White Castle twice," I say. "Where does that fit in?"

Ally is looking at me suspiciously. Has Brian hinted of my "confusing dreams" to her?

"According to *The Book of Naming the Dead*, Azathoth is king of the Outer Gods. He sits on a black onyx throne in the White Castle in the center of chaos. He has the power of life or death in his realm, which many believe includes our life on Earth."

"But there's something more important than all this," says Ally. "The grimoires created in the Middle Ages are creative, but they don't actually work. They might work in a sense. The occult practitioner might use them to go into a trancelike state where things appear to happen to them. Often such practitioners are under the influence of alcohol or narcotic substances during these rituals. It's not surprising that they might think demons really are summoned or controlled."

"But you're saying the *Necronomicon* really works?" asks Brian. "The spells, I mean. If you use the right names, you can actually summon and control demons?"

"It appears that way," says Ally. "Frankly, it's so dangerous to use the book that people are hesitant to prove it. Just reading the book silently has been known to trigger unpleasant events. That's why we keep all the copies under lock and key."

"Or at least we try our best," says Albert. "I'm afraid Terrie Woolworth wasn't quite up to the task when she caught Matt Brown stealing our display copy. Or at least we assume it was Matt Brown. Terrie still can't remember what happened that night."

"Thank heavens she's OK," says Ally.

I'm not sure how to react to this whole discussion of *The Book of Naming the Dead*. A part of me dismisses it. How can words and names have such power? How can eternal life or limitless power be drawn from the life force of others? I start to formulate questions in rebuttal, but then I remember my time in the White Castle. Azathoth seems real enough to me, and I have no explanation for him.

As the evening of conversation continues, I start to feel a little tired. Albert Wilmarth must sense this, because he suggests that he take Ally home, back to the campus. We talk a bit more as the Wilmarths put on coats and gloves to brave the cold weather outside.

My cellphone rings, and at first I think of letting it go to voicemail. Then I notice it's from the university, and I decide to take it.

"This is Mac," I say.

"Is my granddaughter there?" comes a familiar voice. "Ally? Is she still there? I need her to stop at the library on her way to the dorms."

The voice is unmistakable. I'm instantly taken back to the beginning of November and the weird visit to Albert Wilmarth in his basement office at the library. His voice has that strange vibrating quality that sounds like a bad telephone connection. But it's not the phone—it's his voice. I remember the odd smell in his office. I remember the row of miniature diving helmets on top of his bookcase. I remember the odd antiques and steam-punk oddities. I shiver slightly.

"Yes, she's here." I walk past Albert Wilmarth, Ally's grandfather, and hand the phone to Ally. "It's your grandfather," I say, keeping my voice as neutral as possible.

Ally gives a furtive glance to her grandfather in the room. He shrugs, and she puts the phone to her ear.

"Yes, Grandfather," she says. "Do you need something?"

❖

After the Wilmarths leave, Brian and I hold each other on the sofa for a while. It feels good, just the two of us.

"So, what's with the extra Wilmarth?" asks Brian. "Does Ally have an extra grandfather? An extra one here on campus, I mean?"

"At least one extra." I tell Brian about my visit to Ally's grandfather in the library. I tell him about the weird buzzing, the elder's lack of mobility, and Ally's unwillingness to talk more directly about him. I tell Brian about seeing Ally in the graveyard and the "too many" Wilmarths.

"So there are two Albert Wilmarths who say they are her grandfather?"

"I think it's even more interesting than that. There must be a lineage of Albert Wilmarths, including Ally. One of them, who must be at least a hundred and ten years old, phoned tonight."

Brian whistles. "Her name is Albert too, isn't it?" he asks, referring to Ally.

"Yes."

"Do we like her well enough to wade into another mystery at Miskatonic?"

"I think so, but not tonight," I reply.

"Then let's talk about something else." Brian goes over to the Christmas tree and retrieves a present. A small one. I guess it shouldn't surprise me. After all, it *is* Christmas Eve.

I start to protest. "Not fair. I have a present for you, too, but it's back at my apartment."

"We'll get that tomorrow. I want you to have this now. Besides, it's really for both of us."

I see the shape of the small box. I'm suddenly aware of what its contents must be. I'm a little uncomfortable. "I'm not sure if I'm ready for this. We've only been together for five months. Are you sure this will last? Are you sure you want to spend your life with me?"

"I just spent three days thinking I might not have you in my life at all," says Brian. "I'm sure."

I'm thinking of the lifetime I spent away from him while I was in the White Castle. It created a longing for him but also a great sense of loss. Can I be with this man and risk losing him again?

I can see that my silence spooks him a bit. "I think it's just too much at once. A move from the West Coast, a teaching career here in Massachusetts, a new car, a new apartment, a crazy fall term complete with demons. Losing Howie. It's a lot to take in."

"And a new boyfriend," says Brian.

"And a wonderful new boyfriend," I affirm. "The best man I could ever imagine in my life."

He thinks for most of a minute. "How about this," he says, holding the present out to me. "How about if you open this present now and ponder a really long engagement? I'm not asking you to move in or make too many more changes in your life. Not right now, anyway."

He tears off the Christmas paper from the small box and hands it to me.

The ring design is stunning. No stones but instead bands of what looks like white gold and titanium, entwined. There are two of them. Brian gets down on one knee and looks up into my eyes. "Mac, will you consider being engaged to me? We can talk about marriage later, but would you consider being my partner and my love for now?"

Without a beat, I say, "I will. I do. I mean, yes."

We kiss each other for a long time on the sofa.

Later, we get ready for bed. The bed has lovely, smooth, fresh sheets. The parted curtains reveal a dramatic winter view of the river in the moonlight.

Although missing my sweet dog, I could fill up my gratitude journal tonight. Is it trite to say I fall asleep in Brian's loving arms?

Much later in the night, I have this dream.

At first, I'm afraid, because I find myself back in the White Castle. I balk at the thought of being here, and it triggers something that makes my dreams more lucid, more controllable. In the dream, I ask myself, "Are you dreaming?"

"Of course you are," comes the answer.

"In dreams and visions lie the greatest creations of man."

For some reason this calms me down, and I examine my surroundings. The White Castle has changed. For one thing, it's not so bright white. I remember it being blazingly white. Now the white is softer, warmer, more like real alabaster. It's like changing out a stark white fluorescent bulb for one of the warm-white variety.

It's also no longer unpopulated. There are people and creatures everywhere. Now the rooms are being used as they were designed. The banquet room is full of people laughing and dining. The garden with the rainbow falls has small tables, and people are sipping drinks and admiring the silver fish. I walk through the halls and examine the many rooms, familiar from my imprisonment. I marvel at how beautiful everything is. The air is filled with sound and scent.

Before, the castle was a cold, bright mausoleum. Now it is a place for people, for entertainment, for living.

I make my way to the entrance to the throne room, and I see all the velvet draperies are in place. Each one is dotted with stars, and I see that the coverings are translucent, permeable. I feel sure that I could pass through these draperies now. They are portals to adventure, to other realms, to new ways of living and thinking.

The throne room is unchanged. On the dais, the black onyx throne stands empty. The musical piping that I first heard is back, but the melody is different. It is no longer the atonal piping of eldritch madness. Now the panpipes are musical and have a playful melody.

I try my hand at changing the view. I inwardly "bark," and I'm back in my apartment on the Miskatonic campus. I smile at this trick that Howie taught me. I bark again, and I'm back in the throne room. Now there is someone seated on the throne. I approach and notice the steel-gray suit hanging loosely.

It's Howie doing a parody of Azathoth!

He barks, and the suit is gone. He barks again, wagging his tail, and we're on the verdant shore of the lotus field. I kneel down, and Howie jumps into my lap, and we spend some time just loving each other.

Howie is in the best shape of his life. He's gained a bit of weight, and the gray hairs that lined his muzzle are back to their puppy color. He has that bouncing energy that speaks of good times and a healthy curiosity.

"You're doing fine here, aren't you, boy?"

Howie wags his tail and initiates a quick pirouette. He lifts one paw and points to the lotus pond where we made our escape after an eternity of imprisonment.

"Yes, I remember. You saved me. Thank you."

He looks straight into my eyes. There's not a trace of sadness there, only the joy of our friendship.

Howie barks again, and we're in the usual view of the throne room. Now I notice that there are some small differences here, too. The throne has a dog cushion on it! Apparently, Howie's been napping on the onyx throne. There's also a selection of some of his favorite toys at the foot of the throne.

Howie picks up an old tennis ball, and we spend some time playing. I toss the ball across the dais and down the steps, and he fetches, wriggling like a puppy. It's just like the old days, and I'm filled up with playful fun.

After a half hour or so, you can tell he's losing interest. Like all Italian greyhounds, there's a time for play, and there's a time for rest. Howie drops the ball, and it rolls toward me. He gets up on the black onyx throne, on his dog cushion, and circles once, twice, three times. He plops down and is almost immediately asleep.

The ball is still rolling toward me, and I pick it up to return it to his pile of toys.

I look at the ball, but it's not a tennis ball. It's Earth. As I hold it, I can see all the continents. I can see the clouds making up the weather patterns. It's like the view of the earth from space, except it's right in my hand. It's beautiful. After a time, I return Howie's toy and make my way to the entrance hall, back to the velvet curtains of stars that lead home.

When I look back, Howie is asleep, quietly dreaming.

EPILOG

Three months have gone by, and much has changed. The inside of the once-again-famous Witch Tower at Massachusetts Hall has been cleansed according to some arcane and ancient rite by one of the Albert Wilmarths. Its cellar door has been swapped out for solid masonry.

Ally assures me that we don't have to worry about it any longer, that it has been energetically decommissioned as well as sealed up. I hope she's right. I hope the Wilmarths know more about cleansing this piece of land than the Miskatonic tribe that sold it to the Puritans.

Ally's changed, too. She refuses to talk about her family and the various Albert Wilmarths. She's lost some of her easygoing and chatty nature. In my opinion, she's spending too many hours at the library with the elder Wilmarth. I think the Wilmarth family feels responsible for what happened or at least for the stolen copy of *The Book of Naming the Dead* and the part it played. I'm not prepared to lose a friend, though. If Ally requires an intervention of some kind to get away from her family, I'm up for it.

The police find no trace of either Matthew or Emma Brown. Despite my desire for a scientific explanation for what happened, their absence does not surprise me. I saw what I saw, and I'm sure they're exactly where they're meant to be.

A month after the Browns "left," the campus maintenance team came by to put all their personal effects in boxes and ready Condon Hall for another set of tenants. I was walking by and noticed some of the material piled up to go in a dumpster. Among the junk was a surprising quantity of aluminum foil. The foil caught my eye because it was *that foil*. It was the foil we used to line the Faraday cage! I went into the foyer of Condon Hall and asked one of the cleaners about it. She replied, "Oooooh. You wouldn't believe it! There was a whole room in the basement lined with that stuff. We had to peel it off the walls. They must have used miles of it! Tin foil and dog paraphernalia. I kept thinking we might find a dog in there somewhere. What a mess!"

That explains the extra foil that Brian said maintenance needed to finish lining the Faraday cage. Does it also explain Howie's missing month? Instead of vanishing into the White Castle, was he really just two buildings away from our home at Grant Hall? Was he really trapped in the basement of Condon Hall as part of the Browns' attempts at raising and controlling Azathoth?

I've been packing most of the morning. No, I'm not leaving Miskatonic University. Fall and winter terms came and went, and I received excellent departmental reviews. In fact, Dr. Christianson has offered me a significant raise starting next fall and a two-year contract if I stay. Spring term will be starting in two weeks, and I have a full schedule of classes. Although I have mixed feelings about the university, I've made connections here. I have a boyfriend here. My life feels anchored here.

And, no, I'm not packing to move in with Brian, either. I look forward to that day, but it's not this day. Brian and I have made a commitment to each other, and so far, it's working. Recently, he told a friend of our "engagement," and it sounded just right to me. His openness and happy nature are wonderful counterpoints to my sometimes-uptight scientific methodology. Honestly, I'm not sure how I'd manage without his loving manner and warm personality. When he calls me "honey," it always brings a smile to my face.

The packing is for spring break! Brian was able to get ten days off from Three Rivers, and we're headed for Italy! Our plane leaves Boston's Logan Airport in about four hours, and I'm putting the last of my clothes and toiletries into a suitcase. Neither of us has been out of the country before (I'm not counting Tijuana trips when I lived in Los Angeles), so we're both excited. Italy will be a grand adventure.

Brian has his things in the Jeep and is waiting patiently while I finish up. Packing ten days of clothes into one suitcase is not easy, but I think I've finished. I run through a list to make sure I haven't missed anything important.

The last thing I put in the suitcase is a small square package covered in a piece of blue knit. I decided Howie should be wrapped in his blue sweater.

We're taking Howie "home." I refuse to think of him in the throne room of the White Castle. I refuse to think of Azathoth using my sweet friend. Our time together in the castle is beginning to fade from my memory. I remember our connection there, but not all the details of it. I remember Howie saving my life, but perhaps at the expense of his own.

Our flight is to Rome. We'll get a car and drive north and west until we get to the Italian Riviera. Somehow, I know that Howie will like this part of Italy. I plan to scatter his ashes amid the warm Mediterranean sand overlooking the deep blue Gulf of Genoa. I'm not sure where Italian greyhounds really come from, but I'm certain this will be a place where I can think of him being happy, warm, and at peace.

ACKNOWLEDGMENTS

I must acknowledge the Portland Center for Spiritual Living and its writers group led by Kathy Marshack. I would not have managed to put so many words down in a row without its support and encouragement. If you want to write your first book, join a writers group!

I also need to honor H. P. Lovecraft for providing the wonderful and terrible locations of Arkham, Kingsport, and Miskatonic University hidden away in a fictitious version of Essex Country, Massachusetts. A few of his characters (or their ancestors) also appear in the book. If you're a Lovecraft fan, I hope you'll enjoy their presence.

My protagonist, "Mac" Mackenzie loves science and so do I. Because of this, I have chosen to provide scientific explanations for many of the happenings in *Witch Tower*. Where possible I've explained real experiments and given the names of their real-world creators and collaborators. However, I don't claim to be a scientist myself. Where I've gotten the science bits wrong (or arrived at the wrong conclusions regarding them), please forgive me. At the end of the day, this is just a novel.

ABOUT THE AUTHOR

Lawrence King is a Pacific Northwest minister, author, and inspirational speaker. You can find him on Sundays at the Center for Spiritual Living in Portland, Oregon, where he is the senior minister and primary speaker.

You can follow his inspirational Sunday podcasts on iTunes and Google Play.

As an author, he is taking the themes of H. P. Lovecraft to the next level in his "Miskatonic University" series of books and stories. You can always check on his progress at http://www.miskatonic.us.

When asked about the relationship between his writings and his role as minister he explains:

As a New Thought minister, I affirm the positive nature of God and the inherent friendliness of the universe. Heaven and hell only exist as we humans imagine them. As an author of urban fantasy, I reaffirm this notion. Evil only exists as a reflection of our beliefs and the choices we make. When we think positively and make better choices, we experience a better life.

Lawrence King is a fourth-generation Oregonian. As a kid, he watched science fiction movies every Saturday morning and was chased out of the adult-horror section of the library weekly. He always has a stack of inspirational books (including science fiction and horror) on his bedside table along with his gratitude journal. He, his partner, and two dogs live in Portland, Oregon, when they're not at the beach.

Made in the USA
San Bernardino, CA
15 August 2017